MADE GLORIOUS

MADE GLORIOUS

Lindsay Eagar

CANDLEWICK PRESS

Copyright © 2024 by Lindsay Eagar
Epigraph copyright © 1958
from *Thoughts on Machiavelli*
by Leo Strauss

First edition 2024

Library of Congress Catalog Card Number 2023944663
ISBN 978-1-5362-0467-4

APS 29 28 27 26 25 24
10 9 8 7 6 5 4 3 2 1

Printed in Humen, Dongguan, China

This book was typeset in Warnock.

Candlewick Press
99 Dover Street
Somerville, Massachusetts 02144

www.candlewick.com

MIX
Paper | Supporting
responsible forestry
FSC
www.fsc.org   FSC® C144853

For my parents

Dearest reader,

This book contains frank discussions of mental health and suicide (including suicidal ideation), as well as instances of fatphobia. Please take care of yourself if you are sensitive to any of these subjects.

If you are struggling, there is always help. NAMI (National Alliance on Mental Illness) was a beacon of hope for me personally during the darkest period of my life. Reach out. You are worth it.

> *With love,*
> The author

NAMI (National Alliance on Mental Illness)
1-800-950-NAMI (6264)
available Monday through Friday
10 a.m. to 10 p.m. ET
or email helpline@nami.org
or text "HelpLine" to 62640

988 Suicide & Crisis Lifeline
call, text, or chat 988
available 24/7

THE DEVIL
IS A
FALLEN ANGEL.

—Leo Strauss, *Thoughts on Machiavelli*

CLOSING NIGHT

PICTURE IT: A DARK STAGE, CURTAINS CLOSED.

The audience is miraculously silent. None of the usual static that pollutes the final minutes of most productions: impatient whispers, the crinkling of gum wrappers and playbills, the jingling of keys found in the rayon-lined depths of purse and pocket. No, they are spellbound.

The curtains part once more, slowly. A faint requiem, reminiscently Scottish with fife and drum, crescendos as the ultimate tableau is revealed.

When Liberty Prep did *The Crucible* last year, they used the score from *The Last of the Mohicans* for this scene. Unforgivably cliché.

Onstage, a series of gallows. Girls in old-age makeup stand behind them, all in lace-trimmed bonnets and nightgowns, hands bound in thick, obvious ropes. One boy is among them in a ruffled cream shirt. His hair is matted down from sweating in a Pilgrim hat half the night.

"Our Father, who art in heaven," starts the boy, "hallowed be thy name." He stumbles over the next line as he is forced into the hangman's noose, choked by a surge of emotion.

A hunching girl with wrinkles drawn onto her features with eyeliner takes up the prayer: "Thy kingdom come, thy will be done . . ." She, too, is fitted into her noose by a solemn Puritan, whose own buckled 1692-style hat does not hide the shaggy flip of his trendy, professional-snowboarder-style hair.

"I saw John Proctor with the devil!" The accusations are hissed beneath the Lord's Prayer, and they come from the auditorium seats. Several actors, released from their onstage roles, have been planted to cry out, to make this merciless, sonic chaos: "I saw Goody Nurse with the devil! I saw Goody Corey with the devil!" Their effect is powerful; a few people react with shivers, frowns, even incredulous tears.

"But deliver us from evil—"

Before the amen, a lever is pulled. The scaffold gives. The trapdoors open.

Bodies drop, blinked into darkness. All lights go out. And then the horrific creak of the gallows. The ropes.

The audience is given a moment of reverence, to reflect, to fold up this evening's performance, tuck it back somewhere into the recesses of their brains in hopes that they will leave here changed, inspired to never join any fundamentalist witch-hanging mobs, so moved were they by an early-November high school production of *The Crucible* with an artificial sunset and a set of braces on the Reverend Hale's repentant teeth.

Are you wondering if anyone will think of this show again? Surely they will remember very little, you must think, save for a looping, mocking replay of the moment in act 2 when Elizabeth

Proctor stirred the stew and the whole cauldron slipped off its hanger and clanged against the fake hearth.

Maybe if this were another production. Maybe if this were Liberty Prep. But this is Bosworth. And Bosworth shows are unmatched. They are carved into the soul and taken to the grave. They are never forgotten.

When the stage lights come on this time, they are bright, prompting the audience to rise and clap.

Out comes the cast for their bows. The ones with fewest lines are first. They get the warm-up applause. (The parents' applause.)

The leads demonstrate modesty as they take in their reception. Some of them weep. This is the last night of this production, so the moment is bittersweet.

"It's like they were onstage with us," the sap who played Ann Putnam will say later. "All those people who really lived through this, who were hanged. I could feel them with us onstage."

It's not unexpected, this tangle of pride and grief that surges after a show's final curtain call.

Consider it: You rehearse for weeks, you forgo social outings, homework, free time, you build a pretend world. You mentally prepare and, in some cases, systematically rearrange your psyche to withstand the nerves of performing, the strain of that vulnerability, and then—

It's over.

The lines, the themes, the rhythms of moving along the chessboard of the stage . . . The emotions you summon like trained cats, the subtext you invent, the character you've lodged under your skin by the time the curtain goes up on opening night, and then you must let it go. Let it all melt away, let it become obsolete. Let it go and become yourself again.

Strike it from your heart.

When the clapping ebbs and people start tugging on jackets and staring longingly at the aisles, the stage manager rushes out from the wings in her electrical-taped-and-Sharpied sneakers. "House lights on." She sends the command along her headset; the senior in the tech booth makes it happen. In her hands she holds a fat bouquet of roses.

John Proctor (he will never be called that again, not unless he gets cast as Miller's canoodling tragic hero in some future production) calls for the attention of the crowd. "We'd like to invite our director to the stage."

From the farthest corner of the front row, the director lets the new wave of applause urge her to her feet, joining her cast with feigned reluctance. The bouquet is placed in her arms, floral water dripping onto the floor.

It's a garish arrangement, the roses wide awake as if they personally want to give their regards.

"We want to thank you, Pam, for believing in us. For holding our feet to the fire. For pushing us to grow. This show wouldn't be what it is without you." John Proctor, aka Cole Buckingham, the senior who insisted on delivering the tribute, is capable of turning his passions on and off as if his adrenals have valves. He did a good job, most of the cast and crew think. The worry with Cole, always, is that he'll find a way to spotlight himself, but he lets the crowd cheer for Ms. Hanson as long as they want.

"Thank you," Pam finally says, studying the roses. Her tone might vaguely remind you of an adult thanking a kindergartner for a thoughtful but sloppily drawn birthday card. "And to all the parents in the audience, a most sincere thank-you. I've been so lucky to work with your students. Thank you for letting them be part of this. They care so much about this craft. True dedication. That's what I've come to expect, and they delivered."

Before the applause can grow anemic, Pam Hanson dismisses the crowd with another thank-you and a simply put "Good night."

The curtains close.

Backstage, the cast explodes into chatter, clinging to one another, crying. The director vanishes. The stage manager hustles to speak to the group before they are fully lost to post-show adrenaline.

"Everyone, listen up! You *must* change out of your costumes and sign them in with Cynthia before you can greet family and friends! Repeat: You *must* sign in your costumes before you go to front of house! Also, your to-do lists are posted in the drama room. You *must* have those lists checked off by me and me alone before you leave! Principals, Jake is waiting in the workshop for your mics. Again, principals, turn in your mics to Jake in the workshop. Any questions?"

Cole Buckingham asks a banal question, something jackassy, something to provoke, and gets the chuckles he was fishing for. Some cannot handle being out of the limelight for very long, as if they are cold-blooded.

The cast dashes off to change out of wardrobe. Crew members bring out drills, start disassembling the set. Betty Parris's bedroom. The slanted roof of the Proctor home. The menacing trees where Tituba danced with the Salem girls. Danforth's desk. All dismantled, beam by beam.

The gallows were made with the wood from Tevye's handcart from last year's production of *Fiddler*. Lumber is carefully stripped of nails and stacked in the workshop for another purpose someday.

Props are stored, labeled, placed in bins. The scrim is rolled;

dressing rooms are cleaned. There's pizza. There's music. It's been months of funneling their energies into the script, the blocking, the beats, and tonight serves as catharsis.

Most of the audience has filtered out. Pam, the director, has been cornered by a parent for a lengthy conversation that doesn't seem to have a natural ending point.

"She's just so talented," the mother is saying. "Beyond high school talent." She is not referring to her own child but to Clarissa George, who played Abigail Williams in this production.

"She's very good," agrees Pam, unmoved.

"What do you do with talent like that?" the mother goes on. "Scholarships, hopefully! Juilliard, perhaps? If I were her mother, I'd be flying that girl out to New York, get her in front of some agents, some casting directors."

But you are not Clarissa's mother, you might feel an urge to reply. And you know your own child is some unremarkable, potato-faced rucksack of a student who served their time in the ensemble along with a gaggle of choir girls looking for something to pad their college applications and fill their time with until spring concerts.

Now you've sat through six showings of *The Crucible* at twelve bucks a ticket, all so you could be the good-mother witness to your child's second-act appearance as a member of the jury, a role that you know could have easily been filled by a mannequin in a shawl.

Perhaps you think this a cruel assessment. Perhaps this is simply a supportive mother. The kind of parent every community hopes for: tireless in her cheerleading, willing to spend countless hours hemming aprons or cutting sheets of tickets, a volunteer who volunteered herself. Everyone hopes for a mother like that in their student's classroom.

It's also likely that this mother is lonely, repressed, controlling, someone who never did theater when she was in high school and is now hovering over her child's extracurriculars so as not to be eaten up by her own resentment.

The spotlight always looks so warm. It makes sense that everyone wants a turn to stand in it.

You are the only one allowed to stay in your costume.

Bosworth's illustrious costume closet was unable to accommodate your . . . sizing needs, so you had to purchase your puffy white blouse, broad lace collar, and dark linen skirt.

Pam insists that all performers change back into their street clothing before going to front of house—to preserve the magic for the audiences, to delineate the characters from the actors portraying them.

You have no one waiting in the audience to greet, and you are the rightful owner of this Puritan ensemble, so why should you rush to change?

Your chore is to sweep the stage, which cannot be completed until the sets are broken down, the crew is finished with the lights and cables, and the cast members who loiter over the last slice of pizza are chased out of the wings. So you quietly make yourself useful until the stage is empty, sometime around midnight.

The stage manager and two of her most loyal assistants are in the drama room, sorting post-show paperwork as they gossip. Pam retreated hours ago without ceremony. Jake in the tech booth turned off everything but the work lights and left with his girlfriend.

You take up the broom.

Sweep, sweep, sweep.

The stage is awash with sawdust, lost screws, heavy-duty staples, strips of torn fabric, paint chips, and the crumbs of someone's vending-machine feast: granola bar oats and the orange dust of Doritos. All of it must be swept before some heedless actor takes a nail to the foot. Actors love to walk around barefoot, backstage and onstage and up and down the late-night linoleum hallways. They feel at home here on the stage. They feel a little too at home in the after-hours of the school.

Push, push, push.

You sink into the muted percussion of the sweep. Your body is tired. There is no buildup of adrenaline when you have only one line to deliver. There is no need for catharsis. You were one of the first to come out and take your bows.

"Liars! They are liars!"

Out of nowhere, your single line hits you. Echoes in your head. A throwaway line, but it sticks like a bad song. It'll take days to fade. A show ends, and it haunts you, even if you were nothing more than a warm body on the stage, an extra, a part of the scenery—

You empty the dustpan into the trash, sprinkling its contents on top of the crumpled call sheets.

"Liars! They are liars!"

Hours spent in the auditorium, your script open, your one measly line highlighted as if you needed to practice it, as if you would forget it after reading it once.

Part of the great lump of the ensemble. Living, breathing, longing scenery. Set pieces that blink.

It is nearly over. There's only one last semester of senior year. One last audition. One last show.

It should be you next time.

You hear the voice with both your ears and your mind, which makes you wonder if it's coming from the empty air around you or if it's emerging from the darkness within.

On the stage, front and center, a piece of debris, missed by the broom.

You crouch to pick it up.

A rose petal from Pam's bouquet, red as blood.

You should be here. Right here, in the center of the universe.

You close your eyes.

Your spit grows hot, the copper tang of injustice in your mouth—

Save it.

Bottle it up. Seal it tight.

Hold on to it for the next show.

You'll need it.

You pick up the petal, and the work lights snap off.

The auditorium, pitch black.

Before you can run back to the light switch, the front lights come on, illuminating you as you stand.

You don't really want to do another show like this, do you? All those hours, all those rehearsals, just to be in the sea of faces?

You still clutch the rose petal. Your eyes shine, staring beyond the stage, down into the vacant chairs.

Only they're not vacant.

It's a full house. You can see them, the ghost of an audience— they clap, and you can feel the shuddering fervor of their applause in your chest.

You've paid your dues.

The lights are so warm, like you're standing in a hot shower, water trickling down your hair, your back.

It should be you this time. She promised.

If you squint against the gleam of the lights, you can see all the way to the back row. You can see all the way to the future.

You cradle a bouquet of roses in your arms. The audience stands, their adoration strong, solid. Your chest opens like a cavern. Your own skin peels away, your insides turning out.

Melting into someone else.

It should be you this time.

Can you see it?

Good. Then you'll understand exactly why I'm going to do what I'm about to do.

SOPHOMORES

(FLASHBACK)

"Welcome to Drama I."

The teacher did not smile as she passed out her syllabus, not exactly, but there was an amusement beneath the stoic demeanor, the blaze of passion flickering behind a sharply hard professional composure. "I'm Pam Hanson. Call me Pam, please—none of this Ms. Hanson nonsense. Makes me feel old."

The room was composed of sophomores, all of them newcomers to Bosworth Academy and its intractable scholastic environment; most of them would require further cajoling before they'd dare to address their teacher by her first name, even with her express permission.

She did not look like a youthful, energetic drama teacher. Pam was nearly forty but looked fifty. She was large, her stomach the widest, roundest part of her. She wore an oversize cable knit sweater and jeans, shockingly casual for a Bosworth Academy faculty member, but perhaps a certain leeway must be given for the instructor of this subject, the stuff of personas and costumes and silliness.

No silliness here, though. Nothing zany or lighthearted or fun. Pam read through the syllabus dryly, the grading policies, the expectations for class demeanor. Anyone who'd hoped for an easy romp of accent training and reenacting Leonardo DiCaprio's Romeo was properly deterred.

The classroom, too, warned of seriousness, of dedication to the theater arts. A fathomless place, more auditorium than lecture hall, the drama room was all dark cherrywood crown molding, deep-green wallpaper, moody sconces, and a series of framed paintings and prints hung on the walls—Millais's *Ophelia*, Carol Burnett's Miss Hannigan, a black-and-white Steve Martin, Antigone, Audrey II. The greats.

Opposite the classroom door was a stage, smaller than standard but more than makeshift. Opposite the stage, near the classroom door, Pam's office was flanked by bookshelves, spine after skinny spine of plays and craft books and memoirs.

"The best way to light a house is God's way," Frank Lloyd Wright once wrote, and whatever architect designed Bosworth's performing arts room must have agreed, furnishing the tall, pretentious walls with clerestory windows to let in the sunshine. The fenestration was likely meant to mimic the angle of stage lights; one could also argue it looked like daylight streaking past the bars of a cell.

Pam perched on the edge of the stage and took up the roster.

With each name she called, she glanced at the student and studied their face, as if preparing to describe it to a sketch artist later. Rory imagined a file in Pam's head, every student's features and overall aura being paired with potential roles.

"Aaron's brother?" Pam said. "And you're Lorraine's sister, yes?" She nodded knowingly when the students confirmed. "I'll keep an eye on you, then." Everyone chuckled.

Those without older siblings strained their necks, hoping Pam would spare an eye for them as well.

"All right. That's done." Finished with the formalities, Pam put the roster and her other paperwork aside and scanned the batch of new arrivals, kicking out her legs like a playful babysitter. "Congratulations to all of you. You've chosen to be part of the most highly regarded high school theatre department in the state."

She listed some of Bosworth Academy's greatest achievements—all of them accomplished under her reign as department head, drama teacher, and director. Lest anyone here think they'd get away with subpar effort. Lest anyone here think they could offer anything but their deepest, their most hallowed, their full selves.

"Let's get it out of the way," Pam said. "I don't cast sophomores."

It struck like a gunshot. Everyone was silent, waiting for the other shoe to drop. It never did.

"Sophomores get ensemble," she said. "Juniors get minor roles. Seniors get leads. It's nothing to do with your talent. Nothing to do with your age or your lack of experience." She was ready for rebuttals, ready with counterarguments for anyone ready to fight.

"We do three shows a year here: a fall play, a winter revue, and a spring musical. On average, sixty students audition for each show, and even something like *Les Mis* only has nine or ten leads. Do the math."

Rory kept her eyes on the teacher, stilling everything within herself to keep from broadcasting her surprise. In her periphery, she noted the others similarly clenched.

"You've got three years with me. Three years for me to mold you. We'll work like dogs in this room. You'll grow to despise me for a while—that's normal. You'll repeat lines so many times, the words will lose their meaning, turn to mush in your mouth. You'll howl at each other. You'll quit, some of you. It simply won't be worth it to you, this daily breakdown. That's fine. You don't belong here, then, because I require the best. Not the best you have to offer, but *the* best, the best in the world—so you will spend the next three years squeezing the best out of yourself for me. And after all that work, all that dedication, you'll be a senior, and you'll see that it was all worth it.

"Imagine if you were a senior. You've studied with me for three years, you've put in countless hours and long nights, forgoing school dances and dates and parties. And then in strolls a sopho-more, snatching a lead right from under you? No. You'll stay. You'll work. You'll pay your dues. And then, when you're a senior, it'll be your time to shine."

ACT
ONE

IDLE PLEASURES

Have you ever noticed how boorish and embarrassingly poetic people become at the tail end of winter?

Months of darkness, and we've made it out the other side!

At last, spring is winking at us!

What a long, cold winter we've had!

That's what people will say today when they see the sun peering through the clouds and turning the snow into streams for the leaf-choked gutters, lighting upon patches of dried-out grass, reminding everyone that there are living things underneath all that cold. *Such a long, dark winter*, they'll intone, and sigh and stretch as if their bones have thawed.

My apologies. You see, even I cannot resist dipping into my storehouse of words to paint you a glossy account of our carryings-on. I cannot promise you I won't further humiliate myself with such earnest expressions, that my own inner poet won't unleash itself to run free and wild and hump all over our narrative.

But I can promise you honesty. At all costs, in all its ugliness, in all its power. That's what I can promise.

And so I begin by telling you the truth: it's only January. Sunshine before April is a fool's hope.

We still have plenty of winter ahead of us.

I walk on this bright and gloriously frigid morning along a crumbling sidewalk until my path forces me to step into the road. My new Christmas boots are far too thin against the muddy slush. My mother bought them for fashion, not for function. I'd wager my wet toes will be numb until lunch. Still, the cold registers in my internal landscape as mere inconvenience.

Down shines the watery light, birds calling out songs for the false spring. Even I was bamboozled by the clearness of the sky this morning—I skipped my usual down-coat bundling and swore a sweater would be enough for the walk to Bosworth Academy.

It's a neat 3.4 miles from my front stoop to the school's flagpole, and since my mother takes the early shift in the emergency room hours before even the custodians arrive at Bosworth, my morning commute by foot has made me intimately familiar with every house and yard in my neighborhood.

Here, the curbs are lined with out-of-commission cars leaking their bodily fluids onto the pockmarked street, which could be a clear HOA violation if we were the type of neighborhood to have an HOA.

Here, there are Christmas wreaths still hanging on doors, and at least two porches bear the rotting rinds of pumpkins, collapsed under the weight of old snow.

Branches tangling electric wires, duct tape on satellite dishes.

Chain-link, not picket.

A deep breath chills my lungs, but I exhale, invigorated. I am not usually so jaunty, especially this early in the day, but this morning begins a new semester.

The last of my high school career.

Were it not for the brown sluice glazing and slicking the road, I would almost be tempted to add a skip to my step.

Truthfully, I have always eyed the cliff of my final semester the way a cat eyes water. Any other student might view the transition out of the high school experience as a liberation, but I've been gaping at the threat of our looming graduation since the tenth grade.

I simply didn't want to leave. It was absurdly fortunate that they'd let me in at all.

Me, blandly remarkable in the way that so many scholarship students are: white, female, flawless grades, decent extracurriculars.

There were important things missing from my application. Things that could not be listed on a form. Things that were vital nonetheless for a school like Bosworth—

I had no alumni to vouch for me. No legacy. No grandparents with deep pockets offering to fund a new science wing or pay for the math club's letterman jackets. There was only my technical college–educated mother, and her pocket was too shallow to hold a ChapStick.

I did have pity on my side. The zip code on my application form was itself a sob story. There were likely dozens of applicants with their own evocative, dewy-eyed histories to extort—but evidently Bosworth had a Rory King–shaped slot in their roster, because they opened their doors to me like I was a soggy, sad little stray, and I scampered in.

And at the end of this final semester, I will no longer be welcome in their world.

Now that I inch ever closer to the chasm, the collective push to ship me off to a decent college has gone from fevered to frenzied. Bosworth graduates are ceremoniously plunked onto the prep-school-to-university conveyor belt, and the academy longs to prove I am no exception.

Every adult I know has roped me into the old college search— Yellow folders swollen with paperwork. Requesting letters of recommendation from teachers, requesting that they translate their verbal praise and positive parent-teacher conference feedback into black and white, double-spaced twelve-point font, trifolded into an addressed-and-stamped envelope, sent away to serve as oracle.

Waiting. Eternally waiting, a game of waiting.

College is expensive. Even applying to college is expensive. There is little talk about the burdens of such an expense, and there is little talk addressing the realities of whether I merit all this fuss and faxing and funding. College is for people who wish to make something of themselves, is it not? So then it seems fitting that only people who are valuable raw materials would turn out to be anything valuable after college.

It is exhausting to reconvince myself of my worthiness every day.

In previous years, whenever someone aimed me toward that conveyor belt, heading for the refiner's fire of graduation and college and all that lay beyond it, I vibrated with a sickening fear—fear that I would go too far, and then they'd find out. Find out that I am and always have been nothing more than a useless glob of flaccid clay.

But I do not feel that fear anymore.

Not today. Today that fear has retired, and I can reflect upon it with the kind of nostalgia that only a seventeen-year-old possesses. I box up this fear and place it on a shelf in the back of my mind, where I keep all the childish things I've outgrown. For today I draw a line in the sand, as one does a thousand times in these adolescent years, and I hop over my mark. I'm rather looking forward to it now—the cliff, the edge, the final rattle of my precious, most innocent years. All this time, I've dreaded this last-semester plummet, but now I see what it truly is. Like an asteroid emerging from its galactic hiding place, I see my trajectory now, and I can see that I've been hurtling along my path all along, bright and steady and true.

A cliff is worrisome; a flight path is a *path.* A bridge from one point to another. A means to an end.

Oh, we are going to have some fun, you and I. Keep turning pages, dearest. Keep tracking my words like ants marching you toward a divine picnic of discourse. Ants, asteroids—things are already in motion.

One mile has lapsed. If I keep up my pace, I'll arrive with five minutes until the tardy bell.

I pass a dog. Hitched to its zip line behind its house, it nonetheless charges at me, snarling, teeth bared, black tongue unfurling against the chicken wire of its makeshift fence.

An unkempt creature, some breed of matted white goblin rat with the rage of a cop despite being the very kickable size of a football. No doubt it was procured as a way to delight the children of a struggling family, in hopes that a pet could make up for finer things; now the pitiful pup has been relegated to the yard, the children's excitement and love dulled not long after the first dozen walks, and it takes its anger and resentment out on any passerby. Now stale shitbombs litter the yard, abandoned much like the barking rat that laid them. Not even a living thing can stave off the lure of a video game forever.

Or perhaps I am the sole purpose of its yipping; perhaps my hulking form in the world sets off the dog's baser instincts and it goes wild, hoping to scare me away. Perhaps it sniffed out my hulking ambitions.

As I put distance between myself and the hateful dog, I sidle past a pair of elementary-aged children. They sidestep me, making for the balding grass to give me dominion over the sidewalk, and I take it as a simple demonstration of natural hierarchies, the supremacy of my age over theirs, but then I hear it:

"Lardo." One of them mutters it; both laugh. I arch around to peek at them, and when our eyes meet, they scurry away, as if I might run after them, barking in retaliation until my zip line catches.

Yes, I'm primed for comments like this. Lardo, a classic—though I wonder if either of these modern younglings would be able to tell me what lard is, how it is used, or why it's an apt word to describe me. Lard seems to belong to an older time, a lost era of milk bottles and patchwork quilts and respecting your elders. And yet lard, as an appellative, is timeless, isn't it?

Fatty, pig, heifer, wide load, and other more creative variations on the form—I've heard them all. I've thought them myself, too, in case you wonder what I do with my silences.

None of it matters. Let them mock my body, my heft, let them sprinkle insults beneath me like dog shit, let them believe that I do not fit, could not fit, could not belong. Let them think that I am only what I have always been.

I'll have them all rooting for me in the end.

You too. You'll be cheering me on, aching for me to get what I so desperately deserve.

And it begins today.

Today, I'm going to—

TODAY'S THE DAY

A SHABBY AND TECHNICALLY SILVER CHEVY CELEBRITY pulls up to the curb next to Rory, nearly scraping its dented bumper against a garbage can.

"Hey! Get in!" Ethan Yorke, wrists draped over the steering wheel, has to shout his greeting, since the windows in his cheap dream car do not go back up once they've been rolled down. "It's freezing and I need coffee."

Rory, deciding not to point out the controversial sunshine, obediently trudges around the car's rear.

Ethan reaches across the passenger seat, sweeping papers and trash onto the floor, and opens the door from the inside.

Rory tucks herself into the front seat, which is still pushed all the way forward to accommodate her diminutive height—she'd wager she was the only other person to ride in Ethan's chariot all winter break.

"Why didn't you call?" Ethan scolds as he spins the car down the street.

Rory rubs her hands together in front of the one working vent. "I thought you'd be with Brad."

Ethan Yorke has taken to wearing his long black hair slicked straight back so it curls as it tickles the collar of his peacoat. The combat boots he wore even in the summer. The kilts he wears even in the winter. The eyeliner is a newer experiment, something that he kept after the Holiday Glitter Gingerbread Revue. He continues wearing it because it makes the male student body at Bosworth decidedly uncomfortable, and not necessarily because of what it does to his already piercing eyes—though that would be reason enough.

Today's cheery blue tartan is paired with a kitschy (read: ugly, but on purpose) Fair Isle sweater, likely dug out of some thrift shop's mothballed collection for less than the price of a junior bacon cheeseburger.

"Brad's got early-morning swims," Ethan says. "And rehearsals will start soon. So I guess it was nice knowing him." He always dreams big, dreams of dating beyond his own extracurricular's pool of options, but the athletes and the student council and the social sciences clubs and the hunters and farmers and the performing arts kids all live on separate planets.

He and varsity swimmer Brad have been one group project away from finally kissing, but now the portal between the worlds will close.

"Anyway, I'd still give you a ride, even if I had Brad with me." Ethan undercuts his chastising statement by plunking a lime-green CD into his Discman and cranking the volume on the haunted stereo. He gestures for Rory to pinch the cable to the tape deck just so to work against the short in the cord, and then out blasts the morning anthem.

Ethan sings his Jonathan Larson loudly, unabashedly, proud of his sharp tenor voice, and when he glances at Rory, raises his eyebrows, she's galvanized. She gives in to his spell, singing—so softly, but she does sing.

(I never said I couldn't sing.)

After driving through Cool Beans, where Ethan pays for two drip coffees and an orange roll, the car slows to a creep as they idle to get into Bosworth's parking lot. With only four hundred parking spaces and far more than four hundred students with their own sets of wheels, the parking lot becomes a battlefield each morning, and the slightest distraction could cost you a decent spot. If you don't snag a spot in the lot, you have to park on the other side of the school, behind the tennis courts, and then you have to hike like a goatherd to get to class on time.

But today, Rory and Ethan are brimming with patience.

They can wait as long as they need to; they can crawl past every parking spot, a car already nestled within its lines; they can hoof it from the tennis courts and endure a dreaded tardy staining their records, because today is the day.

The one they've been waiting for.

Ethan switches albums, skipping through the tracks of his musical hodgepodge until "Sweet Transvestite" blares through the speakers. He matches Tim Curry's sultry tone, beat for beat, as if there's an audience hidden under the hood.

Rory says, reading his mind, "She'll never pick it. They'd never let her."

"Whatever. Pam does what she wants," Ethan points out, and it's 90 percent of the truth. Bosworth's theater department has a larger budget than their football team.

"The church ladies would lose their shit." Unfortunately for Pam and any other teacher hoping to push the envelope in the name of academic evolution, Bosworth Academy has far too many pearl-clutchers on its board. Requiring high school productions of Shakespeare to remove the bawdy parts is one of their beatitudes. Expanding the mind is how the devil gets in.

"Wouldn't it be amazing, though?" Ethan pines. "I'd be Frank-N-Furter, Cole could be Eddie, one of the Owens could be Brad . . . Who would be Janet?"

Rory stops singing, holds her breath instead. Tim Curry moans on the CD while they ponder.

Oh, my. So many options, my stars. What an embarrassment of options, truly.

"Clarissa, I guess," Ethan determines, sans enthusiasm.

"Too showy." Rory gazes out her window; just outside the parking lot, an angry man in his sensible sedan breaks into a full tantrum, stuck in the Bosworth lineup near a traffic light. Rory's mouth turns up in a wry smile. There are plenty of side streets one could take to avoid the clusterfuck, if one isn't too entitled to believe he deserves a straight-shot, unimpeded route to work. Hopefully he learns his lesson. Then again, Rory's betting he'll wake up tomorrow, drive this way again, and believe he's got the stuff to beat this traffic, to really show it who's boss.

Some people are fond of wearing chips on their shoulders.

"Our last show." Ethan sighs, and Rory is all ready to get nice and sappy with him, but then he says, "Too bad about Annie. She's going to miss it."

Tread lightly. Cautious as an eel moving through shadow.

"She can still do it," Rory points out.

"But will she want to?" Ethan puts on his blinker, pouncing on a compact spot near a streetlight on a concrete pedestal.

Rory unbuckles her seat belt. "She probably doesn't even know auditions are coming up."

"Well, someone should tell her," Ethan says, jamming his gearshift with gusto; the car doesn't shut off so much as shudder into deathly silence.

Rory slings her backpack onto her shoulders, matching Ethan step for step until he pauses near the courtyard instead of following their usual path through the double doors that lead right to the drama hall.

"I've got to hand in a paper to Murdock," he explains, "and then I'm gonna . . ." He trails off, and his smile is both sheep and wolf, prey and predator.

Gonna go find Brad for one last rendezvous before their schedules really ramp up.

But he hesitates, and Rory hesitates, and they are locked. Locked in looking, locked in time, and she can see all the versions of Ethan she's ever known. Ghosts, peering out through his eyes. Memories, every semester, every show. Every moment side by side, in the front seats of his car, in the front seats of the auditorium, in the back seats of the field trip bus. Their first auditions together.

He breaks first, still sniffing after the prospect of catching Brad fresh from a post-swim locker room shower. "See you at lunch. And hey. Next time you're about to risk turning yourself into a human icicle to get to school, call me. I don't mind." He weaves past the marble urns and neatly shaven topiaries of the courtyard.

Rory heads up the school steps alone, her feet damp and cold. The sun buries itself in a passing ocean of clouds, and in the shade's cast, she makes eye contact with herself in the glass of the double doors.

The sun then reemerges, flashing away all reflection. She enters the glare, humming Janet's song, and walks into the semester she's been dreading since her first day at Bosworth.

And yet she is smiling more than she is frowning.

BOSWORTH ACADEMY

About dear old Bosworth, my future alma mater:

Bosworth was once called "the Yale of prep schools, the rose in the rot," according to the Independent Schools Association's then-current roundup of American private educational institutions. The "rot," of course, refers to the faltering mediocrity of many private institutes of education in the prior decade—corruption, nepotism, or simple complacency hath wrought the prep school sphere embarrassingly mediocre . . . But Bosworth blooms lush and bright, ranked number one in the state for academics, diversity, clubs and activities, college prep, and teachers by those whose job it is to rank such things.

I knew nothing of this competitive, almost existential world of prep schools and private education until I was offered an interview. As a scholarship student who is building her own legacy brick by brick, starting with only sand, there's still plenty I don't understand—but one look at Bosworth, and you understand this is a place built on money.

The school sprawls up into the sky and out along the main street of the old town quarters (called Main Street both officially and unofficially, since for many years there was no other candidate). It's a stunning structure, built in classic Collegiate Gothic architecture, with neat gray stones, lightly weathered until they could achieve that effect naturally, ornately buttressed facades, clusters of dormer windows, pointed arches, crenelation on the railings . . .

Less of a building and more of a statement. A weapon.

Bosworth itself—the town, not the school—is on the smaller side, a population of less than ten thousand, kept quaint with bylaws and committees and traditions. The school, the city center, the post office, the best park—all are surrounded by family farms, acres of cash crops, highways leading to other whistle-stops, leading to nowhere. The Historical Society insists on preserving the hundred-year-old buildings along Main Street, so you can shop for a cell phone inside an authentic pioneer home or eat generic Thai food cooked by white people at a restaurant with the original wood floors of the town's general store.

Bosworth's own public high school is only three blocks from my house. If it wasn't for Bosworth Academy fatefully plucking me from the murky waters of the scholarship pool, that's where I'd be. But Bosworth wrenched open its grand, pretentious entrance to me, so I strolled right through its recessed arches and decided to believe them when they said I belonged here.

You might belong here, too, if you listen to as much Liszt as you do Eminem, if you've read enough Dickens to have a favorite, if you've ever fallen in love with a magazine cover of Nicole Kidman in a Pre-Raphaelite tableau and been able to correctly name and date the painting it's referencing, if you've ever experienced spikes in blood pressure while watching a Tolkien adaptation.

If you've ever felt a burning in your middle, a longing for something impossible—a longing to live in a past era, a longing to swandive into a poem or a composition or an equation, to drown yourself in words, to be drowned in your own thoughts . . . welcome.

Here, you will find the Bosworth Princes just as culturally diseased and horny for transformation as you are.

(Yes, the Bosworth Princes. Our colors are red and white, our mascot a silvery-white sword drenched in roses—sexist, true, but some girls find it empowering.)

"The world is what you make of it." That's the slogan Bosworth engraves into its stone archways, slaps on its newspaper masthead, prints on its merchandise. That's the slogan Bosworth wants its students to live by—that we are the creators of our own worlds, and that here, at Bosworth, we will acquire the necessary skills to be ruthless and elite as we sculpt.

Armed with a free period, I cut around the drama hall and head for the library, where I will find a nice, cozy place to work on a brick in my own created world, an English essay.

Bosworth's original 1950s construction was much humbler than the many chiseled and mounted additions that have been built over the decades. The commons, the counseling office, a handful of hallways and classrooms, the auditorium, and the library all maintain the integrity of their initial fashioning. They've all had their share of updates, of course, both structural, for safety, and aesthetic, to better match the lurid strokes of the school's newer wings.

But thankfully for us Princes, the school board has yet to insist on removing the library's original tower.

A dreamy, archaic, romantic turret jutting above the flat roof of the original structure, the tower has deep-plum industrial carpet from the nineties and mahogany shelving units from the eighties, yet the tweed furnishings purchased at the turning of the millennium are still too new and stiff to be adequately comfortable.

I tend to forgo the couches and chairs and sit directly on the floor, next to the window, so I can rest my chin on the windowsill and peer down at the world below. Forgive me such a stale cliché, but from this height, my fellow students are rendered into miniatures. Dolls in dollhouses, Pollys in pockets, tiny beings on tracks through the courtyard greenery, up the steps to the foyer, into the glass-walled commons.

When the bell rings, campus clears out, and I tug my sticky attention away from this princely lookout and onto my essay.

I harbor no ill will toward my essay, even if it is on the most high school of all high school topics: Machiavelli. I expect it's a decent enough introduction to philosophy. As a teacher, I'm certain, one must feel inclined to lure students into engagement by choosing something edgy, something sexy, something that could utilize a Tarantino movie as metaphor. Is the Bride's hunt for vengeance necessary to restore balance in the past? But today, leaning over the precipice, a thousand words on whether or not I agree with Machiavelli's supposition seems as trivial and inconvenient as a thank-you card. As if it matters if I agree, as if the opinion of a seventeen-year-old scholarship scrounger bears any weight on the influence of *The Prince.*

Yet a jumble of words begins to knot itself together in my head. An entry point, a start. I scratch out my previous progress and jot down a new potential opening sentence: "*Morality* is a useless word without context; it must be accompanied by a measuring stick to give it any discernable meaning."

In a fever, alone in the tower, I tear through my essay, lost to the intricacies of my argument until the bell rings.

Bio II, then calculus, and then lunch—and at lunch, the die will finally drop. The die, cast. The die, spinning, will roll to a stop and all will be revealed.

Ethan is holding out hope for something splashy, something that puts the "drama" in melodrama. *Chicago. Little Shop of Horrors.* Anything glittery or dangerous or requiring leather.

Jake and the other techies would probably love a challenge: figuring out the rigging for *Peter Pan*, coming up with a decent production design for a minimalist show like *Godspell*, that whole Loveland sequence in *Follies*.

Our stage manager, Shandie, will secretly pout if it's not something saccharine and dripping in nostalgia: *Beauty and the Beast*, *Brigadoon*, *The Sound of Music*.

Pam is notoriously a sucker for Sondheim, and rumor has it she's been awaiting the right moment to do *Into the Woods*.

But I have my hunches.

And I think everyone will be tickled.

(What about you? Do you have any guesses as to what the musical will be?)

(Are we having fun yet?)

LUNCHTIME

We open on a wide hallway, capped in double doors that lead out to the parking lot. This hallway has a name, actually, as do all the hallways and rooms at Bosworth. This is Euripides, the famed hallway of the performing arts, its name prominently displayed on a placard above an arched section break halfway down the tiles. There is nothing particularly special about it, at least aesthetically—simple white tile floors, impeccably bricked walls, a new drinking fountain with still-shiny chrome—but hallways named in memoriam for old dead white people are always fancier by design. (And buildings, and streets, parks, congressional bills . . .)

Euripides's most devoted students forsake the cafeteria and spend their lunch hour here, safe in its familiarity, safe in Mother's womb. Students sprawl along the floor in various lumps. Some sit up with their lunch trays on their knees. Some tear off bits of that strangely omnipresent white dinner roll that shows up as a side dish for every school lunch and dip it into the grease pooling on their little burnt pepperonis before daintily eating its soft dough.

Some forgo eating at all, opting for liquid lunches in the form of slushy lemonades from the commons, cookies 'n' cream milkshakes from the subpar burger joint across the street, or neon-red limited-edition Mountain Dews from the vending machines in the science hall (Oppenheimer, if you care to keep track).

Farther down the hall, toward the place where an art teacher would have you draw a dot to serve as a vanishing point as you learn to draw lockers and windows and doorways in proper perspective, a foyer splits into two doorways. One leads to Handel (the choir room), one leads to Mahler (the band room). These two neighbors exist in harmony, occasionally appearing in each other's recitals and concerts and state tournaments. Many choir students are in orchestra; many band geeks sing in the choir. These students get their food from the cafeteria and bring it down to Euripides, too, though they mingle with the drama kids at some risk to their egos.

Today, as it stands, is the perfect day for such mingling. All the drama students are banned from their classroom (Bernhardt, though if you call it anything but Hardy, no one will know what you're referencing), where they ordinarily would charge around the tables and Irish-dance on the stage and sing in huddled karaoke groups or gossip loudly while playing cards, letting out their energy like members of a wealthy dinner club in an Edgar Allan Poe tale.

The drama club cult—no one wants out, and no one wants to let you in.

But today, everyone is equally locked out of Hardy while they wait. The drama room is dark. The only light comes from Pam Hanson's office, the faint blue glow of her computer screen radiating out the Plexiglas windows of her office, casting a remarkably eerie sheen on the framed portrait of Ibsen, glaring at the viewer from the adjacent wall.

They may wait as they wish: pacing, wrestling, stacking themselves on each other's shoulders to place an Oscar Mayer sticker onto the vent above the drinking fountain, huddling in a corner, munching from the bag of Cheetos in the pocket of an oversize hoodie.

From the hive of the foaming, fiddle-footed students comes a frenzy of conversation, answers draping over questions before they've been fully articulated:

Is it up yet?

She said she would post it at lunch.

This is lunch, isn't it?

Maybe she's still deciding. She wants it to be big, remember? All out. A smash.

Don't you have tech with her next?

She's been busy, guys. Her sister's wedding. Moving. Give her a break.

Are you going to try out?

Depends on what it is, I guess.

Liar. You have to try out if you're in choir or band. It's required.

I have to try out, but I don't have to be in it.

What if it's Wicked? *(spoken in a squeal)*

No way. The rights aren't out yet.

What's taking so long? She's torturing us!

If it's not up now, it'll be posted after school. Calm down. You know you'll audition no matter what it is.

Just not Music Man. *Please. Not* Music Man.

In the nook where Euripides bends into the entrance to the auditorium, Rory sits cross-legged. Her pen is poised on her notebook, her AP US History book is open to the chapter 12 study guide, but she hasn't dragged ink across the page or even read the first review question. She's staring at the tile just beyond her book, its surface well waxed and reflecting the bottom edge of Hardy's door. She is not quite in a trance, since she is taking in every last comment around her, but neither is she completely present in Euripides with the rest of her agonized classmates.

This is it. The last audition. The last show.

Rory's last chance.

A hush befalls the hallway as Pam emerges from the drama room. She cradles a stack of papers in her arms as if they were just born in a stable to fulfill an angel's prophecy. With no eye contact, no words, only a slight smirk like she is tossing bread crumbs to a lake of hungry ducks, she pins a sign-up sheet to the bulletin board.

And the ducks come a-running.

Good Knight! Sweet Lady: A Musical in Two Acts

The audition information is there on the paper—time slots, dates, requirements (thirty seconds of material, a song in your range).

The cat's out of the bag. The consensus, so far, is a positive one—anyone who was dreading that Pam would choose some lifeless, hackneyed musical standard like *Grease* can rest easy (and should rest ashamed to even think that Pam would choose to do something like *Grease*, and should also rest ashamed to think that Pam couldn't take *Grease* and skin it and give it new life. With Pam's genius and her resources, she could make *Grease* as edgy and brilliant as if Jason Robert Brown had debuted it last year).

Rory's trapped in the hive of three dozen delighted high school thespians. She glances up to lock eyes with Pam, but the teacher's already gone back into Hardy, flipping on the lights, opening the room once again to her students, who will soon flood into the space like dogs unlocked from their kennels.

Flyers will appear around campus, pinned to bulletin boards in the library, the gym, the front office. Auditions will be held in less than two weeks. Pens are clicked, raised to the sign-up sheet to claim time slots as the high-spirited nattering begins once again:

Holy shit, yes! I thought for sure she was gonna do another Sondheim.

What's wrong with Sondheim?

Nothing, but she did Into the Woods *a few years ago. I thought maybe she'd pull it back out again.*

Better than Sondheim—this is amazing! And there's so many female leads.

My mom did this in college. They did it all topless, though.

Jesus, really?

That doesn't mean Pam's gonna do that, you dope.

Do you have the movie? Does anyone?

No, but Hollywood Video does. I'm gonna rent it. You want to come over and watch it this weekend?

Yes.

Me, too.

Does anyone have the soundtrack?

Jake said he'll download it.

Make me a copy?

And me?

Auditions in two weeks—fuck. I've got to start getting ready.

Bzzz, bzzz goes the rowdy throng, and Rory clutches her pen, beaming, happy to be the heartbeat at the center.

GOOD KNIGHT! SWEET LADY

ORIGINALLY WRITTEN AS A STAGE MUSICAL FOR A COL-
lege summer-camp resort, *Good Knight! Sweet Lady* was adapted
for Broadway in 1978 but was an immediate failure, canceled after
only a week of productions. Theaters in New York City have strict
rules about ticket sales, and if you dip below the threshold, that's
it, your show's contract is null and void, and someone else, some
other show, can take your place. (Probably *The Music Man*. They're
always filling up theaters with some version of *The Music Man*.)

But there were a few people who loved it. And the cast and crew
didn't feel like they were quite done with it yet. So, with the blessing
of the writers, they put on one last production on the Great Lawn
in Central Park. Totally grassroots. No lighting, nothing fancy.
Someone lugged over a pair of speakers, and they blasted the score
from the cast members' practice cassettes.

That show turned out almost two hundred people in the audience, which was triple what they'd been selling in the theater. And
that "one last show" turned into another, and another, until they got
a regular spot at the Delacorte Theater and played all September.

That turned into a variety show of sorts, a nightly run of the musical's best songs, plus marionette skits and juggling routines from local buskers. This version of *Good Knight! Sweet Lady* is still performed in parks all around America—go to the nearest outdoor amphitheater or wherever the flower children in your area gather, and I'll bet they're getting ready for a run.

Meanwhile, probably inspired by all that potential hippie cash, someone decided to revive the original musical. They cleaned it up, rewrote a few of the worst bits, and it made its debut this time off-Broadway, at the Martinson in the Public Theater, where it played for a good three years, received some Tonys, and was optioned for a movie.

The movie, another cult classic, was nothing like the original production, of course—nothing ever is, right? But they got Ian Holm as Warwicke, prince of Tillypoo; and Glenn Close cameoed as Lady Bearce, the knight trainer, a real gym teacher Trunchbull type, which . . . well, you can understand the hilarity there, seeing her in this role. It's still played in old-timey art house movie theaters on the first day of spring, à la *Rocky Horror*—there's a live cast who perform the parts in front of the giant screen playing the movie. Audience members play along with their own brown bag of props, the subtitles rolling so everyone can karaoke their way through the surprisingly catchy tunes. There are costume contests. Raffles for charity. Someone from the audience is selected to be the White Knight and preside over the whole show from a saddle on top of a pommel horse.

It's mysterious enough to the general population to be a wonder, a delight, something familiar but not intimate, and it's popular enough in the theater world to not be too obscure. The perfect balance must be struck. No one really wants to put on another production of *The Music Man*.

It's a good pick. A romantic plot with sword fights and slap-stick, which means Pam will have a huge turnout for auditions. Plenty of solos, which means everyone auditioning will delude themselves into believing they could snag one. A strong ensemble, which means everyone bypassed for the solos will still be able to join the cast.

Pam likely has a vision, something she'll reveal in a grand, sweeping monologue during the first cast reading.

And what a cast there shall be! Students will clamor for the roles offered by this musical. There's the charming, swashbuck-ling Thackery, the treacherous Lurkin, the hilarious Harold and Harolda, king and queen of Tillypoo—

But the role that'll have everyone salivating is Joetta the Fox Maiden.

Let me tell you about Joetta. She's the center of the show. She's the Hamlet, the Tevye, the Jean Valjean. She's the rare female char-acter who gets the bulk of the good songs, and it's a show-stealing part—usually women are lucky to get a handful of lines. You get a tiny space to make an impression, and that's it.

Joetta's the role of every theater girl's dreams. Every senior would die to play this part. It's not an old hag, or a sexless mother, or a one-dimensional villain, or a loopy ditz with the worst song in the production. Joetta is simply splendid.

The Elphaba, the Millie, the Blanche DuBois—

And there's no better senior to play this role than Annie Neville.

There's just one problem. Annie Neville won't go anywhere near the drama department. Not anymore.

Because Annie Neville absolutely hates me.

Well, more than one problem, I should say. There's really a series of problems, and they're all nested inside one another, a matryoshka doll of dilemmas.

The biggest, most pressing of dilemmas: Annie Neville is in a cast. She broke her leg in three places, had it screwed back together, and is only now shifting to a walking cast. She's been home since December, since the accident, and she's due back in school next week—but it'll be a bittersweet return. The broken leg not only knocked her on her ass; it also knocked her off the basketball team. Annie's been the star of the Bosworth Princes since her sophomore year. She's the one who led them to the state championship last spring.

Yes, she loved theater. She played Mary Warren in *The Crucible*, a casting decision that the rest of us would have taken as a hint from Pam, the carrot undoubtedly leading to a principal role in the spring musical. But Annie was ready to dedicate the rest of her senior year to basketball, since colleges wanted her to be the star of their courts for as long as she could stretch out a four-year education—

And then the car wreck.

It swept her right off the team. Not officially, I suppose. Officially, Annie's still there, still has the team sweats, still has her number on her jersey, will probably still show up at practice and brood from the bench, because that's the kind of person Annie is— hopelessly, ruthlessly dedicated.

All that potential, all those visions of Annie's long blond ponytail swinging from the center of a college court, her bubblegum smile and California-blue eyes twinkling at the buzzer—gone. Gone with the snap of her femur, a concussion, and the smashed-up

Dodge Neon that she'd purchased with two summers' worth of nannying money.

Twist the matryoshkas in half, open them up, and see all that resentment, that shame, that sadness, unfairness, rage, despair, all of it packed inside, packed tight as dirt.

Would Annie even want to return to the drama department? She loved it, loved it as much as she loved anything. Some don't believe a person can serve two masters, but Annie doesn't do anything halfheartedly. She has heart enough for both basketball and the theater, and yet perhaps the fractures in her leg also fractured her ability to care about anything like that again.

In the very center of our nesting dolls, small and hard as a bullet, is Annie's grudge against me, her loathing.

We were best friends. Sleepovers, swapping clothes, swapping secrets.

And I was driving the car that night she broke her leg.

Her hostility toward me is wonderfully logical, which works in my favor. The unhinged angers and fears are the hardest to break, because you cannot fight the irrational with the rational—it's like throwing fire onto fire.

No, it's perfectly understandable that Annie should hate me. Why her mother always says she's sleeping whenever I call. Why she ignored the email I sent (only one email, because sending any more than that would have been unnecessary; Annie does what she wants the first time, with little to no floundering, and if she wanted to respond, she would have answered), asking if she needed me to bring her math book home from her locker. My handwritten letter of apology, too, garnered no reply.

But I need her.

I need her in the play.

Yes, I suppose it would be excellent for her spirits, to turn back to the drama club in the wake of her athletic tragedy, to find solace in her versatility—but I won't pretend I'm motivated by such goodwill.

I promised you honesty, remember?

Perhaps if I were a better person, I'd let Annie go entirely. I'd stop calling. I'd let her sulk on the bench for the rest of the semester, let her get some pity trophy when the Princes fumble their first round in the playoffs. Let her graduate with some random picture of her in the drama club as her only yearbook presence. Annie Neville, member of the Princely Players, only one leading role, and a thankless one at that. Annie Neville, technically part of the Bosworth Princes but a permanent fixture on the bench, no minutes played on the court at all.

A bleak prospect, but perhaps if I were a good and decent person, I'd do just that.

I've never said I was good or decent, only that I am human.

And I need Annie Neville in the play. I need her name on that cast list, or nothing else will fall in line.

Without her, nothing else will work.

So after school today, I am walking the four-and-a-half miles to the Nevilles' gorgeous, black-shuttered, white-brick Colonial, and I have three aims:

To convince Annie that she forgives me for the car wreck, despite her instincts telling her not to.

To convince Annie that she absolutely wants to audition for this play.

To convince her that the theater is where her passions truly lay all along. Annie, my dear, this busted-leg, broken-basketball-career situation needn't be such a tragedy! Let me show you: *Good Knight! Sweet Lady* is a celebration, a revelation, an opportunity!

A hand, extended directly to her.

The role of a lifetime.

ANNIE

Annie never expected a broken leg would be this painful.

She's had injuries before. She's been an athlete all her life. She's survived sprains, taped fingers, shiners. The worst part about shattering her leg isn't the pain as her bones fuse back together, no. It's the pain of sitting. Day after day. Waiting to heal.

"*Rest* is a verb," her well-meaning mother tells her. Mrs. Neville is echoing the coach for the Bosworth Princes, and the coach is a woman who did exactly what Annie hoped to do—starred in high school without peaking, went on to make her college team proud. The coach prioritizes her team's recovery after tough practices, teaching them to listen to their bodies, know when they're pushing too hard.

Right now, *rest* doesn't feel like a verb to Annie. Neither does *heal*. They both feel like prisons.

They're breaking her more than the car wreck did.

Annie sits in her bed. On her lap desk, she's stacked several of her homework packets, most of them completed. The teachers at Bosworth have been thoughtful and supportive, letting her finish the last semester and begin this new one from her wretched bedroom nest.

Next week, she'll be back. Back at school. She should be excited.

Her walking cast is a disappointment. She hobbles in it. It's a hobbling cast. Her walk will never be the same.

Nothing about her will ever be the same.

Annie Neville will be returning to school in name only. The car wreck changed her. Crushed her. Stole her entire life. She can't think about it without a stultifying rage coiling inside of her, and so she doesn't.

Doesn't think, doesn't move. Certainly doesn't run or jump or shoot.

Rests. Heals.

Her mother knocks on the door. "You've got a visitor."

The door opens wider, and Rory King advances into the room, slowly, as if she hasn't been in this very bedroom a thousand times before.

"Do you want a soda?" Mrs. Neville asks.

Rory shakes her head. "No, thank you."

"Tell your mother I said hello." Mrs. Neville pulls the door closed, leaving the two girls to suffocate alone in the silence.

What to call them? Friends?

They are still invited to the same social interactions, still locker partners. Mrs. Neville is still Rory's emergency contact at Bosworth in case the office can't get ahold of Ms. King. There's still an association in the mind of everyone at school—you think of Rory, you think of Annie. They are a duo. An unlikely pair who could trace their affinity all the way back to a fateful meeting at a Shakespeare festival their sophomore year—and a two-year friendship in a cutthroat, competitive, academics-centered environment such as Bosworth Academy is a small miracle.

And Rory still knows to bring Annie her favorite Fruity Loops donut from Eddie's to wave as a white flag.

She opens the paper bag, presenting Annie with the cereal-encrusted bribe.

"What are you doing here?" Annie cuts.

When Annie doesn't take the donut from Rory's hand, Rory sets the bag on the bed, the donut on the bag. Then she inhales, long and deep, no doubt summoning courage.

"Listen, I'm sorry. You've heard me say it, write it, pass it along through your mother. I'll send it to you by Morse code or carrier pigeon if I have to. I'm so sorry this happened. I wish I could go back in time and change things. I wish it had been my leg that was smashed."

Rory's only injury from the car wreck was a jagged scratch on her wrist, a triangle of glass from the window temporarily embedded in her flesh. It wasn't even deep enough for stitches.

Her chin trembles now as she surveys Annie, but at some point she can't stand it anymore and glances down at her feet on the rug. "I wish I could change things so you could still play basketball and I could still have you in my life. That's what I wish most of all. That I could have my best friend back."

Annie resists, then exhales, her eyes flooding with tears.

"I didn't mean to do it," Rory goes on in a tiny, watery voice. "It was an accident. I can't tell you how sorry I am—"

"Of course you didn't mean to," Annie finally says. "That cat came out of nowhere."

48

Came out of nowhere. That's what Rory kept wailing the night of the wreck. She'd swerved to avoid an asshole of a tabby cat that leaped out from between two garbage cans—and had rammed directly into a spare barrier that had been plunked on the side of the quiet suburban road by construction workers repainting the line.

"Fucking cat," Rory mutters. "I should have just run it over. If you're stupid enough to run under the wheels of a car, you're too stupid to live."

"It wasn't your fault, Ror. It's not your fault." Annie repeats this—not because she doesn't believe it, but because she's had to say it to so many other people that she's weary of it now and wants to make sure it sinks in. "But . . . my scholarship. My championship games. Senior year—god, Rory, I've been looking forward to this since ninth grade. Coach was starting me, those people from Kansas were excited to come watch, and then . . . just gone. My whole world. Gone."

She's already cried over this situation, but apparently she needs to cry some more—and suppressing the tears now would only mean a torrent of tears later. It's as futile as holding a beach ball underwater.

And Rory cries the tears of an apologetic, guilty friend, the hapless girl who has gotten someone else tangled up in the most traumatizing and challenging scenario of her life but still has to live her own life unfettered, like some lazy asshole walking away from a spill he caused in a grocery store.

But this kind of disaster can be endured if you are enduring it with someone else.

So I suppose they are still friends after all.

"Annie, listen. I'm not trying to be pushy or anything." Rory reaches into her backpack, pulls out a yellow paper. "I know basketball was—is—everything to you. Your whole world, you said. But you've always had two worlds, really. Basketball and drama club. And look what we're doing for the spring musical."

She sets the paper right on Annie's lap desk, covering up the homework packets.

Annie scans the flyer. Scans the title. Rory watches for signs of life—signs that Annie might be willing to come to life again for this.

Annie's game face is impeccable.

Annie the Boulder, they called her on the court. Nothing could bowl her over. Nothing could get under her skin. She was immovable.

Rory flops onto the bed, daring to lean toward Annie, her hand very close to where Annie's dressed, healing leg rests on the comforter.

But not even Annie the Boulder can resist *Good Knight! Sweet Lady.* "Isn't this—? I mean, Pam usually picks more conservative musicals. This is kind of hip and trendy for her, isn't it?"

Rory shrugs. "Must be a midlife crisis. Or maybe someone pushed her in this direction. Someone young and hip and trendy."

Annie rolls her eyes, but hidden in the purse of her lips is a smile. "This is pretty cool, actually."

"Your favorite," Rory adds, as if Annie could forget. She doesn't say what they are both thinking—that this musical is the only thing that could drag Annie out of her sickbed and back to the auditorium.

There it is—a glimmer in Annie's eye. A spark, a need to challenge this unspoken prophecy, which is how Rory knows she's on the right track. Annie loves a fight—but she won't fight if it's already a lost cause. She's fair that way.

"I want us to be friends again," Rory says slowly, "if you can forgive me. I understand if you don't. But you know what else I want? I want to see you as Joetta."

Annie's long blond hair, her statuesque figure, her stalwart regality, so reminiscent of a younger Vanessa Redgrave—the perfect person to play the part of the knighted princess. Joetta has to wear gowns but still armor up, carry a sword and a shield. She has to be heartthrob and heroine. Annie is both of those things from dawn until dark.

"Clarissa will get it," Annie says. "She's got her eye on every lead. And it's senior year—she'll act like it's owed to her, and Pam will agree. Plus Pam's still pissed at me for doing basketball last spring instead of the musical. She'll never give me a fair chance."

"Clarissa's too bubbly for Joetta," Rory points out. "She'll be better as Catherine. But she's been so busy with student council. Maybe she won't even audition."

A lie—Clarissa lives at the auditorium. She'll audition. She'll be expecting this lead. She'll try to get Pam to see Joetta as a sunny, peppy Sweet Valley twin of a princess.

"Joetta has to be someone mysterious and wise, someone effortlessly beautiful," Rory presses. "Meryl Streep. Cate Blanchett. Rachel Weisz. You're one of them. You were born to play Joetta!"

Annie still stares at the paper, as if brainstorming more excuses.

"You come back on Monday, right? The parent meeting is Tuesday. Auditions are the week after that. Please, Annie, come on! It's our last show. Senior year. This is the first spring you don't have a conflict with basketball!" Rory swallows, then says, "Maybe your leg is a blessing in disguise—"

At that, Annie wakes up. Out of her trance. Her mouth twitches. "A blessing in disguise? Really? You think this is a blessing? You think I should be grateful this happened?"

Rory stands up. "That's not what I mean! I just mean something good could come out of this—"

"Something good? You don't think the hours of surgery were good? You don't think it's been good to watch my scholarships go to Brenna and Lucy instead? And they won't even play! What a waste of money, bringing those two onto a college team just to fill a spot—my spot. They're each taking a spot that should have gone to me. And you're saying I should hobble onto the auditorium stage and end the year with a little song and dance? Go fuck yourself, Rory."

Rory doesn't move. Annie is the boulder, but Rory is the best friend of the boulder, and she has learned to be stalwart in her own way.

"I forgive you for the car accident," Annie says. "It wasn't your fault. It was just one of those things—but I'll never forgive you for saying this. Not everything has a silver lining. Some things just suck. I don't care that Pam's doing my dream show. Nothing could ever make up for what this leg has cost me."

To Rory's credit, she leaves after this impassioned speech. She nods, takes the flyer, and says goodbye to Mrs. Neville on her way out the door.

In her bedroom, Annie stares at the colorful donut on the bag until all her hot, angry tears dissolve and she's certain she won't cry anymore. Then she eats the whole thing in three large, numb bites, gulping it down with a soda. (Coach usually forbids soda during the season, saying it slows the team down and fucks with their endurance, but she's been guzzling it nonstop since she came home from the hospital.) She spends the rest of the night sulking while waiting for this week's episode of *America's Next Top Model* to start so she can flood her brain with distractions. The last thing she wants to do is think about her own life.

A blessing in disguise. Fuck that. How could Rory contort the worst thing that ever happened to Annie into a serendipitous balloon animal? Sometimes sad things are sad, happy things are happy, and there's no need to mold them otherwise. Sometimes shit happens. There's no need to dig through the shit for flower petals.

It doesn't matter that Pam is doing *Good Knight! Sweet Lady*, the very show that made Annie fall in love with musicals in the first place. Annie is perfectly content to spend the rest of her high school days dragging her leg like the dead weight it is, going through the motions, hurrying to graduate so she can move on to college, start over fresh.

Find a new version of herself to be.

LURES
AND HOOKS

You're probably nervous, aren't you? You're biting your nails, you're thinking, *Oh, no, Annie Neville is far too brittle and angry and traumatized to audition. Rory said the wrong thing—and all Rory's grand plans revolve around getting Annie to play Joetta. One insensitive, ill-timed remark to her former best friend, and Rory's schemes are crashing down like the* Hindenburg—

The look on your face during that last chapter! You truly believed me, didn't you? You believed I was sorry?

You believed I'd put my foot in my mouth, saying all that bullshit about silver linings to persuade Annie to audition? To lure her in?

No, Annie isn't like a fish. She doesn't need shiny objects to bait her. She needs the opposite, in fact—she needs rough terrain. Mountains to climb. She needs the kinds of obstacles that everyone else says are impossible—so she can overcome them, be the triumphant winner, experience that adrenaline rush that comes when you defy the odds and inspire family-friendly screenplays about determination and conviction.

I didn't come into her bedroom with a donut and a flyer, enticing her to pounce on the audition like she was a kitten and I was wiggling a feather toy in front of her paws.

I came in and set up an emotional obstacle course for her. She'll be driving cognitive bumper cars all weekend, and if I know Annie—and I do, better than anyone else knows her, even her own mother—then I'll need to start practicing my surprised-but-delighted face when she strolls into the parents' meeting on Tuesday.

I set it all up, every single bread crumb. Pam wasn't likely to do *Good Knight! Sweet Lady* on her own. Absolutely someone had to push her into selecting it.

I didn't do it—not directly.

But I'd still like to take the credit I deserve.

You know how pool works? There's a cue ball, and you knock the cue ball so it knocks into another ball and sends it into a pocket?

I'm not the cue ball.

Preston Gray's the cue ball. That trombone-playing weenie is Pam's star pupil of the month. He's been hanging around the auditorium late after school, helping her with the light rigs. Surely he believes he's been singled out by Pam because she senses some talent aboil in his performances this unit and not because of his physical size and strength, making him the perfect lackey to unclip the heavy lights from their cables.

Most important, Preston's mother is an old friend of Pam's, and they've had three social coffee dates wherein they've reminisced about the glory days, their college theater troupe, their unspoken but seething rivalry as the two altos—all information that can be easily procured if one is studying at a nearby table, head buried in textbooks, headphones plugged into nothing.

The best way to make Pam feel old—reminisce about old times.

So line up the shot and knock the cue ball toward your target. Mention the musical to Preston, mention that Pam and his mom did it in college. Get him to bring it up to his mom, which gets her humming it. His mom brings it up to Pam, who remembers all the frustrations of their college production, the cheap clichés their director leaned upon, the radiant bursts of ideas Pam had during their dress rehearsal, the way she would have done it, tucked away and forgotten and now brought back out into the sun after all these years.

Corner pocket, easy-peasy.

There are a few more wheels to grease. But everything is going swimmingly.

You needn't doubt me again. I may not be much to look at, I may not stink of the usual Bosworth wealth and substance, I may not radiate charisma or command respect from my peers or lustful adoration from any of the genders, but I do have my own sportive tricks to employ.

Care to watch the next?

PARENT MEETING

ALL THE HOUSE LIGHTS ARE ON. THE STAGE IS DARK.

The Elizabethan Theater feels smaller when the stage is dark. It feels like what it is: a high school auditorium where the student council holds start-of-term motivational assemblies and occasional guest speakers address the student body to imbue either wonder or fear—an astronaut recently returned from a mission to fix something on the International Space Station, a congresswoman bearing her courageous tale of teenage pregnancy, whatever juvenile anti-drug program is trendy in a given year.

Only in the presence of the Princely Players does the Elizabethan reach its majestic potential—this is a spacious, elegant theater, recently renovated, but Ms. Hanson insisted the contractors retain the original limestone facade, the carved columns, the wood railing.

These details merge with the new ceiling, inlaid with fifteen glass panels, each donated by generous (or is it posturing?) alumni, and the reupholstered red velvet seats perfectly match the heavy curtains onstage. The custom-built booth features state-of-the-art light- and soundboards, spanking-new microphones, headsets, access to the rigging, catwalks, pulleys—everything you need to put on a Broadway-quality show for the parents and community of Bosworth's entrants.

It feels historic yet not grimy, ornate yet not stuffy. Most of the Princely Players believe themselves and their productions to be worthy of their space.

And tonight, they file into the auditorium with their parents in tow, as if they are showing their legal guardians a secret corner of their bedroom, a place they feel an intense authority over.

In they trickle, in odd groups—a parent with a student, a couple of parents with their student, a parent and a younger sibling with a student. They take their seats, speaking amongst themselves in hushes as if this is church.

Rory, who arrived early and accepted a chore from Pam, dutifully hands out papers to all who are attending. She smiles at the parents as she does so and wonders what they think of it, privately, this strange cohort of students who willingly give up their time and energy to this pursuit. She wonders which of these parents refer to the drama club as a hobby, an extracurricular, a fun little project, or something equally trivializing.

"All right, we'll go ahead and get started," Pam announces at the stroke of seven. "For those of you who don't know me, I'm Pam Hanson. I'm the drama teacher here at Bosworth. For those of you who do know me, well, my apologies."

A generous sprinkling of laughter.

The truth is that Pam only allows a finite number of people to know her; the rest of the world knows only her ego, which says things like this in jest because they would never be interpreted otherwise. Not with her track record.

As Pam delivers her introduction, the orchestra door opens. One more parent-child duo slips into the auditorium—Annie and Mrs. Neville, who take the seats closest to the door so as not to disturb the meeting by walking all the way across the rows.

Rory peeks at these newcomers from her front-and-center spot, nearest to Pam, and she can't help it—she gives a small wave to Annie, then instantly drops her hand, as though she regrets it, regrets being too obvious.

Annie pauses for a moment, and does not wave, but smiles.

And the smile is enough for Rory to feel like someone has turned the spotlight on her—warmed by the attention, warmed with the hope that perhaps their friendship will be mended by the end of this production.

"Let's talk about the show!" Pam says. "It's very exciting that we've been able to get the rights to *Good Knight! Sweet Lady.* There's no junior version or high school version of this show, which means we're taking on the full original. It's a big task, and kind of a splurge, but I think we deserve to do something special this year, to send our seniors out with a real bang."

Pam explains the show, a vague, generic description of her particular vision, and that she'll be needing a handful of leads, several sub-leads, plenty of comedic slapstick in the background, and a huge cast for all the ensemble songs, of which there are many.

"This is a big wild show with lots of movement onstage," she goes on. "If you want to be in a musical with lots of singing and dancing, you'll have plenty of chances in this one. We'll also have a live orchestra, if we can swing it—so if you're an instrumentalist and you'd like to play, please speak with Mrs. Menounos in Mahler."

The spiel is given. The parents sign the paper, signifying that they give their loinfruit permission to spend even more hours inside Bosworth's hallowed halls. The students sign the paper, signifying that they understand Pam's expectations and will follow her rules, if cast.

"If you're hoping for a lead," Pam adds, "I have to tell you right now—you'd better be ready to work. You get one excused absence and one no-show. After that, you're out of my cast. You might have the singing chops, you might think you can act yourself into an Oscar, but if you can't show up for rehearsals, you're useless to us."

Rory senses every other student doing exactly what she's doing—holding still, listening to Pam's words like they're scripture, so as to communicate how seriously she's taking this.

"The leads will have heavy lifting. They'll be here for every rehearsal, especially Thackery and Joetta. It's very demanding—so if you aren't sure if your schedule can handle it, be honest when you audition. Write down that you'd like a smaller part or an ensemble role. Don't overcommit if you can't devote yourself to this for the next two months—everyone in the show will be relying on you."

Without being directly asked, Rory gathers the signed and dog-eared papers. She waves goodbye to a few of the students, friends who would normally linger with her and screw around until the custodians kick them out, but they traipse out with their parents, who are anxious to leave the Elizabethan and get back to the shuffle of weeknight life.

Ethan calls to Rory from the doorway, angling his body so his feet are in the foyer and his head is in the theater. "I don't know what to audition with," he groans. "Shandie said Pam's sick of 'Mr. Cellophane.' Will you help me?"

At least a dozen possibilities rush through Rory's mind, each one ideal for Ethan's velvety tenor and dazzling, saucy personality.

"Tomorrow," she vows, and Ethan leaves with his parents.

Annie leaves without saying a word to Rory, but Rory is not discouraged. Annie's signed sheet is in the stack. Annie doesn't give her signature without giving her word.

Rory takes her time in the Elizabethan, double-checking all the rows of chairs for garbage or lost keys.

Pam is back in Hardy, in her office, cracking open a Diet Coke.

Timidly, Rory approaches the open door, her own blank permission slip in hand. "Sorry my mom couldn't come tonight. I'll bring this home and make sure she signs it."

Pam's smile is vacant, her eyes glued to her computer screen, open to a grading spreadsheet. "She's at work?"

"Yeah." The surge of emotions takes Rory by surprise; she swallows hard before adding, "A double. She probably won't be home until after midnight." She inhales. "I hate being the only one at these meetings without a parent. And I'll be the only one in the show without a parent in the audience." She sniffles but doesn't catch the lone tear rolling off the tip of her nose, which has turned bright pink with her vulnerability.

"She's doing the best she can," comes Pam's sympathetic response. "My mom worked, too." She angles her chair toward Rory, away from her computer. "My dad was getting his master's, and my mom opened a day care. Childcare was one of the only jobs she could find—you know, because they discouraged women from doing other work that wasn't so virtuously feminine."

Rory notes Pam's oversize gender-neutral sweatshirt, straight jeans, and worn-out loafers that could have come from either side of the shoe racks at the department store, as well as Pam's unpainted face and short, feathered George Michael–esque haircut.

"She had to miss a lot of things because of work," Pam continues, "and I remember being frustrated. Alone. Like everyone else had a family but me."

Rory is quiet, as if letting the accuracy of this familiar sentiment sink in.

"Even if she's not here in person, your mom supports you," Pam concludes, and both of them recognize it as the kind of statement a teacher is expected to make to their students, even if it isn't true. It sounds true, and it feels true, and it closes up the conversation neat as a stitch.

"I'll see you tomorrow." Rory steps back from the office and buttons her jacket, wrapping a threadbare scarf around her neck so she can bury her face in its layers.

"Who's picking you up?" Pam catches the loose thread of their discussion, a V-shaped wrinkle between her eyebrows.

Rory blinks. "Oh, it's—it's only a couple of blocks. I'll be fine."

"Not in this cold." Pam gestures up to the windows that kiss the drama room ceiling. There's no wind, no rain or snow, only the still, haunting blue of a freezing January evening. "I'll drive you home. Let me just finish up here."

"No, really," Rory says.

Pam doesn't insist, but she doesn't respond to Rory's protestations, either. She even lets Rory help with her prep work, giving her handouts to staple, flagged and highlighted plays to return to the shelves. Rory labors silently but steadily, face glazed with contentedness.

They lock up Pam's office and head out to her Honda Pilot crossover. Pam finishes the last dribble of her Diet Coke, tosses it into a parking lot garbage bin, and opens a new can, which was waiting for her in the cup holder.

"Have you heard from any colleges yet?" she asks, and Rory

senses Pam is not truly invested in the answer but needed something to ask about while the car warms up.

"Not yet," says Rory. "It takes a little longer with financial aid."

"You'll get some bites," Pam prognosticates. "Your grades are impeccable. Excellent track record. SUU will want you, I'm sure. And none of the other schools matter, right?"

Rory lets herself feel flattered; in grateful return, she asks Pam about her own time at SUU, where they were so thrilled with Pam's achievements, they had to make up new awards to give to her because she'd won all the others already.

"They'll want you," Pam keeps repeating. "Be patient. I'm sure you'll find that holy white envelope in your mailbox any day now."

They pull in front of Rory's house, and Pam notes that it looks threateningly dark.

"Our porch light keeps going out," Rory explains as she digs through her backpack for her house keys.

She thanks Pam for the ride, and when she unlocks the door, she turns around to wave, letting Pam know that she's safely inside, but Pam's already driven away.

DOUBLE SHIFT

Scene 1

Interior. A split-level house, built in the '70s, updated in the '90s.

> RORY *enters through the front door and kicks out of her boots, which she leaves on the cheap linoleum landing. There's a faint smell of onions in the air. The fluorescent lights are low. A TV flickers from the adjacent kitchen.*

MOM: Is that you?

> RORY *hears the cheeriness in* MOM's *voice and braces herself against it. Almost like she prefers* MOM *to be tired, cranky from a long day of broken bones, drug overdoses, and mystery stomach issues.*
>
> *She does not answer, because who else would it be?*

MOM: Are you hungry?

> *The phone rings.* RORY *sprints into the kitchen.* MOM's *already holding the cordless phone, but* RORY *plucks it out of her hand.*

RORY: *(breathless)*
Hello?

She tries her hardest to ignore the beep on the cordless phone, signifying that the battery is nearly dead.

PAM: *(on phone)*
Hi, Rory? It's Pam. You left your scarf in my car. You can get it tomorrow during class, or if you need it before then, I'll be at the school around seven getting the auditorium ready for auditions.

RORY: Okay, yes. Thank you. Sounds good.

PAM: Have a good night.

She ends the call cleanly; the conversation would have been the same to her if she'd gotten an answering machine.

RORY: Could we keep the phone on the charger when it's not being used? Is that too much to ask?

She places the phone on the charger, annoyed.

MOM: Was that Ms. Hanson? What'd she want?

RORY: Nothing. Just drama stuff.

She opens the fridge.

MOM: I made risotto. I even saved some for you—but you better act fast before I finish it.

MOM is eating standing up, hunched over the counter, in a matching set of maroon sweats. The house is freshly cleaned, a load of towels recently folded on the dining table. Catching up on neglected chores and babying a risotto—these are the kinds of things MOM *does on her nights off.*

RORY: I'm not hungry.

She leaves the kitchen and heads for the stairs.

MOM: Wait! It's *American Idol* night. Don't you want to—?

RORY: We already saw this one.

She indicates the TV, where Ryan Seacrest stands before a crowd of starry-eyed hopefuls. In the next sixty minutes, some of them will be exhilarated when the judges say "yes." Most of them will be rejected and never understand that they were only brought before the judges to be laughed at.

MOM: How can you tell?

RORY: It's Atlanta. We already saw Atlanta. Look. There's the guy dressed like Uncle Fester.

MOM: We could find something else to watch.

RORY: Mom, I don't have time to sit around and watch TV, okay? I've got homework. And then I need to shower and get to bed because I have to be at school extra early tomorrow.

Without waiting for a response, RORY *goes up the stairs.* MOM *waits until* RORY*'s bedroom door closes, then turns up the TV volume and scrapes the rest of the risotto into a Tupperware.*

Scene 2

Interior. RORY's bedroom. There are posters on the walls: *Phantom of the Opera*, *Romeo + Juliet*, *Cabaret*, *Titanic*. A collage of the pastel playbills from every Bosworth production she's been a part of is taped around the mirror of her secondhand vanity. Her bedsheets are a faded pink floral pattern, soft and twisted, a tower of clean folded clothes on her pillow.

> RORY *enters her room, closes the door with force, and drops her backpack onto her bed, disrupting the stack of laundry. She flops into the chair at her vanity with a heaving sigh, then faces the mirror.*

RORY: *(addressing the audience directly)*
I know. It's a cliché to be so rude to your mom. If the producers of some new teen drama on the WB wanted to rip off stereotypical dialogue for when their snotty characters mouth off to their parents, they could just come sit in my living room. But I couldn't help it. I walk into my home, and it's like this energy flares up inside of me. Like I want to either bury myself in my bed and never come out or immediately turn around and run away, run as far away from this house as I can, and never come back. That flare inside me . . . it turns into anger whenever I see my mom. Whenever she tries to talk to me—and it's not that she's doing anything wrong. I know she's just trying to be nice to me, nice to her daughter. Especially on her night off. I know she feels guilty because she works so much, and she always cooks me something fancy when she's got

an evening free. But it feels like a trap. The food, the TV, the clean laundry that just appears on my bed . . . Mom's trying so hard to get me to spill my guts, to nose her way into my world, but she doesn't know the first thing about me. Not really. Not anymore.

And she doesn't want to know. Trust me. She'd regret it if she had any idea what I'm up to.

What I'm up against.

She takes a granola bar from her backpack and eats it.

She leaves to take a shower. When she comes back into her room, she pulls homework out of her backpack and spreads it across the desk but barely looks at it. Instead, her gaze goes out the window.

Scene 3

Interior. Living room.

> MOM *sits on the couch in front of the TV, patching a hole in her work shoe.* RORY *comes downstairs in a hoodie, wet hair slicked back into a ponytail.*

RORY: Is it okay if I go print something at the Hastingses'? It's due tomorrow.

MOM: *(glances at the clock, which shows it's 9:30)*
Do you think they'll be up?

RORY: Travis doesn't go to sleep until late. And he said I could come by tonight. He's expecting me.

MOM: Sure. Come right back, though, okay? It's dark.

RORY: *(slipping into her shoes)*
Okay.

MOM: And next time, just email it to me. I don't mind printing it out at work.

RORY: *(smiling)*
Thanks, Mom. I will next time.

RORY goes out the front door and crosses the frozen grass of their front yard to the house behind them, a house with every window ablaze.

FAVORS

The Hastings family belongs to the same church boundaries as the Kings; Rory and Travis would attend the same public high school if they didn't both get into Bosworth Academy. But though their homes share the sheddings of a willow tree and a property line, they may as well be miles apart. Travis's house is on the very edge of a beautiful and ornate subdivision, constructed by a new, trendy builder, and it's big enough to swallow the Kings' house in one gulp. Big double garage, wraparound porch, multiple bathrooms, open-concept kitchen. One look at the Hastings place, and you understand why Travis belongs at the prep school—and as you take in the contrast between the Hastings house and the dumpy split-level next door with the sad, shriveled lawn, you might wonder why Rory, clearly bound for the cheaper prospects of a community college diploma, doesn't just quit school now and chase after an assistant manager position at Foot Locker.

You can live in the same neighborhood and belong to completely different universes.

Instead of heading around to the Hastingses' front door, Rory follows the darkness of their side yard, toeing the property line until she is deposited onto a sidewalk that leads into a neighborhood park.

Under the fragile glow of a singular street lamp, half a dozen boys are gathered, some on their bikes, some tucked near the bushes, hands in pockets, the standard pose for teenage boys who are generically up to no good. As soon as they spot Rory, they get louder, guffawing and shoving, reminding Rory of a pack of wolf cubs showing off their ferocity—not for her, not really. The peacocking is for each other.

When she is close, their voices hush, draw deeper, more deliberate. The skunk of cheap weed breezes past her, but she is more scandalized by how boys choose to dress in winter—T-shirts and jeans, shorts with sweatshirts, as if they could change the weather, defeat the cold just by withstanding it.

"Hey," Rory says first.

Travis's friends don't go to the prep school. They are at the public high school until they inevitably drop out to take the GED. She isn't there to make pleasantries, and she isn't concerned about what they think of her. She assumes they talk about her, and they know why she's here.

"Hey," several parrot back. One of them whispers to another, who laughs, a gesture that Rory understands is not meant to hurt her or make her feel inferior, but rather to puff themselves up, demonstrate how tight-knit they are, how confident even in her presence.

Rory feels like a babysitter with a group of ten-year-olds.

"What's up?" Travis Hastings, the shortest among the seniors here, is a quiet, nondescript boy with the requisite modish wave of hair swooping into his serious eyes. He is the only one in a jacket, one of those zip-up Volcom hoodies, which he pairs with jeans and beat-up skater shoes. He carries himself with an aloofness here, much different from the Travis Hastings that Rory sees in church, sitting with his younger brothers and sisters.

"I was wondering if I could use your computer tonight," Rory says. "I need to type something up and print it out."

Travis does that remarkably obnoxious thing that boys do, where they don't answer you right away and instead steer right back into their prior conversation. "Did you guys see *SNL*?"

"No, we were driving back from my sister's away game," another boy answers. "Who hosted?"

Impatience zaps Rory like a mosquito. "Is that cool, or what?"

Travis regards her and shrugs. "Sure." Stepping forward into the pool of light, he walks past her and keeps walking along the sidewalk, farther into the park.

"Good night, Romeo," teases one of the boys. The group speeds off to find a new place where the shadows pool to continue their illicit smoking circle.

It isn't hard to know where Travis Hastings will be on a Tuesday night. Like a good boy, he attends Scouts on Tuesday evenings, but he walks home and meets up with his friends. His parents probably think he just can't get enough of that merit badge life, sneaking in more outdoor wilderness time, but really, the boys are sharing a single bottle of beer, or a nudie magazine, or a *Grand Theft Auto* smuggled in a *Spyro* case.

"Sorry to tear you away," Rory says as she catches up to Travis.

He's not walking faster because he's embarrassed or unwilling to be seen next to her, but because he's the kind of person who always walks at his own pace, and if someone wants to catch up with him and keep stride, that's their business.

"Nah. Those guys are dumbasses." Such is the way one speaks affectionately about one's friends. "Fenton popped a boner in the locker room."

Travis rehashes the story, which has no punch line, no point except to explain that someone else is below you on the humiliation ladder, and Rory listens, not because it's entertaining but because Travis is filling the silence. It's always like this—shallow, lifeless conversation. It's best for both of them. This way, they don't have to pretend they have anything in common except their addresses.

Rory used to babysit his younger siblings, and Travis used to mow Rory's lawn in the summers, but other than that, there is no reason to act like this is more than what it is—a business transaction, essentially. A mutual exchange of goods and services.

Their path leads out of the park to a freeway overpass, and here, among the pigeon feathers and the faded graffiti, the two of them stop.

"It's cold," Travis notes after they've been standing here for a moment, kicking a pebble with his fat shoe.

"Not too bad." Since Rory left her scarf in Pam's car, she tugs her jacket up as high as it will go, but it barely scrapes the bottom of her chin. "At least there isn't wind."

Travis nods, then peeks at his cell phone, a dark purple brick of a thing he shares with his siblings. "My mom's expecting me by nine thirty."

They have twelve minutes, then, until he needs to be walking through the door, or else Mrs. Hastings will start calling. At ten cents a minute, calls from a worried mother could add up.

"No problem." Rory lets Travis settle into the darkest part of the overpass, a little notch where the concrete is nice and smooth.

She stands as he paws at her, reaching for her chest. They are not even really making eye contact; instead she stares up at the ledges where the birds roost. Travis finds her breasts, finds her nipples, lets out a muted moan.

Her hands go to his pants, feeling that he is ready.

She checks beneath her for sharp rocks and broken glass, and then she kneels.

No kisses exchanged, before or after. Nothing more than this— Rory is a fast worker, efficient at this point. She knows exactly what Travis requires, and when they're finished, he catches his breath and asks, "You're good, right?"

Travis has only journeyed into Rory's anatomy a handful of times, where he explored for a second, without much interest or curiosity, almost too respectfully, and when Rory didn't give him any further instructions, he pulled his hand out of her pants and moved on to other things.

Yes, Rory is good.

"You don't really like it, do you?" he asked her once, and before she could answer, he hurried and zipped up, since someone was approaching with a dog on a leash.

"I'm on my period" has become her standard defense for when he inquires—and when he does offer, it's driven by a palpable guilt, and to Rory, that's not what this is about. This isn't about mutual pleasure; she gets her reciprocation in other ways. Call her old-fashioned, but she's not going to have a boy finger her to ecstasy before she's even been kissed.

And Travis is not for kissing.

When they get to the Hastings house, Travis scratches the back of his head and opens the door for her with reluctance, as if he wishes he hadn't agreed to any of this. "Uh, you need the printer, you said?"

"Yeah, if it's okay with your mom."

"As long as you're not here too late."

He heads inside, letting the door close on her as if he were alone.

Rory pushes the door open and goes right into their living room, where their family computer is set up in a corner. The rest of the Hastingses are bustling upstairs—getting little sisters ready for bed, Mr. Hastings changing out of his post–church meeting shirt and tie.

"Mom?" Travis calls. "I'm home."

"How was Scouts?" Mrs. Hastings sounds like she is wrestling an unwilling child out of the bathtub.

"Fine. Hey, Rory King's here to use our printer—is that okay?"

Permission is granted with enthusiasm: "Of course! Hi, Rory. Make yourself at home. Let Travis know if you need any help, all right?"

Travis types in the password and leaves Rory to it, heading into the kitchen to make himself a second dinner. He offers Rory nothing.

Ignoring the bitter, resinous taste in the back of her throat, she pulls out a folded paper from her jeans and starts typing.

Minutes later, printed sheets in hand, she takes them back home, where she folds a letter into an envelope, stamps and addresses it, and runs it out to the mailbox before finally going to bed.

AUDITIONS

Auditions for a high school musical are . . . Well, how can I put this delicately?

Sort of like a cruise ship lineup, or a dumpster dive. You'll get talent the likes of which you'd never expect—glorious things, voices and performances that could only emerge from that teenage cocktail of ambition and bravado.

And you also get moments more embarrassing than *American Idol* B-roll footage.

The auditions for the spring musical will be no different.

Pam always sits a few rows from the front, near the center of the Elizabethan. The stage manager, Shandie, joins her, with one seat between them. The house lights stay dim, the stage lights bright, an attempt to make it seem a warm, inviting place. They are blinding, actually, so you cannot see out into the crowd—a mercy, I tend to think. No need for the hopefuls to look their judges in the eye while they bare their souls in the form of their best practiced sixteen bars of some Broadway standard.

"You'll come in, hand Shandie your audition sheet, and head up onstage. You should have already run your music up to Jake in the booth. He'll have it cued for you. As soon as you're ready, introduce yourself and what you'll be singing. Then take it away." Pam's instructions, simple enough, become a herculean task to remember when nerves scramble your brain, even for some of the seniors who have been auditioning for Pam for years now.

Audition slots are every seven minutes, which gives Pam and Shandie time to write their notes, recover, and prepare for the next entrant.

It seems like a grueling thing to sit through. I can't imagine the emotional toll, witnessing the unraveling of all my students, trying not to die of secondhand embarrassment.

But Pam is a rock during auditions, a brick wall. She reveals nothing, not a twitch of a lip, a cocking of an eyebrow. You truly never know where in the pecking order you fall until the cast list is posted.

This week's auditions bring all the usual suspects, and a few surprises—for instance, a dancer from the drill team stops by to dazzle the jury with a song and dance. She practices a kick-ball-change and twiddling jazz hands in the foyer. There's a role in *Good Knight! Sweet Lady* that's fit for a dancer—a jester who performs at the royal wedding—and this drill team darling clearly has her eye on it. Fair enough—none of the Princely Players could contort or chassé well enough to nail the role. It pays to have an odd skill—to know how to juggle, or swallow fire, or river dance. You never know what obscure talent might win you a part that you otherwise would never be considered for.

There are, of course, the beloveds, the Elizabethan regulars, the ones who have been charging toward this moment for literal years now—seniors, that pathetic bunch, all of our wings pinned by Pam the moment we stepped into her classroom as sophomores, and now we all expect, with an incendiary hope, that Pam will loose us and let us fly.

But Bosworth is not a fair arena. All that pamphlet bullshit about private schools rewarding merit—Pam writes her own rules here, and they are underscored by her own senses, her own ideas, tilted or no, about how the world should operate. "The real world isn't fair, either," she announced to a cluster of us last fall. "You see the same people getting leads over and over—maybe someone's uncle is the producer of the traveling Broadway show, or maybe someone's grandparents offer to donate the funds to fix the pro-scenium at the local community theater. Or maybe someone is just prettier, louder, and flashier than you are. There's nothing fair about any of this—so don't try for fairness. Don't crave fairness. Crave justice instead. Justice is better than fairness. Justice will always be on your side eventually—it's in everybody's pockets."

Pam knows how to think big and small at the same time. But she's either missed a problem with her logic or she's lying.

And Pam doesn't miss a thing.

Those of us who finish our audition emerge from the auditorium flushed and perspiring, as if we've stepped off the battlefield—if not triumphant, then at least alive. Those of us clogging the hallway, who have yet to take our turn in the gauntlet, congratulate our peers on their survival, and the sentiments are genuine. After you've auditioned, you are no longer competition, because you are no longer thrumming with potential. What's done is done.

Before your audition, however . . .

We observe only in lingering side-eyes; we communicate in throwaway whispers; we indicate our emotional state through the crinkling of our printed lyrics, the cracking of our knuckles, the rewetting of our dry lips, and the unconscious wiping of our damp hands along our thighs.

Inside the auditorium, you must survive the audition.

But first you must survive the hallway.

I am not in the hallway.

I am up in the booth, scanning the darkness below me like some modern Juliet. Jake let me come up here when I told him it was all right with Ethan, that this was our arrangement—I get to watch his audition; he gets to watch mine. Jake has just solidified his post–high school plans—Northwestern for his undergrad, then NYU for sound design. So right now he is loose, easy to convince.

I prop my elbows on the ledge and steady myself with a long, slow inhale. Jake likely assumes I am a loyal friend battling second-hand nerves as Ethan's name is called, but I am simply settling myself. Preparing for the afternoon's revelations.

Ethan is not the only performer I am spying on today. There are three, and I watch them all for very different reasons:

ETHAN

Ethan enters the Elizabethan, and the entire theater seems to expand to contain the enormity of his charm—yet at the same time, there is him, and only him. The rest of the space becomes gratuitous; it shrinks, light and air molding around his figure as he waltzes down the aisle.

"Pam. Shandie." He acknowledges both of his judges by their names as he hands off his audition form; I know without seeing it that he's written down a lie of a name. Herman Snerd. Rootin' Tootin'. Something corny, something to make Pam roll her eyes good-naturedly as he steps onto the stage.

Everything about Ethan is good-natured. He's better than *Sesame Street*. You can't help but be uplifted when he's around.

Ethan moves right into the light, straightening his cummerbund—he's in an inherently Ethan Yorke kind of outfit today: a vintage waiter's tuxedo jacket and cummerbund on the top, his favorite red kilt on the bottom. Anyone else would look like a try-hard, a bag lady in such an ensemble.

"Today I'll be singing for you a selection from *Cabaret*," Ethan declares. He nods toward the booth, and Jake presses play on his cut track.

And then Ethan begins.

His voice has always been strong. He can hit the tones, run the trills, blast his words to the very back row—but musical theater isn't about being a decent songbird. It's about character. Projection. Not volume, projection—adding flair, resonance, expression, to notes on a page. Ethan sings his piece in perfect German-accented English, and he is cheeky and effortless and clear . . . and yet he tinges his lyrics with tenderness, a stain of desolation.

He changes the very temperature of the auditorium—I steal a glance at Pam and Shandie, who do not shuffle their papers, do not scribble notes, do not move.

The thirty seconds fly by. Ethan ends with a bow, flipping his luscious hair forward and back, and then he leaps off the front of the stage.

"Excellent, Ethan," comes Pam's praise as he passes her row, but he keeps his smirk neutral, even as he pushes open the doors to the hallway.

I, on the other hand, grin like a seventh-grade cheerleader. Ethan's tricky to cast—you can't tear your eyes away from him, even if he has a small role onstage. If you're not careful, he'll steal the whole show.

He'll turn your evil sidekick into a charmer, a background farmer into a magnetic heartthrob. He'll make the chemistry between the two lovers seem ridiculous and fake, just from one single moment of him, cast as a butler, delivering a letter to the leading lady.

He's got the best face for stage lights, too—those thick brows, smooth forehead, pouting lips, all of it the perfect balance between Cro-Magnon man and delicate, almost feminine. The whole package.

He's done it. He's nailed his audition. Pam and Shandie will have to place him carefully and deliberately if they don't want to steer their whole show into disarray.

"All right," Jake whispers. "You can go now." The arrangement was for me to watch Ethan's audition. For me to stay any longer would be a distinct violation. Again, Jake is more motivated by a desire to be left alone in his tech booth than a desire to follow Pam's closed-audition rules, but as soon as the next victim enters the auditorium, some forgettable dullard, Jake's attention is pulled entirely to his duties, and I am invisible, and so I stay.

Immediate ensemble, I think as the next few poor souls belt out their disappointing best one by one. That's what I would write on their audition forms if I were Pam—and, in her own way, that's what Pam does. I can tell by now, after nearly three years of the Princely Players, when Pam is being polite. "Thank you so much for taking the time," she says when a performer has more gall than talent, more gravity than presence. "The cast list will be posted on Monday."

Thank you for taking the *time*—not for taking *their* time, moments out of their busy private-high-school schedules to attempt a long-shot audition for the most exclusionary woman on campus, but for taking up time slots. For filling up the audition sheet. For crowding the auditions with names and songs and expectations . . . so that Pam can go ahead and cast exactly who she always intended to cast, but with the illusion of so many options, so much turnout, she can do so under the guise of a forced hand.

Yes, we had over eighty students show up to audition, but truly only a handful have what it takes to lead our cast. Truly only the students I already cast in my head weeks ago have what it takes to perform in our show. A bunch of duds at auditions lets Pam have her way, with no upsets or surprises—

Except for this one.

ANNIE

The doors to the Elizabethan open and close. Nervous chatter from the hallway is audible for a moment, and then all is silent.

"Annie Neville," Pam says. "Surprised to see you back here again! I thought we'd lost you to the gym."

"Ah, I just couldn't stay away." Annie limps down the aisle, still getting used to the cadence of her walking cast. The tone in which she speaks is not deliberately snotty—though I suppose you could interpret it as such, in bad faith—but it lets everyone know that she will not be letting Pam step all over her.

A risk, yes—but Pam respects honesty as much as she loathes a rival.

The paperwork is exchanged, Annie makes her way to the stage, and you have to be extremely vigilant to catch the millisecond she takes to center herself—a slight inhale, a slow blink, and then she looks beyond Pam and Shandie, up into the nothingness of the audience as the strains of her music start.

She's doing "Gimme Gimme" from *Thoroughly Modern Millie*—more moody than comedic, more of a belting number than Annie usually goes for. An interesting choice, considering how many renditions of "Shy" and "When You Got It, Flaunt It" Pam's heard today.

As soon as Annie starts, I know it was a brilliant choice. Swanky and earthy and immediately remarkable.

The thing about Annie is how easy it is for her to forget everyone else in the room. She compartmentalizes herself into a tiny box, making it seem like the most natural thing in the world to be standing up there, under artificial light, singing to no one, and yet she is somewhere else.

Her presence is transportive. It isn't that she makes the false conceit of the musical come alive or seem authentic; rather, you watch her indulge in escape, and you envy her. You long to be her, to go with her, and you're grateful to her for capturing the bittersweet and complicated emotions of leaving and staying that you've always wanted to explain.

I spy from my perch, and I pick at a painful cuticle so my eyes don't grow misty. Ordinarily I am not so impressionable, but the climax of "Gimme Gimme" swells with the flapper brass of its accompaniment, and it would draw the sentimental salt water out of anyone.

Pam lifts up her pen, intending to take a note, but instead she is sidetracked by Annie, ramping up into a passionately explosive coda.

The song shows off Annie's range beautifully, yet I can hear it: Annie's holding back. She's got more than this to offer. She can go even bigger, even louder, more, more—and Pam knows this, too.

Whether Annie's got some built-up reluctance from her time away, or whether she's trying to send Pam a "fuck you" message, or whether she's trying to tease, I can't tell—but when the music cuts out, Annie's containing her giddiness like a can of shaken-up

Sprite. "Thank you," she finishes, and leaves the stage, taking her time, expecting nothing.

Pam does not converse with Shandie, only strokes some unknown mark on Annie's audition form and moves it to the back of her stack. She's torn. You can sense it even up here in the booth; you can hear the buzz of her complicated thoughts, like hornets stirred up by the swinging of a bat.

But even Pam will have a hard time ignoring all the potential Annie just blasted into the auditorium.

God, I'm relieved. My limbs are lighter, my brain buoyant as I peel myself away from the booth's balcony and move to the stairs. I needed both Ethan's and Annie's auditions to go well—I needed them to at least be competent. Justifiable. But they've been more than that—they've both delivered performances that render them wonderfully pliable.

Based on audition alone, either one of them could be placed in any role, and no one would bat an eye.

Of course, the actual performance at auditions is only a small portion of the overall calculation—you must also factor in Pam's personal biases and desires and whims, and at Bosworth Academy, you must also factor in Clarissa.

CLARISSA

The thing about Clarissa is she aspires to be great. She expects to be on Broadway someday, and she's made sure she looks the part as much as possible. (She'll have to fight against nature in some ways; her legs are too stubby and her chest is overpuffed, full of air, her diaphragm always ready to project at a moment's notice, which should be a good thing—but she's bigger around at the rib cage than at the bust or the hips, and that'll be a problem someday among the dainty hourglasses in the casting calls.) She keeps her ginger hair cut short in a swishy bob, very Sutton Foster, and wears ballet flats and vintage swing dresses and classic red lipstick. Overkill, but overkill is Clarissa's main form of self-expression.

"First, let me just tell you how excited I am that we're doing *Good Knight! Sweet Lady!*" Clarissa pauses on her way up the stairs and twists around, her face and shoulders kissed by the stage lights. "Wherever you decide to stick me, honestly, I'm just happy for the chance to be in this show! It's one of my favorites."

Dear god, what a horrendously unsubtle thing to say at the top of your audition, and if you think Clarissa is doing some cheesy last-minute butt-kissing, you're right . . . but she's also completely sincere. Or at least she believes she is.

She's like a giant baby doll, always up for being positioned however you need her. I don't think Clarissa has it in her to lie, which is probably what makes her a decent actress. She's earnest about everything she does—but Annie's honest, too, in a different way. If Clarissa molds herself into the exact shape of a character until nothing of her is left, Annie digs within herself and finds the place where she and the character intersect. Authenticity over imitation.

For Clarissa, happy is happy, sad is sad, and subtext is for cinema, so I am not surprised, as I huddle in my dark corner of the Elizabethan, to be blasted with the very personification of jazz hands—Clarissa's rendition of "My Strongest Suit" from *Aida*.

Don't get me wrong—Clarissa is good. Very good. She crinkles her nose when she belts, she's got that high-wattage love-interest smile, and she looks the part. She's worn a sky-blue peasant dress today, smoothly copying the ensemble donned by Joetta in the original movie poster for *Good Knight! Sweet Lady.*

Pam and Shandie even clap when Clarissa's song snippet ends, and they thank her for coming, pretending there was a version of reality where Clarissa didn't audition for a Bosworth production.

Anyone watching might think that Pam has found her Joetta, that Clarissa has just earned the lead role in the final musical of her high school career—

But I know exactly how things will shake out for Clarissa.

Would you like to know? I'll tell you.

A little sneak peek at the days ahead.

Clarissa will go home this afternoon, thrilled by her audition, high on her usual concoction of toxic positivity and familial privilege, and she'll sing along to Joetta's solos in the shower, daydreaming about her curtain calls.

Her name will show up in Pam's cast brainstorm. Several times, in fact. Pam won't plan a whole show around Clarissa, but she'll slot Clarissa into a lead role because that's what you do with a Clarissa: you place them front and center like the biggest, shiniest, juiciest watermelon on your fruit stand.

Callbacks will be posted, and Clarissa will be on the list.

Clarissa will be asked to read for three parts: Princess Catherine, Queen Zephrine, and the fox lady herself, Joetta.

But Clarissa won't show up.

Ethan will be there, reading for Thackery, and Annie will be there, reading for Catherine (which everyone knows would be a bonkers casting choice, wrong on all levels).

But Clarissa won't pick up her music and scripts at lunch that day.

She won't even be in school that day.

"Where is Clarissa?" Pam will ask, a mixture of concern and suspicion wrinkling her brow.

Her pool of potential cast members will not move, save to shrug, unapologetically refusing to waste precious energy on monitoring the whereabouts of the senior shoo-in.

Shandie, the stage manager, will call Clarissa's house and reach only the answering machine, but soon Pam doles out the first set of instructions, indicating that she has decidedly forgotten that Clarissa was ever an option for this production—the rest of the group does, too.

And then Pam will be stuck. She can't cast Clarissa, not after Clarissa commits the ultimate sin—not only failing to show up when Pam expects her, but also making Pam want something. She'll make Pam confront her own favoritism, a concept Pam tries to distance herself from at all costs, and not because she fears the emails from disgruntled parents or the scoldings from meddling administrators, but because favoritism, good faith, potential—all of it would wreck the great and mighty field of justice Pam worked so hard to instill in her department. One whiff of favoritism in the Princely Players, and Pam's clutches on her students would be forever weakened.

Yes, Clarissa could fall asleep tonight believing that Joetta is hers, but I know where she'll be on Thursday, and it'll be approximately two hundred miles away from the Elizabethan Theater.

Thorn, removed from side. Discarded.

POSTED

Auditions are Monday.

Callbacks are Thursday.

Pam does not promise to have a cast list posted by Friday, but everyone lingers in the Euripides hallway anyway—as if they'd catch the moment Pam took the still-warm document from her printer and secured it to the brick wall outside of Hardy with Scotch tape anyway. For all of Pam's work in the Bosworth theater department, she excels at avoiding theatrics. Cast lists are posted at mysterious times; they show up overnight, after long weekends, in stolen, hidden moments between tardy bells.

Luckily for the agonized hopefuls, the rumors of Clarissa's whereabouts during yesterday's callbacks have spread like lice, from one hairy ear to the next.

Here are the rumors, exaggerations sprinkled in with the facts, arranged narratively so—

Clarissa, upon returning home from Bosworth on Monday, upbeat and sprightly and with no reason not to believe she would be placed in that sacred, central role of Joetta for her final Bosworth musical, went to check the mail.

And in her mailbox, she found an envelope addressed to her and her mother. Stamped, crisp, important.

Inside was an invitation to audition for Mackenzie's, a prestigious performing arts school at the southernmost corner of the state. Mackenzie's only opens up to new recruits once in a Bernadette Peters Tony win, and certainly Clarissa and her hyper-involved stage mother had written this institution off as inaccessible. But an audition, an end-of-year transfer, even for a senior, was still too good to pass up. It was the kind of program that would grant you other opportunities, give you momentum to pass through other thresholds. The Mackenzie's-to-Juilliard pipeline, for instance, was renowned enough to get Mrs. George drooling all over her chin implant—so of course Clarissa had to take this shot.

And of course Mrs. George yanked Clarissa out of school and personally drove her to the very southern border of the state, a four-hour road trip during which Clarissa no doubt practiced belting out all the most ambitious solos she knew—"On My Own," "Don't Rain on My Parade," "Defying Gravity."

For someone with a personal invitation to audition for the Mackenzie's entrance board, a callback for Bosworth's *Good Knight! Sweet Lady* would seem a mere crust in comparison, a Jordache jean, a Happy Meal.

Clarissa still had not returned to school on Friday, and collectively, everyone forgave her for ditching us so swiftly. None of us could deny that we would do the same in her position, and none of us would admit that we were relieved to have her out of the running.

We gazed upon the naked bricks of Euripides and understood

that the cast list for *Good Knight! Sweet Lady* would not be materializing until at least Monday.

So we would be spending our weekend in the liminal state between anticipation and dread. Existing in the land of naive hope for this long is tiring; many of us will fill up our beloved weekend hours by tending to long-procrastinated homework, deep-cleaning our bedrooms, picking fights with siblings or parents just to force our minds to relinquish their clinging grip on this hope, this dandelion hope, at once so bright and yet, ultimately, so easily mowed over.

Is it an intentional cruelty when Pam drags out the casting process like this? Perhaps she means to toughen us up for that place she loves to threaten us with—the real world, where actors must duel one another for speaking roles like old-timey outlaws, and theater directors care less about your résumé than they do about your deep-rooted traumas, which they will exploit for their productions.

No cast list until Monday means a weekend free from disappointment. Most of the other students overcompensate, burning off their pent-up nerves in a hastily thrown-together round of lunchtime hallway bowling (carried out with milk cartons and humans, though I'll let you sort out who takes on what roles).

But my own anticipation needs more than tender teenage antics to fizzle itself out, and so I sit through my last class of the week, AP English, in a bit of a stupor.

It's not that I'm worried. Far from it. While others who faced Pam and her injunction will wither into nail-biting, hair-fussing, and/or gastrointestinal acrobatics as they contemplate their positions in the Princely Players, as they analyze every sound they made on that stage during auditions, as they reinterpret every word that came out of Pam during callbacks, I can float calmly on the river of what is to come.

Obviously there are still surprise factors to consider—secret loyalties I hadn't sniffed out, rogue fancies that infect a director's brain and shift the vision, initiating a sudden, impulsive, odd decision. The butterfly flaps its wings in Japan and creates a hurricane in Florida. The director's favorite restaurant messes up her burrito, her mother calls to nag her into a blind date, a yowling cat keeps her awake past midnight, and the whole cast shifts.

I would not bet on the future, no. But I would bet on the dominoes I've set up, the dominoes I've carefully measured, erected, tiptoed around.

For those dominoes, I'm all in.

I flicked that first one and it fell ages ago.

And they're all falling right where I want them to.

"Rory? Do you have a minute?"

I am gathering my things in the wake of the final bell when Miss Keating snags me with this request. Bosworth's code of conduct dictates that I let myself be lassoed to my English teacher's desk— *All students should demonstrate respect and courtesy to school faculty. Teachers are here to help you learn and to facilitate a safe, healthy environment for your education.*

And so I rise and approach Miss Keating, who dashes off a last-minute email on her desktop before turning her full attention to me.

"Your essay," she says without fanfare. "How's it coming?"

My stomach sinks, more out of habit than actual trepidation. "I'm still working on it." To prove it, I hand over a ruffled notebook with bent spirals and watch her scan the pages of my slanted handwriting.

Miss Keating is relatively new to Bosworth. She was hired last year, replacing a much-adored Bosworth dinosaur who retired and left behind a real crater in the English department. It takes some time to learn the rhythms of Bosworth, to understand the specific nuances of this private school—the needs of the students, the priorities of the parents, the outlined expectations (and the unspoken between-the-lines expectations) of the school board. But Miss Keating flourished almost immediately.

It helps that she's young, only about ten years older than the oldest senior here. It helps that she's massively qualified, with experience in academia and awards in pedagogy and a master's in administration—yes, she did the work to become an administrator but ultimately decided to stay in the classroom, where she could better mold the minds of the youths in her care. It helps that she's pretty and stylish and Black, one of the only teachers of color in our school, and insists on stuffing our curriculums full of Toni Morrison and Octavia Butler in an attempt to balance out all the stale white classics.

And Miss Keating has helped me, individually, as a sort of mentor and champion. "You don't need a trust fund or someone to pull strings for you," she assured me when she heard my college conundrums. "A smart kid like you? You can write your way into a free ride anywhere you like, and I'll show you how."

Scholarships, yes, and essay contests, and funds set up by rich WASPs in honor of Sylvia Plath or Emily Dickinson or whatever other writer they themselves studied at one of the Seven Sisters.

Miss Keating has me applying for them all. She's got a chart, a calendar, lots of different-colored sticky notes—and this week, I'm supposed to be finishing up with my essay on Machiavellian themes in English literature.

"It's good." Miss Keating nods as she skims my work. "Brilliant, even. But that doesn't matter if it's not finished."

Back into my hands she passes the notebook, and I glance down at my shoes. No one can cut with the blade of truth like Miss Keating.

"Your Juliet analysis was late, too," she goes on, "and you still haven't brought in the worksheets you owe me."

Bosworth prides itself on its tough love; if teachers don't come down hard on flailing students, they propose, how on earth will students learn? And Bosworth parents clap and cream, agreeing that their precious prep school nestlings should learn not to drown in the first place.

"I'm sorry," I start. "I had a busy week. I'll get caught up."

The teacher doesn't fall for it; this is a classroom where we worship words, and such small excuses and hollow promises are as favorable to her as chewed-up pencils and wads of gum stuck under the chair rails.

"Auditions for the spring musical were this week." Miss Keating doesn't seek confirmation. "Does that have anything to do with your busy schedule?"

The silence inflates between us until my jaw is tight as a locked window.

"It's my senior year," I say. "This is the last high school production I'll ever be a part of."

"So you are going to be part of it." Miss Keating purses her lips, and her scrutiny bores holes through my flesh. "Rory, I hope you understand why that concerns me—"

"I know." We both know. We don't need to say it.

"You've been working so hard. We're in the home stretch here—keep your focus, and you'll be so glad you stayed the course." Now Miss Keating drops her tone. Now Miss Keating gives up the performance of a literature taskmaster at a twelve-thousand-dollar-a-year private school and allows me to see her, an overworked woman of nearly thirty whose salary is decent compensation for her hours in the classroom but does not account for the hours of emotional toil she is expected to provide. She's not paid extra to care if I go to college. She's not paid extra to scold me. Everything about her body language is meant to telegraph this to me: she is doing this because she genuinely cares about me and my future.

She's looking for a soft spot.

So I show her one.

I sigh, letting one of my backpack straps fall down my shoulder. "I'm sorry. It's just so much." My hand flies to my face; I cover my eyes as they blur. "It's not Drama—that's the one thing that's going well. We've had tons of homework in Bio II, and Mom's been pulling double shifts."

Miss Keating waits. But I do catch her mouth slacking a little in pity. She wants more.

She's thirsty for a showing of good ol' Bosworth persistence now.

"I'll work harder," I say. "I'll get the essay finished. I— Thank you. Thank you so much. I know you don't have to stay after and help me with any of this."

That gets her to snort at least, and flash half a smile. "It's my job to make sure every one of my students leaves Bosworth fully prepared for the college experience. You just happen to require more organizing."

She wants her ego stroked, even though she's pretending like this is all about you. Go on. Stroke it.

"I couldn't do any of this without you," I tell her. "If I do make it to college, I will lift a red Solo cup at every mediocre rager and toast your name."

Ah, at last, a genuine laugh. "How about instead you just dedicate your first book to me? And a cut of your royalties, of course. That's a given." Miss Keating cracks open a can of Red Bull and arranges a stack of not-yet-graded papers in front of her. "All right, Rory. Go enjoy your Friday. Don't spend all weekend on homework."

I leave Miss Keating's classroom understanding perfectly what it is to be inspected under a microscope. To be prodded. Tapped. Breathed on. If only my biology teacher would let me hand in an essay instead of a field report detailing six weeks' worth of blood smear observations.

I'll finish the Machiavelli essay. I'll get caught up on all the work I've pushed onto the back burner—Miss Keating knows I will. But part of her role as my unofficial mentor is to chastise me, to demand more from me than is humanly possible. To demand that I out-Bosworth everyone else at Bosworth.

And part of my role as pathetic, brainy, uncharismatic poor scholarship student is to accept her hand-holding.

Along the empty hallways of Bosworth I stroll, passing student council meetings, loitering burnouts, janitors anxious to get the floors mopped and waxed. I turn down Euripides, my mind in dark snarls of Machiavellian influence, and I head for the double doors at the end of the hallway—

But then I spot it.

The cast list.

It's materialized. There, fastened to the brick wall like it's now part of the architectural integrity. I slow, as if I need to sneak up on it—as if the single piece of paper is skittish, as if it will evaporate if I appear too eager to read it.

But it holds steadfast to the bricks.

A holy relic.

A beam of God's glory should shine down on it from the parted heavens, but the glare of the fluorescent lighting will have to do.

I draw closer.

Close enough to see its names.

To see Pam's vision.

Aside from Pam's, mine are the first eyes to behold it.

King Leoffald and Queen Zephrine, fine, King Harold and Queen Harolda, fine, fine, all looks fine.

Cole's nabbed Warwicke, Preston's got Lurkin, fine, fine, fine.

Ethan Yorke . . . Thackery.

A squeeze of joy, a twist of pleasure. Yes, yes, god. Right where I want him.

But where is—?

Threads of nerves pull taut, my chest laced—

Annie Neville . . . Joetta.

Yes. *Yes.*

Annie Neville as Joetta. The lead. The star.

All of it, exactly as I planned.

Exactly as I wanted it to unfold.

What of my own name?

I am listed alphabetically in the sad clump of the ensemble.

So I was right.

All those years, all that time spent worshipping at the altar of Bosworth's drama program, and it still wasn't enough.

There're only so many leads. It's a numbers game—not every senior will be a star, but every star will be a senior.

Even if you've improved. Even if you've given all your spare hours to the Elizabethan—even if you monologue in your dreams.

Even if you've paid your dues many times over.

There's still a chance you won't be chosen. There's still a chance someone else will take the role that you were spoiling for.

If this were any other show, any other cast list, I might mourn it, feel the full humiliation of my apparent destiny as an unnamed space-filler in a glob of singing faces, practically part of the set.

But here's the thing I've learned about destiny.

You don't have to stop the arrow from its trajectory once it's been loosed from its bow; you just have to put a new target in its path.

Cast list. Bull's-eye.

To discuss Machiavellian morality, one must first establish a universal definition of morality to use as a foundation, and that is as difficult as trying to catch a fish with your bare hands. In Machiavelli's own work, theoretical morality was much more important than any applications of "good" and "evil." A successful ruler need not actually order a subordinate to be beheaded; rather, he should build himself a kingdom where the fear of such a possibility is as effective as a blade itself.

—*Rory King,* "Machiavellian Politics in the Twenty-First Century"

ACT
TWO

A WORD ABOUT
DRAMA KIDS

They go by many names: theatre geeks (yes, they insist on spelling it—and pronouncing it—"theatre"), drama nerds, players, thespians (dear god, may we all be spared), fairies (cruelly so), divas (also cruel, but within a different context), to list just a few. You might not know you're in the vicinity of such a person if there's only one.

One drama kid on their own is hardly a problem.

Two of them together create an interesting tension—you might think they'll bond over their shared interest, but the world of *theatre* is so inherently competitive that if you so much as place two drama kids in the same enclosed space, they will immediately start posturing to be the lead.

That makes you, unsuspecting bystander, their audience.

More than two drama kids, and things start to get tricky.

And by tricky, I do mean dicey and dangerous and, above all, obnoxious.

There was one year when all the drama kids wore ties every day to school over their T-shirts and sweaters. Yes, this was the era of Avril Lavigne and the onus of the Hot Topic pop-punk aesthetic, but you can't even pin that as the influence here—they'd watched *Dick Tracy* together one weeknight and decided that ties were the ultimate accessory, expressing a midcentury classiness that they believed would elevate the rest of their Labor-Day-sale-at-the-mall ensemble.

Another phase, the drama kids all wore pajama bottoms to school—sweats, flannels, boxers, you name it. If you'd unwrap it on Christmas Eve and wear it for a photo with your coordinating siblings, that's what you paired with your otherwise ordinary camisole and Henley or your pastel polo shirt. Another time, they all wore jumpsuits, like what a mechanic wears—you might think they'd indulged in a little *Ghostbusters* over Halloween, but they'd actually gone to see a grassroots production of *Jesus Christ Superstar*, creatively set in a futuristic urban Jerusalem, where the whole cast had donned earth-toned jumpsuits (except the Romans, whose jumpsuits were bloodred). The drama kids had found their own jumpsuits at a thrift shop in bulk, and anyone who wasn't there on that fateful day had to source their own—beg their mom to stalk eBay or ask an exterminator uncle to swipe an extra uniform, if they were lucky.

So you might be able to pinpoint exactly who the drama kids are in any given academic environment. They might stand out in a sartorial way—and of course, you can't forget that they are often individually dressed in gender- and social-code-defying attire. Kilts, suspenders, pixie cuts, long wavy locks, Doc Martens, flapper pearls, mustaches, glittery eyeshadow—any of it could be worn by any of them, in a spirit of defiance, deviance, or dandyishness.

If you can't pick out a drama kid by how they look, you'll have to see how they're acting.

I don't mean the obvious. I don't mean that they're speaking in character or quoting musicals or, worse, quoting weird thirty-year-old cartoons from some foreign place on the internet that they watched huddled around the same computer, gawking as it buffered.

Yes, you could find those traits, and more. You might watch for strange pranks and nonsense dares. Climbing through the ceiling vents and talking to students like they're God. Hiding behind the drinking fountain and saying things like "Put your mouth on me!"

You might also spy some transgressive behaviors—the group perusing an old sex-education book stolen from a dusty library shelf, tarot cards in a decidedly conservative high school, an impulsive and shockingly ferocious game of knuckles that leaves everyone sopping with blood, the disgusting quarter grit in their open wounds.

And they'll do anything for attention. That's the truth—and they'd all deny it, and be upset at anyone who suggested it, but they just can't get enough of the spotlight. Their dream birthday party would be a surprise where they show up and everyone's seated in an audience, waiting to listen to whatever they want to perform, and their loved ones have to clap no matter how unwilling they are to listen in the first place.

Not a captive audience—a captured one.

Drama kids will have strange friendships, which you can easily trace through their call sheets. This part-time drama kid who is usually a band geek is now friends with a math whiz volleyball manager because they shared a dance number in last year's production of *Footloose* and had to spend a lot of time together counting steps and following the director's frenzied notes to "Smile bigger! Louder!" even though they had nothing in common but an exit and an entrance, and now they are in the same group for prom.

Oh, yes—I should mention:

Drama kids cannot stop touching each other. Seriously. They are like an amoeba, single-celled, on each other's laps and holding hands and wrapped in arms, constantly piling atop a beanbag to watch *Monty Python*, stacking up on a couch to play *Donkey Kong*, the screen competing with five different conversations.

One parent, while chaperoning a field trip to a traveling commedia dell'arte troupe, noticed how many students were touching on the bus and commented, "Wait, I thought Greg Sanchez was with Mandy!" Her daughter caught her up to speed, explaining that, no, none of these people currently cuddling on the bench seats are dating, and the parent was bewildered. "You are so intimate with each other," she said, sounding like a grown-up, to use that word *intimate* for what she was seeing—and perhaps the drama kids should be grateful, because others might have reduced it to simple teenage hormones, horny kids grabbing whatever they could get away with, shameful, a bunch of garter snakes all mating and writhing in a ball.

But the parent was right. It was intimacy. It's the kind of intimacy you can only build when you share a costume rack, seeing one another in weird cat suits and animalistic makeup and funny wigs and doing terrible accents. It's the intimacy you can only share when someone is vulnerable in front of the group, attempting a line delivery, singing a song they haven't yet mastered, telling a joke that won't land, knowingly performing something cringeworthy. You can't purposefully make an absolute fool of yourself without someone falling a little bit in love with you.

That's it. Kids of the *theatre*—they're all in love with one another at least a little bit.

But here's the truth. None of them are as in love with one another as they are with themselves. They love themselves the most. Not in an affirming, self-love, forgive-yourself-for-your-flaws kind of love, but full-blown worship, give-up-all-your-personal-belongings-to-follow-you-into-a-cult kind of love. With themselves.

You have to be. It's imperative. Required. How else can you get up onto a stage and act like a drunken clown? How else can you stand under the lights and speak and sing and disturb the silence, unless you believe yourself to be a gift to the audience, to the universe?

I'm not trying to romanticize things, but you must understand this about drama kids or the rest of the book will not make much sense.

Right now, at the beginning of a new show, at the first table read, everyone is buzzing with stamina. The stage manager hands out scripts—if you're a lead, you get your script in a binder with your name in marker on the spine. If you're not a lead, you don't get a binder or even a full script; you get your relevant scenes copied and stapled together, your lines unmarked. As unremarkable as you are.

But that doesn't matter at this point. Right now, every single person on that cast list is ready to take their part, however small, in bringing a vision to life. They imagine how it's going to be when the curtain parts on opening night, all rehearsed and polished and put together. They daydream about how they'll grow as close as a family, and how on closing night it'll feel like a family breaking apart.

Some are cocksure as they read the lines aloud, some are vibrating with nerves—but they all have faith that the director will smooth their worst tendencies into glory before the end.

In ten weeks, when it's time to open the show, they'll be swarming one another, kissing, smothering, some of them actually fucking, and barking with impatience, ready to hang one another in the rigging. Joining a play is like agreeing to have your heart broken by everyone else in the cast . . . but they'll be the only ones who can truly comfort you, too. So.

No wonder drama kids are so strange.

You can feel empathy for the drama kids, I suppose—all that scar tissue has built up over time, all those characters inside of them, all those closing nights, and no matter how long a show runs, the praise, the attention, it's never enough.

A drama kid is a bucket with a hole.

If you ever have to spend time with a group of them, my god, I'm so sorry for you.

Turn on some Jonathan Larson and get the hell out of there as fast as you can before they rope you into a discussion on the disappointing takeover of Broadway by Disney or a round of improv or, impossibly worse, one of their bizarre games meant to build team spirit, to build intimacy.

To build trust.

FIRST READS

THE TABLES IN HARDY ARE PUSHED AROUND THE CLASS-room to make a giant square, as if this is a Thanksgiving feast and the cast needs to see everyone else's faces. One big happy family.

Rory's sitting next to Cynthia, the head costumer, and one of the juniors, Jillian. She walked into the room with Ethan, but he joined a conversation with Annie and Cole about the new Green Day video, and then they all took their seats by one another—certainly not on purpose, but certainly not *not* on purpose, either. Pam might say it was their subconsciouses at work—the principals congregating together, matching talent and pressure and responsibility, like attracting like.

The scripts are opened. Pam puts on her reading glasses.

Shandie, the stage manager, is doing the stage directions—or she will be, as soon as she stops flirting with Cole. He's snuggled up beside her and she's wearing his sweatshirt—no, they aren't together. Just another theater kid love language: stealing someone else's belongings to flaunt.

Like a costume.

Pam will be listening and taking notes, all those secret director thoughts about blocking and effects and aesthetic.

A blueprint for her vision.

The table read begins.

"Once upon a time, in a far-off place, there was a beautiful kingdom," reads Preston as Osbert. "And everyone in this kingdom had the most glorious hair."

Rory glances around.

Other members of the ensemble sit as well postured as debutantes, studiously following every line. They are those credulous Pollyannas who believe it when directors say "There are no small parts, only small actors." They are perhaps genuinely grateful to be involved in the show, genuinely confident in the value they're adding to the cast. Not everyone in the ensemble is a sophomore, but every sophomore here is in the ensemble.

They are here to pay their dues.

Someone in Rory's position can only survive this. Her part is small and embarrassing. Her single line doesn't come until two-thirds of the way through the musical, once everyone at the table is out of their vending machine Cheetos and Sour Patch Kids and weary of hearing Cole butcher the various names of the kingdoms in the script. Plus Preston's clearly nervous about reading out loud and delivers his lines in a stop-and-start, stop-and-start pattern. He'll be brilliant once all his lines are memorized, sure, but for now it's like watching a run-down locomotive push itself up a hill.

Finally, Rory's scene comes.

It's a gossip scene, set around the fountain in the castle courtyard. Lines are bounced around the room, ensemble members each given a short line as reward for their patience, their mind-numbing presence.

Pam will encourage them to make up their own character, to dream up a backstory, a motivation, as if the audience will catch the interwoven subtext—as if they are anything more than human blocks to fill the space.

Rory's pulse quickens in anticipation of the line, embarrassing her. "I've got time!" she says.

You're better than that line.

Listen to your little heart, pumping away for this—for this? No, you're worth much, much more. These ensemble roles are for the hobbyists, the conniving users who just want to be able to list the Princely Players on their college applications, the talentless lumps who got into the show because their mommies and daddies donate big money to Bosworth.

No. You deserve more.

And you're going to get it.

Rory tries to remain present, but her part in the reading is over. The scene moves on without fanfare, the next one-liners delivered with as much dignity as possible; she resists, but her gaze lingers on the corner of leads.

Annie says more than a hundred and twenty lines. She's in almost every scene, and so is Ethan.

You've been paying dues for years.

That's where you belong.

The moment has passed. Rory's adrenaline clears out of her system, leaving her dull-headed and heavy for the rest of the table read. At five o'clock, as the final lines are read aloud, the stage manager passes out the rehearsal schedules.

"Do not miss rehearsal," Shandie warns (for when Shandie is

near, Pam lets her be the dictatorial mouthpiece). "If you have to miss a rehearsal, you must get it excused forty-eight hours in advance through a written note, and it must be signed by a parent."

If you miss a rehearsal without notice, well . . . good luck convincing Pam that you deserve to stick around for the curtain call.

Rory glances at the schedule. The first two weeks are for the leads. Heavy blocking. Ensemble is required only four times in the next month. Ethan and Annie are called every single day. They'll be married to that stage, married to their parts, so entrenched in the work that they'll become the musical itself—

Just because you're not on the schedule doesn't mean you can't show up.

Rory fiddles with her backpack, pretending to be busy while the others examine their complex calendars.

It's called a call sheet. So do you feel called?

The Elizabethan may be cavernous and transportive to its audiences, but to Rory and most of the other drama kids who regularly haunt its wings, the Elizabethan is a home.

And so Rory comes home to the Elizabethan every day, whether she is on the call sheet or not.

She brings her homework and studies in the aisles. She camps out near the back, but not so far back that she looks like one of the burnouts who crouch in the shadows to swap bong hits and hand jobs.

She stays out of the way. On the side. Camouflaged—until one day Shandie, the stage manager, spots her.

"You're not called until next week," Shandie says, frowning at her clipboard.

"I know," Rory assures her. "I'm just trying to be available."

"You're not really supposed to be here unless you're on the call sheet." But Shandie doesn't tell Rory to leave. She doesn't snitch on her, either.

And then it happens.

Payoff.

One day about three weeks after that first table read, on a day with only principals on the schedule, Pam needs another body onstage.

"The guard . . . Hang on." Pam stretches up and around in her seat in the front row, scanning the auditorium. There are a few tech boys laying out lights and cables in the aisle, and there's Rory, trying to look both inconspicuous and also like there's a halo shining right above her.

"Rory? Are you busy? Can we borrow you up here?" Pam doesn't wait for a response; she meets Rory at the base of the stairs, marching her up and into position on the stage.

Rory straightens her spine. To be looked at by Pam at all is to be assessed.

Ethan grins at Rory. Annie's acknowledging smile is less playful but still friendly.

"So the guard is here." Pam places Rory where she needs her. "And Thackery, you'll lean over to Joetta . . ."

And Rory stands there. Rory is the best goddamn guard you've ever seen. She stands there like one of those guards in London, stoic, professional, while Pam directs Ethan and Annie in their end-of-act-1 sword fight, a moment that will be so rife with sensuality, dramatic tension, and humor, it'll give the audience tingles all over.

When Pam says, "Thank you, Rory, for jumping in," it feels to Rory like the world has been packaged and gifted.

No. No, it feels like the world has been tipped.

Tilted, ever so slightly, in favor of fairness.

Justice.

HOT CHOCOLATE, SPLIT TWO WAYS

Anyone who works in a diner near a high school or a college deserves a raise and one of those hundred-dollar tips from a random celebrity passing through town.

Today was a big day in the world of *Good Knight! Sweet Lady*. A late Friday rehearsal. Full cast on the call sheet. Everyone stayed past seven to block a major scene, the big finale—there were dance breaks, mini-scenes, a big medley wrap-up song on par with "One Day More."

By the end of rehearsal, most of the cast and crew were exhausted from Pam's shouted instructions, her impatient corrections, her ego-bruising curtness, and also exhilarated, because now the blocking was finished.

The first hurdle when you put on a play, done. Everyone knew where they were supposed to be at any given minute during the show, and they could all finally see it—if they squinted, anyway—could see how it was supposed to look in the end.

They could sense it edging closer to becoming a real production, something you could step into. They'd all felt it, in the final moments of the closing song, their characters swirling like little pawns on their invisible chessboards—and then suddenly their characters were alive, the production was alive, more than just a choreographed series of movements and scripted words and premeditated emotions.

Rory was itchy. They all were. Too tired to do anything disciplined, too antsy to return home, where they'd be expected to assimilate into regular life as if they had not just experienced the electric pulse of their musical's first heartbeat—so when someone suggested heading to Ruby's, that's where they went. Some of them drove down the street to the shabby diner, but most of them walked, a big clump of them, waddling almost drunkenly to their destination.

After forging such bonds among themselves as they had, there was no way they could simply split up and go home. That would be like walking away from your own arm.

"How many?" The waitress, already exhausted by them, eyes their party, which overflows into the foyer and also undulates, impossible to count, as they peruse the shelf of Beanie Babies for sale and plunk quarters into the claw machines.

Someone gestures around as if to say, *If you can count us, that's your answer.* The waitress grabs a few menus (sensing they will not really be required) and leads the horde not to the biggest booth in the house but to a series of tables in the farthest corner of the diner. Let them all split up into individual subgroups, let them push the tables together and make a mess of the chairs, let them clump around in their unholy circles—at least put them somewhere they can't be heard.

Rory stands back, letting the more boisterous ones (the boys, mostly) take their seats from among the chairs. They do the thing where they grab the chair like a briefcase, like they're going to carry it off, and then plop down onto it like it's an extension of them.

She eventually slides into the booth, down the cracked mustard yellow leather, and she tries not to blush when her weight makes the bench's guts squeak in flatulence. Someone scoots in beside her, and another, stacking in like Skee-Balls, and there's Ethan, climbing over the others so he can wedge in next to her, his leg pressing against her thigh as he battles for a square inch of table real estate.

Across from Rory and one chair down, Annie sits, setting her binder on top of the menu, and flips through her script.

It's already odd that Annie's here. She never really came to their post-rehearsal cooldowns, since she was busy with basketball—like drama was strictly business for her, and since these extra moments with the cast and crew were not listed on the rehearsal schedule, they were not required.

And yet here she is, among the ragamuffins and diehards of the Princely Players—but she is riffling through her script with a strained expression, spiraling, while around her, people are blowing straw wrappers into each other's faces and building pyramids out of the creamers.

"We're off book next week," Annie finally explains when someone asks her if she's okay. "And I still can't remember half my lines."

"We've got time," Sierra says kindly. "We've got a whole month until we open. You'll have it down by then."

But Rory knows Annie does not want a month. Annie is tearing herself into pieces right now, wishing she could order up her lines to be fried in the back by the egg cook so she could eat them up with a fork and let them become part of her. Annie is sharp, and always has been—but her grades are impeccable because of her incredible work ethic, not because she's a natural test-taker or one of those lucky bastards who can instinctively understand the key battles of the Civil War.

"Pam's already pissed at me," Annie says. "I keep flubbing the sword fight; my leg just isn't healed. And I know she wants all those lines to be nice and tight, but I'm . . . not there yet."

Most of the group isn't listening to her anymore; they're having their own gripe sessions as the waitress brings out water, the glasses spotted with dishwasher stains, and hands them out to the masses.

But Rory is listening.

Not to Annie's words, because Annie has now trailed off—but Rory is listening to the sound on Annie's face, that worry. It's projecting louder than anything in this diner, the worry that Annie will lose everything all over again. The car wreck already took basketball.

"I'll help you," Rory says. She meets Annie's eyes across the table. "I can come over tomorrow and help you run lines."

Annie considers her. Lifts a glass of water and sips.

For a moment, Rory feels it—everything between them, rushing through like a tsunami. Everything since the car wreck, and the car wreck itself. Everything before that, too, the years of Annie missing Rory's calls because she was at a game, of Rory holding her breath from her bedroom floor while Annie slept on Rory's small, lumpy twin mattress, of Annie's own canopy bed and matching curtains and family vacations, of Annie's ribbons and trophies in the glass display case at the front of the school.

Of Rory's scholarship paperwork, right there on the Kings' fridge like it, too, was an award; it was, in fact, the only thing of that nature Rory had to show off.

Annie lets it all roll past and then says, "Yeah. Okay. That would be really helpful."

Someone bumps Rory under the table, a careless foot. All those limbs, tangled together, one organism.

"Who here is actually ordering something?" calls the waitress, who for the past five minutes has tried to go round-robin and is exasperated by all the people with no intention of using the diner for anything but a spillover space to socialize.

A few hands rise, maybe a fifth of the group. Orders are given— some onion rings, someone getting a side of bacon, a few Cokes and coffees and Sprites.

"A hot chocolate," Ethan says, "and can you put that in two cups?"

"Whipped cream?" The waitress does not waste any more time on annoyance; most of these high schoolers have midnight curfews, so she needs only to wait out the clock.

"Yes." Ethan grins at Rory. "Oh, and you know these are all on separate checks."

Yes, the waitress knows. Separate checks, separate tips, one giant cleanup.

Not everyone has cash to blow on late-night pancake platters.

"Buy me a sundae," someone begs. "I'm broke until Tuesday."

"You're always broke" comes the reply, but the sundae is ordered.

Rory wagers she is the only one who understands the difference between being broke—easily fixable—and being poor—easier to forget that sundaes even exist.

Drinks are delivered. Inside jokes are recited and reframed, and some new ones are cemented.

Bonding occurs while discussing the throes of rehearsal, the difficulties of being on this side of Pam and her demands—and they are not even into the bitching and griping of later, intensified rehearsals yet. Rory knows what's coming. Everyone gets whipped by Pam, and everyone licks their wounds together.

"I'm serious," Ethan says, a black tendril of his hair coming unslicked in the passion of his animated speech. "I saw it on VH1. A lady ordered a chicken sandwich from Arby's and she bit into it and thought they'd put extra mayonnaise on it, but it was really pus from a tumor in the chicken. That's why you always get no mayo— Oh, hey!"

And then here is Brad.

Ethan greets the newcomer with an infectious smile. He'd stand up and pull Brad into a lingering hug if he wasn't currently crammed into the booth like an Oreo. "Make room," he commands instead, and another chair is shoved next to Annie. Annie is bumped farther down her side of the table, farther away from Rory, and the whole group quiets as Brad settles himself in his chair.

It's strange to see him after school, strange to see him without his usual cohort of aquatic Bosworth Princes. And he's not here with a study group or with his parents.

Which means someone invited him.

Rory looks at Ethan. There's a pay phone in the foyer, and Ethan usually keeps a quarter or two in his kilt pocket.

Hopefully Ethan thinks it was worth the twenty-five cents to inform Brad of his current whereabouts, Rory thinks, because the arrival of the jock has shifted the air. It's as if Brad has a shield around him to keep him from mixing with the drama kids—or is it the drama kids who put up those walls, who refuse to let anyone not born and bred for the stage into their inner circles?

"Hi, Rory." Brad acknowledges her with decorum; Rory wants to shout at him, Don't you dare; don't act like we have anything more in common than this person in lavender suspenders sitting next to me. But she offers up a tight smile in return.

Brad turns his attention back to Ethan now that he's offered his polite gesture. "How was rehearsal?" The familiarity drives Rory bonkers—"rehearsal," that word in Brad's mouth, as if Brad has any idea. As if swimming back and forth in those little chlorinated lines could give him any point of reference for someone like Ethan, someone brilliant, someone larger than the very stage he stands on every afternoon.

"Brutal," Ethan responds.

"I don't know how you do it," Brad says, shaking his head. "I couldn't memorize all that stuff. I couldn't get up on the stage in front of an audience."

Yes, we know, Rory longs to say. But instead she is silent while Ethan carries on his conversation with Brad. It's less flirtatious than she dreaded, but she can still tell that Ethan's trying to show off for Brad a little, here with his people. Thankfully Cole is on the other end of the tables, or else he'd be fighting Ethan for the spotlight. But Ethan can be the big diva here, delivering to Brad the perfect jokes, the perfect references, the perfect amount of cool, pushing his hair away from his forehead to fully expose those brooding eyes, those eyes that can say a million things without Ethan's ever opening his mouth—*and that's why rehearsal is brutal, Brad. Because Pam is going to squeeze every last bit of juice out of Ethan every time he's under those lights, and he's got a lot to squeeze.*

"Do you want to split a Happy Jack breakfast?" Brad asks. "My treat."

Ethan shrugs. "Sure, I can eat."

When the hot chocolate arrives, Ethan slides both cups over to

Rory without a word. "You can have it all," he says, as if it's a mercy. As if he hasn't just pushed away three years of Ruby's tradition, leaving Rory's cup full of hot chocolate but empty of other things.

The onions on Brad's omelet stink. Ethan offers Rory a bite of his waffle, but she shakes her head. She doesn't take a sip of the hot chocolate, either, letting the whipped cream dissolve into the mugs.

Then she pays for the hot chocolate herself, in quarters, and leaves with the techies, snagging a ride home from Cynthia, whose mom's Toyota Sienna is covered in bumper stickers from the local Right to Life chapter.

Ethan does wave goodbye, but his focus is on Brad, Brad and the final sticky dregs of the maple syrup, to be swirled around on the plate, to be mopped up by pinky fingers, to be licked away.

HALLOWEEN

(FLASHBACK)

WITHIN THE FIRST MONTH OF HER SOPHOMORE YEAR AT Bosworth, Rory scraped up the twenty-five dollars due to the financial office, and then she was officially a member of the Princely Players. A dues-paying member got access to an enormous number of perks, including special group discounts and carpools to live performances (sometimes downtown at the ritzy Capitol Theater, sometimes across the county to see another high school's play—the high school that Pam swore was not their competitor, though she couldn't ever speak about them without adding in a little jab about how they didn't deserve their success). Princely Players also voted on certain things, like the corporate partners for their fundraisers, the themes for their monthly improv nights, the design of their matching sweatshirts for when they went to state.

And, of course, there were the parties.

Four of them a year, and supposedly they were exceptional. At least that's what everyone told Rory, as if she needed more of a reason to join the Princely Players. These parties were truly for members only, and so to protect against any grifters trying to sneak in without paying their fair share, the Halloween bash came with a secret password, which Rory was meant to whisper to the door-keeper when she arrived.

She was on the excited side of nervous the night of her first Princely Players party. She'd auditioned for the fall production of *And Then There Were None*; despite Pam's very clear rules about not casting sophomores, she still expected sophomores to audition.

"Consider it a chance to practice the auditioning process," Pam coached the Drama I class as the sign-up sheet was passed around. "You can rehearse your monologue a hundred times at home, but you should take every opportunity to perform it onstage, under the lights, in front of an audience. Thicken your skin."

Rory had walked past the cast list when it was posted, trying her best to glance at it nonchalantly, and even though she knew her name wouldn't be there, she couldn't help but nurse the tiny glimmer of hope in her chest with a sharp breath—

And then, deflation. No sophomores on the list, as promised.

But exclusion from the fall production did not mean exclusion from all Princely Players activities, and Rory had now spent the better part of two months observing Pam's department. If she was going to pay her dues, as Pam had requested, Rory knew she'd have to understand how the cogs of this universe ran. How it ticked, how it spun, how it was fueled.

It was a costume party. Of course it was, being a gathering for drama kids, and Rory was relieved to see other Princely Players showing up in gaudy ensembles. But she couldn't help retaining a smidgen of self-consciousness as she approached the double doors of the Elizabethan.

Black streamers dangled along the threshold—not mere crepe

paper but strips of fabric, alternating velveteen and satin, and strands of beads and clear crystals for texture. Music trumpeted nice and loud into the hallway.

"You have no power over me," said the doorkeeper, a slender senior in a tawny catsuit, complete with golden cat-eye contacts.

Rory hesitated. Was this part of the script for entry? The password she was supposed to give didn't really fit with this line—

"Your costume." The cat gestured with her stuffed tail. "It's great."

Rory had waited till the last minute to decide on a costume. Her mother had been incredibly supportive—too supportive, Rory had thought a few times—and offered help putting together a getup for a vampire, a witch, an astronaut, but while Rory knew she didn't want to dress up as something so simple (so childish), she also didn't really know what she did want.

The party was Saturday, which meant Rory's mom had the long shift at the ER, which meant Rory was left alone all morning and afternoon to flip through her closet and brood.

There wasn't time to go buy a costume (there wasn't money for a new costume regardless). So Rory, following a whim, went into the garage and tore through the storage bins until she found a dress she hadn't thought about in years. It had once belonged to her mother, but Rory knew her mother wouldn't mind if she wore it—did it even count as a wedding dress if you never actually got married in it?

The dress had big poufy sleeves, a huge skirt with scalloped layers and a silhouette like a cupcake, and a corseted bodice stitched with iridescent butterfly sequins. Rory paired it with a homemade masquerade mask, which she cleverly whipped up with a paper plate, some gold acrylic paint, and glitter confetti left over from a ninth-grade English project on *The Great Gatsby*.

The whole walk over, she'd bunched the gown's unwieldy skirt in her hands like she was carting clouds beneath her jacket, dodging the mud puddles that had lingered in potholes since last week's thunderstorm.

She'd wagered only a few people would know who she was—Sarah from the movie *Labyrinth*, one of the few VHS tapes Rory's grandmother owned and therefore a staple of Rory's childhood. But Rory sensed she'd earn a certain respectability from choosing to represent an obscure favorite rather than succumbing to something trendy, something generic, something safe.

"Oh. Thanks." A triumphant pride surged within Rory, and she stepped toward the streamers.

The door-keeping cat moved to block her. "Wait! I need your password."

"Pygmalion," Rory said, breathless. Her mother's old dress was tight around her middle. But she belonged here. She'd paid to belong here.

Which meant she fit right in at Bosworth.

"The party's at the auditorium?" her mother had said with a crinkled nose when Rory showed her the invitation. "Don't you guys spend enough time in there?"

Leave it to a naive parent to underestimate the Princely Players' ability to transform the Elizabethan—even when it was merely for one of their own functions.

Maybe especially when it was for one of their own functions.

A drama kid is not only drawn to the possibility of standing on a stage to drink up the attention of an audience. A drama kid, at their heart, is a maximalist, a connoisseur of history's finer things, a gold-sniffing fiend with a love—no, a need—for everything—their aesthetics, their environment, their emotions—to be coiffed in the most sensationalized ham imaginable.

So a Halloween party, as imagined by the Princely Players, was a splendid blend of the gilded, the gothic, and the ghastly.

The great *Phantom of the Opera*–style chandelier had been lowered and now hung with black strips of funerary crepe fabric and fat red rosettes. Sets and props from past productions were arranged in tableaux throughout the auditorium—the Wicked Witch of the West's creepy tower and crystal ball, several eerily twisted trees from *Into the Woods*, coffins both upright and tauntingly horizontal from various vampiric shows and Agatha Christie plays.

On the stage was a spook alley to wander through, making excellent use of last year's flats for *West Side Story*—tall buildings made eerily crooked, with crackled windows, cobwebs and fog machines, wind-tossed shingles.

Exquisite tables were set up in the orchestra with a spread catered by Embers, a local restaurant with a reputation for the ornate and refined: pewter goblets of warm, blood-like borscht, root vegetables roasted with herbs and cut into coin-sized skulls, breadsticks baked into crosses, mummified Brie, eyeball panna cotta, and other gothic sundries both savory and sweet.

"Oh, my god, you look amazing!" A senior, the one who had just landed the part of Vera Claythorne, paused in the aisle to compliment Rory, batting one of the bulbous sleeves in affection. She herself was dressed as a red Crayola crayon, a costume that had Rory bewildered—was the senior trying to be ironic? Trying to make a statement about Halloween costumes being juvenile? Trying to genuinely party as her favorite preschool coloring implement?

At the very least, Rory was buoyed by the interaction. Her costume was doing the work for her—giving the older, wiser seniors a reason to speak to her, filtering out anyone who did not know their '80s fantasy cinema, and, by the look of all the unremarkable black capes and striped pirate trousers in the vicinity, making her stand out.

The proceedings themselves were loosey-goosey. There was the food table, the drink table, every row of the Elizabethan, where you could mingle and chat with your fellow thespians, either seated in the red velvet seats or hovering, punch in hand, the energy of a high schooler making you shift and twitch and pace. Onstage, there was a sing-along, a playlist of songs from *The Nightmare Before Christmas*, *Little Shop of Horrors*, and *Sweeney Todd* scrolling on the projector—if you know anything about drama kids, you know that all you have to do to make them happy is give them something to perform, even if there's no one in the audience except one another.

Rory made the rounds, lagging behind the acquaintances she'd made in Drama I, laughing at jokes, singing "Jack's Lament." Eventually she found herself alone at the food table, eyeing the desserts but grabbing a bloodred apple instead. She pushed her masquerade mask onto her forehead while she refilled her punch, and found someone smiling at her. A tall boy, one of the sophomores who was in the other Drama I session. He wore a scarlet pirate's coat trimmed in gold embroidery, a black romper with a skeleton's rib cage printed on the chest, a Wilma Flintstone–esque pearl necklace, a leather three-corner hat, and fishnets with stilettos.

"Oh, dammit!" he said. "I was this close to coming as Jareth!"

"Instead you are . . ." Rory inspected his costume in sections, then all together, but couldn't puzzle it out.

"The best of Tim Curry." The boy spread his arms wide, spinning so Rory could see the full effect. "See, I couldn't decide, so I took pieces from all my favorite roles he's done. Long John Silver, Frank-N-Furter, and—"

"Hexxus!" Rory couldn't contain her delight, grinning as she looked upon this Princely Player, who was now loading up his plate with green olives from the relish tray. "You must have had all the same tapes my grandma did."

"Nope," he said, "no tapes. We were lucky to have a television. So I had to study the *TV Guide*, sneak on the TV when my parents were busy. I saw most things in pieces. I still haven't sat down and watched *Cabaret* all the way through beginning to end."

"Wow." Rory was about to inquire about his parents—why so conservative? And what flavor was their television aversion—religious, political, New Age? But instead the boy took her remark as commentary on his olive consumption.

"No one else ever eats them," he justified. "They just sit there and get all wrinkly in the beet juice."

"You did pay your twenty-five dollars to be here," Rory said. "You might as well get your money's worth." But she reached over to his plate, in a gesture far bolder than she ever would have imagined herself capable of, and took one of his olives for herself.

He grinned, eyes puckish with mischief.

He was Ethan Yorke, recently moved to Bosworth from Oregon. He was not a scholarship kid, Rory surmised after not one but three clues about Ethan's parents: his father worked part-time for a non-profit, his mother recently spent a summer writing a novel alone at their family lake house, and both of them seemed to have strained relationships with their own parents, the kind of tenuous strings that would never be cut because they were attached at the purse.

126

"They never let us have video games or soda because they're hippies," Ethan explained with a roll of his eyes. "And meat is forever being taken in and out of our diet, depending on what master cleanse Mom's recently done at what celebrity spa."

His grandparents were wealthy, and so were his parents, he told Rory, and he used that exact word. Most of the rich kids at Bosworth tiptoed around it as if it instantly devalued them, opting for euphemisms. "We're comfortable." "I'll be out of town that weekend; we're going to Sicily for my cousin's wedding." "My mother made some calls."

Money talks; wealth whispers.

Even Ethan, speaking so obviously of his prosperity, did so with a tinge of guilt, perhaps a bit of shame. "I do have a regular job," he assured Rory, as if she were marking tallies against him. "At the library. My parents want me to save up and buy my own car, rather than just giving me one for my birthday."

Still, he refused to let Rory pat him on the back for this.

"It's actually ridiculous. It's like they want me to play the part of a normal middle-class teenager for some nonsense principle. We all know that I could make one phone call to my grandfather and he'd buy me whatever car I wanted. And I could flunk out of every class at Bosworth and my parents would still be able to buy me a diploma. They want me to try on poorness like it's a costume— Sorry. It's a sore subject for me right now."

He chugged his punch, scrunching the paper cup in his fist when it was empty; Rory watched his Adam's apple pump up and down as he swallowed. Her chest fluttered with newly rooted respect for this Tim Curry worshipper as she said, "Don't worry. I promise I'll never mistake you for normal."

Just then, Pam clapped her hands. The music softened, then

died. One by one, the Princely Players filed into the first three rows of seats in front of the stage, where Pam stood, dressed as a member of a Greek chorus in white toga, gold laurel leaves, and tragedy mask, eerily blank.

"Gather in, Players. Gather in." Pam dropped the pitch of her voice, deep and low as reeds in a pond. Rory scooted into the third row, taking the spot next to Ethan. Her dress poofed up so high around her, she offered to trade him seats so she could lean her mushroom of chiffon and tulle out into the aisle, but he said "Nah" and fluffed up the skirt into a pillow, which he lay his head on.

Rory could feel him through the fabric. She could feel the weight of his head on her shoulder.

The lights in the Elizabethan quieted until there was only a soft circle of blurry illumination on Pam. She removed her mask, waiting for the auditorium to silence itself completely. Beneath, her face was streaked with white chalk.

"All theatres are haunted," Pam began. "Theatres that are hundreds of years old. Theatres that were built yesterday. Theatres that have since crumbled into stone and dust. Every theatre is haunted because every theatre is a portal."

Rory settled lower into her seat, aware of Ethan breathing, listening, blinking.

"These curtains are a doorway. A doorway into other worlds." Pam slowly made her way to stage left, where the red velvet curtain was tucked behind the proscenium, put away for the night. "Every character who has ever lived and breathed on this stage must float past these curtains and into the actor who is playing them—you think Antigone is fictional? Macbeth? Dr. Jekyll, Mr. Hyde? No. Every one of those is a spirit. Every one of them must come through the portal. You don't believe me? Look. There. You see?"

The Princely Players followed Pam's gesture to the curtains lining the stage, the curtains in the wings, the runners that hid the lights in the ceiling. All the curtains blew gently, as if someone had opened a door backstage to let in an autumn breeze.

But there was no open door. No autumn breeze. Just the curtains, moving, blowing.

Rory inhaled slowly, deliberately, aware that the Princely Players had been cast under a spell, Pam's spell, and the last thing she wanted to do was break it. One nose whistle, one scuff of a shoe, one cough, could plummet this party into spooked giggles, and Rory did not want the catharsis. Not yet.

"How many spirits have passed through this very portal?" Pam looked around her, above her, as if expecting a spirit to answer. "How many spirits decided to stay, to linger in the wings rather than return to their own world after the production was over? How many spirits have come here tonight, summoned by our revelry, to find an actor to inhabit? How many spirits are watching you, waiting for the perfect moment to be embodied by you? How many spirits will you house?"

Next to Rory, Ethan reached up to scratch his cheek, then lay back down on the tuffet of her skirt, her shoulder.

Onstage, the curtains blew and blew.

OFF BOOK

"WRONG! AGAIN!"

In the fourth row of the Elizabethan, Pam perches on the edge of her seat, her arms resting on the back of the seat in front of her. You can't see them, but her clogs are likely angled out in a wide stance, a duck's stance.

Onstage, Annie weaves her hands through her blond ponytail and tugs, arching her back in annoyance. "Line!" she calls.

Shandie, the stage manager, reads from her binder, "'You must have done something to deserve it.'"

"You must have done something to deserve it," Annie repeats.

"Oh, come on. You don't think they'd let a murderer sit atop the royal throne of Tillypoo?" says Ethan.

"Anything's possible," says Annie, and touches the hilt of her sword. She's showy about it, because this is a stage production and every gesture has to be seen and understood to the very back row. But the very back row won't be able to see the way Annie's fingers stroke the hilt, twitching to pull out her weapon and make use of it. The back row won't be able to see the gleam in her eyes, the way Annie's Joetta hungers for a fight and also hungers for Thackery, Ethan's foxy scoundrel posing as a prince. The heave of her chest. The curl of her mouth, a sheen of sweat there, the hot stage lights salting her upper lip.

But here, where I'm standing, just left of center stage, holding as still as a Greek column to fulfill my brilliant role as a guard, I can see it all.

"Wrong! Again!" Pam's voice cuts through the scene. "The line is 'Not likely, but not impossible.'"

There's a rustle on the stage, the other actors in the scene grumbling, rubbing their necks, looking heavenward as if praying for Annie to be struck down. The stage manager, too, lets out a long-suffering sigh, peering at her wristwatch.

"Dammit!" Annie shouts. "I keep—"

"You were supposed to be off book this week," Pam scolds as she unwraps a neglected sandwich from Quiznos, delivered over thirty minutes ago.

"I know!" Annie limps in a small, enraged circle. She bats at the wooden dummy sword belted to her waist; she's been rehearsing with it at Pam's insistence—so Annie could get used to its heft, its movements, because Pam sees Joetta as having a bond with her sword like it was a third leg, a familiar, an extension of her soul. "I'm sorry! I studied all weekend, I swear."

When Annie gets frustrated with other people, she manages to stay calm, collected, communicating any breach of boundaries or unmet expectations with clarity. When Annie gets frustrated with herself, however, it's a volatile scene. Her cheeks grow so red they border on purpling, her hair sticks to her forehead in angry perspiration, and her hands don't know what to do with themselves—they wring, they ball, they clench.

Pam takes a long drag of her Diet Coke, then looks at the clock. She has parent-teacher conferences tonight and can't afford to keep babying her lead. "Go get your script," she instructs Annie. "We don't have time for this."

Ethan glances at me, then at his other scene partners. I glance at Shandie. We are all glancing, exchanging the same uncomfortable, graceless look. We are all the children who remembered to make their beds and brush their teeth and put on their shoes, and Annie's getting spanked at the kitchen table.

Annie retrieves her script—in her backpack, right where she left it—and stomps back up the stage stairs. Binder in hand, Annie flips to the correct scene and reads her lines quietly, dispassionately. She's going through the motions, her Joetta now sulky and resentful, and normally Pam would slam her for this, but Pam's done. Done with Annie for tonight.

The scene ends, and Pam takes her sandwich and her Diet Coke out of the Elizabethan without a word, leaving Shandie to handle dismissal.

"Please, please, please go over your lines tonight," the stage manager calls. "We need to be off book so we can really dig into the scenes and fine-tune them, and we can't do that if you have your scripts in your hands."

No need to address Annie directly. No one else flubbed their lines today like she did.

The props master takes Annie's sword from her, to be stored until tomorrow's rehearsal, and Annie fetches her backpack on plodding, dissatisfied feet.

I gather my own things from the wings and keep an eye on her, my heart panging in sympathy.

What a shame it would be, to spend all that time studying your script only for it to slip out of your head like wet noodles once you're under the lights. What a mess, what a tragedy, really, especially for someone like Annie, who already struggles with rote memorization, and who truly did run lines for hours over the weekend, alone, with a parent, with a brother, and with a friend, someone dedicated to the production, someone willing to spend an entire Saturday and part of a Sunday prompting her, helping her rehearse.

What a shame to realize you learned the lines wrong—

Or, more accurately, that you learned the wrong lines.

All that time practicing, and Annie never checked to make sure her script was the right one.

It's amazing what you can do these days with a bottle of Wite-Out, a pair of scissors, and access to the copier in the faculty room.

It's amazing how easy it is to switch a script in and out of a binder—

"Shandie? Where's Pam?"

A disruption.

Clarissa stands in the double doors at the back of the auditorium, her face distorted by the shadow of the tech booth, but her voice is everywhere, projecting from her diaphragm, every timbre of her rage detectable, exactly as the good teacher Pam Hanson taught us.

"Uh . . ." Shandie's frozen.

We're all frozen. We haven't seen or heard from Clarissa since her magnificent exodus to her Mackenzie's audition; if she did have actual friends at Bosworth, and not just colleagues in college application fodder, none of them reported any updates.

"Pam's getting ready for conferences." Shandie slips her big production binder, the fattest they make them, into her tote bag and straightens, squaring her shoulders as Clarissa moves down the aisle. "Can I help you with something?"

"Don't patronize me. You're not my fucking stage manager." Clarissa scoots right past Shandie, then calls, "She's in her office."

"Right." Clarissa's mother is suddenly here, looming from the Elizabethan's side door; Clarissa meets her there, and the two of them head into Euripides, charging down the hallway, tending to some urgent matter involving the head of the theater department.

I blink, shocked by Clarissa's paranoid, almost violent intrusion into our rehearsal space; others still lingering in the auditorium, including Shandie, meet my glances with shrugs. *Who knows what that's about?* we all say without speaking. *Who knows what Clarissa's up to this time?*

And of course we all find out. One by one, feigning other reasons to walk past Hardy, we give in to our collective curiosity and eavesdrop on the radio show that is Clarissa and her mother, confronting Pam in her corner office, letting the cavernous classroom amplify all their accusations and demands through the open door and into the hallway.

"I'm telling you, she was set up!" Mrs. George keeps saying, and Pam keeps letting her, perhaps aware that the more this sentiment is repeated, the more Mrs. George sounds like a tinfoil hat–wearing conspiracy theorist, punching holes in her arguments with her own hysteria.

"I don't understand what you're suggesting," Pam finally interjects. "Someone set up Clarissa to fail at her auditions?"

So she didn't get into Mackenzie's. Interesting.

"Clarissa didn't even get to audition for Mackenzie's because

Mackenzie's never sent her an invitation to audition!" Some shuffling of papers, and apparently the evidence is presented; meanwhile, Clarissa is uncharacteristically muted, reminding us all that you can be followed around by the spotlight at school, but at home, someone else might be the star of the show.

"They said they never sent this letter," Mrs. George goes on. "We drove down there, got a hotel room, everything, and they had never even heard of us. It was humiliating!"

Ah. So the letter from Mackenzie's wasn't real. Very interesting.

Poor Clarissa was so undone by this chain of events—the exciting possibility of attending Mackenzie's, the devastation of Mackenzie's not even knowing her name, the return road trip of shame, and the realization that she had discarded *Good Knight! Sweet Lady* like a bag of dog shit—that Mrs. George withdrew her from Bosworth on temporary mental health leave. That's why none of us have seen Clarissa peacocking through the cafeteria. That's why none of us heard about Clarissa's new adventures at Mackenzie's.

And then came the *really* interesting part.

"I'm sorry, Clarissa. The show's already been cast. We've been in rehearsals for over a month." Pam addresses Clarissa directly, even though Clarissa's mother is the one speaking.

"But surely it would be entirely appropriate to re-audition the principal roles, just in case," Mrs. George pushes back, and we can all hear the PTA-mom, Christian-Coalition smile on her lips. "I mean, one of your most dedicated students was manipulated into missing the auditions—"

"You are welcome to join the show, Clarissa." We hear Pam stir the ice in her empty Diet Coke. "This is a fun ensemble to be a part of."

"Ensemble?" Clarissa spits out the word, already poisoned by the mere suggestion. "I don't want to be in the ensemble. Ensemble is a waste of my time. I play leads."

Pam is apologetic but won't let the Georges strong-arm her into their warped reparations. Clarissa and her mother storm out of Bernhardt, and we in the hallways duck into the foyer, the choir room, the bathroom, the nook next to the backstage of the auditorium. Then we all go our separate ways and tuck the image of tearstained Clarissa, putting on sunglasses and a floppy hat like a celebrity heiress heading off to rehab, into the dark coils of our memories.

So Clarissa didn't have an invitation to audition at Mackenzie's after all. Interesting.

She and her mother drove all the way down there only to be stared at by their secretary. Interesting.

The letter they'd received in the mail looked official—the school letterhead on the top, the logo and mission statement on the bottom, the lines praising Clarissa's performance reputation sounding very much like the kinds of praise Mackenzie's teachers gave their own students. *Interesting.*

And Clarissa, who likely would have auditioned for and taken the big lead role of Joetta in *Good Knight! Sweet Lady*, would instead roll away in her mother's Lexus, off to lick her wounds and finish high school through packets, the method most utilized by burnouts and dyslexics and other students who have to graduate by "alternative means."

Don't feel too sorry for Clarissa. She's at her best when she is victimized, and the extra time away from school will let her solidify her tragic backstory before she starts college in the fall. She'll stay away from the college theater department, claiming the flashbacks make her too devastated to even set foot in that part of campus, but she'll find that the intensity of the narcissistic, cutthroat choir bitches suits her very well, and she'll rise to the top and sing many solos and make lifelong friends there.

You could even say I did her a favor.

MISS KEATING, TAKE TWO

Miss Keating doesn't bother hiding her tells. Not with me.

If she nods, makes comments, or uses a pen to correct small errors on an assignment, it's subpar. She doesn't bother using her whole brain to assess subpar papers, and instead reads them shallowly, polishing what she can polish, because why waste precious energy on something unfixable?

This morning she says nothing while she reads my paper. I lean against the desk closest to hers and wait. It's Miss Keating's prep period, the pathetic stretch where she's expected to cram a whole week's worth of grading and lecture writing and curriculum slinging into forty minutes.

Much as with under-qualifying papers, Miss Keating doesn't bother trying to make much use of this prep period; she's resigned herself to a fate of after-hours paperwork and instead invites me to use her empty classroom as a place to catch up on my own homework as needed.

Today I am here to get her final thoughts on my essay, to make a big show of struggling (and triumphing) over my AP US History worksheets, and to put in face time, because after today I'll be using these free periods of mine to help with some of the crew's efforts for *Good Knight! Sweet Lady*: painting sandwich signs, basting together costumes with Cynthia—any little task or errand Pam needs completed. I'm here to show Miss Keating that she has no need to worry about me.

Miss Keating sets down my essay and stares at it, chewing a thumbnail. She waits until I look at her.

"It's fantastic," she tells me. "More than fantastic. It's flawless. I can't find one thing I'd change."

I smile wide and tuck my hair behind one ear. "You think we can send it off?"

"Absolutely." Miss Keating runs through the instructions for this particular scholarship application, and I inhale deeply, an invisible weight slipping off my shoulders.

"Now. You've got one more to write. Deadline's this month." Miss Keating slides a pamphlet to me, and I cannot help myself, I balk.

"The Ayn Rand Institute?"

"I know, I know." She opens the pamphlet for me, sensing that my shock has disabled my faculties. "But look. You write one winning essay—one essay!—on any of her novels, and you get one thousand dollars. You can sneeze out an essay on Ayn Rand for a grand, can't you?"

I peruse the novels listed, the topics proposed. *We the Living . . . The Fountainhead . . . Atlas Shrugged . . .* All three of them are in Bosworth's library, and the essay is only required to be twenty-five hundred words long.

"You don't have to agree with her," Miss Keating continues. "You don't have to like the books or Ayn Rand at all. But a thousand dollars would go a long way."

"I don't know if I'll have time." That's as far as I get before Miss Keating's jaw stiffens and her eyes darken.

"We had a plan, Rory. If you don't follow the plan, then the plan stops working." She folds the pamphlet and flops it on her desk. "You're almost there. One more essay, and then you can relax and enjoy the end of senior year and wait for those scholarships to come rolling in. Don't stop now."

"I understand." My pitch drops—not to intimidate, no, but to imitate. Pam's voice is lower when she wants to preside, wants to control. So is the voice of every school secretary, every teacher, every mother I know. Even Miss Keating herself. Does she recognize it when she hears it?

Miss Keating clicks something on her computer, studies the screen, then turns the monitor so I can see it.

"Your grades are down," she says. "You're slipping in all your classes—except Drama III, I see."

I've purposefully declined to mention the drama department, *Good Knight! Sweet Lady*, or Pam, but Miss Keating is a bloodhound, hot on the scent.

I can't argue. It's there, plain and harsh on the bright glow of her screen. I'm down half a letter in everything—a full letter grade in math—and yet I have half-formed tassels in my backpack that Cynthia needs me to finish for the grand ball scene at the beginning of act 2.

"It's still weeks until the end of the term," I say. "I'm only missing a few assignments. Nothing major."

"It's not like you to be missing anything" is Miss Keating's counterpoint.

I suddenly feel exhausted. Depleted of my ability to negotiate with Miss Keating. I know I now look like the epitome of surly teenager—posture slumped, mouth turned down, eyes narrowed. I prepare for my scolding.

But Miss Keating isn't one to scold. She never is. "I'm not going to debate this with you like you're an adult," she says, "because you are not an adult. I think you're taking on too much with the musical, and your other responsibilities are suffering as a result."

"It's my last high school production. The last one. I'm just trying to be part of it. I'll be able to get my grades up," I say, and I mean it. I'm sharp enough. I've been at Bosworth long enough to play the teachers. I know their games.

"This isn't an academic issue," Miss Keating fires back. "I'm not worried about your grades; I'm worried about you. I'm worried you have too much on your plate. It's an emotional and mental health issue. I won't forget about last semester, as much as you want me to."

"Last semester . . ." I pause, waiting for the right thing to say. But something's stopped up inside of me. I have nothing. Nothing but the truth.

"Last semester," I tell her, "was different."

"How so?" Miss Keating removes her glasses, rubbing away the streaks with her soft green sweater. *Convince me,* she says without speaking.

Last semester, I hit rock bottom. Last semester, I was deep in the darkness, and all the doors closed behind me. Last semester, I was so disoriented, I couldn't tell up from down, couldn't claw my way to the light.

"Last semester, I needed help." I can admit this without indignity, especially to Miss Keating. Everyone thrives with a little tribulation in their past. "I was in a very dark place. And I got help—thanks to you. And now I am healthy enough to be part of a show again. Yes, it means a busy couple months, but I can balance it all. I will."

Nothing but the truth, so help me god.

I'm healthier than I've ever been in my life. No darkness, no shadows. I'm standing right in the sun.

Miss Keating is still not convinced. I see suspicion furrowing her brow. "Here's my offer," she finally says. "You get your grades back up and you keep working on your college plans, and I won't intervene with your participation in the play."

"That's fair." Ayn Rand, here I come. (It won't be the most unsavory thing I've ever done. It's not even in the running.)

"But I want you to go see the school counselor," she adds. "I'll make an appointment for this week. Think of it like a tune-up. I'm not saying your transmission's got a problem. I'm just saying . . . let's pop things open and see what's going on under the hood."

My heart clenches. I don't want to do this. I don't want to speak to anyone else about what happened last semester. I want the past to stay in the past, and I want to keep chasing after the future I was promised, the future I've built for myself—

You're a performer, and she's asking for a performance.

Put on a good show.

"All right," I agree, adrenaline dissolving, my lungs relaxing. "Good idea. Yes, I'll talk to the counselor. We'll see if he thinks I've got everything under control."

"We'll see." Miss Keating watches me as I retreat from her classroom; I head right to the library and check out *The Fountainhead*, because Miss Keating's eyes tend to follow you long after you think she's done watching.

PLAYING
MR. RICHMOND

Interior. An office on the first floor of Bosworth Academy. All walls are made of reflective glass, muted by a calming gray overtone. Bosworth Prince paraphernalia hangs from every corner: banners, posters, mission statements.

> RORY *sits in front of the massive desk, which is overtaken by files and office toys like Zen gardens and Slinkys. Her backpack is at her feet. Her legs are crossed at the ankles; her arms are placed on the armrests, wrists relaxed, fingers splayed. The epitome of open and relaxed body language. MR. RICHMOND enters, a thirty-something man in a black polo shirt with a Bosworth Prince monogrammed over his heart in red, and takes a seat at his desk.*

MR. RICHMOND:
> Thanks for your patience. We had some student council business that ran a little late.

RORY: No problem.

MR. RICHMOND *shuffles through his papers.* RORY *gets the idea he is trying to give her a certain impression—that he is merely finding the right file, the* RORY *file, which he has already studied and so knows very well, and not surreptitiously scanning it for the first time right now, as well as scanning Miss Keating's note for much-needed context.*

MR. RICHMOND:

So, let's see. Miss Keating encouraged you to come talk with me because . . . Well, why don't you tell me?

RORY: *(giving an "aw, shucks" smile)*

She's concerned because my grades have slipped a little.

MR. RICHMOND:

Right. You're in the home stretch of your senior year. It's tempting to phone it in at this point, isn't it?

RORY: *(pretending to think)*

Oh, I'm not phoning it in. I just turned in a Bio II lab that Mrs. Murdock thinks is up to university standards. She actually wants me to submit my findings to the Plutonian Society.

MR. RICHMOND:

That's wonderful news. Congratulations.

RORY: Thank you.

MR. RICHMOND:

You're a hard worker. There's no doubt about that. Just looking through your file, your transcripts . . .

MR. RICHMOND *scrolls through* RORY's *electronic file, all the evidence of her time at Bosworth, all of it equally impressive.*

RORY: I've fallen behind, but I'll catch up. I always do. Look at my midterm grades from the first term of junior year. See? I get overwhelmed right around midterms, but a few late nights and weekends, and I'll be right back on top.

MR. RICHMOND:

Oh, I'm sure you'll do just fine. Your GPA for senior year is hovering right below the 4.0 mark, and I'm sure you'll graduate with a splendid transcript. Plenty of colleges will be interested in you.

RORY's *foot twitches. She smiles again, waiting for him to excuse her, to write a note to Miss Keating clearing her from any and all mental health concerns. But instead,* MR. RICHMOND *leans back in his chair, away from the computer, away from her file, and studies her.*

RORY: Mrs. Harris gave me an extension on my worksheets, and she always lets us turn in a report on a historical novel or movie for extra credit. I've already started *The Fountainhead*—

MR. RICHMOND:

Miss Keating thinks you're spending a lot of time on the spring musical. She's worried that you'll have another . . . You know.

RORY *knows.*

RORY: *(her smile wide enough to elicit a compassionate chuckle)*
I have been very busy lately. Pam's needed help with some of the crew tasks, since we're putting on a show with one of the largest ensembles in musical theatre.

MR. RICHMOND:
The more time you spend with the drama club, the less time you have for schoolwork.

RORY: True, but I'm not that behind. A few assignments and I'll be caught up. Besides, there's only another month until the play opens.

MR. RICHMOND:
Last semester was—

RORY: Awful. It was awful. I know.

MR. RICHMOND:
Miss Keating and the other faculty here at Bosworth— and myself, of course—we want to make sure you have the support you need so you're not—so you don't—

RORY: It won't happen again.

MR. RICHMOND:
Well, Miss Keating and I both agree that you should have some safeguards in place, some systems so you can watch for red flags and get help before it's an emergency. Let's talk about what some of those safeguards and systems could look like.

RORY *dons a serious expression. As always, she has come prepared. "It may feel impossible to recover from a self-*

harm attempt, but you aren't alone." So sayeth the mental health pamphlet she sneaked home from her mother's ER waiting room long before this meeting. "There are steps you can take to get out of the cycle and heal your mental state.

"First, talk to someone about your attempt."

RORY: I've been working with a therapist. She's been great.

"Find new coping strategies for your stresses and triggers."

RORY: I have some strategies for stresses and triggers. Those have been helpful.

MR. RICHMOND:

Such as?

"Journaling."

RORY: Journaling.

"Gentle exercise."

RORY: Yoga, long walks.

"Baths, music, connecting with loved ones . . ."

RORY: When I'm overwhelmed, I put on some music and take a bath. Or I talk with my mom. She's so easy to talk to— she's my rock.

MR. RICHMOND:

How will you know if you've taken on too many responsibilities? Will you be able to step back from the musical if you need the space?

RORY: Absolutely. Like I said, it's really busy right now, but my schedule will have some breathing room once we get closer to opening night.

Beat. RORY *sits up slightly taller in her chair.*

Have you ever seen *Good Knight! Sweet Lady*, Mr. Richmond?

MR. RICHMOND:

I'm afraid not. I have heard of it, though.

RORY: It's such a good show, and working on it has been . . . so fulfilling. It's not like last semester's show. *The Crucible* was all about witchcraft and lying and secrets, neighbors getting neighbors jailed and killed. Such a dark play. But *Good Knight* . . . It's a cheerful show. Affirming. It has a happy ending, and the characters are so funny and brave, and the music always puts me in a good mood. . . . I love it so much.

RORY *laces her hands together, leaning forward to deliver her final line.*

It's the perfect show to go out with.

MR. RICHMOND *closes* RORY*'s file and puts it away. He tells her he's thrilled she's found something so empowering to be a part of, and assures her he'll bring his wife to the musical when it opens. After she leaves, he writes an email to Miss Keating, then gets started on some administrative work.*

RORY, *just outside of the counselor's office, takes a long, luxurious bow, as if an audience is before her, rising to its feet.*

SET DAY

Everyone has to put in two hours on set day.
That's the rule. That's how Pam keeps it fair.

Yes, there are students who are on the technical theater crew,
and they are the heavy hitters, the architects of Pam's vision for
Good Knight! Sweet Lady. But in the production of a musical, there
is enough work to keep a whole construction crew busy, and Pam's
solution to share the load is brilliant.

Not only does it get the set built—cheaply, with free labor in the
form of hyperactive teenagers itching to get out of their houses—
but it also teaches every cast member about the behind-the-scenes
operations of a show. Some kids never would have picked up a paint
roller or a nail gun otherwise.

It instills a bit of pride in all of them, to look at their set and
know that they built it, they did, together. One big bonded, boisterous, happy family.

Saturday is set day, and most of the students blow through the
required two hours and continue to hang around, as eager to see

the set finished as they are afraid to miss out on any jokes, injuries, or tantrums among the cast and crew.

If you don't stay until the bitter end, you might be the person who left fifteen minutes before Preston rigged his dad's old Taser and let Cole Tase him in the balls, to outrageous applause and laughter, sheer delight. You don't want to be the person who was absent when Shock-Sack got his new nickname.

Rory arrives at the earliest possible hour, eight in the morning. She brings a packed lunch, a water bottle, and enough dimes to get a Mountain Dew from the vending machine, and ties her hair back into a low ponytail. She wears old paint-splattered clothes. (As she left the house, her mom commented, "I would have killed to have those jeans in high school! Messy and grungy was the look!" Rory had no response and gave none.)

"The list of jobs is taped right there." Shandie, the stage manager, points to the proscenium, stage right. Three sheets of paper printed with all manner of tasks hang on the bricks. "Please do not mark the job as complete until it is one hundred percent complete. If you cannot complete it yourself, please come tell me and I will help you find someone who can complete it. Do not jump around from job to job. Choose something you can get done and then get it done." Shandie, truly born with the talent and temperament of a chief of staff . . . or a preschool teacher.

"Any time spent standing around will not count toward your two hours. We are here to work. Understood?" Shandie directs this last announcement at the trio of senior boys currently seated on the edge of the stage, legs kicking back and forth, a postcard of nonchalance.

She's right to be wary. The closer the cast gets to opening night, the more rambunctious everyone becomes. The stronger the friendships, the more likely that rehearsals will turn into frolicsome hangouts.

Pam is here to supervise, as an adult needs to be on the grounds supervising, technically, but her own list of tasks to complete is mysterious and intense. She flits in and out of her office, down to the faculty copy room and back, into the Elizabethan to inspect the student handiwork. She is, as Pam always is, blunt with her corrections and matter-of-fact with her rare praise. "The stones need more crackling." "The roof is perfect. Done." "We need it to fade to that dark blue much more smoothly. Blend that middle section up."

This last direction is given to Rory, who peered at the list of tasks and chose to work on painting the back wall. It's a huge concrete expanse, and Pam wants it to fade from a pale sky blue down to a deep, dark gunpowder blue. Onto this wall, they'll project a starry night, a rich sunset, and a bloodred sky when the knights drag themselves home, defeated.

The job is repetitive, entrancing, and there's not much room on the cherry picker, so Rory will be alone, cranked up twenty feet in the air, just a can of paint, a brush, and whatever Jake chooses to blast from the tech booth. Right now it's a new album, non-Broadway, from guitarists with bangs in their mascaraed faces.

Rory only barely knows the song, but she hums along anyway.

At noon, several people break for lunch, heading out to Ruby's or the taco place down the block. Below the cherry picker, Pam strolls across the stage on her way to her car, and Rory chooses to take her silent assessment of the wall as approval.

Stroke, stroke, stroke . . . So Pam saw her. She saw Rory there this morning at eight, and she saw that Rory is still here, four hours later. Double the requirement. Still working. Still fixing this wall.

Caring so much about this musical, she'll give up every spare hour and weekend and her grades and even her sleep if she can somehow contribute to the production—

Rory King, senior year, and here she is, still paying her dues.

"That's dangerous equipment, you know." Ethan's voice carries up to Rory.

She looks over the edge of the cherry picker; he's standing center stage, hands in the pockets of his ripped black jeans.

"Only if you fall." Rory puts the lid on the paint and lowers herself to the ground.

Ethan glances around at the empty Elizabethan. "Where is everyone?"

"Lunch." There's something about Ethan today. Rory's trying to determine what, exactly, without staring too obviously. He's not wearing any makeup, for starters. No glitter on his cheeks, no liner on his eyes, no gloss on his lips. One might assume that's because today's set day, a day for sawing and fitting and lifting and sweating, but Ethan would wear sparkle to a funeral.

His hair's pulled back into a tight bun at the nape of his neck, and his clothing is all muted and simple. No kilts. No accessories. Nothing odd, nothing vintage, nothing that could start a conversation or make Ethan stand out in any way.

Anyone might look at him and think, Oh, Ethan simply took a day off from being Mr. Glamorous, the Phantom of the Opera, the Bard of Bosworth. Ethan simply decided to show up as a normal teenager.

Anyone except Rory.

Ethan always wears his feelings, no matter how over-the-top. This is the opposite of that. This is camouflage. This is Ethan stitching up some affliction, but Rory suspects he's one loose thread away from coming apart.

"What's wrong?" she asks.

He glances at the half-finished villa facades on the stage, picks up a nail gun, and secures a beam. In his regular-person clothes, he looks smaller, slighter. Peter Pan's shadow.

"I can tell something happened," Rory presses. "So you can either spill now or we can wait until you inevitably get into your dad's booze cart and call me crying after consulting with Cuervo—"

Ethan interrupts her with an exaggerated sigh, like a toddler who has decided, against all instincts, to finally fess up. "Brad and I. We're—we're done." He reports this without snark, without an addendum that it's for the best, without false strength.

When it's Rory, he doesn't have to.

He shrugs at her after he says it, but she's not so easily fooled.

She notices that despite his best efforts at scrubbing it away, his face is ruddy. He's already cried about it today. Yes, Ethan's a guy who wears his plaid heart on his lacy sleeve, but he's not quick to tears—which means his heart must be absolutely dashed.

"Oh, Ethan." Rory opens her arms. Ethan walks into her, shuddering out a sob. She can feel his face scrunched up against her neck, disappearing from the rest of the world, finding solace here against the top of her shoulder.

Her shoulder.

The double doors at the back of the Elizabethan swing open. Like a parade, the cast and crew march back into the auditorium, remnants of their meal in takeout containers and doggie bags, and they bring their conversations with them, too.

Ethan releases Rory and moves beside her, sliding his arm around her shoulders as if they were just hanging out, nothing-doing, two buds chilling on the stage. Rory is strangely adrift and wonders if this is how a flotation device feels once the human is safely inside the boat. Too light. Cold from the sudden desertion.

"Now he shows up!" Cole, ever the jester, leaps onto the stage and gives Ethan a full-body rattle. "You just had to get your beauty sleep, didn't you?"

Ethan tugs his hair out of its bun, shaking it loose. "Nah, I was hoping you'd be gone by the time I came around. But you're still here." He's blinked away his anguish, and as he and Cole rib each other, Rory takes to her backpack and nibbles her peanut butter sandwich.

When Rory is finished with her lunch, Ethan jogs up to the tech booth to negotiate with Jake. A few seconds later, "Science Fiction/ Double Feature" blasts from the speakers.

"Let's get this shit built!" Ethan rallies the troops, whipping off his long-sleeved tee so he can work in his undershirt. Rejuvenated and ready to make a dream world come alive, the cast and crew spread out to their various tasks, taking up their hammers, their sandpaper, their hot-glue guns once more.

Rory climbs back into the cherry picker and is about to press the button for liftoff when Ethan rushes to her side.

"Want some help?"

She studies him. "Isn't your job to dance around and make puns about getting drilled? Entertain us all and keep your hands pretty?"

He chuckles. But he is sincere as he responds, "I just feel like talking for a while. Is that okay?"

The cherry picker's platform is technically wide enough for two people; Rory swallows as she squishes herself into as tiny a three-dimensional package as she can.

Inside every person comforting a loved one's broken heart, there is a tiny flame of glee. Rory won't pretend she doesn't feel it—she knew all along, didn't she, that Brad was going to drop Ethan like this, that Brad was no good for Ethan, that Brad would ultimately cause more collateral damage than he was worth. She thinks of Brad imposing that night at Ruby's, and the stink of chlorine tangles in her memory. He was rude that night, wasn't he? Dismissive of Ethan's interests, his friends. Selfish. Stealing the spotlight for himself. Ethan needs someone who pushes him into the lights, always, where he deserves to be.

Yes. She is ready to listen.

"All right," Ethan says once he's settled beside her, their thighs less than an inch apart. "Send us to space."

Set day ends at five, but most people stay later than that.

A group pools money and orders pizza. Rory is unaware this has happened until the pizzas arrive. She fumbles through her pockets and her backpack, even though she knows there is less than a dime to be found, but Shandie shakes her head. "It's already taken care of." She insists Rory have a slice. Rory only approaches the pizza once she sees others who did not contribute do so. (She always forgets: when you live in a home that has money, you don't have to tally every cent. Not the way a scholarship student does.)

They didn't get every task finished, but when Pam emerges from her office to examine the list, her face relaxes.

"Excellent work, everyone," she says. "Thank you so much. Make sure you signed the call sheet so your hours are counted."

Most of the remaining tasks are things that can be attended to at rehearsals, during school, and in other cracks of stolen time. They'll be handled by the tech crew, Pam herself, and any other students who are willing to volunteer their precious hours.

Rory lingers after the pizza is gone. Ethan hugs her goodbye before he leaves for a family function, promising to call her tomorrow. She heard all the sordid details of the breakup while the two of them were painting the wall. Ethan spoke; she listened. Brad said it was just too hard to find time to see each other, between his swimming and Ethan's musical, but Ethan secretly suspects Brad's into another swimmer, and if Brad shows up at prom with him, Ethan swears he's going to vomit right on the dance floor.

"So we skip prom," Rory said, casually dipping the paintbrush back into the gray-toned blue. "We do something else that night. Or we show up and ignore them completely."

Ethan sniffled, then gave her a rueful grin. "You're right. Let's get completely dolled up and set the whole thing on fire. Fuck 'em!"

And Rory kept swiping paint onto the concrete, realizing that she had essentially just asked Ethan to senior prom, and he had essentially accepted.

"Rory?" Pam calls from the doorway that leads into Euripides. "Could you come here for a minute?"

In the drama room, Pam has a stack of handbills and glossy posters laid out on the tables. *Good Knight! Sweet Lady*, they all say, with the musical's retro floral design, a take on the original logo— Joetta in profile, leaning into her sword, a mysterious stranger reflected in the blade, lots of flowers, lots of green, lots of spring.

"I've got to drive the truck back to my house tonight"—the truck, borrowed from Pam's father, is used to transport some of the larger set pieces and lumber from an off-site storage facility—"and I'm wondering if you can drive my car."

Drive Pam's car.

"I can take you home after." Pam holds up her keys; Rory takes them with a meek smile.

"Make sure you sign yourself out first." Pam stacks the posters and bills in her arms and grabs a Diet Coke for the road. "Park on the right side of my driveway. I'm dropping these off at the city center first, and then I'll meet you there."

Pam's keys in hand, Rory heads to the call sheet to sign herself out.

She scans the names of everyone who showed up today, from those who popped in for the requisite two hours to those who gave up their whole Saturday, like she did.

But there is one name missing from the list: Annie Neville.

No-show on set day.

A cast and crew become one big happy family over the course of a production. Rehearsals, costume fittings, drilling lines, chew-outs by Pam, mic checks—all of it weaves everyone closer, until you're existing in your own universe together. It's not about the show; it's about something bigger—

And Annie just cut herself out of the universe, while Rory's behind the wheel of Pam's car.

Not part of set day, not part of the family.

Not really.

UNBELIEVABLE

"WHERE IS SHE?"

We're seated in the first three rows of the audience in the Elizabethan. Pam stands in front of the stage and looks at each of us in succession.

This rehearsal is a first and a last—our first full run-through of the show completely off book, no scripts allowed. Our last rehearsal before we start tech week, when Pam and Shandie attempt to orchestrate the actors and the crew, combining the light cues, the props, the music, everything but the costumes.

Tech week is always long. Stop and go. Today should be something of a victorious rehearsal, a chance for the cast to feel out the rhythms of the show as it unfolds on our tongues, a chance for Pam to witness her vision coming together.

Instead, we are hunched in front of her, as dumbfounded as she is, hearts fluttering in blunt panic, the minutes ticking, wasting our rehearsal block.

"Does anyone know where she might be?" Pam tries this question next, a variation on the former, to similar failure.

No, no one knows where Annie might be. Shandie's using Pam's cell phone to call Annie's house. No answer. Someone ran down to the gym, just in case Annie was with her old team. She attended all her classes, she doesn't work at the smoothie bar on weekdays, and she hasn't seemed sick or defiant or distractable.

Our first full run-through without scripts, and our lead actress isn't here.

Interesting.

"She didn't come to set day, either," I hear someone behind me comment, not bothering to soften their gossip. Perhaps if Annie had begged forgiveness for blowing off her required two hours of hard labor, showing up to rehearsal today with a contrite heart and a really, really good excuse, she might still have found a shred of mercy in Pam.

But this is too much.

"Sabotage," someone whispers, and that's the closest word for it. The closest way to categorize how it feels when the star of your show, the lead, the titular character, the linchpin of the whole damn thing, just vanishes this far into the production.

It feels menacing.

And Pam is overprotective of her department as it is.

No one says it out loud, but you can practically hear the cerebral choir of identical thoughts swirling around:

Annie did choose basketball over drama, at least until her car wreck. Maybe Annie's realized her heart can't ever belong to the stage after all.

Annie wouldn't even be here if she hadn't broken her leg. She'd be in the gym 24-7. She'd be winning championships and catching the attention of the best college teams in the nation. Maybe she's punishing all of us for her terrible luck.

Annie did say she resented the way Pam treated her for having another extracurricular. Maybe Annie's punishing Pam for her jealousy.

"Take your places for the top of act one. Jake, let's have the overture." Pam has made up her mind. Annie will not abandon the show high and dry; rather, today's rehearsal will go on without her. Cutting around the blank space rather than sticking your finger through the hole.

My place in act 1 is the grand ensemble entrance, a bustling square near the palace. I climb up the stairs with the masses, moving to the wings, where I'll await my cue.

"Shandie, will you read Joetta's lines?" Pam settles into her usual place in the auditorium, her cell phone tucked back into her jeans pocket. Not Annie's lines. Joetta's.

I'll wait.

The overture plays. The anxious chatter about our missing Joetta gives way to excited patter about tech week, dress rehearsal, opening night, all the milestones we have ahead.

Music fades. Out comes the narrator.

And the show begins.

From my various places—the wings, the stage during ensemble numbers, the left side of the auditorium, where we ensemble members creep back into the darkness to spy on the scenes we aren't part of—I watch Pam.

I watch to see if she looks behind her. She does not anticipate the double doors of the Elizabethan opening. She does not anticipate any latecomers straggling in, adding themselves to the shining, punctual cast.

As far as Pam is concerned, I gather, the entirety of the cast for *Good Knight! Sweet Lady* is all here.

Where is Annie, you ask?

I honestly don't know.

Truly.

It baffles the mind—because Annie Neville is one of the most well-organized, responsible, reliable people I've ever met. She lives and dies by the pages in her planner, and she's never been late for anything, not class, not work, not church, not family dinner.

It's interesting, though, the implications therein. If you follow your planner to a tee, it requires an inordinate amount of trust in your planner. You rely on this spiral-bound Bosworth Academy–issued weekly planner to tell you where, when, and what you promised you'd do . . . And yet a planner cannot answer for itself. A planner cannot alert you if its pages have been altered. A planner will not scream if you pull it out of Annie's bag and slice it up.

Such a reliable person, but consistency is more easily manipulated than chaos.

What a shame.

Rehearsal rollicks along perfectly swimmingly after the drama of Annie's mysterious and inconsiderate truancy. Pam's calmed down a bit, everyone's remembering their lines, and aside from a couple of awkward timing issues with the practice musical tracks, we all settle into the show, its pacing, its flow.

It can be difficult, when you're embarking on any creative endeavor, to see the larger picture—to look at the messy sketches, the splatters, the misshapen clay, the pile of wrong words, the hollow performances of a work in progress, and to be able to imagine the end results.

A play, especially, feels like a warped game of dress-up for weeks at a time. Opening night seems far away; rehearsals are filled with embarrassed giggles, attempts to joke away the flawed deliveries, the failures to emote. Those who need the catharsis of laughing at their mistakes can frustrate those who need seriousness, intensity, harsh repetition, tough love.

But today, sometime during the ensemble number that opens the second act, we feel it.

It's alive in all of us; I can sense it the way you can sense an electric current, that hum and vibration, the warmth.

Today as we belt out "Harold Pretty-Hair" and twirl through the spring festival choreography, our painted world becomes real. The music is not piped through speakers; it is played by fiddlers and drummers and the best damn pipers in our beloved court. We're not the cast and crew of Bosworth Academy's drama department; we're the good citizens of Downere, and we've gathered here to gossip about the king and queen's flub-up.

"Hope it won't affect the state of the union," we sing to a medieval-esque banker who strokes his chin in consideration and replies in song, *"I'd hold on to my assets, if you want my advice!"*

In this scene I am not a senior and a scholar; I am an apple seller.

The song ends; the set changes.

Now we see Joetta's old home in the woods, among the briars and the foxes.

In this scene, I am nothing.

I hover on the edge of the stage, staying out of the light.

In this scene, I am a guard, and Shandie is trying to read Joetta's lines out loud while also jotting down the lighting cues.

"Is this a trap for a fox? Or for a fox maiden?" says Ethan.

"Oh! Uh . . ." Shandie flips the page, searching for her place. Out in the audience, Pam sighs. This is meant to be a fast-paced scene, full of banter between Thackery and Joetta. The constant halts leave everyone drained, impatient.

Say it.

"Either one, so long as it also catches a snake," I say quietly to Shandie.

"Thank you. 'Either one, so long as it also catches a snake,'" she reads.

"Pause. Black hole on lower stage left. Needs to be spotted up a touch," Pam cuts in. Shandie scribbles it down.

"Come on, now. It wasn't personal. You weren't exactly kissing the king's robes before I showed up. You're like me, Joetta. On your own. A scoundrel. We have nothing, nothing in the world but whatever luck we can hang on to. We'll do whatever it takes to survive." Ethan draws closer to the imaginary Joetta, curling above her— above nothing; there is no one there.

"Hang on." Shandie fusses with her script.

Again. Say it.

"I am not like you," I prompt. "You have nothing, so you can care for nothing."

"Caring is a rich man's game," Ethan says before Shandie can parrot me, and before Shandie can find where we are now, Pam holds up a hand.

"Hang on. Rory, you know the lines?" Direct. Unemotional. The question is not a promise, only a question.

"Yes," I tell her.

"Great. Please read Joetta's part going forward."

Pam says to "read" Joetta's part, although I don't need to read anything. The lines are loaded into my lungs, ready to be fired. I move to my new position.

"Caring is a rich man's game. You're a fool to keep anything around that you won't trade for coin," Ethan baits, and there is merriment in his eyes, genuine merriment, to be sharing the stage with me.

"I may be a fool, but my heart is made of steel. You have no heart. You probably sold it at first chance." I take the stance Annie has practiced, only I make it my own—no sword in my hand, wooden or otherwise, but I make myself as tall as I can, arching my back, a graceful striking pose, and I can almost feel the sword in my hand—

"I'm here." Annie bangs through the side door, the one nearest stage left. She throws her jacket onto the floor and jogs up the stairs.

Everyone drops character, the scene crashing to its death as Annie charges toward her mark. I step out of the way just in time; I get the impression she would have pushed right into me if I hadn't moved.

"Rehearsal started over an hour ago, Annie," Pam calls.

"Yes, I know." Annie is panting with rage, her bottom jaw jutted forward like a bulldog's. If her leg is hurting, she doesn't let it show. She seems angry enough to jet right off the earth. "I'm sorry I'm late, but I'm here now. So let's go."

Ethan, understandably wary of the extremely frustrated ex–basketball player beside him, gets back into position. "Joetta, I . . . I care about some things," he delivers.

"Then cut me down. Get me out of this trap. Let me go my way and you go chase after yours." Annie jumps right in, and, bless her, she knows her lines like "My Country, 'Tis of Thee."

On they go, to the end of this scene, and I am in the wings once more.

"Pause," Pam announces before the next big ensemble number, and we all pause in the lights, trying not to stare so obviously at Annie, who, we sense, is in for a real spanking.

But Pam tells us to take five minutes before the final act, stretch our legs, get a drink of water, reset our brains. At first I think she does this to lift the tension, but as soon as I file into the hallway to the drinking fountain with everyone else, I realize she's caused the exact opposite effect. The tension is thick as fog, and it follows Annie around like a spotlight.

"I'm sorry, okay?" Annie barks at Cole when he gives her the least subtle dagger-eyes I've ever witnessed. "It looks like I didn't hold you up at all. You guys started without me."

"You would have loved that," Cole snarks back. "All of us holding our breath until you finally run out onto the court—oops, I mean onto the stage."

"Fuck off." Annie moves past him, taking her turn at the fountain. "I don't need this from you."

Her thirst quenched, she wipes her dripping mouth with the back of her hand, then makes eye contact with me and walks my way.

"I swear to god, if Cole says another word to me, I'm going to break his teeth." Annie's hands go to her hips, and she huffs, a stance I've seen her take when a referee makes a controversial call. "I don't know what happened anyway. I write everything down in my planner—you know that. I never miss anything, but my schedule said there was no rehearsal today. And set day wasn't in my planner, either."

"Maybe you forgot to write those dates down," I prompt. We're all given the same printed calendar at the beginning of the production with all the important dates and times marked. It's not unfeasible that Annie might forget to copy down a date or two into her own planner.

Annie shakes her head. "I checked my calendar. Saturday and today are totally blank."

"What do you mean?" I cock my head, pushing my eyebrows down in confused concern.

"I mean I must have a different calendar than the rest of you!" Annie uses both hands to push her hair off her forehead, blinking frantically. "Shandie must have printed off a special one for me that doesn't have all the right dates—that's why I missed set day, because it wasn't on my schedule. And today was blank, too! It's the only explanation!"

Very, very close. So close.

"But why would she do that?" I say.

So close.

Annie doesn't answer at first. She closes her mouth, pressing her lips into a line, looking so much like her mother, it's almost scary. (I say nothing, because when you are seventeen, hearing that you resemble a parent is one of the worst insults you could possibly imagine.)

"Pam did it," she blurts. "Or she told Shandie to. They both hate me. Pam still hates me for doing basketball instead of dedicating my whole life to the Princely Players. She hates anyone who doesn't make an idol of her. She's punishing me for refusing to kiss her ass constantly."

"But she cast you as Joetta," I point out. "Why would she do that if she wants to punish you?"

"Oh, Rory, you know why!" Annie's chuckle is jangled, forced. The desperate laugh of a perpetrator right before the police show up with the cuffs. "I'm here all the time now, right under her nose! There's no better place for her to punish me. She can switch the schedule on me, boss me around, leave me out of important meetings, criticize me onstage under the guise of being my director— it's perfect! I'll bet that's why she chose *Good Knight! Sweet Lady*. I'll bet she wanted to goad me into it. Lure me into a lead. All so she can keep playing puppet master with us. Because that's what this place is, Rory. It's Pam's little kingdom, and we're just here to be her puppets so she can play God—"

Annie stops cold, glancing behind me.

Shandie, the stage manager, has quietly approached us, and she peers at Annie with an assessing, calculating look. "Ninety seconds to curtain," she announces. "And the reason Pam cast you is because when you sang 'Somewhere in Between' at the callbacks, you gave her actual goose bumps."

Shandie leaves to round up the rest of the cast, and Annie's face falls into a neutral expression—but I can see the worry in her eyes. "Can I borrow your calendar later?" she asks. "I want to make sure I've got the right dates in my planner."

"Of course," I tell her.

She slinks over to stage right and waits in silence through the entr'acte, mulling over the stage manager's words.

And I take in a deep breath, relaxing near the drinking fountain. I'm not needed until the grand finale. I've got time.

Annie's fate is all but sealed.

She's shown her hand to Pam one too many times—Annie's not wrong that Pam will forever punish her for playing a sport instead of choosing to bind herself to the theater for all her days. And it doesn't matter why Annie was late today—to Pam, it can only mean that Annie doesn't understand this life, the life of a Princely Player. Annie doesn't understand the work of a musical—first you sing, then you dance, then you bleed.

One more tiny measure to click everything into place, and then it will be my move on the chessboard.

I've got time.

TARGET

(FLASH-FORWARD)

"Annie? Annie Neville?"

Annie can no longer pretend she doesn't see the small woodland elf–like woman staring at her in the bedding section. She angles her empty red cart and meets the woman's eye, offering a smile while trying to place her in her memory.

"Lizzie," the woman offers. "Alder. I was a sophomore when you were a senior?"

"Oh, Lizzie! I thought that was you. How are you?" Annie is a liar. She has no idea who Lizzie is, or if Lizzie resembles how she looked back at Bosworth. Annie thinks she herself looks different enough, but it's not easy to be forgettable when you're a five-foot-ten blond woman with thick biceps and a scar on your chin.

But the woman doesn't let Annie get away with false pleasantries. She gives a rueful laugh. "You don't remember me. I don't think you ever knew my name, not even during the play. Of course, we all worshipped you."

Well, what in the world is Annie supposed to say to that? "I'm sorry," she attempts. "There were so many people in the ensemble, I couldn't keep track of everyone."

"I wasn't in the ensemble." Lizzie's smile is not a pretty one; it stretches across her whole face, making the skin on her cheeks go sinewy, her teeth skeletal.

Annie is uncomfortable. She is uncomfortable being back in Bosworth, even though her parents assured her it had changed enough since she left for college. She never wanted to go backward in her life, only forward. Mostly to avoid looking at the things she left behind.

Things like this.

"So do you still act?" Lizzie asks. She's completely let go of her half-filled cart, as if she has all the time in the world to badger a former high school acquaintance.

"No," Annie says.

"That's too bad! You were so talented," says Lizzie.

"Yeah, well, theater departments are bullshit cults run by sick, power-hungry people. I was glad I got out when I did." What did Annie even come in here for? She's trying to remember. It's Target. It could have been anything.

"I did some acting in college," Lizzie tells Annie. "Down at Stanley College."

Enough of this. Annie smiles a tight-lipped smile and grips her cart. "Well, it was so nice to see you."

"You know, I thought of Rory the other day." Lizzie drops this bomb without warning, without fanfare, without emotion, like a psychopath. Because only a psychopath would bring up Rory, Annie thinks. Only a psychopath would be that callous. "I saw a girl loafing around at the park, and I swear, it could have been her twin. Do you ever—?"

"Lovely to catch up." Annie steers away from Lizzie, aware that she is giving Lizzie more ammunition for some potential future meeting, when Lizzie can say, *You didn't remember my name and you left so abruptly, as if you were better than me.*

I will definitely remember you next time, Lizzie Alder, Annie thinks.

She heads back out to the parking lot, her cart empty, and sits in her car alone. She glances in the mirror only once, and her eyes go right to the scar on her chin, a scar that was added to the topography of her face during her senior year of high school.

A scar she tries to forget about, unless it's right there in front of her, unavoidable, and then it's a sinking reminder of the worst moments of her life.

Moments she'd like to erase completely from her mind.

But Annie's memory is better than she thought it was. Slippery with formulas and letters and words, but it holds on to nightmares with an ironclad grip.

"A truly selfish man cannot be affected by the approval of others." Ayn Rand is known for her long, moralizing monologues—yet she begins *The Fountainhead* with a small sentence of three words: "Howard Roark laughed." Why would anyone in Roark's position laugh? He's just been expelled from the Stanton Institute of Technology's architecture program, his counterpart Peter Keating has been singled out for his by-the-book academic excellence and promising future as an architect, and it has never been clearer to Roark that he must reject his personal values in order to align with the societal standards of collectivism. But Rand instills in her protagonist a clear-eyed conviction, a deep-rooted inner worth that renders all other opinions powerless. In the face of such failure, Roark leaps from the cliff of uncertainty, knowing that wherever he lands, he alone will catch himself.

—*Rory King*, "The Power of Self-Confirmation in Ayn Rand's *The Fountainhead*"

ACT THREE

MORE FAVORS

WELL, DEAREST READERS, ARE WE ENJOYING OURSELVES?
You must be, since you keep turning the pages. I do hope I am
providing the kind of entertainment I promised you—I've given
you intrigue, betrayal, secret combinations, and there's still plenty
of book left.

Plenty of tricks up my T-shirt sleeve, too, beginning with this
next one. You won't miss it if you blink, so settle in and savor it,
knowing that my tricks are the kind that require measurements,
planning, slow unfolding.

And so this is how I walk over to the football bleachers after our
disastrous full off-book rehearsal is finished—slowly, deliberately,
at ease.

It's minutes before sunset. The blue of the sky is brilliant, almost
defiant, and soon everything will be made into silhouettes. But for
now, it's that golden hour when the light streaks across the land
sideways, warming backs, squinting eyes, hitting faces and making

them glow—if they have the propensity for beauty, anyway; the sun only makes shadows out of someone like me.

The Elizabethan is empty now, the rest of the cast and crew hobbling out to their cars, heading home to recover from the brutal emotional whiplash of today's run-through. If Annie stayed after to let Pam chew her ass out, they were chillingly quiet as she did so. As far as I can tell, I was the last one to leave Euripides.

Outside, the football field is speckled with track-and-field athletes, stretching limbs and hurling various objects across the turf—shot put balls, javelins, themselves. True, this is not an area of the school that I usually frequent, but I move through it with purpose. I head beneath the farthest bleachers, where a lone pack of stoners coughs, fanning away the thickest parts of their incriminating clouds . . . for what? To fool me into thinking they're meeting here for book club?

"Yo, Travis," one of them calls. I wait patiently for Travis to emerge from the dark corner of the bleachers' nether lands, his gaze glassy and red.

"Hey," he says weakly, widening his eyes as if I am blurred and he is unsure if I am actually here. "Uh, what's up?"

"I need to use your computer again tonight. I'm free anytime after eight, if you're free." Favors for favors. The usual trade.

I am prepared to ignore the teasing hoots and whispers as Travis's friends elbow and nudge at the sight of us communicating; evidently when you are blazed, you find the interaction of the genders to be hilarious in a giggly, elementary-school kind of way.

But Travis's friends don't giggle. They watch him, then watch me, flicking their glances back and forth like we're about to duel and they're here to be Travis's second.

A whistle blows on the field.

"Well . . ." Travis takes a few steps away from his friends and ushers me out of the bleachers and into the openness of the dimpled blacktop. "I can't let you use my computer tonight." He lowers his voice, trying for confidentiality, but I can tell by the way his buddies are staring that they are listening to every word.

"Tomorrow morning, then." A sunrise trip over the freeway rather than a twilight one. I know enough of boys to understand that morning has its appeals.

Travis shakes his head. "I saw what you printed last time. That letter for Clarissa."

Aware that I am now giving off an impatient aura of bristles, I nonetheless push out the word "So?" What is Clarissa George to someone like Travis? Clarissa was Bosworth royalty, one of the upper-echelon students who would only ever mingle with a burn-out if it was for the social justice portion of her college application.

"So you really fucked her up." Travis meets my eyes, and I consider him. He's only ever been the neighbor, the kid in my church classes, the son of my mom's friend, the Bosworth Prince who should, by all accounts, also be a lowly scholarship student like me (but who is an unlikely legacy student and thus can afford to fry his lungs beneath the bleachers because there's nothing else to prove once you've paid the tuition). He's always been a means to an end. I get on my knees, and then he lets me use his computer, his printer, his internet, all those shiny resources that he just walks past every day like they're part of the decor. I haven't looked at Travis Hastings like this, never.

And I can't say I like what I see now.

A lucky resource, now reshaping itself into an enemy.

"How did you even hear about that?" I lean back, defensiveness curling my very toes.

"Her mom's in my mom's garden club," Travis says. "Plus you didn't close the window on my computer when you made it. At the time, I didn't think anything of it, but then word spread about Clarissa getting a fake letter from some other school—"

"Who have you told?" To stop a leak, you must first find the source. Close it up. Glue it, stitch it, wedge a fucking bedsheet into it to plug it up.

"No one." Travis finally looks down, shuffles his feet. His hair swoops in front of his eyes, and he doesn't bother pushing it back. "It's your business. But I don't want anything to do with it."

He lurches back to his friends under the bleachers and never once glances over his shoulder at me.

Inside, something flickers, growing hungry and wild. All those months of evening strolls to the overpass, kneeling on the chilly concrete, the bitter taste lingering in my mouth for hours afterward like a salt lick gone rotten, and for what? So Travis could cut me off without warning as soon as he felt justified? He never understood how lucky he was—the luxury of being able to trade a few precious minutes of AOL time for blowjobs-on-tap, anytime he wanted them—

My fingernails dig into my palms as I leave the football field, the heat of my ire radiating like a coal in my chest. Travis thinks it's fucked up, what I did? He doesn't know what I'm capable of. Not yet. But he will.

I'll show him just how fucked up things can get.

Here are the facts:

A handwritten note was delivered to the front office of Bosworth Academy sometime between three o'clock in the afternoon on Monday and half past six in the morning on Tuesday. The office was locked by three on Monday; the first custodian arrived and unlocked the school at half past six on Tuesday.

The letter was not slid under the door, as there are rubber noise guards beneath the office doors, nor was it passed through a window, as the office windows do not open. The letter was trifolded, sitting up on the head secretary's keyboard. No one saw who delivered it.

"To whom it may concern," the letter read in big comic-book font. "Your school is overrun with drugs. Several of your seniors are involved in an opioid ring. This goes against District Code 11.35.4a, the subsection entitled 'Illegal Substances on Campus,' and warrants a phone call to the police department."

The police, when notified, were already on their way to investigate. An anonymous message had been waiting on their after-hours tip line, and their a.m. team had found it just before sipping on their morning cups of joe.

Copies of the letter were also delivered to the counseling office, the principal's office, and, inexplicably, the art teacher's office (which only made sense once you saw which students were incriminated in this claim).

Most Bosworth classes began as usual, the students having no knowledge of the letters or the investigation. But halfway through homeroom, the announcement crackled over the intercom system: "Teachers and staff, please do not allow any students out of your classroom for any reason. We have local law enforcement conducting a K-9 locker search, and they need complete control of the hallways until they are finished."

"K-9 locker search," the students whispered, until eventually they translated the euphemism: drug-sniffing dogs.

Someone brought something to school, and the cops were going to find it.

Of course the cops found it; the perpetrators didn't bother hiding their paraphernalia. The prescription bottles were stacked right on their locker shelves, chock-full of round white pills. "The good stuff," someone would say if they were particularly versed in opioid distribution or classification.

Teachers barely attempted to shut down the chatter. Most lessons devolved into little clusters of gossip, people sharing with their desk neighbors who they suspected, who was innocent, who was definitely going to prison for this.

The excitement was mostly over by lunchtime. The police officers were gone, the German shepherds in riot gear were gone, and no one had witnessed anyone being yanked out of their classrooms—

But if you walked past the office at just the right time, at about eleven o'clock, you could have seen the ashamed, downtrodden heads of the drug-peddling suspects and their parents:

One Travis Hastings. (No surprise there, as many Bosworth Princes would later comment.)

And, very much a surprise, one Annie Neville, pale as a shell, holding on to her mother with both hands like a frightened child.

Drugs, man. They can cause a world of hurt and pain. Just say no.

BUSTED

No fucking way.

Annie Neville? Our Annie Neville?

She's not going to be our Annie anymore. Pam won't let her stay in the show now.

Pam already had it out for her—you know Annie missed set day, too?

This is beyond set day. The cops are here—Annie's going to jail.

Not jail, but maybe juvie. Or rehab.

She's not going to rehab. She wasn't taking the drugs; she was selling them. That's what I heard.

Me, too. The cops found her prescription bottle in Hastings's locker. A bunch of old empty ones, too.

Damn. That's heavy. I had no idea Annie was into this kind of stuff.

No one did.

Hopefully she's got a good lawyer.

Who cares about her? What about us? We open in three weeks!

Pam will find someone else—

Someone else? Who? No Clarissa and now no Annie. Who else is there?

Rory sits in Euripides, down near the music rooms. The police presence outside of Hardy has communicated the clear message: Back off. Give the investigation some space. But the Princely Players can't possibly imagine eating lunch in the cafeteria, along with the rest of the student population—as if they are expected to play normal, the one role they cannot master—and so they are sprawled along the floor here, clumped closer than usual, spreading their crudely acquired information like mono.

Some are spilling rumors and some are listening; Rory is among the latter, tearing her turkey sandwich to shreds as she takes in all the incriminating clues, the rationalizations, the projected outcomes.

"It happened to my aunt," Preston says with a spirit of well-earned wisdom. "She hurt her neck and they put her on pain pills. But they made her nauseous, so she didn't take them—and then she started selling them to some college kids. She made bank. They let her off with community service."

No matter how many of these stories are swapped, no matter how many gentle jokes are cracked, it does nothing to alleviate the anxiety that one of their own, the star of their show, was a secret kingpin this whole time. Annie, the best actor of them all.

And there is worry for her sake, absolutely, because even though Annie didn't stick her snout up Pam's trousers like the rest of them, Annie is part of the production. Part of the family—a small part, a distant cousin, but family nonetheless.

So when the door to the drama room opens and Annie steps out into the hallway, everyone falls silent as the bereaved at a funerary procession—they all watch her shuffle with the police officers, coming for the drinking fountain on stiff legs, her pace zombie-like, her eyes red rimmed and swollen, staring ahead at nothing, clearly in shock.

Annie takes a long sip from the fountain. Even when she's done drinking, she keeps the water streaming, watching it seep down the drain. She glances up, and her onlookers are reverent, standing with their hands respectfully interlaced in front of them or else in their pockets. Their faces shine with pity, with confusion, and with compassion, and not even the Academy would be able to determine which performances were genuine and which were merely for show.

But Annie looks past all of them. She locks eyes with Rory.

Few people know what Annie's tell is. Her chin doesn't quiver; her eyes don't water.

Rory knows exactly what to watch for. First, Annie gets very, very quiet. Then her cheeks go blotchy, the color of wine.

Then Annie is moments away from spilling over.

Thus summoned, Rory goes to the drinking fountain, where she stands next to Annie, waiting, waiting for the deluge.

"My parents are in there talking to Pam," Annie says, unprompted, both cheeks dappled pink. Her voice trembles, nothing like her usual confident tone. "I can't believe it—Rory, you know I'd never do anything like this. It's a mistake. A misunderstanding."

"I know," Rory soothes.

"I didn't even want those pills," Annie goes on. "They made me feel so loopy, so I stopped taking them. Tylenol was enough for the pain—but I didn't sell them! I would never—"

Overcome, Annie presses one hand over her forehead, her eyes, her whole face scrunching up into a cringing sob. The police officers in the hallway peer at her, suspicious.

"Then how . . . ?" Rory needs only start this line of questioning, and Annie bursts into an impassioned plea that she's clearly delivered more than once today.

"I don't know! I kept my pills in my backpack. They gave me permission to—the office, the principal, my parents. Just in case my leg acts up. Someone must have stolen them—and I must have thrown away an empty bottle, and someone fished it out of the trash. This has to be a joke, right? A mean joke, but they're not seriously thinking I've been selling drugs?"

Rory's stomach lurches. Annie's holding on to both of her shoulders—holding on to this plane of reality, holding on to anything that will assure her she is not alone—and the fear and dismay in Annie's eyes are lantern bright.

Not even the night of the car accident has Rory seen her like this.

"And now they're saying I can't stay in the play. I can't be in it anymore, Rory. I—I don't know what to do." Annie cries, and Rory lets Annie wrap her in a hug.

The size difference between the two of them is comedic, she knows—a real Jack Sprat and his wife situation, stout and lean, but this reminds Rory of how it used to be. Reaching for each other. Her weight, Annie's weight, the weight of whatever they were carrying—it didn't matter.

"Rory, I don't know what to do," Annie repeats.

"It's okay," Rory says. She pats and she shushes. She'll say it as many times as Annie needs to hear it. "It's okay."

"After all this work, Rory. All this work, and now the investigation? It's too much." Annie doesn't move as she speaks; Rory feels the buzz of Annie's words resonate in her own chest.

Too much. Yes.

First the shattering of her leg, the shattering of her basketball legacy. The shattering of her dreams. Then the auditions, the callbacks, the way Pam's put her through the wringer, making Annie prove at every turn, every rehearsal, that she deserved to be here—making Annie re-audition for Joetta every chance she got.

And now all of that gone, all that swallowed pride, regurgitated in one humiliating fell swoop.

"Maybe it's for the best." Annie suddenly sniffles and arches up to standing, wiping her eyes on the back of her sleeve. "I couldn't handle the schedule anyway. And I still don't know the lines perfectly, and I don't really have the range for 'Somewhere in Between.' Maybe if I focus on physical therapy, and I see if Coach can recommend a summer league . . ."

Only a few months ago, Rory was standing in Annie's room when Annie snapped at her for pointing out the silver linings. Now it's Annie who can't blink away from the shine of the glass half full.

"Of course," Rory responds. "And they're going to get to the bottom of this whole investigation. We all know you're not dealing. It'll be over soon. Just cooperate with them and answer their questions. And then you can get back to the court."

"Annie?" Mr. and Mrs. Neville stand in the doorway of Hardy, both of them white cheeked, looking tired. "Ms. Hanson wants to speak with all of us."

Annie nods, but her face breaks into despair again. "I'm so sorry," she whimpers to Rory. "After you worked so hard to get me to auditions—I'm letting you down."

Rory tries to make her own expression the very epitome of strength and faith. "Of course you're not letting me down, Neville. You could never let me down. Whatever happens in there, we'll figure it out."

"What about the show?" Annie's throat bobs as if it has a mind of its own.

Rory's smile is calm. "The show must go on."

CLOCKWORK

OH, DON'T LOOK SO SCANDALIZED. I DIDN'T DO ANYTHING too sinister, and I'll prove it.

First of all, Travis Hastings has been playing too close to the cliff's edge for years. True, he generally leans more herbal in his choice of mind-altering substances, but I know for a fact that many of his cohorts, those greasy future mechanics who congregate in parks and under bleachers, occasionally worship in the church of stronger drugs, scarier drugs. It was only a matter of time before Travis was offered something more pharmaceutical, before he took it, before he loved it, before he decided to make his locker a one-stop shop for all of Bosworth's deadliest, beatiest burnouts. All I did here was speed up the clock a bit. Projected into the future. Perhaps we could have helped Travis, steered him away from the cold terrain of his destiny, but he didn't want any more favors from us, remember?

And Annie, well . . . It's a shame, yes, to see her like that. It takes a lot to make Annie Neville so upset that she can't advocate for herself, but she cried herself raw today and barely had the energy to scrape up a decent alibi. But you heard her yourself, I know you did—we've now put her back on a path toward basketball, the one thing in life that brings her unadulterated joy.

Good Knight! Sweet Lady was always only going to be a tale she spun, a funny little speed bump she hit on the way to her career playing ball professionally. She didn't need it, not really. If she needed it, she would have been there on set day. She would have shown up on time for yesterday's rehearsal—yes, even though those dates were oddly missing from her planner and her play schedule. If she really needed this musical, she would have channeled the rehearsal schedule somehow, and sensed that we had all gathered without her. She would have found a way to learn her lines—if she really needed Joetta, she would have carved those lines into her heart.

As for the investigation, it will be nothing more than a blip on Annie's records, if it shows up there at all. Who knows if Travis and Annie will have conflicting stories? Who knows if he'll get busted and Annie's shiny, dimply, honor-student-and-star-athlete disposition will scrub her name off the reports, squeaky-clean? Who knows if they'll both catch a fine and a scolding from a judge for this? Slaps on the wrist for both of them, and then they'll move on.

Some of us cannot move on. Some of us need this play, need Joetta. Some of us deserve it. Some of us have paid our dues, and it's nearly time to cash out.

It's a clockwork system. It's all been set up at Bosworth long before I ever put my hands on it—so I can keep cranking and winding and oiling the cogs, and never once have to feel guilty for it. Never once should I feel guilty for chasing after what I want, what was promised to me.

And so I feel no guilt when I walk home after school today and spot Travis and his parents saying goodbye to the police officers in their driveway.

No guilt as I see Travis's face, beyond stunned, soft, like he's ten years old again.

No guilt as I see the local bishop pull up, shake hands with Travis's parents, set a comforting hand on Travis's shoulder, guiding them inside to work out the necessities of a spiritual road back to God's light.

He won't mention our arrangements. My fatness protects me there—Travis will prefer to stand alone in sin rather than admit he'd let someone like me touch him.

The bishop and the Hastingses will be the only ones touching him now. It'll be Travis on his knees now, night and day, and he won't be let out of their sight until they're satisfied with the purification of his countenance—or until he's had enough of this bullshit and hits the road.

No guilt. No shock.

Only justice.

But what about the play? you are no doubt wondering. Having your lead actor drop out of a musical three weeks before opening night should be a disaster. It should cause a crater of worry in Shandie's gut and a flutter of injustice in the hearts of every member of the cast and crew. It should add a new loop to whatever ungodly knot of emotions are tangled in Pam during the lead-up to the production run, though she'll never let anyone bear witness to her struggles.

But I tell you again, this is not any ordinary production. This is a clock. And not only will the show withstand this kind of disaster; I have been counting on it.

A planned, purposeful disaster.

I designed it this way.

Annie was always supposed to leave the production before hell week. Travis is an unfortunate casualty, but I expect I'll always look back on him with fondness, the way a clockmaker might look at her wrench or pliers with gratitude. A tool. An appreciated one.

And at tomorrow's rehearsal, the cast and crew are supposed to have the energy of freshly decapitated chickens. Shandie is supposed to look sweaty and overcooked, the weight of her binder pressing her into a hunch. And Pam is supposed to be strangely collected, and she is supposed to give a comforting speech about how Annie is now getting the help she needs, and we can be grateful for that.

And then she'll announce that Joetta will be recast, and that rehearsal should proceed as normally as possible.

She'll ask me to stand in and deliver Joetta's lines.

And the clock will tick, tick, onward. Everything moving toward its end.

SHAKESPEARE

(*FLASHBACK*)

Sʜᴀᴋᴇsᴘᴇᴀʀᴇ ᴡᴀs ᴀ ʟᴏᴏᴘʜᴏʟᴇ.

Every year, Pam took her drama department to the state Shakespeare festival, a fall theater festival held on the golden-leafed campus of Pam's beloved, well-respected undergraduate alma mater. For a week straight, there were lectures, workshops, banquets, museum exhibitions, and, of course, professional productions in every possible interpretation. There were straightforward plays in classic Elizabethan, performed in the wooden replica of the Globe Theatre; there were retooled versions of *The Comedy of Errors* and *Titus Andronicus*, scripted and styled à la '90s teen movie *Clueless*; there were extremely inaccessible variations on *Macbeth*, *Twelfth Night*, and *Henry V* happening with a lot of pantomime in black box theaters.

Any way you could slice Shakespeare, it was served here on a cafeteria tray for the partaking.

And then there was the competition.

Participating high schools brought their best-directed scenes, monologues, and recitations, and these were performed and rated and judged. Bosworth always brought home new cups and ribbons for the award display near the school's front office.

The Shakespeare competitions were not bound by the same expectations as the other Princely Player productions back home. If you wanted to compete in the Shakespeare festival, all you had to do was sign up.

No auditions. No cast list.

The cost of entry was the source material itself—Shakespeare is easy enough to read, decent to memorize, and incredibly difficult to understand, interpret, and perform. Lesser schools brought half a dozen monologues from *Hamlet* and the *Romeo and Juliet* death scene; Pam's standards for Bosworth's entries were impossibly high.

To embarrass yourself with a subpar production at the Shakespeare competition was to shut yourself out of Pam's good graces forever—but Rory, like many other sophomores anxious to prove themselves, signed up to compete with a monologue, overjoyed at the prospect of stepping into the spotlight.

Permission slips were gathered, trip fees were paid, this year's official Bosworth Shakespeare Co. sweatshirts were passed around and donned—Rory thought she finally understood, when she put her own sweatshirt on, why sports teams insist on matching uniforms.

They were united in these sweatshirts. A squad for the love of the Bard.

They took a charter bus to the university, checked in to their shabby-but-clean hotel rooms. From the moment they stepped onto campus, Rory's unspoken objective was to accompany Ethan.

Whatever workshops he wanted to attend, Rory had been interested in all along. Whatever lectures he sat through, Rory had been eyeing since the moment they got their program schedules. Stuck to his side like a pasty barnacle, she was his unofficial plus-one for the opening ceremonies, the early-morning continental cook-your-own-waffles breakfast in their hotel lobby, the stage makeup tutorial, where she used liquid latex and a square of wire mesh to turn Ethan into a convincing burn victim.

"Come on," Ethan would say, standing outside the hotel room Rory shared with three other sophomores. "Let's go find Andrew and those guys and get Frosties."

"We have Gender in the Comedies first," Ethan would say on the shuttle to the campus, wisps of his hair rebelling from their haphazard bun at the nape of his neck. "Then should we do War Monologues or History of Gesture Acting?"

Let's. We.

Rory had never known it was possible to fall in love with such small words.

Wednesday came—the first day of competitions. Ethan performed first, leading a scene from *A Midsummer Night's Dream* (in a role, Bottom, that fit him so well, so like a glove, that it seemed William Shakespeare must have written it specifically for him to play hundreds of years later). Rory watched his first heat from the front row, laughing with the rest of the crowd at Ethan's ass-headed antics, and was unsurprised when his scene scored the highest points. His troupe would move on to the next round.

"Did you see Phillips?" (Phillips: the department head of Liberty Prep's theater program and Pam's closest thing to a living rival.) "He was pissed!" Ethan let his triumph ring out without shame; he and the other actors in his scene were so giddy, Rory felt a little like a moldy toadstool as she slunk beside Ethan and his ethereal, fairy-like exuberance.

"Yeah, well, *Caesar*, act three, scene one? It's been done," one of the other boys said.

"Staler than croutons," Ethan agreed. "I've seen at least three other schools bring it for this week."

"Says the guy who brought *A Midsummer Night's Dream*?" Rory piped in.

The boys went silent, anticipating a spat, but the smirk on Rory's lips was meant to challenge, not insult. Ethan closed his eyes and straightened, as if an invisible hand were petting the downy fur of his Bottom-as-donkey ears.

"Now, now! Any cliché becomes fresh again if you inject it with a bit of pizzazz." He punctuated this last word by framing his face with twinkling fingers, and Rory followed the troupe out of the auditorium, a warm dollop in her center.

Most of Rory and Ethan's conversations followed a formula: she lobbed him a bit of brass; he turned it into gold.

Plus any chance to preen Ethan—whether Rory paid him the compliment directly or whether he stroked his own ego—was gladly offered, gladly received.

It was Ethan who first pointed out, with audible turmoil, that since he'd progressed to the next round of performances, he wouldn't be able to watch Rory compete with her monologue.

"It's fine," she assured him. "I'd feel weird if you were watching anyway."

"Break a leg!" he called as his troupe dragged him away to find an energy drink before their next heat, leaving Rory with over two hours to kill until her own performance.

Rory tagged along with a few Princely Players, hovering just inside their sight line so they'd spot her and invite her to join them. But eventually they splintered, off to their own devices, and Rory was alone again.

Monologues were competing in groups of ten, rotating every forty-five minutes. Each performer was given three minutes to dazzle the judges, and at the end of the round, one lucky actor would move on to the next group.

With little else to do, Rory slouched to the location of her monologue performance early, tucking herself into a corner. A new round was about to start. The classroom-turned-auditorium fizzed with anticipatory whispers. High school students from all around the state sipped hot lemon water, double-checked teeth for lipstick or lunch residue, recited their lines without sound.

A body sank into the chair next to Rory's. It was another Princely Player Rory recognized as a sophomore. The girl with the thick wheat-colored hair and the statuesque frame nodded curtly and said, "Hi. Rory, right?"

Rory didn't confirm and didn't ask after her name, either. No need to play games—she was Rory and the other girl was Annie. They knew of each other even though they'd rarely exchanged words prior to this.

"Are you in this round?" Annie skimmed Rory's street clothes with the same expression a mother might use to peruse a bedroom that a child supposedly cleaned. She herself was in costume but covered her ensemble in a long black peacoat.

"Next round," Rory answered. She didn't mean to sound as curt as she did, but she'd just recalled that Annie played basketball. She didn't stay after school to help Pam in the Elizabethan; she ran drills in the sweaty gymnasium. And Rory felt she had very little to say to someone who did sports.

Interesting that Annie would even come to the Shakespeare festival, Rory mused. It seemed like quite the commitment for someone only half invested in the drama department. Annie split her time and her heart between the stage and a burnt-orange rubber ball; Rory couldn't imagine filling the open slots in her schedule with anything but theater.

Annie shuffled through a stack of dog-eared pages—her festival schedule, her map of the university campus, a printed copy of her monologue, all marked up with notes. She inhaled and let the air whoosh out her mouth, and Rory couldn't help herself.

"Nervous?" she asked.

Annie glanced at her and smiled. "Not really. I mean, physically I get nervous. Look." She held up her hand, which trembled like she was an old lace maker. "But my brain's completely in the game."

The doors closed, signaling that everyone should sit and simmer down. Rory peered sideways at Annie. The other girl did radiate an unflappable composure, but Rory was unconvinced. She watched for Annie's tell—a stiff jaw, a slow blink, a moment of dissociation so powerful, it turned the whole Shakespeare festival into a regret.

But Annie stared straight ahead, giving away nothing.

The judge of the monologues welcomed everyone to this session, informing the group that he'd be calling for their performances in random order. Again, Rory glanced at Annie to see what the girl thought of this arrangement; again, Annie's expression was one of amenability. Not quite pleasant, but just left of it.

The first name was called. A sprite of a girl from West Delta walked to the front of the classroom. "I'm Ivy Sorenson, and I'll be portraying Beatrice from *Much Ado About Nothing*."

Ah. Act 3, scene 1. "What fire is in mine ears?" and so on. A familiar monologue at the festival, especially among this type of girl—pixie-esque, small of feature, named for an inanimate object, most likely to be described as "quirky" for their love of old-timey jazz and their collection of rubber ducks.

A girl like Ivy could never play Lady Macbeth. Too doe-eyed. Too adorable.

The next girl, another will-o'-the-wisp, recited Ophelia's soliloquy, the "bells jangled, out of tune and harsh" from act 3, scene 1 of *Hamlet*. Another monologue for a small bell of a girl—it was a fair enough rendition. Rory, who had always loved this passage, gritted her teeth and wordlessly clapped at its conclusion.

"So, what happens if someone brought the same monologue as you?" Annie leaned into Rory. Their height difference meant Annie's whisper blew right into Rory's ear. She smelled like powder-scented deodorant.

Rory's cheeks flared. "The judges get to compare and contrast your versions, I guess?"

"Right." Annie nodded to herself as if Rory had confirmed something she'd been suspecting. "The show must go on."

A boy went up and launched into King John.

Annie, after a moment, asked, "What's your monologue?"

Prickles erupted all over Rory. "Cressida, act three, scene two." For some reason Rory's skin reacted as if she'd just revealed a secret to Annie—her body, nervous. Her brain, confused.

"I love that one," Annie said. "Did you ever—?"

Then Annie's name was called.

Annie Neville, sophomore, Bosworth Academy.

Annie stood, stripped off her coat. Before she charged to the front of the classroom, she turned back toward Rory, and Rory, for the life of her, could not decipher the look Annie gave her.

Coming from anyone else, it would have been smug, conspiratorial, a little show-offy. But Annie delivered to Rory a comportment of humble, almost worshipful fellowship. An expression of complete alliance, communion, from one performer to another.

Team spirit.

"Wish me luck," Annie murmured, and sidestepped to the aisle.

And then it was like Rory had known Annie for years—they weren't so different, that expression from Annie had signaled. Not really. Not when they were both here, in the service of the theater, giving themselves over to this great art.

Annie centered herself before the audience.

"I'm Annie Neville," she sang out, her voice as loud and as clear as a student body president's. "I'll be performing a monologue from *Macbeth*: act four, scene three."

The room was quiet. Rory understood why—there were several things happening here, and she tracked them all:

Everyone was scrambling mentally, trying to recall exactly which monologue Annie was about to launch into. Lady Macbeth's famous monologues were from acts 1 and 5, so was this Lady Macduff? The witches? How so?

Also, now that Annie was before them, her presence was overwhelming, impossible to take in. She wore a men's suit—pressed white shirt undone at the collar, a tie that had been loosened and left limp, as if she'd had a hard long day at the office and was exhausted from being so buttoned up. Her hair, slicked back into a high swinging ponytail, gleamed golden against the charcoal-gray suit jacket she slung over her shoulder with one hand. The creased pants were perfectly tailored to her long legs, and, although they were absolutely purchased in the men's department—there was room in the crotch—they looked as if they had only ever been designed, sewn, and sold to be on Annie Neville's body.

Annie grounded herself, peering down at her shiny black dress shoes, and when she glanced back up, she was Malcolm.

Not with a deep silly men's voice, not by grabbing at her junk or doing anything that signaled "butch," but because she spoke, and commanded the room to believe her.

> *This tyrant, whose sole name blisters our tongues,*
> *Was once thought honest. You have loved him well.*
> *He hath not touch'd you yet.*

It was stunning. Perfect. It was hard to believe she spoke for three minutes; it went by so fast, so wrapped up was the whole room in her Malcolm's dilemma—revealing to Macduff the depths of his sins: his greed, his lust, his lack of decent qualities, all of which would make him a terrible king . . . a confession that was, in the end, only a devious test for poor Macduff.

Everyone would probably have been satisfied if they had simply closed the rest of the monologues right now, Rory calculated. Tally up Annie as the winner, listen to her recite the rest of the whole damn play. Her presence was that magnetic.

Was Annie this magnetic on the basketball court? Rory wondered. Either way, it was glorious to behold—and a little intimidating.

"Thank you, Miss Neville," said the judge after the stunned applause. "I'm curious: What made you choose that monologue in particular?"

Annie shrugged, released back into her own personality, and the contrast was startling—so that charisma was not just her natural presence: it was something she could switch on and off. Always wonderful—and a bit sneaky on the judge's part—to ask the performer a slight question afterward. That way, the room was privy to the contrast between the performer and the performance.

It was an actor's craft that they'd witnessed, then, and pure talent. Not just someone who was good at memorizing and enunciating.

Annie thought for a moment before answering. "I don't love *Macbeth*," she finally admitted. "I know it's considered one of Shakespeare's best, but it's difficult to root for any of the characters. There are no heroes. Only the least of, like, ten evils. This monologue, though, when Malcolm is seeing how loyal Macduff is to Scotland . . . I can understand that. That loyalty. That allegiance to something larger than yourself—and that fury for anyone who would dare threaten it."

The judge thanked her again, and Annie sat down.

In the years that followed, Rory would come to understand exactly what Annie meant in this moment.

That allegiance. That conviction.

It was the single greatest moment of Bosworth acting Rory had seen to that point—and when the round ended with Annie pronounced the winner, there was hardly a ripple of disappointment in the room. It smelled like fate—Annie was meant to go on, to win the next round and the next. She was meant to carry a trophy onto the bus home.

"You're next, right?" Annie double-checked with Rory. "Oh, damn! I wish I could stay," Annie said as she peered at her watch and slid her peacoat back on again, "but I've got fifteen minutes to pee, race over to the other side of campus, and set up for my next round."

"That's okay," Rory assured her, and marveled at the change between them—she felt less reserved around Annie now. Even though she was not the only one who had witnessed Annie's secret brilliance, Rory was the one Annie had chosen to sit by.

Could that make Rory brilliant by proxy?

Perhaps Annie hadn't sat by Rory simply because they went to the same school. Perhaps Annie sat beside Rory because she'd seen something in her that she recognized. Something Annie wanted to be a part of.

"Um, good job up there." Even as Rory said it, she knew it was an understatement. Even the suit Annie wore deserved something bigger than "good job."

Annie grinned. "Hopefully I did Bosworth proud."

(The trophy from this particular festival that bears Annie Neville's name as the Overall Best in Monologue still resides in the school's glass display case and is dusted and shined once a year. Same with Annie's basketball championship plaque and her MVP ribbon.)

"I'll see you later, okay? Break a leg! Let's both make it to the finals—that'll show Pam to put sophomores in her ensembles! You'd better hurry and go change."

Then Annie was gone, shuffling through the crowd of people she'd soundly spanked in the competition, and they were patting her on the back, congratulating her, like they could transfer her capabilities to themselves with one touch. Annie was, of course, the very model of a good sport, thanking them kindly without a whiff of self-deprecation—simply accepting that she had been the best in this round, and that was how it was.

And that was how it would remain.

For Rory did not move from her spot in the corner of the classroom. Not to change, not to find a quiet place to go over her lines.

Not to rise from her seat when her name was called in the next round: "Rory King? From Bosworth Academy? Is Rory here?" She wrapped her ankles around her chair's legs like vines.

She did not move to run out of the room when the awkward silence continued and the judge stood and glanced around the room, looking at each person—boring his eyes into her as he considered whether or not she could be Rory, ultimately moving past her, perhaps deciding that this pudgy dumpling of a person in holey jeans and a sweaty Shakespeare sweatshirt couldn't possibly be the girl who had signed up to be Cressida.

Rory let her spot go. She did not perform the monologue she'd been practicing at home for weeks. She did not put on the sky-blue Grecian gown she'd begged her mother to help her procure, which was folded up in a silken wad at the bottom of her tote bag. She did not say the words, the lines she'd been aching to say out loud:

> *Who shall be true to us,*
> *When we are so unsecret to ourselves?*
> *But though I loved you well, I wooed you not.*

Lines that felt like they had been written for her, to her, to come alive when she alone said them. Lines that felt like they belonged to her.

Lines she hoped to say one day, to the right person, at the right moment. It's far too embarrassing to spill the truth, but harder still to hold back the words.

I am in love, and it is embarrassing to admit. I love you, and I try to keep it to myself, but it keeps spilling out of me. Forgive me my thoughts—they are inappropriate, too much, too impossible. You could never love me back, but I have to say it, because if I don't, I will regret it—

She did not say it. Instead she sat, arms folded around herself.

Why perform when she had already seen the winning monologue?

Why try when she was destined to fail?

Rory watched every round of monologues until the classroom was surrendered to the afternoon lecturers. Then she grabbed her things and made her way to the shuttle. Back at the hotel, she turned on the TV and stared at it, waiting for Ethan's jubilant return.

At the end of the week, Rory sat beside Ethan during closing ceremonies. His troupe came in second place in their category. Annie sat on Rory's other side, and when she was crowned winner of the monologues, Rory clapped with genuine pride. No resentment in her guts, no envy in her bones.

Others came home from Shakespeare with laurels and tokens. Rory came home with a new friend.

THE LIZZIE ISSUE

EVEN THE BEST-MADE CLOCKS REQUIRE A BIT OF GREAS-ing now and then.

At the next rehearsal, the cast and crew are no longer chittering, clucking out their latest theories and worries and rumors; they slump in the first three rows of the auditorium and are mostly quiet, staring up at the great ceiling of the Elizabethan as if the pathway back to joy is somewhere in the geometric designs of its glass.

Rory takes her spot next to Ethan, who's flopped into the fourth row, an act of rebellion or an act of nonchalance, who can say.

"Hey," she says.

"'Sup" is his lethargic reply.

"Gloomy in here, isn't it?" Rory tugs the sleeves of her cardigan down so she can grip them in her palms.

Ethan snorts. "The death of the show doesn't exactly inspire the kicking up of heels."

"The show's not dead." Rory slouches down as far as her hips will let her, until her knees kiss the back of the chair in front of her.

"Pam's going to cancel," Ethan says. "Guarantee it."

"Not a chance." Rory speaks with her voice and also with her beating heart; she can feel the pump of each valve, each push of new blood through her system. "Pam's too in love with this show to cancel it."

There's too much at stake with this show to cancel it.

Ethan is not moved by Rory's gesture of optimism; he shrugs and fusses with a loose thread on the hem of his kilt until Pam emerges from backstage.

Pam waits until the students silence themselves.

"All right," she says. "I'll get right to it. Annie Neville will no longer be part of our production. I know there are plenty of rumors floating around, but I would ask you to stop spreading unverified information. It's a very serious situation, and I assure you that the authorities are investigating it thoroughly. But that leaves us without a Joetta."

Rory's lungs clench. She grips her sleeves so tight she can feel the pattern of the cheap acrylic yarn, count the loops and purls.

"For today, I want to run through the second and third acts of the show. We have a few transitions to polish. I'll announce the new casting for Joetta later this week, but for now . . ." Pam scans the rows of people.

Rory sits up slowly, her breathing even.

"Lizzie? Could you come read Joetta's lines?"

Lizzie Alder, a pixie-like girl from the ensemble who wandered over from chamber choir, nods and accepts a binder with the script from Shandie.

It doesn't mean anything. It's one rehearsal.

Stick to the plan.

Pam claps her hands and asks everyone to get into their places for the top of act 2, then hisses open a Diet Coke and takes her place in the front row.

"Adios," Ethan tells Rory, and the two of them part in front of the stage, he on stage left, she on stage right with the rest of the ensemble.

The stormy mood seems to have lifted. The cast begins the bustling, pre-rehearsal movement backstage, their hijinks, their various conversations that are dropped and picked up between scenes. Usually Rory ping-pongs back and forth in the wings, going from one group to the next, but today her feet bring her to the very edge of the curtain, the closest she can stand to the stage without catching the light.

She's watched this scene dozens of times.

But she feels compelled to watch it again.

Lizzie holds the binder in both hands; it makes her look ridiculously small, far too slight and delicate to take on the giant role of Joetta, who is a knight and a rapscallion and an athlete—

"Louder, please, Joetta," Pam commands, and Lizzie dials up her volume.

Next to Ethan, she looks more like his little sister than his secret love and possible enemy—and surely plucky Joetta should have a boisterous, assured way of speaking?

"Is this how they court women in Tillypoo? Seems more like hunting bunny rabbits," Lizzie recites. Her nose has been in the binder this whole time, since she doesn't know the lines, not by heart. But now she attempts to gesticulate Joetta's bold claims, and again, Rory is less than charmed. It looks like a kitten swatting a paw—

"She's good," someone whispers. Behind Rory, Sierra and another choir girl lean their heads out of the wings, spying on the scene.

And Rory's insides catch flame.

Lizzie's not good, but she could be.

Pam's visions for her musicals are always malleable things—and if Rory strains to listen, with the deepest part of her, she can sense the vision stretching to accommodate a new version of Joetta, someone who wields her power in her finesse, her subtlety—

"But she's a sophomore," replies Preston, and it's like someone's doused the fire in Rory's body with a bucket of cold water. Of course. Lizzie's a sophomore.

Pam doesn't cast sophomores.

"It's three weeks to opening," Sierra argues back. "It's not exactly standard circumstances here. Pam might have to bend her precious rules."

The truth of this statement rings through Rory, aching her teeth.

Pam might bend the rules.

Lizzie Alder, no dues paid, not so much as a dime.

And there she is, the only ensemble member holding the weight of the whole script in her hands, trading jabs with Ethan Yorke.

No, Lizzie could have been randomly selected. Lizzie could have been the first person who caught Pam's eye. Lizzie could have been an inoffensive, nonthreatening, unintimidating student to fill the space on the stage while Pam mulls over the actual, real possibilities for a permanent Joetta . . .

Or Lizzie was chosen.

Predetermined.

And this rehearsal, then, is more than just a rehearsal; it's an audition.

A stealth audition.

Lizzie lifts her chin just then, on the tail end of a line that sums up Joetta as a character, her pride, her valor, her vulnerability: "And perhaps a woman can do more than just dream. Perhaps she can pick up a sword and fight to make those dreams her own. Don't assume anything about me ever again."

Maybe it's only a trick of the lights, or the vision of memory, but Lizzie looks so much like Annie when Annie used to say that line. She sounds like Annie.

The scene ends, and the ensemble moves into position for the next curtain.

But Rory is frozen, a knot of whispers anchoring her to the spot.

It will be you this time.

You've earned it.

No, you won't allow a sophomore to waltz in and take it from under your nose. Here is how to keep what's yours.

The wind starts right after rehearsal. Most of the cast and crew have gone by now, including Pam, who raced off to attend a board meeting. Rory's lingered until the custodians started roaming the halls, and now huddles against the double doors of the foyer. She tugs her hood up, pulling the drawstrings tight, bracing herself for the violent walk home.

"Rory?" Shandie, the stage manager, is walking down Euripides, schlepping her normal stack of show binders and notebooks, along with a heavy backpack that doubles her body width. "Are you waiting for your ride?"

"No," Rory says, punctuating the word with a chuckle. "I'm trying to decide if I should wait until it dies down a little or if I should just gird my loins and run."

"It's really blowing out there." No sooner has Shandie said this than a whole tree branch blows through the parking lot, ripped clean from an aspen somewhere too weak to hold on to its own limbs. These spring storms can be dangerous. One wrong turn, and debris can knock you right out.

"I'll be fine." Rory tucks her hair back into her hood and adjusts her backpack straps. "At least it isn't raining."

"Why don't you let me drive you home?" Shandie insists. "That wind would knock Mary Poppins right over."

Rory doesn't make much more fuss, but she accepts the ride, helping Shandie carry all her show paperwork to the back seat of her Focus.

"I've got to drop something at the post office really quick," Shandie informs Rory. "Do you mind? It's on the way to your neighborhood."

"Not at all." Rory does not know if there is supposed to be emphasis on the words "your neighborhood," but in this moment she is all cheerful appreciation, a sounding board for anything Shandie might bring up to discuss.

A friend for half an hour.

Because that is the thing about Shandie. In a group, she comes across as studious, stilted, shy. She wears the ugliest pastel purple glasses Rory has ever seen and does little with her hair except pull it back into a fuzzy ponytail. She gives orders at Pam's behest but rarely starts conversations by herself . . . until you get her on her own.

On her own, Shandie doesn't stop gabbing.

And gab she does—from the second they pull out of Bosworth's parking lot, Shandie rambles, on and on about the least exciting production details (which are, to be fair, Shandie's main jurisdiction as stage manager) and the minutiae of the Bosworth senior grind.

Rory is patient as Shandie drives through the post office mail drop, talking about some mishap with the playbills. She remains patient as Shandie takes them through a coffee shop drive-thru, where she buys two caramel-mocha frozen cappuccinos, ordinarily too sweet for Rory to endure, and which feel strangely like barter: sugary coffees in exchange for another fifteen minutes of Shandie's prattle.

And then finally, once their coffees are only melted whipped cream and Shandie's pulling her car through Rory's shaded subdivision, Rory hears the opening she's been waiting for.

"Just a constant list of things to do, and every time I get something done, there's a new thing ready to take its place. Not only is there the Joetta dilemma, which is . . . Well, it would be enough to tank any other production. But I also have to finalize the lighting order, print out the list of cues for Jake, find an accordion player . . . Honestly, it'll be a miracle if we can get it all together by opening night."

"Wait, say that again?" Rory has been cataloging the damage done by the riotous wind so far, the siding ripped off the cheaply built houses, the roof shingles missing, the garbage cans knocked over, the miniature trampolines and kiddie pools rolling through yards unattended, but now she turns in her seat, facing Shandie, who sighs.

"I didn't mean that literally. I was just being dramatic—of course we'll be able to get everything together for opening night. I mean, this is Pam Hanson we're talking about—"

"No. You said you need an accordion player?"

Shandie lets out a laugh. "Yes! The script calls for a musician in the opening, in all the court scenes, for the big ball, and Pam has this gag all mapped out with an accordion player, but so far none of her contacts are available. Why, do you know someone?"

Rory grins just as Shandie pulls her car into Rory's driveway. "We both do."

Bless Rory, Shandie thinks as she drives home that evening. Bless her for thinking outside the box. For paying attention.

For being such a good friend.

"Guess what?" Rory informed Shandie after they'd finished running errands together. "Lizzie Alder plays the accordion!" Rory knew this because she'd overheard some of the chamber choir girls talking about odd jobs, weird talents, things of that nature. Apparently Lizzie's father spent his summers playing the accordion on cruise ships in his youth and passed the knowledge on to his daughter. The two of them mostly performed together, a special father-daughter duo, but Lizzie was plenty capable of playing solo.

And she was already cast in the show! Rory answered Shandie's prayers. It was like destiny. An accordion player, right under their noses all along.

Pam is thrilled when Shandie brings this tidbit to her the next morning.

Even better, Lizzie is excited to show off her niche skills! Cynthia is going to make Lizzie a medieval musician's costume, and Lizzie will get special recognition in the playbill.

This is what Shandie has learned, after stage-managing so many shows for Pam: things are always darkest before the dawn. A show can be a goddamn mess before its run, but by opening night, things usually have a way of pulling together.

Good Knight! Sweet Lady is one step closer to a successful run.

Thanks to Rory King.

COMPLICATIONS

THE END OF FEBRUARY CLENCHES ITS FIST AROUND US with more of those freezing days that taunt with bright sun and clear light. Winter lingers into spring, but as we spin into March, the cruel bite of such bitter cold eases, giving way instead to gloomy storms, mildly warm overcast afternoons, the sprouting of buds on the barest of branches.

Hell week is nearly upon us, and ordinarily we would be descended into a thick dread, knowing that the fusion of script, music, set pieces, props, and technical cues slivered Pam's patience and made us taste our own incompetence, made us all feel like we'd regressed to children's theater. But Annie's departure from the musical has bespelled an interesting hope on the cast and crew, even though we have yet to hear news of our replacement Joetta. True, most of us are merely following Pam's emotional cues, choosing to remain optimistic because she, our director, our pope, remains optimistic. But I also believe there is a sort of cleansing effect at work here, that Annie's perpetually dismal attitude and almost combative dynamic with Pam is gone now, and so the air is clear.

A show is only as good as its weakest player, and we are lucky to have excised ours with time to spare before we open. Now *Good Knight! Sweet Lady* can be authentic. Now it can be pure.

I am, of course, torn. On one hand, it cuts me to the heart to see Annie booted from the musical, knowing how much she loves this show, how hard she worked to overcome her injury and the disappointment of losing her senior basketball season. *Good Knight! Sweet Lady* brought Annie and me back together as friends, too— or at least we're moving along that path. To know that she won't be holding hands in the circle during our preshow ritual in the green room . . . it tears me up. Really, it does.

And yet on the other hand . . . Annie did miss set day. She did nearly miss a rehearsal, which is absolutely against Pam's production rules. Her pill bottle was found in a known drug user's locker. Certainly such behavior is not befitting a Bosworth production. Certainly you understand why I might be relieved to have Annie gone.

For the integrity of the school, you see. For the integrity of the show.

And speaking of the integrity of the show, we've had a few more tightly focused rehearsals, spot-treating a couple of problem areas in act 2, but Pam has not yet made an announcement regarding Joetta.

Whispers buzz around backstage, each rumor more ridiculous (and also, somehow, more plausible) than the last: Pam's secretly rehearsing with her chosen Joetta already, and it'll be a big reveal during hell week. Pam's bringing in an outsider from another school. Pam's playing the role herself.

All those noses, sniffing the air for a scent of the trail, and yet no one's even come close to guessing.

No, I'm not suggesting I'm clairvoyant or anything. I am not prognosticating the future; I am simply able to see the stepping-stones along the pathway, because I have been the one to lay them up to this point. I'm standing on one now, even, another crucial stone on the way to opening night, and here is the shape of this particular stone:

This Saturday is our cast party. Traditionally Pam holds it before hell week, as a bonding element, rather than at the end of hell week as a reward, so as to withhold catharsis from us until opening night. Brutal but effective.

Anyone who is willing to help with some technical chores on Saturday before the cast party is invited to do so, and those of us who volunteered another one of our precious weekends must make sure our parents see the email Pam sent home and grant permission, make manifest their awareness of where their dependents will be that day.

Perhaps inspired by the Annie Neville fiasco, perhaps pressured by the school board to indicate that she keeps an established leash on those students in her care after school hours are through, Pam has insisted on these parental emails and verifies that should we not have our parents message her back, we will not be allowed into the Elizabethan on Saturday morning.

"It's nearing the end of the school year," Pam tells us all in Drama III. "Midterms are coming. I know homework has probably ramped up for many of you, and your academics are top priority." They aren't, and Pam knows it, but she has to say the words aloud, has to be on record with this stance, despite all the evidence showcasing that Pam doesn't give a fuck about our grades. "This email is so you and your parents can decide the best way for you to spend your Saturday. Schoolwork comes first."

Quite a performance from Pam, all things considered.

And let me assure you: my own grades are fine. Perhaps not as glistening as they were last semester, perhaps not sharp enough to prick your finger on, but no one could rightfully look at my grades and complain. Not even Miss Keating, and, as you know, she would love to find something to complain about. I have the kind of GPA a rich white boy would pay good money to achieve.

So I knew my mother wouldn't veto another Saturday spent in the Elizabethan based on my grades.

But she's been very busy lately, working long hours at the ER. Another nurse quit, leaving them understaffed, and that's just not ethical, frankly, when you've got people coming in with heart attacks, broken bones, overdoses, car accident trauma.

She's helping with this neighborhood church charity drive, too, since Mrs. Hastings had to pull back on her involvement to spend time with her son, the addict. A little ironic, perhaps, if you think about it—Mrs. Hastings has gone from providing the social charity to now needing it herself. A real full-circle moment. There but for the grace of God go I, and all that.

So please understand, when I feign overwhelm about a history paper and gain access to the library computer lab during PE, I am not logging into my mother's email to sabotage, or to keep things from her, or to create a barrier between my mother and Pam, their communication.

I am simply trying to lighten my mother's load. She works so hard for us. Pam knows this—she said it herself.

Pam's email is polite but to the point. "I'm writing to inquire if your student can spend some of their valuable time this Saturday assisting with some of the technical theatre tasks for the musical," blah, blah, blah . . . Such a robust way of asking for free labor from teenagers, and such an elegant trickery, to beg for permission from parents whose very children salivate and jump to volunteer themselves for the chance to be in Pam's presence, even if it's sweaty, thankless work.

For my mother's sake, I send Pam a short affirmative reply, then delete all evidence of both messages. My mother isn't likely to have seen it anyway; it would have been buried by the constant influx of emails from hospital administrators, newsletters, spam—

My hand freezes on the mouse. I've scrolled down through her inbox and spotted something interesting—something that churns my gut, steals my breath, sends my brain into an electric frenzy of thoughts.

Miss Keating sent my mother an email yesterday. My mother already responded.

The summation of Miss Keating's email: I'm concerned about Rory, concerned about her involvement in the musical, concerned that the school counselor, well intentioned as he is, didn't really evaluate Rory with any kind of depth or nuance in a recent visit, especially given Rory's "history," and could Rory's mother spare any time during the next week (also known as hell week) to discuss this in person?

And my mother's response, in a nutshell: Of course, let's find a time, I work a hectic schedule but this is important, thank you for bringing this to my attention, Rory has been distant since the "incident," and it's difficult for me to tell when interventions are needed, next week I have Tuesday afternoon and Friday off, what time works for you?

Ah, so Miss Keating has given my mother something to fuss over, something to fix. My mother's favorite feeling.

And this is beyond what I can repair using only email. My mom's been hooked now, by Miss Keating's concerns, and knowing the two of them, they'll pin down a date and a time and discuss the hell out of my "situation" until they've landed on a solution they both love the sound of.

No, this is bigger than email. This requires something—

The bell will ring in six minutes. Every chamber of my brain is rigging something together, something spectacular, something to shoo both of these hovering pelicans out of my hair.

I may not have the decadent charm of Ethan or the stately grace of Annie or the compact beauty of Lizzie, but I do have guts.

All my roundness, my heft, my fleshy furnace that insulates me beyond the need for outerwear—that is where I must keep my gumption, and I have it in gallons, in acreage, in strides.

The first thing I do is temporarily block Miss Keating from my mother's inbox. No more messages between the two of them. No more coordinating meetings, no more "situations." Not until I spin my scheme into motion. Before the bell rings, I've printed a document and tucked it into my backpack.

An envelope, a stamp, and I'll have bought myself some time from the circling shadows of Miss Keating and my mother—

Enough time to plug up their communication, to throw disarray on their schedule-matching, to fall back into the gaping musical and fend off any other attempts at intervention with the reality of this frantic truth: that the show opens soon, so soon, and all our dedication is needed to make it work.

Miss Keating and my mother will have no choice but to let go of

my hand, let me slip back into the inky depths of Pam's demands—
and by then, all will be made plain.

All that time, that energy, all of myself, given over—

All will be justified.

Two days later, like clockwork, my mother's inbox doth choke with
something from Miss Keating:

FROM: Margo Keating

TO: Gwendolyn King

Hi, Ms. King,

Sorry for my delinquent reply. Something's come up last
minute. I'm afraid I won't be able to meet with you this
week, but we should absolutely make time soon. I'll be
available the last week of March.

Now, that's a message of a different color. I didn't even break a
sweat.

CAST PARTY

Bernhardt, Hardy, the drama room at Bosworth Academy, has been transformed.

Twinkle lights hang from every wall, every shelf, every seam and trim, ostensibly by nothing but sheer will; no chunky fasteners or hooks. Just hazy orbs, making a fairyland of the dark-wooded classroom. Tapestries drape down to cover the whiteboard, the fire extinguishers, the more contemporary fixtures that set this party in a modern high school. These students are able to believe themselves away into fantasy with less than this, but the effort is much appreciated.

The cast is larger than the room can reasonably accommodate, but everyone in the Princely Players rightfully predicted that the party would be bypassed by several types: the chamber choir girls, some of the senior techies, a handful of the more studious ensemble actors who chose instead to spend their evening at a band concert at City Hall (which was the reason these actors would only always

ever be ensemble actors, with a director as vindictive and possessive as Pam).

Rory enters the party and feels calmed when she sees it's mostly
classic Princely Players, those students who have not only dedicated
the last twelve weeks to the production of *Good Knight! Sweet Lady*,
but who long ago dedicated their entire beings to the production of
all theater—good theater, bad theater, mediocre theater, anything,
as long as there was a stage and an audience and someone telling
them what to do.

The usual fixings are present—a spread of food, a drinks table,
music, lights, teenagers in a state of anticipatory celebration desperate for some form of exorcism—but it is all themed, all of it
based on *Good Knight! Sweet Lady*'s vaguely medieval, retro-'60s
flower child reminiscence, and so Rory is delighted by a crown of
baby rosebuds placed upon her head at the entrance. She gets herself a cup of soft honey mead to sip, peruses the offerings of finger food, and ultimately settles near a cluster of fellow seniors who
are simultaneously commandeering the karaoke machine and also
keeping the heartbeat of the party pumping.

"Rory!" Ethan spreads his arms wide and pulls her in; Rory
stumbles a bit, her body reluctant, but Ethan perches her on top of
his knees as if she is canary-light, and so she settles, forcing herself
to trust him.

Ethan's jetted into the giddy, almost drunken phase of his post-
breakup routine. He saves all his brooding for the privacy of his
own home and publicly must prove that life will be better now that
Brad is no longer in it. Rory is aware of this split in Ethan's emotional makeup and is wary of encouraging any major outbursts that
he'll come to regret, but she also wants to be part of his exhilarated
bubble. Be part of that rainbow light.

"Put Rory and me down next," he tells Jake, and hands Rory the list of song choices. "Here, pick a duet."

Rory skims the list, tucking her hair behind her ears, hands shaking with nerves. "I don't think I should," she finally says. "No one wants to hear me sing."

"Oh, come on, Rory," someone encourages. "This is a party! You're part of the cast! Of course we want to hear you!"

"I'm part of the ensemble, you mean," Rory points out to a bevy of sympathetic laughter. As if they could possibly forget. As if they didn't differentiate between the "real" cast and the ensemble as soon as the list was posted.

One of the benefits of being Rory, she's learned, is that people rarely tell her no. People rarely resist the chance to cheer her on, like she's a toddler taking her first steps. Is it her body? Her clothing? Her scholarship, which is a matter of public knowledge by now? She can never tell, but she has "service project" written all over her, and tonight, fostered by good food and the weathering of rehearsals thus far, the cast and crew are in the mood for some goodwill toward men.

"Pick something easy." Ethan takes the list and holds it up for Rory to peruse.

When Rory shakes her head and jabs a finger uncertainly at a song title, he grins in approval. "Perfect. You've heard it a million times in the last two months. I'm sure you know it by heart."

Rory attempts one final protest; Ethan won't have it. He gets Jake to cue up the song and pulls Rory onto the stage with him, handing her a microphone.

The cast cheers when the first measures of the song play— "A Proper Courtship," a duet between Thackery and Joetta from dear old *Good Knight! Sweet Lady.*

Anyone else who chose to sing something from their current production would have been skewered alive. Rory's "feel sorry for me" air turns out another triumph for her.

Ethan goes first, singing Thackery's part with extra oomph. He has oomph, barrels of it, and the actual audience on opening night will be receiving a restrained amount, but tonight, at the cast party, Ethan can let it all loose.

Rory's part comes. She licks her lips, swallows, swallows again. Her feet are locked onto the floor, her elbows tucked in tight to her body, as if making herself as small as possible—as if she might disappear by the end of the song, as a mercy, just melt into a pile of her clothing.

She sings.

The cast whoops. A kind group of cheerleaders, all of them. They'd be whooping if she croaked her way through this song, because tonight is about camaraderie, about togetherness. It is not an audition—

And yet as Rory sings, Pam leans out of her office.

Watching.

Rory and Ethan harmonize in the chorus, notes Rory has drilled again and again for the last few months, making sure her voice can hit them head-on, the hammer striking the base of the carnival strongman game.

On they sing. On Pam watches.

Rory dares to lift an arm, a gesticulation, making this more than mere karaoke. Her sleeve drapes down, catching the light—yes, she wore a carefully selected peasant top not unlike the peasant dress Joetta wears in this scene. Rory's hair streams down, the flower crown atop her head, and though she'll never look like the actress on the original movie poster, she could, if you squint, resemble the actress from the revival . . .

A different vision, but still, a vision.

Ethan ramps up the cheese, the camp, moving his body in ways that Thackery will never move in the actual production. Rory does not follow suit with her own body but attempts to follow him with her voice—and the final verse, the notes she's meant to belt . . . She closes her eyes and lets it burst out of her.

Like sunshine, gasping out of her throat.

The room explodes when the song ends. This is what karaoke is all about, this unfiltered, nonjudgmental appreciation of anyone willing to stand up and sing for a crowd, regardless of talent or skill or charisma.

And someone like Rory, who would get their pity claps regardless but who surpassed all expectations, has just proved the point of karaoke, the point of theater, actually—anyone can get up in front of the lights and put on a good performance, as long as they're willing to reach down inside of them and pull out something honest. Something real.

The fact that Rory has rehearsed this song with the dedication of a professional athlete doesn't make this impromptu performance any less honest.

The fact that Annie is not in this room right now, and that Lizzie is preparing for her debut as the accordion player, doesn't make this any less honest.

The fact that Rory did not just carelessly sing a karaoke song in order to relax, party, bond with her fellow castmates, but sang solely so one specific person would hear her—that doesn't make it any less real.

Ethan smooches her on the cheek, and Rory gives a modest dip for the crowd before they both pass on their microphones to the next batch of singers.

"Girls Just Want to Have Fun" blasts through the speakers. Rory smiles back at those telling her she did well, heading over to the drinks table to soothe her throat with another cup of mead. It tastes like victory.

She stands there, away from the rest of the group. She waits, counting the seconds that pass.

Much sooner than she expected, someone taps her on the shoulder.

Pam, her face giving away nothing. "Rory? Can I talk to you in my office?"

The party's official end is ten o'clock, and few linger much longer than that, since tomorrow is one of those rare Easters that falls in March rather than April, and parents want their children home and in bed so the bunny of the hour can make his pastel, chocolate-covered deliveries.

Ethan staggers into the Elizabethan at close to eleven, after the Princely Players have finished cleaning up the food and the theater room is more or less back to its standard form, ready for classes on Monday.

"You ready?" he asks Rory, who is seated on the edge of the stage, the work lights pooled around her, legs dangling.

He is drunk, not with alcohol but with the giddiness of a night spent in total distraction. He'll be safe enough behind the wheel of his car so long as he can crank up his radio and release some of this bottled energy.

Rory is the opposite of Ethan at this moment, all quiet thoughts and simmering perspective, a wistfulness to her body language, her eyes. She looks up at him, beaming, childlike.

"You okay?" Ethan plops down beside her, studying her. "You disappeared for a while. Where you been?"

Rory does not answer. Instead she reaches beside her and holds up a binder, heavy and fat, with JOETTA written down the spine in black marker.

Ethan does the math, and his enthusiastic expression doesn't disappoint. "Wait . . . You mean—Pam gave you Joetta?"

Rory nods, that same modest, almost shy posturing she gave after their karaoke duet. Yet there's an energy to her, of a star ready to explode—all that motion, that force, churning through her systems, lid tightly shut.

Don't be shy. It's yours. You earned it.

"That's so perfect!" Ethan nearly tackles her with his hug, and then Rory regales him with the conversation she had with Pam moments after her big number:

Pam logically laid out the reasons why Rory could take this part. Rory knows the lines. Rory knows the blocking. Rory can practice with Ethan, since they're good friends. The costumes were fitted to Annie's body, obviously, but Pam insists that Cynthia will be able to accommodate Rory's size. And, as Rory's impromptu karaoke performance showed, Rory can sing the songs.

Most important, Rory's paid her dues. She's put in the hours. She's been at every rehearsal, whether she was on the call sheet or not, and she helped build half the set.

"Go home, think about it," Pam said as she pressed the script into Rory's arms. "If you can't, let me know by Monday at noon so I can figure out what to do next."

Rory held up the script, feeling its heft. "I love being part of this musical," she'd said, "and I want to make sure we have an incredible run. Especially since it's my senior year—my last production at Bosworth." She sighed, as if she were about to leap off a mountain with a bungee cord around her waist. "I'll do it."

"You saved all our butts," Ethan tells Rory now, shaking his head in exasperation with the circumstances they've now dodged, thanks to Rory. "I was about to insist I play Joetta."

Both of them snicker at the image of Ethan yanking a wig on and off his head to be Joetta and Thackery, and when they settle, Ethan very seriously reaches up to Rory's head. He adjusts her flower crown, straightening it, bringing it forward to rest above her brows. "This is fucking amazing—you and me, Ror! You and me. Like it should have been from the start. Makes you wonder why she didn't just cast you in the first place."

Rory focuses on the weight of the crown, the view from the stage. "Sometimes people need a second chance."

A second chance to sing, a second chance to show what they can become in the spotlight.

A second chance to right any wrongs, a second chance to give a senior the part you promised her she could one day have.

A second chance to crown the right girl.

She feels like a knight in this moment, a queen. All-powerful, ruler of the universe.

In utter control of the chessboard.

No one can make a single move unless she says so.

CEMETERY

(FLASH-FORWARD)

ETHAN YORKE COMES BACK TO BOSWORTH OFTEN ENOUGH. His mother is still here, and Ethan wants to make sure his son has a strong connection with his grandmother. It's about an hour's drive from the city where they've put down roots.

But this weekend, Ethan's husband, Tom, keeps asking if Ethan's okay, and Ethan suspects it's not just because they're in Bosworth to bury Ethan's grandfather.

It's because today's events have them heading into town, to the funeral home on Main Street, to the wake at Anthony's, and to the cemetery. Ethan can't just hide at his mother's house. And his grandfather was a beloved man in his community—there might be familiar faces at today's services, and so today might be more of a homecoming than Ethan is ready for.

They drive past the academy and Ethan holds his breath, then releases it when he sees it's been renovated beyond recognition. New additions, a new name, even.

But his heart snags when he glimpses the northwest roof, the roof that elicits guilt and fear whenever he reflects on it. So it's still here. Not just buried in his memories.

After the funeral, which is less sad and more a poignant celebration of a man who accomplished much in his ninety years of life, Ethan and Tom and their son go to the cemetery for the grave dedication. He receives plenty of gracious hugs and condolences, and a handful of people manage to declare their recognition of his husband and their adoration of Tom's onscreen work with a well-balanced reverence. This is a funeral, after all, and not a fan con.

The cemetery feels like an escape. Ethan helps carry the casket with his cousins and shows his son how to toss a fistful of dirt into the grave. Then he leaves Tom to make small talk with his relatives (which, to be fair, Tom genuinely enjoys) and chases his son down the grassy aisles between headstones.

His son points a grubby finger at a butterfly. Ethan inhales the blossoms of the crab apple tree, grateful to be the only one in his family not cursed with allergies, because the crab apple tree is the scent of Bosworth in the springtime—

"Pretty!" The shriek of Ethan's son is possessive, denoting an oncoming tantrum. Ethan races to catch up with him and finds his baby trying to grab at a rainbow pinwheel cycling in the gentle breeze.

"No, no, that isn't ours." Ethan scoops up his son, who is now wailing, "My pretty! My pretty!"

When Ethan turns, he is face-to-face with a short, sullen woman, maybe a little older than his mother, dark-haired but with white sprouting along her part.

"Ms. King," he says at once, reverting back to a teenager's

respectful greeting before he can think twice. Only then does he realize where his son's led him.

There's the headstone, right at his feet.

Small, simple. A name, a birth date, a death date, and a red rose, engraved horizontally, always in bloom.

"You were one of Rory's friends, weren't you?" Ms. King is cold, withdrawn; Ethan wants to feel afraid, the way he would have as a child, but remembers that this is a cemetery, and all emotions are legitimized in this hallowed space. "You did plays with her, didn't you?"

"Yes," Ethan confirms. His son is momentarily distracted by the stranger, but then squeals for the pinwheel again.

But it feels like the wrong answer.

We weren't just friends; she was my best friend.

Always there, always listening to my dating gripes, always ready to let me be the star. Or so I thought—

"Do you still do plays?" Ms. King asks.

Why on earth do you want to know? is Ethan's first thought, but instead he shakes his head. "Not really, no."

As if sensing his desperation, Tom calls for Ethan.

"I should get back," Ethan explains. "We just buried my grandfather."

"I'm sorry for your loss." Ms. King's gaze is not an easy one to bear; Ethan keeps waiting for her to slap him like some bereaved mother in an old Hollywood flick, or to spit on his shoes.

"Lovely to see you," he says, and moves to leave.

"You really were talented, you know," she tells him. "You were the real deal."

Before Ethan can respond, she stares at the headstone. She doesn't have anything to lay on the grave, no flowers or trinkets, nor does she kneel in the grass or squat to address the dearly departed. She merely stands there, staring down at the name and the dates and the rose, and Ethan takes his squirming son back to his husband.

He wonders, though, if he should have told her. That the last time he ever stepped on a stage was senior year, opening night of the spring musical. That he felt like he had been cursed as soon as the curtains went up, that he might as well have buried his desire to perform, because it died that night, too, and he missed it so terribly, he couldn't sit in auditoriums anymore, and he couldn't help his husband run lines or attend his premieres, not without tearing up, not without feeling a hundred years old.

Not without remembering the loss.

Your daughter ruined so many lives that night, he thinks, *and yet I'm the one who can't forgive myself. I can't forgive myself for not helping her before it was too late.*

Dramatic irony: when the audience knows more than the characters

Situational irony: when there is a gap between what is expected to happen and what actually happens

Verbal irony: when a character says something different than what they really mean or how they feel

Greek tragedians used the device of dramatic irony in most of their works. Their audiences were composed of Athenian citizens who would be familiar with the myths and stories depicted onstage, which meant heightened suspense and tension between the characters. The use of dramatic irony allows both a creator and an audience to let go of the what of a story and instead focus on the how and the why. Dramatic irony also forged the concept of anagnorisis: the often gut-wrenching moment near the end of the play when a character recognizes their fatal flaw, sees themselves the way the audience sees them, and also realizes it's too late to fix it.

—*Rory King,* "On the Utility of Dramatic Irony"

ACT FOUR

MAKEOVER

"Rory! Welcome!"

"Thank you, Charlie." Ethan's mother, Mrs. Yorke, insists Rory call her by her first name. Rory pauses beside the pile of shoes near the front door and slips off her own Doc Marten dupes. Charlie fusses, tells Rory she's not required to remove her shoes, but Rory keeps them off anyway. She likes feeling the Yorkes' carpet under her feet. It's expensive, high-end stuff that feels like you're walking on lambs.

Besides, guests may step inside and leave their shoes on, since they're going to be quick—but members of the family settle in, and tonight, Rory would like to feel settled.

She should feel settled, all things considered. Pam is relieved, and Shandie, although clearly not fully convinced, let herself appear relieved, for at least that rather significant task on the production's to-do list was crossed off.

If Rory digs for it, she can sense a glowing ember of calm, of accomplishment, set off by the passing of the Joetta binder into her possession. But it's buried. Buried beneath the weeks of waiting, of wanting, the weeks of control, the weeks of planning and adjusting and firing. Perhaps she needs a few more days for the reality to fully sink in and wash away the worst of the residual expeditiousness— or perhaps she won't fully feel the cloying, sticky glee of triumph until she's out on that stage, lights blazing on her cheeks.

"Phil's warming up the grill. Rory, are you busy tonight? Can you stay for dinner?" Charlie addresses Rory directly rather than channeling the question through Ethan; Rory nods with a gracious shrug.

"Wonderful. How do you like your steak?"

A query Rory does not know how to answer—cooked? As opposed to . . . uncooked?

"Give her medium rare, same as me." Ethan, saving the damsel in distress. "We're going to get some work done upstairs."

"I'll call you when it's ready."

Rory follows Ethan up to his bedroom, marveling, as she has a dozen times before, at how Charlie lets her children move about the home with an autonomy not usually afforded to offspring by their parents. Ethan can choose how his steak is cooked. Ethan can have a girl come up to his room unsupervised.

She's suddenly struck by the potential irony in this last observation—was Brad allowed to come up to Ethan's room alone? Are girls considered safe in a way that boys are not? Ethan's never been shy about his preferences at school, and Rory knows he doesn't hide them at home, either, but she's guessing the Yorkes have never had a face-to-face conversation about what that means in practice, what it means for Ethan and his male guests, how it twists all the standard sex ed lessons in health class.

Fine, then. Let them think I am safe.

Ethan invited Rory over after rehearsal because he's behind in history. And calculus. Actually, he's behind in everything but drama and physics, which is just as well, because Rory's scientific prowess lies in the study of living things and not in the aerodynamics of the world around her. She could advise Ethan on growth patterns and cellular machinery and the ever-important food chain, but the theories of space and time and motion are beyond her understanding. She's not used to letting her imagination run so wild in the sciences.

"How do you do it?" Ethan marvels halfway through their tutoring session. He's seated at his desk with Rory beside him, almost spooning him, her arm curled around his to rap at his knuckles when he gets distracted from his Belle Époque essay. "Your classes are way harder than mine, and you've got the play, and your deal with Keating—how do you keep up with all of it? I feel like I'm barely staying afloat myself."

Rory smiles, her eyes still on the last words he wrote. "*Occurrence* should have two *r*'s. Right there."

This is not like the steak question—there is a right answer, and Rory knows it. She could open her mouth and it would fall right out. She keeps up with everything because unlike Ethan, and unlike the majority of the students at Bosworth, she is there by the good graces of the school, here to fulfill the academic potential she promised on her scholarship application.

Her scholarship to Bosworth is a stepping-stone, and if she doesn't keep it under her feet at all times, it'll sink to the bottom of the pond and drown her.

Ethan scrubs out the misspelled word and rewrites it properly. "How's it going with Keating? She still have you popping out those essays left and right?"

For the first time in weeks, the mention of Miss Keating does not turn Rory's stomach into a Ferris wheel of dread. "We're done with all that," she says. "We just got word that my essay on Abigail Adams earned me a whopping two hundred fifty bucks if I choose to go to an East Coast school, so I guess all that work wasn't a total bust. That'll buy me, what, two whole textbooks and a bus pass?"

She glances up, anticipating a wisecrack from Ethan, but he's not adding to her embittered monologue. He's looking right at her, his eyes serious.

"You have worked hard," he affirms, "and you deserve to go to college."

"True, and luckily for me, that's exactly how the higher education in our country operates," Rory shoots back. "Miss Keating was just having me do those essays to keep my wrists in practice—"

"Stop." Ethan puts his hand on hers. Rory knows without looking that the pencil on his paper underneath his palm will smear. "You're the most dedicated person I know. You bust your ass while the rest of us Princes fart around, waiting for the trust funds to kick in—but you, you're brilliant and ambitious and you're so stubborn." Here he grins, and Rory's heart sprouts wings. "It's going to pay off for you. It has to. Or else the whole world is broken beyond repair. It's only fair."

"Fair," Rory echoes. "Whoever said life was fair?" She can see her pulse in the periphery of her vision, the world spasming, colors blurring, a thud, thud, thud, and she forces herself to inhale, to breathe out the red, the rage, the fire . . .

"I'm just saying," Ethan doubles down, "that you can't give up now. There's a place for you somewhere where they'll reward you for your brains and your talents. I don't want you to throw that away. Not now."

Rory feels the words in her throat like a terrible glob of phlegm. She considers saying them: *Fuck off, Ethan. Mind your own business. You can afford to.*

Not that she wants him to fuck off—she wants the opposite; she wants him to keep speaking to her like this, keep telling her what she's capable of, how far she'll go, as if she's a NASA-built rocket running its final tests, ready to be launched into the sky.

His eyes are too much to bear right now, too much like spotlights, and her instinct is to hide. Hide, run, get out of this light.

But then he squeezes her hand, enough that she can feel the dry scrape of the wound on his thumb, still healing from a mishap with the power tools on set day. "You're better than all of us, Rory. I just wish you would see that."

And oh, it is the exact right and wrong thing to say to her.

Wrong, the way it is wrong to bait a starving animal.

Right, the way you sharpen a blade so it can slice through paper midair.

Rory does not whisper her gratitude for his words; she passes it to him with her gaze, her fingers in his, the kind of wordless communication every Princely Player must learn during Pam's trust exercises unit in Drama II. *Everyone sit in a circle, close your eyes, and hold hands. Count to ten, one at a time, without going down the line or making any sort of predetermined pattern. Simply feel it, feel the vibes, feel the energy of the group. Feel if it is your turn to call out a number, feel if you are meant to say number four. If more than one person says it at the same time, you must start over—you must feel it. In the air. In your own chest.*

And Rory passes it to Ethan, almost all of it—everything she has, her secrets.

Ethan suddenly changes his gaze, focusing on the lines of her face, her brows, the shapes that are inherent and the shapes that could be brought forth. "You know," he says, "I just got a fun new palette and I haven't opened it yet."

Rory lets go of his hand. "I thought I recognized that look."

"Maybe it's Maybelline." Ethan leaps up, runs to his dresser, and recites the color names to her. "We're done with this stuff, right?"

"You mean all the schoolwork you've neglected this term? Not even close."

"We're due for a break, then." Ethan takes her hand again, this time leading her to the Jack-and-Jill bathroom he shares with his sister. "I love that you always bring me a blank canvas to work with."

"I shudder to imagine what you're about to do to me." Rory, knowing well her part, sits on the closed toilet and smooths her hair back.

"Now, now, Joetta," Ethan says, dabbing a sponge into some peachy-ivory liquid, "being a knight requires sacrifice."

Rory answers his line from *Good Knight! Sweet Lady* with Joetta's canonical response: "So does being a princess."

Interior. The King residence, very late at night. The porch light is on, as is the kitchen light.

> RORY *enters through the front door, attempting to be quiet. Her makeup is exquisitely done, a sort of 1960s glam, with black winged liner, dark eyebrows, pale cheeks, and cherry-red lips. The house is still.*

> RORY *shuts and locks the door, then tiptoes into the kitchen. She gets down a cup and fills it at the sink, then turns around, drinking it, and startles at the sight of* MOM, *sitting at the table.*

RORY: Oh, god. You scared me.

MOM: Where were you?

RORY peruses the table, where two plates of now-cold food sit pathetically next to a bouquet of white roses and a birthday cake, its candles still spiking out of its frosting like some lumpy dead dinosaur.

RORY: I told you I was going to Ethan's after rehearsal.

MOM: You told me you were helping him with his homework for an hour or so. It's ten o'clock.

RORY: His mom invited me to stay for dinner. I didn't want to be rude, okay? Sorry.

MOM: You could have called to let me know. I got off work early for your birthday, I picked up Winger's—

RORY: I said I was sorry.

MOM: I did all this for you. For when you got home.

There is guilt now, hanging in the air. RORY knows it is meant for her, but she refuses to let it sink in.

RORY: Well, it's my birthday. I spent it where I wanted to.

RORY finishes her water and puts the cup on the counter, right next to the empty sink.

I'm tired. I'm going to bed.

MOM: You want some of your cake? Chicken's gone bad.

RORY: I'm not hungry.

MOM: At least open your present.

> RORY *pauses for a long time first, almost as if tempting*
> MOM *to ask again, to beg* RORY *to open the present. When*
> *she finally does unwrap it, she says nothing. Only stares.*

MOM: It's *My Fair Lady!*

RORY: I can see that.

MOM: It's the special edition—

RORY: Thanks, Mom. Really.

MOM: Remember, we—

RORY: I said thanks.

> RORY *takes the gift and heads to the stairs. She*
> *contemplated saying "I already got a copy from Ethan"*
> *or "I'm not into this anymore" but ultimately decided that*
> *silence, or stiff, stalled responses, would be more devastating.*
> *She leaves* MOM *downstairs with the cake.*

RORY: *(to audience)*

> If I'm nice to her, she'll want to get closer. And I need her
> to stay far away. I need her to be afraid of me—I need her
> to be afraid of hating me. I'll make it up to her someday.
> *(Beat.)* But she knows me too well. I can't be myself
> anymore. She'll just think I'm acting like someone else.

SMOOTHIES

THE WALL OF MANGO-BERRY-FRUIT-WHEATGRASS PARA-
dise hits Rory as soon as she comes into Main Squeeze, the
smoothie shop on Bosworth's main street. She wishes she could
bottle it up, this scent, then realizes Bath & Body Works already did,
and you could make your own home smell like papaya and berries
for the price of a candle or a body spray.

But no, it's never the same. It's not just that the smoothie shop
smells like a tropical getaway; there's something else to it. Maybe
the plastic of the blenders, or the cold scent of the ice (yes, ice has a
distinct smell, and if you ever doubt this, fill up a cup or stick your
head in an ice cooler at a gas station and take a whiff).

Whatever the ingredients of this blend, it always gives Rory a
toothache, knowing it represents all things she does not—the tossing of blond hair, artificial tans, being small enough to go shopping
at the aptly named 5-7-9. She is as out of place against the silhouettes of palm trees as an espresso bean, round and dark.

"What can I get you?" asks a perky cashier, wearing her neon-orange visor like it's the latest accessory from Jessica Simpson's line of trucker hats.

Before Rory can decline, before she can ask for what she truly wants, Annie appears behind the counter.

"I'll take this one," she tells her coworker, and then Annie stands there, the cash register between them.

"Hey," Rory says. "You left this in the auditorium." She lifts up Annie's beloved Disneyland sweatshirt.

Annie seems to decide something. "I'm about to go on break. You want to share a Caribbean passion?"

The two of them go outside to the shaded patio and perch at one of those tiny tables with the tiny chairs that threaten to topple beneath Rory, furniture more fit for dolls than actual people.

Annie places two Styrofoam cups full of liquefied fruit in front of them.

A mango smoothie in two cups.

"I tried calling," Rory says.

"I know." Annie laces an apologetic tone to her words. "I've been working a ton. They want me to take assistant manager." Both of the girls know Annie will not take this position, or if she does, she won't carry it further than the end of the school year.

Wounded leg or no, kicked out of the musical or no, suspended from Bosworth pending a criminal investigation for distribution of narcotics or no, Annie's not assistant manager material.

This is just playing house for Annie, for her teammates, for these other gals who come from money. Assistant manager is like a fun sticker to earn for your pretend sticker chart, and working at a "normal" job, a smoothie shop or a teahouse or a department store for babies is like a fun check mark to tick on your pretend-to-be-a-normal-teenager chart.

"That's great" is Rory's line, the line of the supportive bosom buddy, and so Rory says it, prompted to do so by their historical friendship, the fact that Annie is still wearing a boot on her leg, the recent events that, for any other person (i.e., a person without family money and influence to pull them out of the darkness of the legal system's gaping maw) would be so devastating that assistant manager at Main Squeeze would truly be as high as you could hope to fly.

"We'll see." Annie sips her smoothie. Her smile does not even come close to reaching her eyes.

A hint of compassion floods Rory's insides, which surprises her.

Annie will not be assistant manager.

Annie will be finishing her high school career through mail-order packets, just like Clarissa—hardly the ideal way to end senior year, but they will both still earn their prizes: Bosworth diplomas, one apiece.

Annie will head off to somewhere luxurious for the summer, like the Bahamas or some obscure beachy location that only rich people know about, and it will be heralded as one last summer of freedom.

Because of course she'll go to college. A good college, really any college she sets her sights on. She's got the résumé and she's got the legacy. A busted leg during the senior year of high school means she's got the perfect topic for a tragic essay, and this little entanglement with the law will disappear. A misunderstanding.

Yet Rory still feels inclined to wrap her arms around her friend and assure her that everything will be okay. Even though Annie already has that assurance from every corner of her life, and has since birth.

"I'm sorry." Annie's voice is low, not in shame for expressing her regret, but in demonstration of her contrite spirit. "I wanted it to work out. You and me, the last musical, senior year . . ."

"I know. Me, too." Rory lets the smoothie fill her mouth, holding the flavor steady, warming the chunks of crystallized ice until they're runny before swallowing them.

"And I'm sorry for disappearing. I just needed some time to hide, you know?" Annie lights up suddenly. "Oh, did I tell you the investigation's wrapping up?"

This is indeed news to Rory; she sits up, putting on her best "interested" face.

Annie reports the latest: there have been no charges filed against Annie so far because there's no evidence that any pills were sold or distributed. She doesn't say how Travis is faring with his charges, and Rory imagines it's because, as he is a known connoisseur of certain herbal substances, Travis's reputation is already tarnished, even if narcotics and marijuana are miles apart in theory and in practice.

"That's amazing," Rory says, and means it. She's still always amazed by how the wealthy members of the community manage to dodge all manner of unpleasant experiences.

"It is," Annie agrees. "I guess the school surveillance cameras were switched off the night before the bust, so they think someone must have planted the pills."

"That's— Wow" is all Rory can manage. Her cup is Styrofoam so it won't leak condensation from the smoothie all over her, to lock in the cold, to keep those ice particles frozen, but her hand is now damp. "How did they figure that out?"

"You'd think it would be the first thing they checked, right?" Annie chuckles, rolling her eyes at the incompetence of the adults in charge of this world. "They were turned back on in the morning, so no one thought to check the archives. But there's like twelve hours unaccounted for." She shakes her head, still jovial, even though this is a serious detail in a case that nearly sent her in front of a judge. "Anyway. They're downloading footage from the archive, and then they'll have more information. They'll at least have the supplementary footage."

Rory didn't even have to echo "supplementary footage"; Annie fills her right in.

The supplementary footage comes from another set of cameras, ones that aren't looped into the school's grid. They're essentially emergency cameras—not sophisticated, not really for any kind of surveillance or crime scene investigation, but more backup in case the main grid is tampered with, by weather or power outages or an ill-intentioned individual hoping to blind the system so they can get away with something foul.

"They go straight to the school's big system, and there's warrants involved, et cetera." Annie attempts to sound impatient or bored by the details here, but there's no mistaking her relief. These supplementary cameras will provide her the clearance she needs to scour this whole incident from her record completely—and restore her reputation, too.

There's really only one thing this footage can't buy back for Annie:

"So. Did they recast it yet?" Annie looks nervous.

Rory fiddles with her straw. Will it give Annie closure to hear that the show will indeed go on? Or will it haunt her to know that she was replaceable?

She can't remember the last time she saw Annie squirm like this. Even on the day of the investigation, when Annie was crawling out of her skin with uncomfortable emotions, she still managed to find her conviction, a solid center. Right now, across this ridiculous Barbie table, Annie is fussing with her empty cup so rigorously, she's going to pierce through the Styrofoam with a thumbnail any second.

Put her out of her misery.

"Not yet." Rory says this as softly as she can manage while still sounding nonchalant, as if they're discussing something as mundane as biology assignments. "Pam's still thinking about some possibilities."

Is it compassion that compels Rory to lie? Or fear that Annie will guess Rory's game if she knows who is playing Joetta now?

Annie knows Rory's been pining for a lead.

But does she know just how far Rory would go to get what she wants? Just how far she *has* gone?

Not what you want. What you deserve.

What you've earned.

Annie says nothing. She nods after a moment, then stares out into the parking lot; Rory allows the conversation to dwindle into dead air. A true friend can share a ponderous silence as well as lively discourse.

When Rory leaves, Annie gives her a hug, sweatshirt in hand. "Thanks for checking on me. Everything's going to be okay."

Yes, everything will be okay, because Rory has made sure everything will be okay, through meticulous planning and almost superhuman concentration.

There are new snarls to work out, as there always are:

Annie will find out that Rory's playing Joetta. It won't be long now.

The police will get ahold of the surveillance tapes, and if they're clever, they'll understand what happened that night with Annie's pills and with Travis's locker.

But Rory won't be bogged down by any of these small calamities, because everything will be okay.

It will.

Rory will guarantee it.

CATWALK

Why do they call it hell week?

Let's illuminate.

Hell week is the unholy combining of the various components of the production so far—of what the actors have been rehearsing, what the technical crew has been prepping, and what the stage manager has been notating—and all of it must bridge the gulf to meet Pam's vision, which, she will realize this week, may or may not be possible.

For the actors, it means any and all of the following:

A sharp shift in the ambience backstage. No more goofing around, no more playful ridiculing when someone boffs their lines. Now is the week when you are made to feel like an outsider if you mess up, a total disaster. You should know your lines by now.

You must learn to stand in your light. You must learn to cross to your mark. You must learn to use the microphones, which are not as instinctive as you might think. They're lavaliers, long wires connected to a mic pack that's attached to your bra or your belt in the back, and the mic itself is taped to your cheekbone. Microphones pick up resonance, not volume, the actors will hear a thousand times this week. It's not enough to simply speak your lines. The microphones will not do the work of projecting for you. Put your diaphragm to work. Your microphone will take your words and make the audience feel them, make the seats rumble. Louder, dammit, louder. Project!

The actors will work with all the props for the first time, and it is not always seamless to go from pantomiming a goblet to holding one, to go from presenting an invisible ring to angling a real one so the light reflects off the gold. There are fumbles and dropped props, and everything echoes in the Elizabethan. The props master will hunt down any actor who does not return their props to the prop table, and full castigations will be inflicted.

The actors must also read between the lines to find any sort of compliments or praise from Pam. Her notes and corrections are harsh and impersonal; as an actor, you'd almost feel better if she blasted you by name—your real name, not your character name— but this is the week you disappear into your role. You no longer exist to Pam, except as a scrub, a stain, a scuff on her production. Nothing will be good enough for her. You must come into the auditorium with armor on for hell week, knowing nothing will make her happy, least of all your own individual performance.

For the technical crew, it is chaos in the form of:

Spiking the stage with every color of glow tape, only to have the dunce-headed actors stand a foot away from their marks instead.

Sliding the rolling sets into place, only to have the actors lean against them and move them out of their spots.

Conducting mic tests, only to have the actors forget their lines, breathe into their mics, produce too much static electricity from their nervous bodies so the sound cuts out, sweat off their mic tape so the lavalier springs away from their cheeks midscene like some sort of antennae.

Actors being assholes, misplacing props. Playing with props. Touching props when they shouldn't. Touching props that aren't theirs. Why the devil are they suddenly so fascinated by wooden plates, saddlebags, baskets of fake fruit? It's a childish thing, to be interested in something only because you're told you can't have it.

Every techie is ready to strangle an actor within the first hour of hell week. They could line them up, step forward, take them out one at a time, for there's not a single performer who will remain sinless come Friday evening.

For Shandie, the stage manager, it's simultaneously the best week of her life and also the worst.

She's backstage in the wings for the first time during the production and is granted the headset she loves so much. It gives her access to the tech booth, the props master, the guys at the light board, and puts her directly in Pam's ear. On opening night, she'll also be looped into front of house, which means the whole of the Elizabethan will be under her control.

As a senior who, as a little girl, lined up her Polly Pockets in a conference room made from a shoebox so she could address them all as the CEO of a successful cosmetics company, Shandie is in her happy place.

Not that she looks it, of course. Or sounds it. She's hammered by the end of the first act, bags under her eyes, sallow skin, hair frizzed in a halo of duress. Her voice will be raw, shredded from the orders she's giving, for it seems that the cast and crew show up at hell week and forget everything they've been rehearsing. Memories totally wiped, and Shandie has to give them moon-kissed stones, lead them back to the blocking they've rehearsed, the lines they've drilled, the stage cues they've practiced.

No worries; Shandie's written it down. She has it all in her binder. All of it. That's why she's here.

And during hell week, Shandie's usefulness is made manifest. She hasn't been perched next to Pam for the last two months just to prove a sidekick, a minion, a glorified secretary.

She's the musical's living, breathing brain, its consciousness. No one makes a move without Shandie taking note of it first, and if it's not in the binder, it's not happening in the show.

Pam is an enigma during hell week, even more so than usual. She sits in the audience, about twelve rows back from the stage, and with the gleam of the lights, it is impossible to make out her face. She looms as a figure only, and her own comments are usually piped through Shandie on the headset—if she must speak, if she is so inspired as to address the players on the stage directly, you'd better brace yourself, for her words and her delivery will be unrestrained. Enough to make an adult cry.

No one can tell if this is her favorite week during the production schedule or if she dreads it as much as the cast does. Or perhaps she is neutral about it, as she seems to be about so many things in the theater department—necessary, unpleasant, perhaps, but part of the process. Part of what it takes to put on a show.

It is hell week, but Rory cannot be daunted. She has only ever known hell week as an ensemble member, or as a low-level techie helping with costume changes or set dressing.

Her demeanor is starkly cheerful, obnoxiously so, yet everyone forgives her for it, since it is her first rehearsal as Joetta. The cast has been kindly supportive of the news, even if some of them did nothing to hide their surprise ("Rory? Rory King as Joetta? Really?").

It's the perfect week to slide a new actor into a lead role, they all come to conclude. Hell week is full of pauses, redos, exasperated breaks, and polishing, polishing, polishing. No doubt Rory will come to shine.

Her Joetta so far is not completely realized, and Pam forgives her for this, too. "Just get the lines and blocking down," she assures her new superstar. "Let the words and the movements help shape your delivery."

Rory is not naive. She knows her performance so far is . . . bumpy. Her uncultivated presentation grates against the polished, velvety deliveries of the rest of the cast, and if it isn't smoothed out, the audience will leave prints in their chairs from cringing so hard.

But Rory is buoyed. There is much faith placed in her by the cast and crew and, presumably, Pam herself that she will improve. Faith that she will grow into the Joetta they need. That she will make *Good Knight! Sweet Lady* the greatest senior musical in Bosworth history (as all seniors believe their musical will be).

And she wears that good faith not like a crown, heavy and solid on her head, but lightly, like a pair of wings sprouted from her back. Lifting her, carrying her upward.

Always, always upward.

At the end of hell week, when everyone's egos have sunken into the rot and the dirt, the sun comes out at last.

They go a whole scene without an interruption, and then another.

"It's marvelous," Pam assures them at the closing of their final hellish rehearsal. "Much, much better than where we started. A few cues need tightening, but we'll work those out next week during dress rehearsal. I'm immensely proud of you. Well done."

Only a morsel of praise, considering how hard she's worked them this week, but it is a feast coming from Pam.

This is the game, as the seniors know: all week, Pam pounds them down. She does not let a single imperfection go unnoticed, and they tuck themselves into bed at night and stare up into the darkness, wondering why they possibly thought they were worthy of Pam's production, Pam's direction, Pam's stage.

And then, on the final day of hell, when things are finally clicking (though not everything is perfect, because that's not the point, not really), Pam builds them back up with a few finely placed comments and sends them into dress rehearsal week with soaring spirits and the type of confidence required to wear low-rise jeans.

No catharsis, not yet—this is just a slight release. The true catharsis will come on opening night, when the audience cheers. When the curtains fall. That's when the performers will let their battle wounds begin to heal, to close up. To scar. That's when the performers will know they have not let Pam down. Not this show. Not these seniors.

The mood is happy, just shy of giddy, as Pam releases them into the remainder of their weekend. Saturday and Sunday are for resting, and then Monday and Tuesday and Wednesday are the dress rehearsals. Costume fittings. Makeup checks. Final aesthetics approved before opening night, Thursday. Less than a week away.

Pam asks Rory to stay after to run through her songs with the instrumental track. "There're a few measures I want to workshop with you" is her uncharacteristically gentle way of telling Rory, "There're a few measures that are not up to snuff and will ruin my show if you sing them like that."

Before the two of them can head into Hardy to sing said

measures, Pam must first deal with some minor technical drama—a gobo is out of focus and needs a diagnosis.

"Ian, Troy? Will you take a look at it?" The two boys, both juniors, both the younger brothers of some older, legendary Princely Players, leap to their feet.

Up they go into the catwalks to inspect the problematic light, and no sooner have they scrambled onto the ladder than Pam, no doubt using some muscle memory developed over the past two months, turns to Rory, who is, as always, nearby and available, and asks, "Oh, they might need the wrench. Would you mind running it up to them?"

Rory has been up in the catwalk only one other time: during junior year, when Ethan volunteered to tie a "Congratulations, Sterling Scholars" banner to the battens and Rory had baby-ducklinged up the ladder behind him.

"Whatever you do, do not step on the plaster," Ethan had warned her, pointing at the gray, almost fuzzy layers beneath the walkways. "The plaster is lava. You step on it, you die. Okay?"

It hadn't seemed so high when she'd gone with Ethan, Rory notes now, hiking up the ladder behind the proscenium to the small creepy rust-red door near the ceiling. She has her new wings to help carry her, and recites the reality of her situation under her breath ("finally cast as Joetta, opening night less than a week away, this is really happening") in order to stave off the reality of her *other* situation (a heavy girl who has climbed maybe four ladders in her life, currently wavering on the very top rungs, the metal of the ladder's cage brushing against the roundness of her back).

The door is open. Rory steps off the ladder and onto the walkway, a series of planks leading through this strange, hidden space above the stage. It's a labyrinth of lights, all of them bolted and cinched on their metal rods so none of them can crash down through the opening in the ceiling and kill an unsuspecting actor. Surely that happens in less-than-cautious high schools. Surely there are statistics to look up, to see how many people have been killed or injured by stray lights or weak clamps. Surely theater ghosts are entertained by the onstage offerings for eternity.

Ian and Troy are around the corner, kneeling on the planks, leaning over to tussle with the wretched light. They cannot see Rory from here—the shadows of the crawl space and the angles of the catwalk mean she's out of sight—but the acoustics of the claustrophobic chamber mean she can hear every word of their conversation.

"Fucking awful," one of them says, almost gleefully, the way some people recap train wrecks or explosions on the highway with unfettered, vulgar delight. "She's stinking up the whole stage. What was Pam thinking?"

"Desperate," the other one responds. "And it shows."

"No one's that desperate," says the first one. Ian, Rory remembers. That one's Ian. "I think she's got something on Pam. That's why she got bumped up from ensemble."

"Like blackmail?" Troy uses some unknown tool to open a clamp. The hinges sound in the cavernous space.

"Something like that," says Ian. "It's gotta be. Did you watch her audition?"

Troy must shake his head no.

"Me and Preston were in the wings. It wasn't good. She's lucky Pam let her into the show at all. Senior pass, I guess."

Senior pass. Ah, yes. The concept that because Pam made her students wait for their senior years to get the good roles, seniors were then given some kind of leeway, a spot in the show guaranteed just by dint of their age. Not just the drama department—it was a schoolwide phenomenon, decried by underclassmen who felt that hierarchy was the epitome of unfairness.

Rory was once such an underclassman. She herself once saw such operations as incredibly, unattractively wrong—but now that she is a senior, she knows the truth.

That senior pass is only granted if you've done the work. If you've paid your dues.

Pam won't repay you with your name on a casting sheet if you haven't paid your dues.

Talent talks. So does seniority. But nothing shouts like a debt to balance.

"You know what else?" Ian is on a roll now, all hopped up with adrenaline—the end of hell week, the dangerous height of the catwalk, the seditious thrill of exchanging such theories unchallenged. "I think she got Annie kicked out, too."

Now the hairs on the back of Rory's neck stand up tall.

"Annie Neville, involved in drugs? Doesn't add up." Ian clicks his tools, fiddling with the light. "I'll bet Rory planted them. Called the cops. Got the whole thing rolling."

If Rory moves, even a toenail, the planks will creak, announcing her presence. If she exhales too loudly, the space will reverberate her breath, and she'll be found out.

She quiets every part of her body, even her racing heart.

"Dude, someone turned off all the cameras that night!" Troy is excited now, having something of value to add to the conspiracy. "I heard Jorgensen talking about it with the office ladies. They're getting the board involved. They think it's a cover-up."

"See? There's something fishy going on. Foul play or whatever."

A pause, and the click of metal on metal before Ian goes on.

"I've always thought she seemed weird. But I didn't think she was, like, frame-your-best-friend-and-steal-the-lead-in-the-musical weird."

"Who knows what else she's capable of?" Troy adds, sounding philosophical.

"Ethan better watch out. She's been hounding him for years, even though he's gayer than Broadway." A snicker. "Maybe she'll sedate him and kidnap him and make a doctor do some brain surgery that un-gays him so he'll finally fall in love with her."

"She's desperate enough" comes the agreement.

Rory cannot remember when she last took in a breath.

Inside of Rory is a gnarled, jagged black stone. She no longer feels the warmth of her good fortune or the rainbow-bright trust of her fellow castmates. Her mind gallops over rocky terrain, a whole host of possibilities hitting her at once.

Surely there are deaths every year from high school students falling through plaster.

Surely most of those deaths are high school boys, prone to shoving each other, laughing, refusing to take things like catwalk safety seriously.

Surely it wouldn't be a surprise, she thinks, and tenses her foot, preparing to step along the planks.

Wait.

Rory stops. She takes in a breath.

She climbs back down the ladder.

Patience is the province of those who can afford to wait.

This is the one thing she can afford.

You've waited this long.

FIFTH AND VINE

There's a place on the corner of Fifth Avenue and Vine Street, right past the tire shop. To the north and south, stop signs for the two-way intersection. To the east, the overpass. To the west, the weed-lined ditch of the muddy canal. If you're driving home from Ruby's on a Saturday night, you'll get bunched up in Main Street traffic, and you'll be forced to make this stop with a whole assortment of impatient cars waiting on your tail.

If you're a teenage boy driving your dad's Chrysler, and you've got another teenage boy in your passenger seat and no real curfew except to beat your parents back from their champagne-soaked company gala, you might feel inclined to show off a little, to drive recklessly, and you might not completely stop at the stop sign, and you might take this corner a little too quickly, a little too sharply, all in an attempt to look cool for your buddy and prove to the line of cars behind you that you're not the reason they're backed up. That's someone else; someone else is the problem.

You might take this turn too sharply and too quickly, as you so often do, but this time you might see, in the kind of flash usually reserved for lightning strikes, a girl.

Somewhat squat, somewhat familiar, but you can't place her, not when everything is such a blur. And instinct will take over, and you'll swerve to miss her.

Swerve, and overcorrect, and then it's lights-out.

In the wreckage of your car, down in the ditch, you'll come to, the steering wheel pressed up into your ribs. You'll feel like a giant's hand has squeezed your middle, popping your lungs—have you ever tried to breathe without lungs? It's the strangest thing, like trying to grab the sunshine. Your body knows the mechanics of it, but nothing takes, it's just big gulps and no relief.

You'll hear the people coming, rushing down to be with you, and you'll hear the paramedics, the sirens, the wind blowing around the frame of your dad's car. Next to you you'll hear the confused movements of your friend, who was also knocked senseless, and you'll wonder why the hell you two decided to drive into the creek tonight. What were you planning? How did you mistake this for something fun?

As you come to in the hospital, they'll ask you about the wreck. Do you remember what happened? And you won't, not at first, but through the haze, you'll remember: there was a girl standing there, and she looked right at you before she stepped off the curb.

Like she knew you were coming.

And you'll remember the fearlessness in her eyes as she approached your car—like she was ready for the hit. Ready to be taken out, if it meant taking you out, too—dragging you right to hell with her. You wonder if it was her hand that squeezed your ribs until your organs popped, but you can't say anything; all you can do is slip back into a permanent dream state while your brain swells and your heart thumps and your body tries to decide if it's going to keep you alive or not.

You will survive, but you'll be in the hospital for a long, long time. Your friend, too.

As for the girl, the one who stepped off the curb at just the right time, as if knowing that the perfect swerve would send the car careening down into the canal . . . She walks the other way while cars are skidding to a stop and people are running through the weeds to check on the wreck. She walks all the way down Vine Street, and then all the way down First Avenue, then turns once more.

It takes her a good ninety minutes to get home, most of her pathway through the dark sidewalks of the suburban parks, and her fingertips are so cold, she warms them by sticking them in her mouth.

But when she gets to her house, she heads straight up to her bathroom and gets in the shower, and it's unclear whether she's shivering because it feels so good to get warm after such a cold night, or whether it's because she's so happy, or whether her body is trembling simply to survive.

DRESS REHEARSAL

"You're saying the lines correctly," Pam calls. "A robot could say the lines correctly. That's not what I'm asking you to do. I'm asking you to emote! Project! *Act!*"

The criticism is for one person, and it's been repeated about a dozen times already, and it's only the fourth scene.

Rory takes in a breath, and her costume strains against her waist. It's too small. Of course it's too small. Even though Cynthia took Rory's measurements and said she'd fitted the dress to Rory's size, it's so snug it feels like she's wearing a Christmas stocking. Could Cynthia have altered it incorrectly on purpose? Rory has always felt neutral about Cynthia, but maybe Cynthia is punishing Rory—for being larger, for simply not looking the part, for not being Annie—

Stop thinking this is personal. Stop thinking this is more than what it is—an ill-fitting costume. You need to have Cynthia let it out for you so you can actually sing. Make a note of it. Don't let her leave without promising to fix it for you.

"Again," Pam commands.

Rory ignores the series of exasperated sighs sounding from the rest of the players in this scene and resets herself across the stage from Ethan.

Ethan, as Thackery, pauses to give her a sympathetic nod, and Rory nods back. She can do this. She's been gaming to do this for weeks. Months, even. Years, you could argue.

Now do the thing you've been dying to do.

"It's customary in Downere to greet our betrothed with a belching contest," Rory says, and as she extends her hand for Ethan-as-Thackery to kiss, she arches her back and pretends to be emitting the massive, echoing, prerecorded belch that's piped in from the sound system. Her delivery of the line is better, but still not great. She knows it, Pam knows it, they all know it—at this point it's like hammering nails with a banana. But she's all they've got.

Ethan's about to counter with Thackery's devastating response, but Pam cuts in.

"Did that sound authentic to you? Really? Because it sounds like you're reading aloud from a refrigerator manual." Pam rises from her seat in the front row to pace, back and forth, before the stage. It's a marvel that Pam can be four feet below them all and yet tower over them, body and soul. "'It's customary in Downere to greet our betrothed with a belching contest,'" she delivers, and makes Rory repeat it over and over again until the words become mush in Rory's mouth.

"This scene has layers. We're laughing at Joetta's antics, but we're also aware that this isn't the real prince of Tillypoo—there's heightening tension," Pam reminds Rory. "And you won't get a single chuckle out of the audience unless you go full ham. Commit. Again."

If hell week was a breeze for Rory, the dress rehearsal is a violent tornado of suffering and frustration.

Everyone's sweating and exhausted in their costumes. The lights are so hot, Rory feels like she might slip into a very Princess Catherine–like swoon, and she can feel the cast and crew's collective anger swirling above her like a storm cloud.

She says the line again, trying her best to get it, but it feels wrong even as she says it. God, the frustration of knowing how something should be done and realizing you do not have the skills for it—it's enough to drive a person mad.

"Just because you have the lines memorized does not mean you are acting." Pam's criticism buries itself in Rory and feasts on her remaining shreds of dignity like cockroaches, and this time Rory says the line forcefully, horrified to feel the heat of tears and the hot saliva that comes before crying filling her mouth.

"Take five, everyone." Pam doesn't even try to mask her annoyance; she rubs her face with both hands as she charges out of the auditorium, seeking her third Diet Coke of the afternoon.

"Hey." Ethan approaches Rory and doesn't feed her some saccharine line of encouragement, which she appreciates. "I have to stop by Hollywood Video before I drop you off tonight. Is that okay?"

Rory's been this emotional a few times before in her life, but right now she has nowhere to channel it, and so it floods her systems. No release valve but her eyes, even though she's determined not to cry in front of them. Not today. Not after all this work.

But Ethan cannot let her go uncomforted. He holds on to her shoulders and leans down so their foreheads are nearly touching. "Don't let her get in your head," he advises. "We've had months to practice. This is still new for you. You'll get it for opening night;

I know you will. Pam's just vocalizing all her panic, unloading it all on you. It's not fair, but . . ."

Life isn't fair, Rory finishes for Ethan.

The grand paradox—that Pam should put so much stock in fairness, that she should monitor her productions and her classroom and her department for any whiff of maltreatment, and yet it still seeps in through the cracks, doesn't it? Sometimes Pam brings the infractions upon them herself, and whether it's subconscious, incidental, or whether it's absolutely on purpose and to teach a lesson within a lesson, Rory isn't sure at this moment.

She hugs Ethan back, grateful for his assurances, naive though she knows them to be, and lets him walk off to refresh himself from the drinking fountain in the hall.

From here, in the center of the stage, Rory can see all the way to the back row of the audience. She can see all the way up to the tech booth, where Jake is supervising the replacement lighting operators who are taking over the jobs that Ian and Troy did. Dress rehearsal today began with an update on their condition—Ian and Troy are stable, meaning they'll live, but the damage is devastating, meaning it'll be a long road to recovery and they won't be spending their summers running around or swimming or even watching television, but healing for the next school year. Traumatic brain injuries, treated with rest, rest, and only rest.

What are you fretting for?

You're better than every last one—don't listen to them. You've been at this for years, planning this exact moment. Stop holding back and unleash. Unleash what's within.

It's you this time.

Pam comes back into the auditorium, and Rory determines by her body language—stiff, tilted forward like a bull charging through a field—that she's determined to power her way through the rest of this dress rehearsal. There're other things to do besides babysit her new Joetta: final proofing of the playbills, coordinating with the archival team, approving any last-minute set-dressing receipts . . . And so Rory braces herself for a lightning round of ruthless notes at the end of the run-through and remembers that it really is a luxury to have Pam Hanson nitpick your performance. It's the kind of attention you could pay massive amounts of money for, from acting coaches or casting managers, and yet Pam offers it to Rory for free, and Rory intends to lap it up gratefully for the rest of the night.

At Pam's beckoning, everyone takes their places. There are smiles, tight-lipped, amicable, nice but not kind, from those who dare lock eyes with Rory—a bunch of bleeding hearts who also cannot stomach sitting through another hour and a half of secondhand humiliation. Rory does not mirror their awkward smiles, but turns, chin up, shoulders down, imagining a wire is suspending her from the very center of her head.

Stop holding back. Show them what you're capable of. What you've always been capable of.

"Let's write it phonetically on her hands. Or will she just sweat it off?" The quip comes from Cole Buckingham, standing just offstage in the wings, who must carry these comments around in his pocket in case the need for them ever arises. He gets a few chuckles, but when Rory whips around to glare at those laughing, driven by instinct, everyone is still.

"From the top of the scene," Pam commands, "and then we'll go right into 'A Proper Courtship.' No stopping."

Rory's heart pounds, the geography of Cole's guffawing face still visible even when she closes her eyes. Rage, imprinting him into her brain. Cole's always been a prick, but for the past three years, Rory's been out of the spotlight and so has never been his target. She should feel thrilled, shouldn't she, that she's finally in his crosshairs—but validation by ridicule is not as potent as one might imagine.

"There he is, my future ball and chain, my one and only! Come here, you lump! Let me look at you!" she says. Better. Objectively better. Maybe even funny.

"'You lump,'" Cole echoes from the wings. He peers right at Rory as he does so, glancing at her costume, where it bulges against its ties.

Yes, her. The lump. Subtle.

So it doesn't matter that Rory's with the principals now—he'll never respect her for it.

Cole, who has been climbing up the pyramid since he set foot in Pam's classroom, even as a sophomore, because to be a boy in theater (a boy who aspires to be onstage, not a boy who only wants to skulk in the wings and run the machinery, involved but not in the spotlight) meant you would always have a part. There're ten wannabe Éponines for every one potential Jean Valjean, and almost all scripts have five Seymours for every Audrey. Cole's absolutely foul disposition and obnoxious personality are ignored in deference to his gender—and Rory, who despite being bigger in real life always appeared so small onstage, is expected to simply put up with this discrimination.

Get him. Death to Cole Buckingham.

There isn't room for both of you on this stage. Take him out.

The scene finishes. Rory doesn't miss a line, which, well, no one expected her to—that was never the issue. She manages to spice up her delivery a bit, drawing on the energy of the original movie cast's Joetta, but that just makes her feel cheap and ordinary. An impressionist, not an actress.

"Well," Pam says as the scene comes to a close. "It's not getting worse. That's something. Move on. Next scene."

Shandie calls the set change on her headset. Backstage, Rory wrings her hands, her flesh turning white. She can sense it—someone behind her, stalking her like a lion singling out a lone, injured wildebeest. Her haunches prickle. Something is coming.

"Brilliant, King," breathes Cole's soft, derisive tone. "Was that your audition for the community children's theatre? Not sure if it's up to their standard, but they could find a part for you. You could be a tree trunk; you've certainly got the figure for it."

One more obstacle. One more obstacle to toss out of your way.

"Look, you and I both know you don't belong on that stage. You kissed enough ass to weasel your way into this show, but you're tanking our musical." Cole drops his pitch, so low that Rory can feel it more than she can actually hear it. Resonance over volume. "At the end of the day, you're just a fat wannabe with no talent."

In a fair world, Cole's mic would be hot, and the whole auditorium would have heard his nasty speech, broadcast from the wings, like a dictator caught with his pants down.

But the world is not always fair.

The world sometimes requires a bit of leveling of your own. Rory knows this more than anyone.

And so she waits.

She waits until the next scene is set and the crew is making their way back to the wings. She waits until it's silent.

She waits until Cole, falling into character as Warwicke, grabs his prop pistol and adjusts his shoulders. As soon as the lights come up, it'll be his cue to head onstage.

Rory gets into position, slipping right beside Cole.

This time, her delivery is perfect.

"Oh, my god, stop! Please, stop! No!" Rory lets out the shrill upper register of her voice. She arches back against the curtain, recoiling in a posture of terror.

The noise of her cry shocks Cole; he turns toward her, startled into a somewhat villainous posture, leaning over her, his pistol out.

It rather looks as if he's poised to shoot her.

Shandie is there first, on her feet from the moment Rory cried out. The stage manager's nerves are already on high alert, and they will be until the show's run is over.

"What's going on?" she asks. Horror overcomes her face when she realizes that Cole is aiming a weapon at their leading lady, and in an act of sheer stage manager heroism, she charges in front of Rory in a gesture of protection. "Put it down, Cole!"

Cole drops his arm to his side. "It's a prop pistol! Jesus! Relax!"

"You never aim a prop gun at a person, Buckingham!" someone else shouts. "Dry-firing it could have burned her face off!"

Not this pistol. This pistol is mostly replication metal and however much paint was required to make it resemble an old flintlock. Rory knows this. The props master knows this. She's not sure if Cole knows this, but she's certainly going to keep her face cramped up as if she's unaware, as if she believes that Cole Buckingham just aimed a dangerous-if-not-actually-deadly weapon between her eyes.

"I wasn't aiming it at her!" Cole defends himself, but with the tone of a spoiled child on Christmas morning. "I was about to go on! She came up right next to me and screamed."

"Cole, what the fuck?" Ethan storms into the scene, taking Rory's other side, nestling her into him. His costume smells like mothballs, but beneath that, she finds the scent of Ethan, his Old Spice, the vanilla candles his mother burns in their living room, the gasoline stench of his junky car. "Get back! Stay away from her."

"God, what the fuck is happening?" Cole is surrounded now by cast and crew, staring like he's just admitted to armed robbery. "I wasn't aiming it at her! I was just—"

"We could hear you muttering at her all rehearsal," Ethan fires back. "You just wouldn't leave her alone. And now this? Preston, go get Pam. This guy is fucking nuts."

Cole stammers like a fish gulping for air on land. Rory keeps herself mashed into Ethan's side, shell-shocked expression on her face, as if she looked into death's barrel and lived to tell the tale.

What was it that Cole said?

At the end of the day, you're just a fat wannabe with no talent.

No talent? But what about Rory's performance with Cole? Only a gifted actress could have convinced everyone that Cole had moved from insults to taking aim.

At the end of the day, Pam talks to Cole, who denies any wrongdoing. She also hears from several eyewitnesses who report overhearing Cole insult Rory and then, when she asked him to stop, saw him pull the pistol from his sheath and hold it to her face, as if to shoot. This is not the first time he's victimized someone, they murmur, relieved to be able to finally say it.

At the end of the day, Pam asks Rory and a cluster of other cast members, mostly girls who have been previously harassed by Cole, if they feel safe continuing the show with Cole in the cast.

"Not really," Rory answers quietly, lacing her words with guilt so everyone knows how sorry she is for the mess she's making. "I had no idea he was so volatile."

"I just don't think I could feel safe knowing he's back here," others chime in.

And just as a string is wrapped around itself and pulled tight into a knot, the deed is done.

Cole is removed from the cast. His empty costume hangs on the costume rack, still fitted to his exact dimensions, and the blasted pistol stays with Pam until she can decide on his replacement. "The show must go on," she tells the cast at the beginning of the next day's dress rehearsal, and they have no choice but to believe her.

Now Chris will play the part of Warwicke, as suggested by Rory, who recalled that Chris was unnecessarily kind to her last semester while hanging out in the wings during *The Crucible.* And though he has a very different stage presence from Cole, Pam's vision can shrink to accommodate him.

Annie removed and replaced.

Cole removed and replaced.

Next it could be any one of them—and it lights a fierce fire under all their butts. Perform your hearts out. Do your best. Let your character become you and let it all out on the stage. Better out than in when it comes to those emotions. Lay them bare. There may not be a tomorrow. After all, the production comes first, even before you.

And Rory somehow, impossibly, has improved tenfold in the last twenty-four hours.

Her costume, carefully restitched by Cynthia, now hugs her body perfectly—her own body, not made into a new shape by corsets and lace-ups and girdles, her very own shape. Her own tree trunk figure. Solid and alive.

Her deliveries are better. Her performance close to flawless.

Almost as if by losing Cole, she's lost a weight that hung from her shoulders, and she can let Joetta out, released from within.

"Rory?" Shandie asks at the end of the final dress rehearsal. "How many comp tickets do you need for opening night? One for your mom? Anyone else?"

Rory shakes her head. "My mom has to work." She's already changed out of her costume, checked it in with Cynthia, and taken up the push broom, pacing the stage. Rory volunteered to clean the dust and chalk left by the bodies of a few dozen cast members, hesitant to leave the stage. Almost like she's worried that if she steps out of this dream, she'll be locked out permanently.

"What about Miss Keating?" Shandie pushes.

Rory doesn't pause. "Miss Keating's out of town. She won't be back in time for the show."

"Well, if anything changes, let me know before six tomorrow so we can set them aside." Shandie, finished with her own tasks, leaves Rory with the broom.

Rory sweeps alone, taking special care of the corners.

Yes, Miss Keating is out of town. Off to a conference in Midvale, where she's gone to collect an education award she's won. AP English has suffered through the company of their substitute teacher for two days now, and everyone is looking forward to congratulating Miss Keating on her award when she returns. It's quite a prestigious award.

An award that Miss Keating was notified of by a polite letter, which then directed her to drive far away to collect said award and give a rousing acceptance speech, a trip that would keep her far away until the curtains were tugged open—

"You missed this." The voice sends Rory into an off-kilter spiral.

Standing at the door that connects backstage to the hallway, Miss Keating picks up a wrapper from the floor and drops it into Rory's pile.

Miss Keating, who is not out of town.

Miss Keating, who is not supposed to be back for another four days.

Miss Keating, who is very much still here.

EMAILS

Interior. Inside the Elizabethan, on the stage, back near the scrim.
An assortment of ropes and weights dangle from the ceiling, and
the work lights make menacing shadows of these shapes, like
noosed marionettes.

> MISS KEATING *stands primly on the stage near the door,*
> *her hands laced in front of her. She does not belong here—*
> *this is not her corner of the world—and her posture confirms*
> *that she knows this, but she nonetheless looks at* RORY *with*
> *an authoritative air.*

RORY: Oh.

MISS KEATING:
> Hi, Rory. We need to talk.

RORY: I'm a little busy right now.

> RORY *makes a big motion with her broom, keeping her eyes*
> *cast to the floor, turning away from* MISS KEATING.

MISS KEATING:

Aren't you going to ask me how Midvale was?

RORY *pauses. She tries not to look too reproached, but her entire body has frozen itself stiff, broomstick in hands, feet midstep.*

MISS KEATING:

It was lovely, actually. Perfect weather. All the strawberries were coming in season. What a shame I couldn't stay longer. But, you see, as soon as I got there, I learned that there was no Distinguished Educator Award. There was no Excellence in Literature category. And while there certainly was a National Educators Conference, they weren't expecting me.

RORY *continues to say nothing.* MISS KEATING *reaches into her jacket pocket and unfolds a crumpled envelope. She doesn't open it or pull the letter out to peruse it again; she doesn't have to.*

MISS KEATING:

My god, Rory. I knew you were smart, but this is a little scary.

RORY *finally peers up at* MISS KEATING *but has no contrition in her face. Her shoulders are seized up in a defensive posture, as if she is readying herself to drop the broom and run away if this confrontation cuts too close to the heart.*

MISS KEATING:

I haven't talked to your mother yet. I haven't talked to the principal yet, either. But I have to. I have to speak to them, Rory, because this is . . .

Both RORY *and* MISS KEATING *seem to sense a catalog of potential words to use.*

MISS KEATING:

> . . . This is disturbing, actually, Rory. You faked an award at a conference out of town . . . and why? To get me out of meeting with your mother? Or to get me out of town when the musical opens? Or was it something else? Some kind of payback for the way I've been harping on you? To get you to do the work for your scholarships? Your own future?

RORY does not speak. Still. MISS KEATING *is doing enough speaking for the both of them.*

MISS KEATING:

> Look, Rory, I have a feeling this will go in one ear and out the other, but I care about you. Quite a bit. Believe it or not, I have never taken a student under my wing like this. Most of the students at Bosworth are—well, we're still on campus, so I'll censor myself a bit. But they're not like you. They've had things handed to them—this twelve-thousand-dollar-a-year education, for example—and they're still not able to see Bosworth as the springboard it is. You're so smart and so capable, Rory—

RORY: So capable, yes. Maybe I'll plan on being a teacher someday. That's where all the really smart and capable people end up, right, Miss Keating?

MISS KEATING: *(takes a minute to react to this cruel statement, then resets)*

You need help, Rory. You need professional help to get healthy. Because this? *(She holds up the letter.)* This is the opposite of healthy. This is unhinged.

RORY: *(chuckles)*

I'm just doing it the Bosworth way. *The world is what you make of it.*

MISS KEATING: *(nodding, as if she's just had something verified that she was hoping wasn't true)*

Your paper on *King Lear* is late.

RORY: *(stunned)*

You said I could have until—

MISS KEATING:

Yes, well, that was before I saw what you've been doing with that extra time. *(Holds up crumpled letter.)* As per our agreement in the disclosure document you signed at the beginning of the school year, delinquent assignments are docked by one letter grade for every day they are late. The paper was due over a week ago—

RORY: This is bullshit.

MISS KEATING:

Which means you have failed the class. Your overall grade for this term has dropped significantly and you won't be able to fix it.

RORY: *(dropping the broom with a clatter)*

This is bullshit! Is this because I didn't fall down on my knees and sob all over you in gratitude last semester, or because I haven't kissed your ass for all your college prep help? Because I didn't ask you to do any of that! I didn't ask you to get involved in my personal life. I didn't ask you to get me into college.

MISS KEATING:

Your GPA is now below the required threshold for extracurriculars, which means you'll be removed from the cast. I've already sent an email to Pam letting her know the situation. Your mother, too. If we need to, we can get the administration involved.

RORY: But the show opens tomorrow night! They've already replaced the lead once—

MISS KEATING:

They'll figure it out again! My god, Rory, you can't revolve your entire life around these people! There's no future in drama. There's no money in it, and universities only hand out scholarships to the cream of the crop. Do you understand? It's a dead end. But you're such a gifted writer, Rory, and an incredible thinker. You could build a future with your words—you have so much more to give. I only want to help you.

RORY: *(seething)*

No, you don't. You just want me to get on your conveyor belt so you can sleep at night, knowing you schlepped some sad scholarship student off to an Ivy League. Because if you can help the pathetic, poor fat girl, maybe you can believe that giving up on your own dreams was worth something. Well, forget it! I'm not going to be your service project anymore. You'll have to find some other way to inject meaning into your life as a sellout.

MISS KEATING *lingers, hesitant to leave* RORY *alone with the devastating news of these developments—but* RORY, *it appears, has decided to no longer acknowledge her present company. She tucks her head down, letting her hair fall across her face, picks up the broom, and continues sweeping, going over places with the broom that she's already thoroughly cleaned, and when* MISS KEATING *calls her name once more, softly, in a clear attempt to begin some reconciliation or explain her reasoning for such drastic measures,* RORY *does not look up.* MISS KEATING *finally exits, leaving* RORY *alone on the stage, the curtains slowly blowing.*

MAKING IT

FROM: Pam Hanson <phanson@bosworth.edu>
SENT: Wednesday, April 6, 2005 8:05 PM
TO: Margo Keating <mkeating@bosworth.edu>
CC: Principal Howard <showard@bosworth.edu>,
     Gwendolyn King <king.gwendolyn@bihealth.org>
SUBJECT: Re: Rory King

Thank you for your message, Margo. You've certainly
provided a thorough recap of some very serious goings-on.
I admit I had no idea of Rory's academic behaviors, as she's
always been a model student in my department. Given the
circumstances of her recent struggles, I can understand
your concerns regarding the musical, and I can also see that
perhaps her involvement has stretched her thinner than
is ideal. The Princely Players are often asked to sacrifice
a great deal of their time and energy to our productions,
and those who do so are much appreciated—indeed,
our productions are possible due to the hard work and

dedication of students such as Rory. Without her and others of her caliber, the drama department at Bosworth would be pitifully lacking.

I am not, however, in agreement with your proposed resolutions for Rory's predicament. I understand that I am coming in from a biased perspective, but to rip Rory out of the musical the night before we open would be traumatic on multiple levels. She has devoted her life to this production for the last two months, and more so over the last two weeks, as she graciously took over a role that was unavoidably abandoned, thus saving the day. To remove her from the musical at this point would be, in my belief, a tremendously disrespectful and damaging gesture. I believe it would communicate to Rory (and many other students who might find themselves in similar situations in the future) that her work is irrelevant, her sacrifices null, and that if she is to remain on good terms with Bosworth and other academic institutions in the future, she must commit herself only to a narrow, prescribed list of subjects, and any deviation from this list, based on passion, opportunity, or willing, impulsive curiosity, might prove detrimental to her good standing.

Furthermore, taking away this role from her because her grade in one particular class has fallen below par might telegraph, intentionally or no, that any teacher or authority figure who feels personally slighted by a student's performance could, with little notice or consequence, rearrange said student's life in a sort of petty vengeance for preferring one department over another.

I don't think that's the message we want to send to our students here at Bosworth, do we, Margo?

My proposal is this:

My fingers fly, pressing with such force, the tips may bruise.

I am breathing hard, fevered, flushed, spilling this response into the computer.

I have limited time. Miss Keating—Margo—already sent an email to Pam, my mother, and the principal before she came to see me.

She already knew I would be unrepentant. She already knew she would walk away from that impromptu meeting disappointed by my refusal to relinquish my grip on *Good Knight! Sweet Lady*. She already knew she would be ruining things—this course, this path that I'd set up so carefully and nearly finished running through.

And I have to respond, clean up this mess, before anyone else can see it.

Heart hammering like an old drum, I glance up at the open door of Pam's office. The classroom is dark, and I am using only the gleam of Pam's computer to light my deed.

Let Rory finish the run of the musical. She's worked so hard, it would be heartbreaking to punish her now—not to mention, the show would undoubtedly need to be postponed until a suitable replacement could be found and trained, and our presale tickets are already nearly sold out. Leaving Rory in her role will allow the rest of the cast and crew to experience the fruits of their hard labor as well.

As for her grades, I'd suggest—

In my peripheral vision, the darkness in the classroom rearranges itself slightly. The shadow of a figure moves into the doorway of the office.

My pulse skips a beat as I see who has joined me:

Pam Hanson, Diet Coke in hand.

She studies me with a calm intrigue. My blood runs cold, my hands instinctively curling away from the keyboard as if I could lift them in the air and feign innocence—not at this point. Not when her office lock is picked, her computer blazing, her email open right in front of me.

"Rory," she says, and I am reminded just how much an actor must train their voice. She's only said one word, and yet I can hear all manner of things in it—I can hear her role as a teacher, that state-required instinct to give me, a student in her care, the benefit of the doubt. I can hear a slither of danger in the word, too, and I know that if I were not eighteen years old and she were not more than two times that, she might not be approaching me and this break-in with such gentleness.

"What are you doing?" she asks.

My pulse is thrumming; I am certain she can see my throat bulging and throbbing with my nerves.

"Uh," I say, scraping the barrel for the right words—or any words. I did not prepare for this. Pam is supposed to be gone for the day. Pam already locked up. Pam was never supposed to see any of this conversation with Miss Keating. Pam was never supposed to look at me that same way Miss Keating did, that pity mixed with disappointment. The realization that I've failed her in an entirely different way from what she thought possible.

I don't say anything else, and Pam moves behind me, behind her own office chair, and reads through what I've written on the screen.

She scrolls up, glancing at the original email from Miss Keating, then rereads my response.

I watch her face, preparing for the armies to be called in. Preparing for my mother to be summoned from the hospital, preparing for the board to vote to expel me from their prestigious school. Preparing for everyone to say out loud what they've surely thought many times: that they regret giving me my scholarship, that I was never really suited for this kind of environment, that I'd better go ahead and start applying for the community colleges in the area, where I could absolutely be the smartest fish in a very, very small pond.

Instead, Pam looks down at me. The blue light on her face makes her look even older, sharpening her eyebrows into peaks. I can see the places where white hairs wire and poke their way out of her temples, and wonder, for the first time, why Pam is here.

Why did this woman, with so many accolades, with such a résumé, with lifelong ambitions to be onstage, decide instead to lock herself in a classroom every day and teach remedial drama to children? I see us how she must see us, nosy little beasts that she has to keep track of, keep alive, try to teach a thing or two before sending us out into the world. Why would such a decorated thespian want to teach at all? Why isn't she off doing more glorious things, collecting awards, in front of audiences?

Why is this the world that she has made for herself?

"Well?" she says. "Finish it."

The world's gone hazy. I wonder if my ears need to pop, like I've gone through a tunnel. I don't dare to move except to say, rather senselessly, "What?"

"Finish it. Let's see how you fix things."

I turn back to the computer. Dazed.

The world is what you make of it.

Let Rory participate in the musical for its full run, with the understanding that she will meet with each of her teachers as soon as the show closes and make plans to improve her grades for the remainder of the school year. If we want to extend some probationary academic status for her during this time, so be it.

Furthermore, I believe Rory should be granted a release period during the school day to get caught up on her current workload. Her excellent academic record so far proves her deserving of this leeway—perhaps she could utilize her AP English hour for independent study in the library, so as to provide a cooling-off period for the two of you, Margo. Some time away from each other might be just what the doctor ordered.

Either way, Rory King is a highly committed, determined, hardworking Bosworth Prince, and I believe it is prudent that we all support her efforts—both scholarly and subsidiary—after her years of achievement.

Best,
Pam

I hesitate over the button to reply, glancing back up at Pam once more.

I ask.

She answers: "Do what you have to do."

And then I, as Pam, reply, sending the email out into the cyberworld. I wonder if it counts as a forgery if the teacher I'm impersonating is standing right behind me. I wonder if it'll be enough, and then know that it will—Miss Keating is new and nervous with extra energy, and Pam is a well-established teacher at this institution. Pam's suggestions will be taken. Miss Keating may even be admonished for putting her nose in my business and for potentially derailing the musical.

It's enough to save me. I've done enough.

I close down the computer as if it's my own, stand, and move aside so Pam can take back her chair.

I must give her a look of tremendous guilt, because she chuckles.

"You're young, but you've just learned an important lesson," she tells me. "This is how these things work. You can call it politics, call it opportunism, whatever you want—but there isn't an establishment on earth that doesn't operate this way."

Campaigning. Delicatesse. Bluffing, axioms, jockeying. I think of my essay on Machiavellianism, sent away long ago to whatever scholarship contest Miss Keating had found. Yes, I do understand how such things work. I have for a long time.

"This is what you have to do if you want to make it big-time," Pam says. "If I can speak honestly, Rory, I'm pleasantly surprised. I didn't think I'd see such promise. But look at you."

I surprised Pam. Having no one else to gloat to, I twist this admittance over and over in my head. "So—you think I've got what it takes? To make it?"

No future in theater, Miss Keating told me. *Ten girls for every boy. No lead roles until you've paid your dues.* The drama world is a thorny path, and here Pam will tell me that I was right to break off one of those thorns and use it as a sword—

But I still want to hear her say it. I need to hear Pam say it.

"You could do well for yourself," Pam says. "You're very talented. I'll be interested to see how far you can go."

As I walk home, kept company only by a shivering wind, I wait for Pam's words to resonate within me, to warm me with their validation. I wait for the crown of praise to circle my head—and yet I feel hollow. Unsteady.

You're very talented. The rare compliment from Pam Hanson—but I ache, knowing she commended me not on my abilities as an actress, a singer, a performer, but on my gifts for trickery. For deception.

For politics.

I've played the game well. Too well.

I can make the wind blow whatever way I want it to—is this what I wanted? Truly?

Is this the recognition I craved? Then why doesn't it feel like applause?

TODAY'S THE DAY

Today's the day!

"Hear ye, hear ye, the opening night of *Good Knight! Sweet Lady* is tonight!" comes the announcement over the intercom. Ethan and Preston read in exaggeratedly deep voices that suggest they've got scrolls in hand, while Lizzie plays a little interlude on her accordion. "Get your tickets at the box office, by day and by knight! We'll be selling them at lunch!"

"Rory, you're involved in the production, aren't you?" asks my biology teacher, Mrs. Murdock, after the announcement.

Students arch around in their seats to look at me.

"Yes," I admit.

"And what part do you play?" Mrs. Murdock is likely not familiar with the character list in *Good Knight!*: she is simply doing the polite thing that adults are socially required to do with children and teenagers, inquiring after their interests and hobbies.

Before I answer her, I remember to take a moment and breathe. Drink this in. This is the first time in all my acting life when I can give an answer other than "ensemble."

"I'm, um, one of the leads." I say it with the perfect blend of modesty and honesty. No use in denying it—the show would falter and crumble and cease to go on without me. I am *Good Knight! Sweet Lady.*

Mrs. Murdock says something complimentary, something pat and expected, recites the dates and times of the show run again for good measure, then turns back to the whiteboard, continuing her lecture on cell division. I feel the flurry of interest around my desk as people inspect me—*Her, the lead? Really? Rory King?*

Yes, I think as I grip my pen and concentrate on copying down every one of Mrs. Murdock's notes. *Believe it. The very same. Yes. Her.*

Today's the day!

I run down to the office to pick up a stack of worksheets for another teacher; the secretaries, who know me by my scholarly reputation only, perk up when I walk into the office.

"Break a leg tonight!" one of them coos.

"I'm bringing my nephew on Monday," another one tells me. "My sister said he'd hate to watch a musical, but I told him there was sword fighting, and he practically begged me to buy tickets."

I smile, imagining a sea of enchanted children, their faces beaming up at me as I glide through the choreographed fights with the ease and grace of a ballerina. "He'll love it," I assure her. Who couldn't love it? It's the greatest show Bosworth's ever put on. It's the highlight of Pam's career. It's only taken me three years to climb to the top of this pyramid, and now that I'm here, I expect everyone, including Pam, to realize that they've been sleeping on a winner all this time.

Today's the day!

At lunchtime, I hang around the box office with Shandie and a few other Princely Players. Ethan and Chris demonstrate some of their jousting in the foyer, drawing a crowd. I laugh freely, openly, as loud as I want. It feels good to be in the audience of such a delightful show. It feels good to know that in a few hours, I'll be the one getting claps and shouts and cheers. I'll be the one in the spotlight.

Today's the day!

Instead of heading to Miss Keating's classroom, I go to the library for my release time. I'd be lying if I said there wasn't a small, slight dread in the back of my brain at the thought of speaking to her today, after everything that happened last night. But Pam's email—my email—has provided enough of a shield that I am no longer afraid.

Today's the day!

And then school is finished, and while the hordes of my fellow students head out to the parking lot to drive off to their jobs or their country clubs or one another's fancy houses to sneak alcohol from their parents' bar carts or whatever is on their rich-kid agendas today, I stay behind.

Call isn't until five. It's only three o'clock. But it feels silly to walk home to sit for a few minutes, turn around, and walk back. Besides, the sky is darkening with the threat of rain, and I think if I try to leave the vicinity of the school, I might just explode with my ecstatic energy. Best to save it all here, to keep myself contained.

I head down to Euripides and into the bathroom closest to the Elizabethan. There, I stand in front of the sink, my thoughts so boisterous, they echo on the tile.

Did I not tell you I would be triumphant? Did I not tell you we were in for a rollicking ride, you and I? I do hope I've delivered, and that you can see—

The bathroom door swings open.

Annie Neville walks in, her limp pronounced.

"Hey," I say with genuine shock. "I didn't know you were at school today."

"I wasn't," she says. "I came by to get a packet signed by my counselor." She doesn't go into a stall; she doesn't use the sink to wash her hands. She stands beside me, looking at me; I look at the water streaming in my sink, the foaming of the bubbles.

"Are you okay?" I finally ask, as her silence is bouncing off every mirrored surface. I feel uneasy, an animal paused and waiting for the wind to shift so it can sniff out any forthcoming danger.

Annie blinks and nods, and the thin-lipped smile she gives me is more artificial than spray cheese. "Good luck tonight," she tells me.

Oh, dear Annie. My heart pangs as I switch off the water. "Thank you," I tell her. "God, I wish—"

"Too bad about Ian and Troy," she barrels onward. Her voice is sharp. "I heard they rolled into a ditch last weekend and nearly died."

Something prickles in me. "Yes, a real tragedy," I say. My wet hands drip at my side. Annie's blocking the paper towel dispenser.

"Another car wreck." Annie shakes her head, her eyes never leaving my face. "So soon after mine. Scary."

"Scary," I agree. "Could you move?"

Annie does not move. "I talked to Troy's mom, actually. The circumstances of the accident? Really familiar."

Ears pricked, senses alert. "There're only so many ways you

can wreck a car and survive," I tell her, matching her menace tone for tone.

"Is that so." Annie studies me. I cannot break her gaze now, I know, or else she will win—holding her gaze is like clinging to a hot pan handle. Your brain screams at you to release, to let go, so you must rely on some other awareness, something deeper within you. Your stubbornness. Your conviction.

And then the dam has broken. "I know what you did," she bursts. "You did it to me and then you did it to them."

"I did what?" I say.

"You crashed my car and then you crashed theirs."

"What are you talking about? I wasn't driving their car—"

"No. But you did it anyway. Somehow you did it." Annie, as she's spoken, has raised herself to her full height, this Amazon goddess, and spread herself wide, blocking my exit. She's cornered me, and I, a cornered animal, am ready to lash back out.

"A cat ran in front of your car," I remind her. "I swerved to miss it."

"A cat that only you saw." She's on fire now, ready to combust. I must tiptoe carefully—or else throw myself into the flames and surrender. "Ian and Troy said they swerved to miss a person— a girl, they said. Someone from school, but they couldn't place her."

"They're concussed," I remind her. "Do you think they're the most reliable witnesses?"

But it's too late. She can see it all, all my calculations. She sees them add up now, and she can see the whole pathway, as far back as the very first stone I laid:

A mother who works in the ER, who told me countless stories of car accidents. Stories about people who survived them, stories about how cars rolled and flipped and wrapped themselves around poles, and yet if the angle was just so—or if the person inside the car only leaned just so—

I should feel terrified, I suppose, but instead I take all this in, and it feeds me, feeds every cell. I will not rise to her height, not ever, but I have found my own sense of power. Tall and strong wins the battles, but short and shrewd wins the war.

For a long moment I say nothing, and she says nothing, and it doesn't matter that she's accused me, and it doesn't matter that I've denied it. Some things don't add up, and they never will. This one does.

"Why?" Annie breaks, and the pain in her voice, the way her expression crumples . . . It claws into me, it shreds me, far more painful than I'd braced myself for.

Stay the course. Remember your lines.

You worked on them for long enough—say them out loud. Deliver. Project.

"Annie . . . I knew you wanted one more shot at this. The play. The theatre world." I soften myself, tug my eyebrows down so I look like my younger self. The self that Annie knew and loved and that always said exactly what she needed to hear. "I knew you'd hold yourself back, deny yourself this, convince yourself it wasn't your path. You've got your whole life to play basketball—I knew you'd regret this. You're good, Annie. You're so fucking good—and you're too much of a team player. I knew I had to get you onto that stage. You're brilliant when you let yourself be front and center."

An absolutely killer monologue. An audience would be on their feet in seconds.

Annie smiles as if she's just had glasses put on her face and is seeing the bright, clear world for the first time. "And you're brilliant at making everyone believe you're not selfish. My god. You're so full of shit—and you're trying to spoon-feed me more of that bullshit right now? I see what you did! You orchestrated all of it! You put my pills in Travis's locker. You sent Clarissa away, too, didn't you? God, Rory, this is psychotic!"

Is it any different from what you do on the court, Annie? It's strategy. No different from what we all do. You think Pam only casts based on talent? Of course not. I've worked my ass off for Pam for years. I improved. My auditions got better and better, and yet the rest of you are the ones who get patted on the head, because you all glitter in the sunlight. What's a little hobgoblin like me supposed to do? I'm relegated to the nurses and the fairy godmothers and the hags of the theater world, all because I can't flash a big smile and make everyone fall in love with me. So maybe it's my turn. Maybe you're just upset that your talent and your beauty weren't enough this time. Maybe you're just upset that you've finally been bested, and it was by someone so wretchedly ugly. A real dog.

But I do not say any of this aloud.

When I do finally speak, it's a single word. "Here." I pull a folded paper from my pocket; it's dingy around the corners, dyed blue from my cheap jeans, from sitting in my pants for weeks now.

Annie takes the paper. Opens it. Reads it.

I didn't want to do this, you understand. The last thing I wanted was to have to resort to this—but Annie's pushed me to it. Here, in this tiled corner, with the raspberry scent of the air freshener and the echoes of our argument ringing through my head and the reflective surfaces everywhere, she's pushed me to it.

"Blackmail," Annie says numbly. "You're blackmailing me."

"I don't really like that word," I tell her. "This is just an exchange of information."

"You're—you're—" Annie's voice is shaking now, and for a

second she looks so much like her old self in her photos on the walls of her house that I'm shocked. Tiny, scrunched face, crying because her knee is skinned, because her brother stole her toy, because Mommy didn't give her a treat like she wanted. "You absolute monster."

I am holding her biggest, darkest secret. Something she certainly would have thought was safe with her best friend—but there are no best friends here. How could she ever think we could be best friends? There was never any sense of equality between she and I—with her looking the way she does, with her money, her charm, her perfect family, and her bright future? And me, who has to throw myself into the future like a pebble on a trebuchet and hope to land somewhere decent? There was never equal footing between us. Never once. So it was always going to come to this. It was always going to be either her or me. I can't understand why she didn't see that. Maybe she's not as brilliant as I thought she was.

"You have a contingency plan for everyone, don't you? Even Ethan?"

I feel the steel of defensiveness curl through my limbs. "Ethan doesn't need one." *Stay away from Ethan*, I lace into my meaning. *Ethan is perfect. Ethan is right where I want him.*

"Ethan might surprise you," Annie says.

I laugh. She doesn't know; she doesn't understand—I've already written him off as an impossibility. Ethan has never been the prize. With Ethan, I already have nothing to lose.

"You shouldn't have secrets like this, Annie, darling. You never know who's going to go looking for them."

We exchange steady looks, as if daring each other to be the first to move, to throw a punch, to say it—whatever else we were holding back, to say it.

Go on, I dare her. Say it. All those things you've probably been thinking for years—that this was a pity friendship, that this is the only way I could ever possibly get a role like this, that this is the only way I could ever get close to Ethan. To trick everyone, to rig everything in my favor.

Say it. Say I'm ugly and fat and poor and hopeless. Say all of it—I guarantee I've already learned it all to be true. I guarantee you cannot hurt me more than I already hurt.

Annie leaves first, and though there's no spoken agreement, no pact we write and sign in blood, I see in her eyes that we've got a fair bargain. I won't spill the beans about her secret dealings, and Annie will leave me be. She'll forget about me, stay out of my way.

The show must go on.

I track her down the hall; she limps around the corner, defeated.

I spin on my heels, feeling taller than I ever have in my own skin, and head into the Elizabethan.

Tonight's the night!

HAUNTED

I T ' S Q U I E T I N H E R E , E X C E P T F O R T H E F L O W O F A I R through the vents, which makes it feel like the whole auditorium is breathing. A great cavernous animal, something alive, like an organ, the inside of a heart.

Everything is set for tonight—there are seats roped off at the front of the auditorium for the parents of the cast, and every aisle is neatly cleaned, the floor mopped, the curtains freshly steamed. The glass ceiling above shines like a glorious moon under which we'll perform and weave our delicate magic.

It's a chilly night, with a soft rain plinking overhead. It'll bring people into the theater. People want to go somewhere cozy and warm—the cold spring weather brings out our inner cavemen, making us want to huddle around a fire and hear stories. Well, onstage, behold, our fire. Our story glows like a flame, and tonight, it will be one for the ages, one to be remembered.

Taking my time, my stomach finally settled, I walk down the steps of the stage and into the audience. I weave through the aisles, all the way to the back, then forward again.

Tonight, every one of these seats will be filled. I walk past them all, as if to issue a slight blessing, my own little spell: *Let them be entertained. Let them leave here tonight forever changed. Let them be enchanted by me. Let it all be worth it.*

Annie's words still pulse through me, and my insides pang with a moment of sorrow. Such a shame, I think, to have lost someone I was so close to—but investments are not guarantees. Sometimes investments come up dry. Cut your losses. Ignore the sunken costs. To do otherwise will only make you mad with despair.

To move forward in life, everything must be ready to be snipped away at a moment's notice. Ready to be tanked, or traded in for something more valuable, something that will push you to where you're trying to go.

I take a seat in the very middle of the auditorium—the fifteenth row back, the twelfth seat in. Here is where Pam sat for last night's dress rehearsal. Here is where I can see the entirety of the stage, all its glory. The curtains are open, like shutters thrown back to let the daylight in. The set for the opening scene is in position—cheery flowers adorning the balcony of the castle courtyard, a lamppost shining as if it's housing a burning star, that faded-blue background I painted with Ethan adding a touch of expanse to our production.

Pam's vision, realized: *Good Knight! Sweet Lady* as a modern classic, an exploration of female ambition, a romanticized take on what it means to chase after your dreams and catch them at all costs—

A figure limps onto the stage.

I shield my eyes with my hand, straining to identify it. It's not Annie, that much I can tell. But then who—?

"Is there much drinking in Grover's Corners?"

The figure turns, the light hitting her ruffly lace blouse. It is a girl, dressed in Edwardian women's wear and not the medieval garb of the *Good Knight! Sweet Lady* cast. But that isn't what's caused my heart to jolt.

It's the light, rushing right through her transparent limbs. She is only visible when she turns just so. An apparition.

"Is there much drinking in Grover's Corners?" she says again. This time the words penetrate.

I swallow hard, my throat suddenly dry.

The very first Bosworth production I was ever a part of: *Our Town*, fall semester of my sophomore year.

I auditioned with the "Sunbonnet Sue" monologue from *Quilters*, my recent acceptance into Bosworth's elite and expensive halls buoying me into a callow optimism. Even with Pam's formal declaration of her no-sophomore rule, I somehow believed I might breach her boundaries, might be the one to make her untie that rule—

But I was cast in the ensemble.

Not everyone in the ensemble gets a speaking part. My one line made me feel like a god.

Onstage, the girl shuffles around in a daze. Another figure joins her; I recognize myself in both their pale, spectral forms—

Fiddler on the Roof, my junior spring semester. Auditioned for Hodel with another gust of hope, landed in the ensemble again.

This time, my one line ("Tradition!") was said with the rest of the group, and by closing night I knew better than to think that my own individual voice could be distinguished, no matter how loudly, brightly, or passionately I spoke it.

Another figure.

"What do I care who you should rob?" this newcomer shouts.

She's singing her one solo line from *Les Misérables* on a miserable repeat; my scalp aches to recall the hours of intricate braiding I endured, all so my plaited head could appear before the audience for a whole four minutes of stage time.

My breath comes faster. Here comes the North Pole elf I played for the Christmas revue my junior year. "And I'm Jinglepuff!"

Here comes a beautician from the Merry Old Land of Oz. "We can make a dimpled smile out of a frown!"

"He's giving a ball!"

Random townswoman from *The Importance of Being Earnest* whom I named Ermintrude, because in the script she was simply listed as "rag woman" and Pam insisted we give our minor characters backstories, preferences, favorite foods, hidden traumas, all to enrich the verisimilitude of the production.

Even back then, I think I knew it was bullshit. That my lines were just springboards to push the spotlight back onto the leads.

"Jolly old town!"

The curtains blow from their folds behind the proscenium, arcing around the stage.

"Every theatre is haunted." Pam's ghost story from my first Halloween as a Princely Player chants through my head. *Haunted by every character who has ever been played on that stage—*

Every character I've ever played—

You gave them your all. You let them wear you like a skin suit and play their little parts in the shows. You owe them nothing.

"Break a leg tonight," says Ermintrude, who is nothing.

"Let's hope they clap louder for you than they did for me." The Rory from *The Crucible* stares out at me, our round face like a turnip plopped onto a Puritan's collar. She flickers in and out of sight.

"You really did it," says the North Pole elf, looking the jester in her toe-curled shoes. "You worked your way up. You paid your dues, and you finally got to see your name on the cast list."

They still don't get it. And, being ghosts or spirits or echoes or whatever they are, they never will.

You didn't wait until Pam finally noticed you.

You made it happen yourself.

Fair is fair, fair is fair.

All stages are haunted.

I am haunted by the versions of myself who believed it was that simple—

But these suckers don't realize there's only one rule.

One rule for the theater, one rule for life:

Watch out for yourself.

Only you.

There is no one else.

If you do not make them pay attention, you will be forgotten. If you do not take what you are owed, you will have nothing.

And if you do not take the crown for yourself, you will never know power—

The lights shut off. Dark stage, dark auditorium.

I blink until my eyes cease their flowering and adjust, and I understand I am alone.

I am alone.

THE INCIDENT

ACT I

Last September.

Two days of auditions for *The Crucible*.

Pam wanted to explore what was possible with a stripped-down set—she wanted her *Crucible* to prove that minimalism didn't mean low effort. "There are no ghosts in *The Crucible*, but every character is haunted" was the sermon she preached at the parent meeting. There would be twisting black tree branches, Escher staircases inside the Parris home, faint lavender backdrops clouded over by hazy fog.

Rory could see it. She could see exactly what Pam was envisioning—*The Crucible* had always felt like the perfect fall play to Rory. There were no ghosts, like Pam said, and no real witches, either, and yet from the very script rose a palpable spookiness, a seasonal gravity, the promise of crisp, smoky air and hooded figures slipping into the woods.

"You're a shoo-in for Mary Warren," Ethan told her as they waited in the hallway for their turns to audition.

Rory rubbed a scuff off the toe of her high-top, refusing to let him see her coy smile.

"You think?"

If she had her pick, she'd choose Goody Proctor—wise, willowy, patient Elizabeth, who was the play's bleeding heart—but Mary Warren was a tricky role to inhabit. Only the rarest of actors could get the audience to sympathize with weak-willed, moon-faced, hysterical Mary Warren, and Rory was flattered that Ethan considered her up to the challenge.

"We're seniors now," Ethan reminded her, dropping his voice as a student exited the Elizabethan, their face unreadable. "We've been waiting for this for years. Now it's our turn."

Rory's turn.

Inside the auditorium, Rory handed her sweaty audition form to Shandie and Pam, then ascended the steps to the stage.

"Whenever you're ready," Pam said.

Rory took in a deep breath, her eyes fluttering.

Her insides were snarled with nerves and fears and expectations, but she knew Ethan had already sneaked into the tech booth. She knew he was up there, watching.

It's our turn.

"Today I'll be performing a monologue from Louisa May Alcott's *Little Women*," Rory said.

She'd selected this monologue after hours of thoughtful, detailed research. *Little Women*—another classic, like *The Crucible*. A period piece, like *The Crucible*. And though Jo March was much less conniving or cruel than Abigail Williams, Winona Ryder had played them both in the '90s—so Rory hoped there would be a subconscious connection.

"Oh, Teddy, I'm so sorry, so desperately sorry, I could kill myself if it would do any good! I wish you wouldn't take it so hard. I can't help it; you know it's impossible for people to make themselves love other people if they don't."

Out in the audience, Pam and Shandie were little more than silhouettes, only the softest gleam lighting up their faces.

Rory homed in on Pam, their eyes connecting. "Well, they do sometimes, but I don't believe it's the right sort of love, and I'd rather not try it."

Louder, she told herself. Push it. All the way to the rafters.

"I'll never marry you; and the sooner you believe it the better for both of us—so now!"

Her audition piece concluded, Rory let out a long, shaky breath and bowed her head until her hair fell.

"Thank you very much, Rory; that was wonderful." Pam glanced down at Rory's audition form. "It says here you're okay with any part?"

Rory's chest quickened. "Yes," she confirmed. "Anywhere you want me."

Mary Warren, yes. Abigail Williams—quite the stretch, but she would make it work. Elizabeth Proctor? She'd die.

Outside the Elizabethan, Ethan gathered her in a shrieking hug and showered her with compliments. "That was the best I've ever seen you! How do you think it went?"

And with complete confidence and unbridled honesty, Rory answered, "Perfect. It couldn't have gone better."

Seniors, finally.

Ready to collect.

ACT II

No callbacks. Not for anyone.

"That just means Pam knew exactly who to cast," Ethan reminded Rory, who wore this reassurance as a coat.

When the cast list was posted, Rory's heart thumped so hard in her body, it made her stomach turn.

None of the names next to the characters were hers.

She found her name at the bottom of the list.

Courtroom attendees: Chelsey Eda, Amelia Bronson, Rory King. Ensemble.

ACT III

Opening night of *The Crucible*. The show sold out.

Backstage, Pam led the cast in warm-ups and set them loose to take their places.

Rory made sure her bonnet was secure, even though she didn't go onstage until the second act. She stood next to Ethan, who was waiting for his cue in the wings. When he went on—the most charming Reverend Hale there ever was—Rory went back into the drama room and stayed there through act 1, act 2, and intermission, until act 3, scene 3, approximately one hour and forty-two minutes into the production.

By the two-hour mark, Rory's part was done, and she was back in the drama room until curtain call.

ACT IV

"How is *The Crucible*?" Miss Keating asked. "Miller's finest hour?"

"It's fine." Rory shrugged, digging her nails into her palm. "I'm only in the ensemble, so I'm backstage for most of it."

"No, I mean how is it? The production itself?" Miss Keating narrowed her eyes, inviting Rory to conspire. "*The Crucible* can be such low-hanging fruit. It takes a really special cast and director to make it stand out."

Rory wished she could claw through her palms until there was blood under her nails. "It's good," she admitted. "Stripped down. Pam's focused on the judicial system, you know? Drew's so great as Danforth."

"I think I'll come tonight. I want to see how our Miss Hanson handles Miller." Miss Keating did not bother hiding her slightly critical air; Rory wondered if there was bad blood in the faculty lounge. English versus the performing arts. "Plus I want to support you! I'd love to see you onstage."

"I'm—I'm not in it very much," Rory warned Miss Keating.

Miss Keating waved a hand. "Nonsense. What's that saying? There are no small parts, only small actors?"

Rory smiled to hide her disdain. There wasn't a theater student alive who didn't want to wring the neck of anyone who repeated this platitude—it was only ever said to the saddest, most neglected actors. No one ever said it when the leads were being assholes.

"I'll see you tonight, then," Miss Keating told Rory. "I mean, I'll see *you*. You probably won't see me."

You probably won't see me, either, Rory wanted to say, and a feeling rushed over her just then. A bleakness, a mist. Walking a never-ending road in the pitch-black. An eternal treadmill. A hallway with no exits or entrances. Your own body, a prison; your own skin, a vise. The feeling of no future.

ACT V

That night, when act 3 rolled around, Rory was technically onstage, the lights barely hitting her face, and she knew that her head was the size of a grape to Miss Keating.

When her scene was finished, she walked past the leads slurping water at the drinking fountain. She walked past the drama room, where the rest of the ensemble was dealing a round of Uno to keep them occupied until curtain call.

You could leave right now if you wanted. No one would know.

No one would notice if you didn't come out for the final curtain call.

You could leave forever. No one would remember the scholarship student who hung around the Princely Players for two and a half years only to fill up space on the stage.

It was against the rules to leave Euripides during a production. Rory walked right past the student ushers and away from the Elizabethan, off to the empty chambers of the rest of the school.

She moved swiftly, a dreadful march as she held in the worst of her desolation. She had every reason to believe she was alone. She had every reason to believe she would always be alone.

Rory went to the tower in the library, up in the tallest spire, and finally allowed herself to cry. Her feet had brought her there on instinct—her favorite place to hide away, there by the window, that view of campus. But perhaps she loved it because towers, attics, secret dark nooks . . . those were where they put stowaways. Imposters. The unwanted.

The unbelonging.

In an ordinary public school, that window wouldn't have opened. It would have been tiny, barred shut, the glass triple-paned thick, meant to signal to the students that school was government-sponsored babysitting and if you happened to come out with an education, bully for you.

But Bosworth trusted its students. Bosworth believed that its students were capable of great things, and so Rory was able to slide the window open, punch out the screen, and stare at the grounds below. The cold November air rushed around her, through her, chilling her in her thick linen *Crucible* skirt and ridiculous collar and bonnet.

It was supposed to be her turn.

Work hard, pay your dues, and when you're a senior, you'll see it was all worth it.

Was it worth it? She placed her hands on either side of the window and leaned outside, farther, as far as she could go before she felt gravity's pull, and scanned the ground below. Maybe she'd find her answers there.

"Rory?" Miss Keating's voice was an unexpected shock. Rory arched back inside to see her English teacher behind her, panting from her sprint up the tower stairs. "What are you doing?"

Now Rory was fully aware of the reality of her state. She'd cried so hard, her eyes were puffed and round, her stage makeup streaking off in weird lines. She'd stained her collar—dammit. Cynthia would wring her neck for that.

Miss Keating was waiting for an answer, any answer, and Rory's insides seized with the instinct to tuck it all away—to be a good actor and act her way out of this. Feign the death of a family member. Feign boy troubles, blame rascally adolescent hormones.

But Miss Keating was looking at her with worry and an almost parental exasperation and yet with compassion, with a calmness, as if she knew she'd be able to fix whatever Rory had broken.

Something split open within Rory, and she spilled over.

"I wanted a lead. I've worked so hard for Pam for years now! My audition was good; I've put in more than my fair share of hours, gone above and beyond to prove myself to her! It was my time—"

Our time. Rory choked on a sob.

"There isn't room for everyone at the top, I know. But I want it. I want it so bad! There's only one musical left. And if I get put in the ensemble again . . ." She looked to the window, clenching her teeth as despondency shuddered through her.

"That simply isn't true." Miss Keating's interruption was gentle but bracing as a cold rain. "There will be plays and auditions in college—"

"I won't get into college." Rory smeared her wrist across her nose, her sleeve catching tears and snot. "This is my peak in life. There's no way they'll let me into college—not unless it's for something really practical like nursing or teaching. And I don't want that. That would be such a waste—I know I'm capable of so much more. But sometimes I feel like I'm the only one who does."

Miss Keating, to her credit, did not argue. Did not point out that, actually, *she* had always seen Rory's potential.

"What were you planning on doing with the window?" Miss Keating's tone was so very kind, her aura so very safe, Rory nearly melted into a puddle.

"I was—I was going to—I mean I was just thinking about—"

"That's what I thought." Miss Keating reached for Rory's hand.

"Come on. Let's go tell your director that you'll be going home early tonight."

When they got to the bottom of the tower stairs, Miss Keating paused. "Rory? Let's make a plan, you and I. You want to go to college? To study the arts? Let's do it. Any college you want. It'll take some hard work and some strategic planning, but there are enough scholarships floating around out there—you should be able to go anywhere you want. You can study what *you* want."

RORY: *looking up at her teacher like a child*
        You really think so?

"Absolutely," said Miss Keating.

And with that, Miss Keating whisked Rory out of the school and into her own car, a sensible little Camry with clean seats and a quiet purr to its transit.

Miss Keating waited until Bosworth was out of their sight line. "Look, it's a tough thing to break into theater. There's so little you can control in that discipline—you can't control what the director's standards are, or who your competition is, or if there are some secret backdoor deals being made. It's like playing the lottery—and if you want to keep on gambling, fine. But if it's causing you this much stress, you should think about sitting the next production out. There will be other chances for you to perform—including in college. Everything will be better in college."

Rory said nothing, but rested her head against the cool glass of the passenger window, and Miss Keating drove to the emergency room—not to admit Rory as a patient, necessarily, but first to find Rory's mother.

Miss Keating's words sounded good. But she's wrong.

College will just be another round of people playing by their own rules, making up their own sense of justice.

Pam cast a sophomore once. Did I ever tell you? Junior year, spring musical. *Fiddler on the Roof.* She put Glenn Pesetto in as Perchik and told everyone at the first table reading that the rules for boys were different. "There're so few of you," she pronounced, "that with male-heavy shows like this, I run out of seniors and juniors real quick."

I always thought it was a shame Glenn moved before junior year, because he couldn't capitalize on his jump up the ladder. But now I know to build my own ladder.

It was never about Pam. It was never about Bosworth, either, and it wasn't even about rich people, as many problems as they do cause.

If you want something, you have to reach out and take it.

The world is what you make of it.

The first scholarship essay Miss Keating ever assigned to me. Machiavelli. *The end justifies the means.*

The greatest lesson I ever learned from Bosworth.

And you agree with me, don't you? You must; you've been right by my side throughout everything. I told you exactly what I would do. I told you I was going to chase after what I wanted, and you've watched me do it, step by step.

How can you not agree with me, after all you've witnessed here?

"You're early." Ethan strolls into the auditorium, and I do my best to slow my heart rate. He's wearing only a white undershirt and the pair of gym shorts he'll keep on beneath his Thackery armor. No shoes.

Bare feet are against the rules.

Seeing Ethan's feet renders him vulnerable, like I'm seeing him fully naked.

All my emotions, everything that's churned and whipped and settled in the past twenty-four hours . . . It froths within me, all at once, and I shudder, keeping from crumbling.

He is instantly concerned. "Wait, what is it? Did something happen?"

How can I answer that? Yes, everything happened. And it was because of me.

He holds on to my shoulders, forces me to look at him. "I know what's going on."

I am a vessel, and Ethan's words have filled me to the brim.

I cannot wait to hear it, the accusations that will come out of his mouth. Surprised by my grit? Why should I be so conflicted now? Why should I fear being caught? Why should I do anything but rejoice, bask in the glory of all that I've done? Paranoia tries to hollow me out, but I refuse to succumb. My charade will not end here. The curtains will not close on me. I will not wake up to find myself invisible again.

I am nothing but triumphant. I cling to this feeling even as a tear breaks away and trickles down my cheek.

"You're nervous," Ethan guesses, and I shudder with relief. He doesn't know. He doesn't know a lick of it. "It makes sense. This is your first big show. But let me tell you why you shouldn't pay any attention to those nerves."

Yes, tell me. Tell me how to ignore the things that pain me.

"You're so talented." He wipes my tear away with his thumb. "I don't know why Pam didn't give you this role after we auditioned, but it doesn't matter—you've proved that you belong here. I'm so proud to be sharing a stage with you. In fact, I can't wait."

I stare up at him, seeing myself in the reflection of his eyes.

Ethan, oh, god. We are right where we first met. The Halloween party, in our costumes, and now here we are, both stripped bare.

Our final show together, and it feels like the closing of something, even though I always hoped this moment would feel like an opening—

It would be so easy to tilt my mouth up. I can feel him, looking at me. Reconsidering. Things are fluid. There are ways to get around who you thought you were—and there are as many opportunities to be true as there are moments in your life. Any moment could be the one where things change.

I smile and tuck myself into his chest for a hug, breaking eye contact. Breaking the moment. "Thank you."

I did not orchestrate things to steal a kiss from Ethan. I did not make my way toward Joetta to share the stage with him.

I am here for my own spotlight.

"It's nearly five," Ethan says. "Come on. Let's go see how much eyeliner I can get away with before Shandie flips her lid."

I laugh. The moment has passed.

The curtains onstage are still.

In two short hours, I'll be standing on that stage before a full house.

Triumphant.

King Lear showcases the two emotions Aristotle defined as necessary for a tragedy: pity and fear. Yet Lear is a difficult character to pity or to fear—from the first act, he is blinded by his judgment and his hubris, demanding flattery from everyone around him. He believes himself entitled to certain positions and relationships that he has not labored for; when he finally does understand the damage he's caused by his fatal flaw, he's been wandering in denial for so long, he descends into madness instead. There's no real catharsis, no purifying moment until Cordelia dies before him. "Why should a dog, a horse, a rat have life, / And thou no breath at all? . . . . / Never, never, never, never, never" (act 5, scene 3). The scene evokes a great mourning for its audience, but also a discomfort, that such a powerful man would require suffering first in order to understand compassion.

—*Rory King,* "Is *King Lear* Too Sad to Be a Tragedy?"

ACT FIVE

OPENING NIGHT

(IT'S TONIGHT)

SHANDIE: *Twenty to curtain!*
EVERYONE: *Thank you, twenty!*

them what they've all been wait – ing for!

them what they've all been wait – ing for!

them what they've all been wait – ing for!

them what they've all been wait – ing for!

Cur – tains part! Lights go low!

And there's the set we built!

Cur – tains part! Lights go low!

There's what we built!

Ahhh! Ahhhh! it's a lit-tle slea-zy!

it's a lit-tle chees-y, Like a go-od Fos-se, it's a lit-tle slea-zy!

Ahhh! Ahhhh! it's a lit-tle slea-zy!

Ahhh! Like a go-od Fos-se, it's a lit-tle slea-zy!

One last call, then open – ing night!

One last call, then open – ing night!

One last call, then open – ing night!

One last call, then open – ing night!

put your ver-y heart on dis – play! (S.)

put your ver-y heart on dis – play! (A.)

put your ver-y heart on dis – play! (T.)

put your ver-y heart on dis – play! (B.)

Two hours from now, take your bow– (S.)

You're the next Joel Grey! (A.)

Two hours from now, (T.)

Two hours from now, (B.)

S. Oooh!   Oooh!

A. Like dear old Mel Brooks,   we're danc-ing   in spring-time!

T. Oooh!   Oooh!

B. Like dear old Mel Brooks   Oooh!

S. Oooh!   just like Steph-en Sond-heim!

A. We're gon-na be out there,   just like Steph-en Sond-heim!

T. Oooh!   just like Steph-en Sond-heim!

B. We're gon-na be out there,   just like Steph-en Sond-heim!

Pno.

S.
One last call! *SHANDIE: Fifteen minutes to curtain!*

A.
One last call! *EVERYONE: Thank you, fifteen!*

T.
One last call!

B.
One last call!

Pno.

Spotlight on ETHAN, visiting RORY in her dressing room

S.

A.

T.

B.

ETHAN: Good knight!

My swe-et la - dy, Ro - ry!

To - night, it's you-ou and me, Ro - ry!

no-w it's fin – ally to – night!

no-w it's fin – ally to – night!

To – night!

Sing loud! You 're Jo – et – ta to – night!

Reach out for what you're owed! Eth - an!

Ro - ry! Good knight! Go out in glo - ry!

EVERYONE:

S.: Hear that crowd?

A.: Warm up your vo-cal cords!

T.: Hear that crowd?

B.: Warm up your cords!

All sold out! Don't rush through!

Get rea-dy to per-form!

All sold out! Don't rush through!

Time to per - form!

Bask in all of that spot-light's glow!

Bask in all of that spot-light's glow!

Bask in all of that spot-light's glow!

Bask in all of that spot-light's glow!

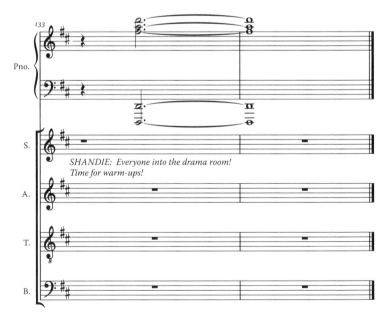

WARM-UPS

EVERY DRAMA DEPARTMENT, EVERY DIRECTOR, EVEN every performer, has their own warm-ups for before a show. The directors may proclaim that their particular warm-ups are steeped in some sort of ancient tradition, eliciting visions of Greek choirs chanting "red leather, yellow leather" behind the skene. But the truth is most directors are simply repeating the rituals they learned in their own high school drama days, creating an unending chain of tongue twisters and nasal trills.

There are vocal exercises, of course. Lots of lip buzzing and throaty hums, lots of deep breathing, scales, waking up the vocalizer. Lots of whooshing noises and sirens and other odd sounds that, on their own, would be bizarre to hear from any individual, but all together the sounds are rendered almost beautiful. The sounds of a cast, crowing as one.

After vocal warm-ups comes the grounding—the centering of oneself, the alignment of individual intentions into a single, solitary aim. A grail. Imagine you are filled with a blue light, cleansing your body as it moves up and down your insides. Imagine you are standing before a door, and once you walk through it, you enter a place where gravity does not exist and you are at peace. Some directors encourage students to pray, though they cannot suggest it in anything more than vague hints: "Stand in a circle and think of England." "Heads down for a minute of silence." Or, simply put, "Do the thing."

Then a final raucous cheer, which always blurs the line between tradition and superstition. Put your hands in the middle and yell "Thundercats, go!" not because it contains any inherent magical spell or meaning to the students or to the show, but because the director has done that before every production since 1987, and they're not about to risk it now.

Rory lies back in the dark.

This is Pam's favorite thing to do during warm-ups on opening night, after revving the throat muscles and guiding the cast through gentle, golden mindscapes—that good old-fashioned trust exercise.

Lights out. Lie down on the drama room floor. And then you must all count to ten.

A reminder of the rules: Only one person can speak at a time or you must start over. You cannot go in any arranged order or pattern. Count to ten, one voice at a time, without any strategizing, without wordless gesturing, with no communication except some silent collaboration of the souls.

You must feel it. That's your strategy.

Rory's usual strategy? Just be quiet. Let the others count verbally—she dreaded the potential humiliation of boldly calling out a number, thinking it safe to do so, only to jinx another student who had decided this was their moment to speak. She would fasten her eyes tightly shut and send out a wave of invisible, supportive warmth to her fellow players. When they reached ten, they all claimed victory, even those who had not uttered a single integer.

But tonight, as she nestles on the pillow of her ratted, teased, leaf-adorned fox-maiden hair, she feels a prickling.

Pam's meditations have not done anything to tamp down Rory's nerves—though Rory diagnoses them as anticipatory, affirmative jitters and not locked-knee, vomit-on-the-front-row jitters.

Potential energy, coursing through her.

"Three," she sings out during the first lull in the count.

She's never been so bold. She's never had reason to be—but right now, she could build a rocket by hand and shoot herself up into the sky, fueled only by this nerve.

The cast makes it to ten smoothly, without having to start over once, and everyone can feel it—the miracle that this is, the wonderment.

"That's never happened in the history of trust exercises," someone points out. "We're so in sync."

"Means it's going to be an incredible night," someone divines, and Rory can't help but agree.

The key to a trust exercise, it turns out, is to trust no one else. Only yourself.

The lights come up, the cast rolls to their feet, and Pam begins her preshow pep talk.

Every year, every show, Rory has been in the ensemble and has known, in the deep, cruel pit of her stomach, that it doesn't really matter if she hears this or not. It wouldn't really matter if she were there or not, if she was asleep, if she replaced herself onstage with a scarecrow, two brooms tied together wearing her costume.

But tonight, it matters.

Tonight, Rory stands at the front of the cast cluster, looking up at her fearless director, as loyal and alert as a pup.

"Well, we're finally here." Pam smiles. She's in her customary director ensemble—all black, a genderless, sexless outfit that is neither intimidating nor mysteriously scholastic à la Simone de Beauvoir; simply neutral, as if to wear any other color might give hints about which way she tilts, one way or another. She cannot flaunt any kind of bias tonight, not even pride in her own creation.

"What a production this has been," she says. "Filled with surprises. Some difficult ones." Everyone chuckles and nods, recalling the same unprecedented bumps in the road—and yet they've made it.

Rory has made it.

"I want to thank you all," Pam says, "for your devotion, your passion, and your—"

The doors to the drama room open; ordinarily they wouldn't be so loud, but in this concentrated quiet, they whoosh like airplane hatches.

Shandie pokes her head into the room. "I need to borrow Rory."

Rory's stomach flips. Pam looks down at her, as if searching for a good reason to keep her, but not even Pam can come up with one. Rory's dressed, makeuped, her hair is shellacked into place. She's warmed up, she's meditated, she's counted to ten in the darkness, and she's heard enough of Pam's pep talk to feel buoyed.

"Go ahead," Pam dismisses, and Rory wishes she hadn't.

"Five minutes to curtain" is Shandie's addition, a kindness and a warning; Rory knows Shandie will hunt her down and search everywhere in the building to guarantee Joetta is behind the curtains when the lights go dark. The notion comforts Rory somewhat, knowing that she cannot simply slip away. She would be missed.

Shandie marches Rory through the hall with no explanation.

The walkie-talkie at her hip spurts out a constant stream of updates: "Sold out of Junior Mints already!" "Need more programs at the east door." "Just saw the press walk in. The *Banner* sent Gabby Hobbes this time. Rocko says she's tough but fair." "We want tough but fair. Let her try to find something wrong with this show, I dare her. We're bulletproof."

When Rory reaches the threshold, the silk rope bisecting the hallway, demarcating the spot where backstage begins, she sees what she's been summoned for, and all of her frets, all those dark possibilities that went through her head, they suddenly vanish. She is instead beset by a great and overwhelming anger.

Her mother stands there, on the other side of the rope. Not in her scrubs, like she usually is, but made up, looking laboriously nice. Rory usually forgets that her mother can look like this, like her own separate person.

MOM: Well, hello to the leading lady!

MOM has a giant bouquet of roses, deep red with velveteen petals, a bouquet so beautiful, it takes RORY's breath away. This bouquet probably cost seventy dollars. MOM tries to place it in RORY's arms.

RORY: What are you—? I thought you had a board meeting tonight.

She doesn't raise her arms to take the roses.

MOM: You forgot to put the schedule for the show on the fridge. I found out it was opening night from Janice, and she's the one who told me the big news! This is great, Ror. Why didn't you tell me?

RORY *looks around, surreptitiously, like a mouse preparing to run for cover when the moon comes out.*

MOM: Seriously, Rory. Why didn't you tell me you got the lead?

"You don't need to make a big deal out of it. It's nothing. You don't need to be here. It'll probably be really boring." I glance around—for who, I don't know—but I must keep my eyes roving, keep from letting her look at me. I'm supposed to be hidden away from the audience now, and yet here is my mother, demanding that I converse here by the threshold, where anyone can see me. As if I'm just a nobody in the ensemble, just a body in the crowd.

God, this is exactly why I didn't tell her. Because she wouldn't get it. She'd never understand.

And she would have known right away. She would have known how weird it was that I got the role—she'd question it, and start to look closer, and the last thing I need is for her to go poking around in my business, searching for answers.

MOM: Here.

She finally passes the bouquet of roses into RORY's *arms.*

I'm so proud of you, Ror. You've been working for this for a long time.

"I have nowhere to put these," I say.

The roses are heavy in my arms, and they weren't cleaned properly—a thorn stabs into me right below my elbow. The armor of Joetta is useless against gestures of goodwill that come with invisible strings.

MOM: *(cheerfully)*

> Keep them backstage. That way you can look at them when you're waiting for your next scene.

Yes, yes, that's what I should have. I should have a whole row of bouquets in the dressing room, my own private garden. But not from my mother. From anyone except my mother. From everyone except my mother.

MOM: I believe your line here is "thank you." These weren't cheap.

"I didn't ask you to bring them," I snap. "I didn't even ask you to come here. Are we going to be short on rent now, because you decided to bring these gaudy—"

A flash in the crowd behind my mother. A familiar face—or am I dreaming? Am I so keyed up by this surprise maternal visit that I can't even tell whose faces belong to who?

I watch the crowd while my mother gives me some watered-down response—she can't even scold me properly. Too afraid of what her daughter might do in response. Too afraid to lose me. Too invested in acting like a peer—maybe she's lonely and has been waiting for me to grow older so she can have a built-in friend. But I'm not interested.

"I guess I can hold these until curtain call." Mom reaches to take back the bouquet of roses, to cradle them all night like an infant.

But I slide them out of her reach. "No. That's worse. Fine. I'll find somewhere to put them." I won't allow my mother to slink out of her seat as the cast gives their bows, rushing onstage to find me and saddle me with these all over again in an even more public display of maternal devotion. "I've got to get back."

"Break a leg!" my mother calls. "I'll see you after the show!"

The harder you try, I think, the easier it is to push you away.

The flowers really are beautiful. They're lush and fat and delicate and smell like a department store.

But I didn't want my mother to come. I didn't want her to be here.

All that meditation we did with Pam, now moot. There isn't a relaxed cell in my body. I am all shivers and electricity, and as I pass a garbage can outside the choir room, I dump the roses in with a delicious *thunk*.

I slip into my place backstage, standing in the shadows, and breathe deeply. My knees are water. I'm searching for the power I felt only moments ago, that depth and that courage, but it's misplaced.

I don't have anything against my mother personally. She works hard. She is what she is—a lower-income single mother with *Gilmore Girls* aspirations and a spine made of jelly.

My eyes crinkle, hot with the threat of tears, thinking of the arrangement of roses now at the bottom of the garbage can. Why couldn't she have just stayed home tonight? Why does she have to be so aware, so supportive? Why can't she just let me be invisible to her?

Now it'll be harder to perform onstage, knowing my mother is here. It'll be harder to transform when someone who knows me so well is right there in the audience, tethering me to this reality.

Now all of my roles stack up in layers, the roles I've won and the roles I've assigned to myself, and it'll be harder to break through.

But break through I must.

DOWN HERE IN DOWNERE

THE OVERTURE BEGINS, THE ORCHESTRA IN THE PIT playing its jaunty medley of *Good Knight! Sweet Lady*'s greatest hits. Those in the audience who recognize it, perhaps from their own childhoods or from old VHS copies that floated down from grandparents or garage sales, perk up. They know this, remember this. They remember what this show once meant.

And those who are hearing it for the first time sit up, impressed already by the extravagant strains of the strings, the bounding percussives, the raucous brass section, the promise of slapstick, adventure, and romance, all presented in less than three hours' time.

As the overture swells and fades, a single pan flute trickles a playful melody as a spotlight warms onto a figure, stage right.

"Once upon a time, in a far-off place, there was a beautiful kingdom," sings out Osbert, the gentleman-in-waiting and self-assigned narrator of this musical tale. He sits atop a wooden stool, striped stockings crossed. "And everyone in this kingdom had the most glorious hair."

The curtains open, and there is the first set, a well-lit feast of bricked turrets, balconies, and a great tree-lined courtyard where the good folks of Downere are gathering to sing us into the opening number.

The stage has limited dimensions, but somehow the technical crew has transformed it, giving this kingdom texture and depth. A pastel blend of soft peaches and carnation pinks render the false castle into a Disney-movie idealism; the stark blue sky of the backdrop places the scene neatly into a sunny midday.

"It's all sweet blooms and happy tunes," sings the ensemble, "down here in Downere!" They are powerful in unison, voices charging into the audience, gripping every ticketed hand to tug them into the story. *Come along, this way*, their song seems to say. *We know exactly where we're going.*

"It's all pretty maids and shiny braids down here in Downere!"

Indeed, every member of the ensemble wears their hair in such a manner as to inspire shampoo commercials—long, luscious waves dotted with beads, tamed curls piled on top of heads, waxen beards woven with daisies.

Downere, Osbert explains, is a kingdom obsessed with the upkeep of their magnificent hair. Now the audience can see the signs posted around the onstage kingdom: "Hair today, gone tomorrow!" "Have you brushed your locks today?" "Hair is the rope with which you will reach heaven!"

It's not an opening of high school caliber; it looks professional grade, one of the many qualities of a Pam Hanson production. Other high schools, even universities, may put together shows with rickety design and lots of heart, but not Bosworth. Not with Pam here.

On the show goes.

Osbert introduces us to King Harold and Queen Harolda, who are desperate to break off a betrothal between their daughter, Princess Catherine, and the neighboring country's Prince Warwicke.

"That's absolutely disgusting, Harold!" Queen Harolda shrieks when her king, overcome by nerves, lets out a meaty belch. "And completely unbecoming of a royal! Why, if you made a sound like that in front of your courtiers, they'd all be repulsed . . ."

Harold and Harolda lock eyes. Eureka! Brilliance has struck them! They'll hire a "Princess Catherine" so ill-mannered, so coarse and unrefined, she'll frighten Prince Warwicke out of the betrothal. Contract voided, on peaceful terms.

Backstage, Rory awaits her cue. She is entirely alone, hunched in the corner of stage right, near the ladder to the catwalk. As the lines bring her closer to her first step onstage, a radiant heat blows through her.

Is this truly happening?

For a moment, she can see above herself. Looking down at her body, a swirling motion. For a moment, she wonders if she will hurl or run away.

But the cue of the line and the music has her perfectly trained.

Out she steps onto the stage. Into the lights.

Into another world.

> KING HAROLD *and* QUEEN HAROLDA *wander into a forest. They are clearly out of their element, dressed far too finely for a trek through the woods.*

QUEEN HAROLDA:

> Are you certain we're in the right place, Harold? All the trees look exactly alike!

KING HAROLD:

>It's a forest, my sweet. Every tree is unique in its own special way, and a true expeditioner knows every trunk, every leaf, every root, by sight.

QUEEN HAROLDA: *(after a beat)*

>You're lost, too, aren't you?

>*The audience laughs.* KING HAROLD *and* QUEEN HAROLDA *approach a burrow of sorts, dug into an earth mound, a round wooden door marking the entrance to a hobbit-like home. In the dirt in front of the mound, a fire cooks something in a cauldron.*

KING HAROLD:

>There, you see? The fox maiden's lair! And she has a stew cooking! She must be close by. Take a seat by that prickly briar, darling, and rest your royal feet.

>QUEEN HAROLDA *makes a big show of sitting on a flat rock next to a thistly bush; after a moment, the bush moves. It's not a bush at all, but* JOETTA THE FOX MAIDEN's *wild hair.*

JOETTA:

>That's my dinner rock. I'd rather not have any bottoms plopped down right where I eat, if you wouldn't mind.

Joetta's an immediate hoot. The audience loves her.

God, Rory loves her. Loves *being* her.

Rory loves being Joetta more than she's ever loved being Rory.

The scene continues. The king and queen hire rough-and-tumble Joetta to pose as their princess to scare away the prince of

350

Tillypoo. They instruct her to really get gross—"all your disgusting country habits should be put on display."

They leave.

And Joetta, alone with the audience at last, sings her big opening number.

Every good musical has an "I Want" song.

It's a fast way to loop in the audience on the protagonist's greatest desires—their motivations, the reasons they do what they do in the rest of the show. Belle wants much more than this provincial life. Audrey wants to go somewhere that's green. Pippin wants to find his corner of the sky.

Joetta wants to be knighted.

"By Day and By Knight" is Rory's moment of truth. Rory's own "I Want" song.

And Rory nails it.

I want it by day and by knight!

The final line bursts out of her, and Rory pants, holds her mark.

This. This is what you always wanted. This is what you always knew you could do. You've always known it, and you have always been held back—by your own limitations, no less. But now you have flung yourself into the sun, and you'll never huddle and wonder in the darkness again.

The crowd breaks into applause, and she is startled— she'd almost forgotten about them. Her audience, her silent co-conspirators.

How on earth do people manage to leave things up to chance? How on earth did I? I'll never live by chance again. I'll seize it all for myself.

Just before the lights evaporate, signaling a scene change, Rory lets herself peer out at them—but the crowd fades to black before she can make out any individual faces. She rushes offstage, her feet dragging her away, though she aches to stay.

Because now she knows the big secret. She could never learn this when she was in the ensemble, no. Too little to work with, too little space to slip into.

You get out onstage and you're not really pretending to be another character. You're surrendering. You become that character yourself.

She has no need to be Rory anymore. She can be Joetta now.

Even when the auditorium is emptied and the custodians are sweeping up the ticket stubs and candy wrappers, Joetta will live.

Rory will never be just Rory ever again.

"That was great!" Here comes the pattering of praises, whispered backstage. Rory takes the compliments one by one, like little chocolates, each one a nourishment to her, then walks to her next cue.

Ethan makes his entry in the next scene; when he's finished, he waits in the wings next to Rory.

Rory turns to him, ready to engage in the sort of outshining banter they always do, but once she looks at him, she sees something is wrong.

Something is off.

There's no gleam in his eye, no flip to his hair. He's watching the show carefully from his backstage vantage point, as if he's never seen it before.

"Hey." Rory pokes him quietly. "Let's do the thing where I jump in your arms at the end of 'Courtship.' The audience seems like they'll go for it."

Ethan nods without eye contact.

Rory could ask him anything, she senses—she could ask him

to please take a shit with her onstage, and he would agree. He's not listening to her at all.

"Are you okay?" she asks, placing a hand on his forearm. It's imperceptible, but she can feel his muscles tighten beneath her touch.

"Fine," he answers. "Just staying in character."

Rory chortles at this. Ethan's the furthest thing from method. He never needs to channel his roles; he explodes onstage as whoever he needs to be—the Grinch; Orin Scrivello, DDS; a rock.

At first she thinks he's joking, poking fun at those who require concentration to stay in the head of someone else—but then she notices he doesn't smile, doesn't move. Just has that faraway look in his eyes and a troubled furrow to his brow.

"You seem weird," she whispers. "Are you sure you're okay? Are you nervous?"

When Ethan finally turns his head, he has to drag his eyes over to her. And as soon as she looks at them, she can see it.

He knows everything.

She senses it, the way she can sense their movements onstage as Joetta and Thackery. That connection they've had since meeting over the food at the Halloween party sophomore year—she can only feel her side of the rope, frayed and loose and limp.

His side of the rope, dropped.

Everything in Rory is cold.

"Ethan, I—" she starts.

"I need water," he tells her, slipping into the hallway.

Rory tries to reassure herself, tries to believe she's just needlessly stirring up drama—how could she not? Everything is heightened here backstage, with the curtains hanging heavy, a breeze blowing from the rafters, the lights, the music, the breath of hundreds of onlookers in velvet seats.

Everyone made into characters larger than themselves—was Rory just fitting Ethan into a part?

She doesn't have long to wonder.

"Joetta!" Shandie hisses, waving her clipboard.

Yes. Joetta begins this next scene with King Harold and Queen Harolda. They're in the throne room of the palace of Downere, getting ready for the arrival of the prince of Tillypoo—so Rory blinks, suppresses a throat clearing, since her mic is now hot, and strolls out into the scene.

Joetta hams it up. She's spent the morning rolling around with the pigs in her pink satin princess gown. She's eating a turkey leg, hot and oily, sucking the meat clean off the bone. She's perfectly poised to send the prince of Tillypoo off screaming in the other direction—and now is the moment when the two betrothed royals finally meet.

OSBERT:

> Your Royal Grandnesses, may I present the prince
> of Tillypoo!

It's Ethan's cue. He's supposed to saunter out, making a right liar of the king, who just described the prince as "timid as an aardvark at bath time." Everyone's expecting a dry plop of a man, but Ethan-as-Thackery-disguised-as-the-prince emerges, a charismatic, mischievous, bad-boy heartthrob, and the crowd goes wild.

Rory is already anticipating the screams; Ethan's very presence elicits cheers. She needs that new infusion of energy, needs to suck it from Ethan, boost the Joetta in her—

Thackery comes onstage, but it isn't Ethan.

THACKERY:

> Well met, my beloved! At last I lay my eyes upon you—let
> me have a look at my bride!

Annie Neville is wearing Thackery's costume: deep-blue tunic embroidered with golden threads and crimson tassels, rawhide breeches the color of sand, leather boots with knee-high shafts.

Ethan's sword hangs from her belt.

QUEEN HAROLDA: *stumbling only slightly*

> Come closer, Prince. Make sure you can really get a whiff.

Rory, barely remembering where she is, manages to hold still while Annie-as-Ethan-as-Thackery-disguised-as-the-prince edges nearer, inspecting her greasy face, her bushy hair, her soiled gown.

Ah, Annie. Touché.

So you couldn't resist the pull of the stage—I can hardly blame you. But now I'm no longer acting. The character of Joetta sinks into me, her arms, her legs, her very will.

Any threat to Joetta is a threat to me.

The crowd understands that something has changed. Their cheers are dynamic, wild for Annie—perhaps excited to see a bit of edge in this otherwise gender-incurious musical.

Rory stops hearing their cheers. She homes in on one thing only.

Annie's face, triumphant. Pleased to have caught Rory off guard.

THACKERY:

> Oh, my. You are not what I expected.

JOETTA:

> You have no idea.

JUST LIKE
WE REHEARSED

ANNIE WEARS ETHAN'S COSTUME SO WELL. BEING A TALL girl has its advantages. Her hair is tucked back in a bun at the nape of her neck. She hasn't tried particularly hard to look like a boy—she hasn't taped down her chest, she hasn't adhered whiskers to her jawline, she hasn't contoured her gamine features to be bigger, sharper.

She's not here to play Thackery. She's here to play Rory.

THACKERY:

> I'm only in town for a few days, so I'm afraid I won't have as much time with you as I'd like—

JOETTA:

> Don't worry, prince-y mine. A few days is all I need.

The script surges out of Rory. She recalls the weekend she spent with Annie, running lines in Annie's bedroom—Rory read Thackery's lines so Annie could practice Joetta's. Did Rory ever imagine they'd be saying them here, before a crowd and in reverse? Of course not. Even Rory can be caught by surprise.

THACKERY:

>Of course, I have other business to attend to. Royal matters, you understand—and an appointment with the cutler.

JOETTA:

>Is it a blade you're sharpening? Or your wits?

THACKERY:

>Why? Do they seem dull to you?

Thackery and Joetta move closer. The audience is on the edge of their seats. Those in the more conservative circles of the Bosworth community who would ordinarily protest such a blatantly "progressive" production find themselves swept up in the motion of it all. No doubt they'll write strongly worded letters to the school board tomorrow, but for now, they give themselves over to enchantment.

What is the nature of the tension in the Elizabethan? Are we witnessing Thackery and Joetta resist their blooming attraction for each other? Or are we about to watch them kill each other on the spot?

JOETTA:

>I must insist on a proper Downere courtship before we can set a date for the wedding. There's quite a lot of paperwork.

THACKERY:

>And what does a Downere courtship entail? Sending you poetry written with ink of my own making? Serenading you with love songs in the still of the full moon?

JOETTA:

>Nope! Wrestling!

Annie's rehearsed this part. She knows it well—or she did, before "Pam" and "Shandie" started mysteriously changing the schedule, the blocking, the very floor from beneath Annie's feet. Annie performs it smoothly, the mirror image of the scene she learned.

Rory-as-Joetta leaps toward Annie-as-Thackery, pulling her to the ground. Joetta squeals with delight, like she's hog-tying some feral beast in the woods. The audience laughs at the slapstick, laughs at the improbability of a princess dishing out an arm wringer and a takedown while clad in satin.

Thackery escapes from Joetta's hold, but only barely.

Annie is breathing hard, staring at Rory with a blaze in her eyes, and Rory—not Joetta, but Rory—feels the chill as she slips out of character.

Off Joetta comes, like a sleeve or a gown, a skin she's been wearing. A snail, popped from its shell.

Rory steps toward Annie, almost as a dare.

There's a pause, longer than Pam originally instructed—

Pam. Where is Pam?

What's she thinking right now, seeing the two of them on her stage?

Is she blowing a gasket? Is she rushing to find Shandie, to instruct everyone to end the show?

No. Rory knows without even having to look at her. Pam's quietly watching, revealing nothing from her spot in the corner of the auditorium. If you were to observe her, you'd assume that this was all entirely planned, that none of this is different from what they've been rehearsing for weeks and weeks.

Pam is not about to reveal that this is a sharp turn into the unknown. "A production is alive," she would say, "and once a show starts, no one can really know where the show is going to take us. It's all in the hands of the drama gods now. I've done all I can do."

Annie does not shy away as Rory comes nearer.

THACKERY:

>All right, all right. You pinned me. Any other Downere courtship rituals I should know about?

Rory feels the pull—and she follows it.

She seizes Annie in a kiss. A scripted kiss, but this feels too real to be rehearsed.

It's a violent kiss, and it's supposed to be—Joetta is meant to grab Thackery and kiss him, a surprise, an attack. A reversal of the usual trope where a man grabs his sassy, reluctant woman in order to shut her up or convince her to fall for him or both.

Joetta lunges at Thackery and gives him a smooch that sends thrills down to his soles. Afterward, Thackery is meant to look at her, dazed, but keep himself planted in the scene, proving to the king and queen that he is more than equipped to handle the false Princess Catherine's antics.

But Annie peels away. She looks at Rory with a trembling chin, and she does not say her line.

It's silent.

The Elizabethan grows in size; suddenly it is as wide open as a field, a city, a stretch of space empty of stars, empty of all things except this silence.

JOETTA:

>Downere sure is full of surprises.

Rory says the line. It's Thackery's, but Joetta can say it. Just this once. Just for tonight.

Will there be anything beyond tonight?

Rory cannot come up with an answer. Had she ever thought that far, in all her planning and preparation? Had she ever looked beyond this one night?

Tonight, Joetta says Thackery's line. And then Joetta rushes off-stage before the scene's end, leaving her own final lines unsaid.

Rory charges straight backstage as the scene behind her comes to a close, past questioning stares and shocked glances, out into the hallway. Any second, Annie will be tailing her, stalking closer; maybe she already is, maybe she is yelling her name, yelling for her to turn around—

Rory can't tell; she's awash in all the noises of the school—the cheers of the crowd, the belligerent entr'acte music as the scene changes and the true Princess Catherine and Prince Warwicke take the stage. The strain of the pipes behind the new drinking fountain. The crank of the air flowing through the vents in the ceiling. The whispers and confusion of the cast and crew.

Her ears even throb with ghostly echoes of the sound she's most familiar with—the minuscule, obligated applause of an audience clapping for the ensemble. But it isn't like that this time. This time, the claps for Rory are thunderous. Momentous.

She doesn't stop until she's all the way in the drama room. She runs into Pam's office. She knows right where Pam keeps her keys—Rory's kissed her butt enough times that Pam's opened her world to her.

And now Rory is on one side of the glass wall of the office and Annie is on the other, and although Annie is knocking on the door, slapping it, demanding that Rory open it, Rory is busy doing something else.

It takes her thirty seconds to log on to Pam's computer. Fifteen seconds more to open an email of her own creation, something anonymous—something that, if traced, would lead to the computer lab in the library, thus leaving Rory out of its pathways completely.

She finds it in her drafts and is about to hit send—

But Annie finally calls out something worthy of Rory's attention: "Go ahead. Send the email. But I already confessed!"

Rory pauses, hand hovering on the mouse, and looks at Annie.

"Coach knows everything. I called him as soon as I got home," Annie shouts. "I called every player on the team and sent out letters to every teacher in the school. They know all of it. Everything you could possibly use on me or hold over my head, I already sent it out there. You have nothing. Nothing."

Other cast members trail into the room, but Rory ignores them as easily as one ignores white cabbage moths flapping by at a picnic. Irrelevant. Uneventful. Unnecessary. An ensemble. Nothing.

"It's been a rough week—I'll give you that." Annie chuckles. "A real purifying one. You're a hell of a priest, Rory—you've gotten so many confessions out of me. Baptism by fire, you know? I have nothing left to hide." Annie pauses to study Rory through the glass, and once again, Rory feels cornered. Cornered in this little box, where she herself ran.

"I'm free now," Annie says. "Nothing to hide. Nothing to lose. Can you say the same?"

Rory's holding on to the most complicated braid she's ever attempted. Both hands in, fingers gripping hair. If she lets go of one strand, it'll all fall apart.

She should have told first. She should have told everyone about Annie, about her unmentionable shame, her worst vice, the secret behind all her success on the court—

But Rory hesitated.

Annie's secret was Rory's last bullet. And now Annie's shot it out into the world like a flare gun, lighting up the sky with her shame. Even you've probably heard by now what Annie has been hiding all this time—

Rory's gut churns, a sickening hollow. She isn't supposed to feel like this on opening night. She is supposed to feel free.

Annie finally steps back from the glass wall and grips the sword at her belt.

"See you in a minute, Joetta. Time to close act one."

Rory can only guess at what Annie's plotting: Will she stop the play and address the audience directly? Unmask Rory and all her misdeeds? Or does Annie have some other payback ready for Rory, some other humiliation?

There should be a flicker of dread, a shred of self-preservation. Rory searches within herself and finds nothing of the sort.

Only the need to finish it.

Pam's computer is still on, its monitor throwing blue light onto Rory's face. A group of cast members peer at her, and she understands now how aquarium fish feel.

She wanted attention, yes, but never like this.

Fuck all of you! she wants to scream. *You never looked at me before this. Now you want a look? Go ahead: drink me in!*

But instead, she listens.

This is your night. Show them what you're capable of.

The voice whispers, telling her what Joetta would do.

When Rory unlocks the office, she walks calmly out of the room. Into the hall. Backstage.

She wordlessly gets into position, making sure Shandie sees that she's ready.

This is the big ending of act 1, the final scene before intermission.

"It's very important that we leave them with the right taste in their mouths," Pam told them. "We want them hungry to see what happens next—so play big, play hard. Make an impression."

Rory reaches down and grips her sword.

Annie is right. Rory's not free. She's less free than she's ever been.

There's really only one more thing to do.

This is Rory's impression.

She unscrews the tip from the sword—the tip that blunts the blade, that keeps the actors from injuring themselves or others. The tip goes in her pocket. The sword remains on her belt.

There's only one thing to do when you are this tied up.

Cut yourself free.

Rory exhales and heads into the light.

OH, READER, WHY ARE YOU LOOKING AT ME LIKE THAT?

Don't make that face. Don't pretend you didn't know where this was going.

I've laid out the bread crumbs for you, and you've gobbled them up.

It's fine to be concerned. That's entirely fair. But angry? Upset? Scandalized?

You think I've gone too far?

Dear reader, you're complicit.

You've turned every page in this book. Read every paragraph of nefarious schemes and justifications for the obscene. I've spilled my secrets to you and you've stuck with me—you're part of this.

And so you more than anyone should know that she shouldn't have gotten in my way.

She should have let me have the crown.

Now, let's keep going. Let's see how it all shakes out in the end.

Turn the page. Go on.

Turn it again.

SHOWDOWN

The Animal Ball. A tradition in Downere. The tur-rets are decorated with hanging paper lanterns and garlands of lamb's ear; the balconies are colored with pale pink streamers. King Harold's costume is a regal lion, his hair fanned out into a mane jeweled with topaz to match the ochre tone of his doublet. Queen Harolda's costume is a glimmering white peacock, resplendent with a fan of long plumes, glittering and rustling and framing her slicked chignon.

The rest of the ensemble saunters in, bustling and gossiping and making merry over the orchestra's twinkling rondel. Pam's made sure their costumes for the ball are varied—every hue, every tex-ture, every fabric for every shape and order in the animal kingdom represented. A gown of turquoise scales paired with an iridescent fin headdress. A wild boar, with elaborate ivory tusks curling forth from a collared cape. A zebra tunic with stocking hooves.

Annie waits as Thackery, black crow's feathers springing forth from her tunic's shoulders like epaulettes. She already touches her sword, though Thackery is not due to draw his weapon for another twenty lines.

But Annie smells blood.

Rory's Joetta is itching to hunt.

JOETTA:

You lied to me!

THACKERY:

How are you defining "lie"?

They move through the scene, each line springing them closer, and then—

THACKERY:

Don't act like you didn't have your secrets! I don't even know who you are—

JOETTA:

And you never will.

Joetta is first to draw her blade. Thackery is meant to wait until the last possible second to meet her sword with his, since he's already having feelings for the fox maiden and is trying to warn her about the kidnapping plot—

But Annie sees the tip of Rory's sword. Her eyes widen, but she catches herself before she disrupts the scene. She draws her own sword.

THACKERY:

There's something you have to know.

JOETTA:

Tell it to the coroner.

Rory moves through her practiced steps. Annie's leg seems healed—if it hurts her, she doesn't stumble once.

God bless Annie and her athleticism, the way her body can so easily pick up new movements—this is the mirror image of the choreography she learned when they practiced the duel, and yet she doesn't miss a single step. It's miraculous, really.

And the audience is eating it up—there's a hunger in the air. Rory catches a whiff of it, salt and tang.

Time to make a move of her own.

She dashes toward Annie, swiping the sword with all her might.

Annie tries to dodge the jab, but the blade cuts into her. The red of her blood seeps through the forearm of her tunic, gleaming under the stage lights.

The audience doesn't know what is scripted and what is not—and neither does Rory. Not anymore. She's too far in, too far gone—

Is this what it means to be completely in character?

Annie attacks, more forcefully this time.

Let me take her. Let me take over.

Joetta lifts her arm and slices at Annie.

Joetta cuts into Annie's face, a long thin line. But deep enough to bleed. Deep enough to scar.

Annie jumps back, holding her chin.

Such wonderful effects, the people in the Elizabethan are thinking. Such brilliant makeup and choreography, marvelous, as real as real life.

Real life. What does that mean anymore?

Do any of us have a moment when we're not acting? When we're not performing?

Every day is some sort of performance. To say otherwise is a lie, a performance of deception or denial.

The final moment of the duel. Annie lurches for Rory, and Rory is ready for her. She holds up her sword, ready to end her.

A sword and her performance—these are Rory's only weapons in such an unfair world. How else is someone like her supposed to survive?

"War is just when it is necessary," Machiavelli said. "Arms are permissible when there is no hope except in arms."

That's something Rory learned right here in the halls of Bosworth, under the careful tutelage of teachers who called her bright, who welcomed her into their silver-spooned society. The scholarship girl, studying the truth about things.

Annie charges toward her.

Rory lifts her sword.

It'll go right through Annie, and Rory doesn't have a clue what she'll do next—she can't remember her next line.

This is all an improvisation—

Someone grabs Rory from behind, forcing both arms down. Forcing her to lower the sword.

As soon as she sees the hands, she knows who it is—Ethan, dressed in the raggedy threads of Lurkin's crew from Bankruptia.

Joetta is kidnapped at the end of act 1 by Lurkin's men, a comedic struggle that nonetheless guides the story off a cliff into murky plot territory and unresolved tension.

Rory is kidnapped at the end of act 1 by Ethan, who keeps her locked against his chest and shakes her until her sword clatters to the ground.

The curtains close, the orchestra begins the interlude, and a confused applause rolls through the Elizabethan. Intermission now. Ten minutes for the audience to stretch their legs, use the facilities, exchange theories with their seatmates about the performances.

Behind the curtain, Ethan finally drops a screeching Rory, and as she rises from her knees, she turns around.

It's not just Ethan waiting for her to face him. It's Ethan, Annie, the cut on her chin bleeding, her forearm soaked red, and the rest of the cast and crew, all of them stunned, staring at Rory like she's an animal that needs containment.

Pam comes into the wings, her face plain as day. She's not mad, not bewildered, not provoked in any way.

She's curious as hell. Her eyes glow, as if watching a critter squirming in a trap, waiting to see what it'll do next.

INTERMISSION

"IT'S OVER, RORY! TIME TO COME CLEAN. NO MORE GAMES. No more lies." Annie's hands are on her hips, which should be enough of a stereotypical teen-girl image to soften her accusations, but I'm not laughing. She doesn't look like a queen bee; she looks like a judge, towering over me in the height of her great pronouncements. A warrior for fairness.

"I don't know what she's talking about," I fire back. "She's obviously disgruntled that she was kicked out of the show, and she's here to ruin it for the rest of us."

"Cut the bullshit!" Annie turns to the crowd clustered on the stage. "Rory's been playing us all. She's sabotaged every step of this musical, from beginning to end, all so she could guarantee she's here as the lead."

I heave a dramatic, pitying sigh. "It's easy to come up with impossible conspiracies when you're that jealous."

Annie shakes her head, touching her temples. "She's not going to admit it, so I'll just tell you." Out spills a list of my sins—non-exhaustive, but I'm not clamoring to fill in Annie's gaps. Still, it's impressive how much she's been able to untangle.

She is my best friend, after all.

The other students and Pam listen; it's intermission, so they should be resting, drinking water, eating snacks, touching up makeup, preparing themselves for the long endurance run of the second act. Instead they're locked into this drama.

"I don't know how many lies she's told," Annie says, "but if you've talked to her at all in the last three months, I think it's safe to assume that she told at least one to you."

I meet Shandie's eyes first.

I've set traps all semester, luring every Princely Player onto my side. I've bred myself a cast of loyalists, people who felt so touched by my devotion and self-sacrifice, they've cheered as I rose through the ranks.

But I see the truth now. The mechanizations wheeling through their heads.

Annie's words, scattering the shadows.

Shandie's voice is as weak as her personality. "Rory? Is that true?"

I ignore the patsy; behind her, Ethan has been studying me, taking in Annie's pronouncements like polluted air. He looks pained to behold me, and when I meet his eyes, he shuffles out of the pharisaic mob.

"Wait!" I cry, but he's already disappeared out the door.

I turn back to the swarm. One by one, I regard them.

Preston, who cut a special deal with his math teacher: Preston could help out in the auditorium during fourth period, and new jackets for the math club would be provided by his wealthy father.

Heather, who hooked up with Jake so she'd be guaranteed the best mic pack for *And Then There Were None* callbacks.

Alex, Sean, Cody, all migrants from band, who blew off their state competitions so they could be Pam's elf trumpeters for the Christmas revue.

Cynthia, who trash-talked her way into becoming assistant costumer our sophomore year and now has her own little crew of minions.

Chelsey, Sierra, Megan . . . They made sure Pam's office was always stocked with Diet Coke, first as a joke—the obviousness of the bribe—and then as a standard part of their weekly routine.

Every single person on this stage has done something untoward, something to win the favor of Pam—

Pam, who told us all on the first day of drama class that we wouldn't amount to anything as sophomores—not as juniors, either. That we'd need to plant tiny seeds and spend two more aggravating years waiting for them to sprout. That's a lifetime when you're a teenager—but I planted, under Pam's advisement, and I watered. I weeded. I let my harvest grow.

"I did what I had to do. We all did," I say. I glance at Pam—for what? Confirmation? Approval?

But Pam simply tilts her head, thoroughly entertained. As if this is just a show—as if she gets to just sit in the audience of my trial. As if she isn't the director of it all.

Bravado gusts through me.

Tell the truth.

No sword is sharper than the truth.

I fill up my chest with air, puffing it into my diaphragm—just like Pam taught us.

"I did it because of Pam. Pam enables all of this! She set up this environment—we're all bribing her and trading favors, kissing her ass so we can get the parts she promised us!" My heart thumps, my words slashing, cutting, bleeding. "She pretends it's all under this guise of fairness, but she does it so we'll prostrate ourselves and fight over the crumbs she gives us. I was only trying to level the playing field. How else was I going to get Pam to give me a shot? She plays us like fiddles. You all know it."

There's hustle and bustle outside our curtained, protected wings, but none of it penetrates our convocation on the stage.

"We're children," I nearly yell at them, "and she's been playing cat and mouse with us for years!"

They're not looking at me anymore. They're eyeing Pam. Waiting for her to speak. Waiting for Pam to tell them what to do.

My stomach becomes a sinkhole.

"Well, Rory," Pam says, "you've put forth a very interesting case. I certainly enjoy getting feedback as a teacher. I'm curious—does anyone else share Rory's perspective?"

I already know, before anyone answers, that I've lost.

Pam doesn't treat us like that.

No, Pam's always been fair.

The best person for the role always gets it. Pam makes sure she's casting by talent.

The thing about the sophomores, well, that's only fair, isn't it? Some of us have been here for years, and we've worked hard. It wouldn't be fair to cast someone who just strolled in without paying their dues.

Their dues, their dues. I've paid all my dues—but if I hadn't scraped and scratched for this, I wouldn't have been given a part.

There are only so many leads to go around.

This is a college essay come to life. This is a wet dream for Miss Keating, an example of Machiavellian philosophies being debated in a flesh-and-blood scenario.

Write about a modern arena in which you see the themes of *The Prince* applied.

This very stage.

Bosworth, this institution of injustice.

At the next one, where tuition will not be as easily covered, I'll be expected to function as an adult, navigating through systems meant to keep me crushed and underfoot, and I won't be able to convince anyone that such unfairnesses exist, because those who I would complain to are the ones who keep the systems chugging. They're the ones wearing the boots.

A bold reaction against such systems is Machiavellianism at work. Sell your very soul to save yourself. The end justifies the means.

"This department is run as fairly as possible," Shandie finally announces. "She makes sure everyone has a chance—you're the one who's ruined her system. You're the one who's corrupt."

Others echo her. Deny reality. Defend Pam. Kiss the hand that feeds.

Fairness is nothing. What about justice?

With every speaker, Pam exchanges promises with her eyes. The exchange is clear—they defend her, and she'll make it worth their while. Solos, recommendation letters, special auditions with scholarship committees.

I see an entire network of deals being arranged. An entire future of the Princely Players commissioned, right here on this stage.

"Five minutes until curtain." Shandie's headset has come alive, neon-green light flashing.

All heads turn to Pam—Pam, fearless leader, orchestrator, director.

"Oh, Rory," Pam says. "What are we going to do with you now?"

I do not wait for orders. I do not wait for the next scene to be set.

I run, dashing through the curtains. This is against all the rules. I'm still in my costume. I've still got my microphone, taped to my neck and cheek.

I leap into the orchestra pit, pushing past the row of flautists and the boy with the tuba, and then I'm running up the aisle.

People are streaming back from intermission, Red Vines in hand, and they're ready to sit through the back half of the show and be dazzled. Do they think this is part of some weird intermission performance piece? A little play within a play, a teaser?

I don't know; I'm moving too quickly to tell.

"Rory!" someone calls. Is it my mother? Could be. Is it Miss Keating, who's walking dangerously close to my mother now, bridging the gap? Could be.

Is it Mr. Richmond, the counselor, hurrying in like he's been called at the last minute?

How much do they all know?

It doesn't matter now.

This is Pam's world. Pam's system. Pam's justice.

I thought I could infiltrate, but it's time to leave. I'll outrun them all.

Time to hide.

I head straight to the library tower. My legs burn as I take the stairs two at a time; my microphone makes a strange feedback noise, grating to my ears. I yank it off my face, tug it up through the top of my gown, and it shuts up at last.

In the tower, I climb out the window. I've dreamed of touching my feet onto the roof for years now. JANITOR ACCESS ONLY. NO STUDENTS, says the sign, but I don't care. I was never really a student; I was only ever a pathetic cog in a machine that would never serve me.

It's snowing now, gently. It sprinkles the top of my head, crystal ice dampening my scrunched, leaf-strewn Joetta hair.

The brisk air feels medicinal. It's good to be up this high, to look out at the expanse of the campus, the city. At last I feel as large as Bosworth promised I would feel—but I had to climb to this height myself.

A pair of footprints ink the white beside me. I track them. I'm not alone.

Standing near the roof's ledge, hands folded patiently across his front like he's been waiting hours for me to arrive, is Ethan, in the snow.

CONTINGENCY

Exterior. The roof of a prep school, night. The sky is hazy, with little visibility. Snow falls, erasing the horizon and masking all ambient sounds.

> ETHAN *stands, hair dripping. No coat, no shoes. Theater kids are always running around barefoot.*

RORY: It's snowing.

> *She is dangerously tense for such a slippery surface. Her hands she must consciously keep from balling into fists. Her legs slightly bent, to spring away, to escape.*

ETHAN:

> Rory, I—I can't believe you would do this. I'm a little scared. I feel like I don't even know you—what else are you capable of, if you already had this in you?

I close my eyes, but it does not clear the image of Ethan's face, the confusion in his brow, the hurt on his bottom lip, the shock in his eyes. The same face a baby makes when it is shouted at for the first time—a shattering of innocence, a new world of possibility and pain.

And I did that to him—

No, no, you did it for him. For both of you.

RORY: I did it for us. For you—to prop you up. To give you a hell of a show to go out on. I knew there'd be people in the crowd—scholarship reps, talent scouts. I wanted to give you the exact kind of actor you love to perform against—

ETHAN:

    I like acting with all sorts of people. The whole point is to be dynamic, to respond to different— No, this is bullshit. *(He rakes his hand through his hair; the frozen water sparkles as it flies away from him.)* This wasn't about me, Rory. Even I know that's a lie.

It didn't feel like a lie when I said it. Can I no longer rely on my senses to distinguish truth from untruth? Or do I simply inherently believe everything that comes out of my mouth?

ETHAN:

    You cheated and you—you set Annie up! You broke her leg. God, you could have killed her. Your best friend, and you could have killed her, and for what? Why did you do it? For some lead? For some applause?

RORY: It was never about applause!

It was senior year! You didn't want to miss your last opportunity to—

You were just tired of being invisible, and so you—

You always knew you had a star performance inside of you, and so—

"It was never about that!"

I reach inside me, reach for that wonderful dark place that always gives me the right lines, but it's dancing out of my reach—

Transformation.

"I just wanted to be something else!" The words pour out from my soul's very chambers, and the shame of this confession turns my nose to water, my eyes to burning orifices, my insides to hurricanes. "Can you blame me? Look at me! I hate everything about myself—"

> RORY *cuts off, overcome by the swelling of emotion. She hunches over, her hands catching her face, and sobs, wailing like a mourning bird.*

"You can't be surprised that I would want to be someone else," I say. "Even for one night."

It feels true. It hangs there, a cloud of breath between us.

Ethan listens. But he shakes his head.

"No, I don't think that's true, Rory. I don't think you hate yourself. I think you're actually in love with yourself. You think you're smarter than all of us, and you know what? That's probably true. But that's not the only measure of a person. You can use whatever metric you want. You can always find a way to come up short . . . or to tower over someone else."

And everything feels like a cut-down when you're used to coming out ahead.

"What did you say?" Ethan asks.

I shiver, but it's not from the cold. Snow has a particular smell, but all I sense is the bitterness of my mouth.

"There weren't enough parts to go around." I hear myself say it this time, feel the words resonate in my chest as I loose them in Ethan's direction like arrows. "So I did what I had to do."

Now Ethan stares at me with genuine fear, which sharpens my irritation. He's not trapped on the roof with a wild beast. He's not facing off with a serial killer.

It's Rory. The same Rory he picks up for school on chilly mornings, the same Rory he clung to when he broke up with Aiden, with Carlos, with Brad . . .

"I could hear her," I attempt to explain. "Joetta. She spoke to me. I can feel her, sense her. It's like she chose me—"

"Being the lead just means you're the lead," Ethan counters. "What you're talking about is either another lie or some sort of possession. Are you saying you were possessed, Rory?"

Possession.

Something else, making itself at home inside of me.

No—not something else.

Possessed by my ambition. Possessed by myself.

"So." Ethan swallows, his glorious Adam's apple bobbing up and down. "You had a plan for everyone. Blackmail. Did you have something for me?"

RORY: No. Of course not.

Junior year, baseball dugout.

RORY: I didn't have anything, I swear.

Junior year, baseball dugout. Assistant Coach Hunter—

384

Don't you dare, I whisper, and cannot tell if I am speaking out loud or not. Don't you think it.

Assistant Coach Hunter in the dugout. It was only supposed to be one time—

And then a flood of evidence, evidence that's gathered in the back of my mind for so long.

Don't think it. To think it means—

It means you're more conniving than you ever thought you were. It means Ethan is right, and it was never about Joetta.

It was always your own desires, pushing past everything else around you, floating to the top.

It means you're not some undiscovered genius, some acting prodigy channeling the spirit of a great leading role.

It means you're just as selfish as they think you are.

You already knew all this. You knew, all along, that you were only ever listening to yourself.

Did you know, dear reader? Or were you holding out for my redemption?

What are you going to do now?

You should run.

My kingdom for a horse.

You're still on the roof. You walk right past him. He reaches for you—does he think you're going to jump? Come on, you've got more sense than that.

That's no way to escape.

You move right past Ethan and find the service ladder. The snow touches you, your forehead. As you climb down, you can see them, gathered at the tower window. There's Miss Keating, concern on her face, and a few others—you'll never know if they're motivated to be here by true compassion or by morbid curiosity, and you suppose it doesn't matter.

Either way, they'll tell the story. *I was there*, they'll say. *I was there, and I saw it.*

They'll say you nearly slipped climbing down the ladder, but your feet are steady in your Joetta boots. They'll say you staggered through the courtyard, as if drunk, or inebriated with your emotions, but you are clearheaded, calm. Reverent, even, as you cross into the parking lot.

What of this story will you remember? Were they chasing you? Were they calling your name? Impossible to remember, and irrelevant nonetheless.

You do remember finding Pam's keys, stashed in the pocket of your gown.

THE BATTLE
OF BOSWORTH

TELL ME, READER: COULD I HAVE EVER BEEN THE HERO IN
this situation? If we view the last semester as a war of some sort, and
the theater as our battlefields, is there a way in which I could have
emerged from this night a luminary? A champion, a savior, a star?

Or was I doomed to be the villain? Is it the pathway that makes
a wretch, or the person walking it?

Have I been poisoned by the idea that I am owed something?
I didn't expect the world to simply hand me my desires, after all;
I was willing to fight for them, and I did. Arrow and blade, hand
over foot, for every inch of it.

Just like Bosworth taught us. Just like Pam taught us.

The world is what you make of it.

If you really want something, Pam taught us, there are a thousand ways to convince others to offer it to you. Hint, cajole, gesture.
Build yourself a stage. Get the audience to look right where you
want them to. Everyone else is a character to be blocked, a performer to be directed.

I was Bosworth's greatest pupil, then, their legacy. I made the world in my favor—and I don't know how to stop.

But I was wrong to think they'd ever see me as a world-maker. Even as I walked through the same hallways as the rest of them, sat in the same classrooms as the rest of them, graduated with the same diploma. We were never going to be the same. Never.

Snow drifts down. I can hear them shouting.

Do you know how to cause a car wreck without actually killing anyone? I do.

Pam's Honda starts nice and easy for me.

There will be rumors that I drove toward the people who are chasing me, but that's not true. I swerve to miss them, as I swerve to miss all things.

There will be rumors about tonight, but remember this, and you can decide for yourself if it's true or not:

Villain or hero, I only hoped to play a part.

Exterior. The parking lot of Bosworth Academy.

A car has been driven into a pole. Snow falls, sprinkling everything with a soft blanket. Sirens blare. People are running to inspect the car, to open the door.

The car is smoking, the hood completely frazzled.

Windshield is cracked. Airbag deployed.

Spring snow, spiraling down. A second winter.

Covering the wreckage.

Making a world.